Amelia A. B. Edwards

Pharaohs, Fellahs and Explorers

Amelia A. B. Edwards

Pharaohs, Fellahs and Explorers

ISBN/EAN: 9783337387617

Printed in Europe, USA, Canada, Australia, Japan

Cover: Foto ©Andreas Hilbeck / pixelio.de

More available books at **www.hansebooks.com**

PHARAOHS, FELLAHS

AND

EXPLORERS

BY

AMELIA B. EDWARDS

ILLUSTRATED

NEW YORK
HARPER & BROTHERS, FRANKLIN SQUARE
1892

PREFACE.

THE following chapters contain, with large additions, notes, and references, the substance of a course of lectures on ancient Egyptian subjects recently delivered in the United States of America. While necessarily recasting the form of these lectures, I have to some extent preserved the colloquial style—in the hope, I confess, of being the better remembered by those who have heard them.

For permission to reproduce various illustrations from the works of Professor Maspero, MM. Perrot and Chipiez, Sir John Lubbock, and Mr. W. M. F. Petrie, I have to offer my grateful acknowledgments to Messrs. Grevel & Co., Chapman & Hall, Longmans, Williams & Norgate, and the Committee of the Egypt Exploration Fund.

The reproductions from Mr. W. M. F. Petrie's series of original photographs are executed by special arrangement with Mr. Petrie.

AMELIA B. EDWARDS.

WESTBURY-ON-TRYM, ENGLAND,
  March, 1891.

CONTENTS.

I.

THE EXPLORER IN EGYPT.

Our knowledge of Egypt ever on the increase—Continuous march of exploration—Foundation of the Egypt Exploration Fund in 1883—Egypt an inexhaustible mine of antiquities — Funerary customs of the ancient Egyptians—Approximate number of mummies embalmed during 4700 years — Egyptian mounds — How these mounds were formed, their growth and decay—Story of a typical mound—Excavation of a typical mound—Objects likely to be found in Egyptian mounds—Exploration in Upper Egypt—The tomb-pits of Upper Egypt—Exploration in Lower Egypt—Excavation of Tell Nebesheh in the Eastern Delta—Interesting antiquities discovered at Tell Nebesheh—Tell Defenneh—Hardships incidental to the work of exploration in Egypt—Necessary qualifications of the explorer—Homer in the Fayûm—Definition of archæology—The explorer "born, not made"—Discovery of Naukratis by Mr. Petrie—Ruins of the temples of Apollo, Hera, Zeus, and Aphrodite mentioned by Herodotus — "The potter's quarter" — The house of the scarabmaker — The house of the jeweller — Evolution of Greek from Egyptian art—Discovery of Masonic deposits—Great historical value of this discovery—Ceramic riches of Naukratis..................Pages 3–36

II.

THE BURIED CITIES OF ANCIENT EGYPT.

Extreme antiquity of the ancient Egyptian monarchy — The *Horshesu*, or "Followers of Horus"—Probable age of the Great Sphinx—Wealth of Egypt in building material—The ancient Egyptians a nation of builders —Destruction of the mounds of the Delta by native laborers—Excavations conducted by the Egypt Exploration Fund—Archæological survey of Egypt recently undertaken by this society — "Pithom and Raamses"—The Hebrews in the Land of Goshen—Tell Abû Suleiman identified by Lepsius with Pithom and Tell-el-Maskhûtah with "Raamses" —Excavation of the mound of Maskhûtah by M. Naville—Tell-el-Maskhûtah proves to be "Pithom of Succoth"—Identification of the route

of the Exodus—Store-chambers of Pithom—Bricks of Pithom—Mr. Petric's excavations at Tanis (Zoan)—The great temple of Tanis—The
largest colossus ever sculptured by the hand of man—House of Bakakhiu at Tanis—Great discovery of papyri and other manuscripts—The
granite shrine of Saft el-Henneh—Daphnæ of Pelusium—The camps of
Psammetichus—Occupation of Daphnæ by Greek mercenary troops—
Siege of Jerusalem (B.C. 585) and flight of the daughters of Zedekiah
into Egypt—Settlement of the Hebrew fugitives at Daphnæ—The
prophecy of Jeremiah—Mr. Petric's excavations at Daphnæ (Tell Defenneh)—Palace-fort of Psammetichus I.—Masonic deposits of Psammetichus I.—Identification of the palace-fort with "Pharaoh's House
in Tahpanhes"—Discovery of the brick-work, or pavement, mentioned
by Jeremiah—Historical testimony of the ruins of the palace-fort of
Psammetichus—Conflicting testimony of Egyptian and Babylonian inscriptions—Discovery of clay cylinders of Nebuchadnezzar. Pages 37-69

III.

PORTRAIT PAINTING IN ANCIENT EGYPT.

Egyptian sculptures and paintings the oldest in the world—The art of
drawing more ancient than that of sculpture—Prehistoric art—Subjects of the earliest Egyptian paintings—Treatment of the human figure
by ancient Egyptian draughtsmen—Conventional coloring of ancient
Egyptian artists—The skill with which Egyptian artists reproduced
the ethnic types of foreign nations—Errors of ancient Egyptian artists
—The same errors common to early art in all the nations of antiquity
—Ancient Greek painting—The art of painted vases—Ancient criticisms
and anecdotes of Polygnotus; of Xeuxis; of Apelles—Unparalleled
luxury of the early Greek painters—The Proto-Homeric vases of
Athens—Pliny on the priority of ancient Egyptian painting—Early relations between the Pelasgic Greeks and the ancient Egyptians—Inscription of Sankhara in the Valley of Hammamat—The Greeks in
Egypt under the Eighteenth and later dynasties—Mr. Petric's discoveries at Tell Kahûn and Tell Gurob—Inscribed potsherds found in these
mounds—Traces of Foreign settlers at Gurob—The Tursha identified
by Lenormant with the Etruscans—Etruscan alphabetic signs at Tell
Gurob—Comparative antiquity of the earliest Greek alphabets—Foreign captives in Egypt during the Nineteenth and Twentieth dynasties
—Momentous results of Mr. Petric's discoveries—Special characteristics
of the Egyptian School of figure-painting—The "four races" of men:
the typical Syrian, the typical Egyptian, the typical Libyan, the typical Ethiopian—The tomb of Hui—The Sardinian in Egyptian art—The
charioteer of the "pre-Homeric" vases—Archaic Greek painted ware of
Daphnæ—Egyptian conventionalities reproduced in early Greek painting—First appearance of the Sphinx in Greek art—The Sphinx-plate of

Naukratis—The wall-paintings of Etruria ; their relations to ancient
Egyptian art—The Cervetri tomb of 1889—Etruscan reproduction of
the conventionalities of Egyptian art—Genealogy of the French eagles
—Discovery of the laws of chiaroscuro and foreshortening by Apollodorus—The Labyrinth ; its destruction by the Roman Government—
Excavations by Mr. Petrie on the site of the Labyrinth—Ruins of the
Roman town on the Labyrinth platform—Mixed character of its ancient
population—Successive styles of mummification practised by the inhabitants of this town—The evolution of painting on panel from painted
cartonnage and painted canvas—Painting in Egypt in the time of Hadrian—Reaction of Greek art upon Egytian art—Great discovery of
panel-portraits in the Fayûm—Methods employed by the Græco-Egyptian portrait painters of this period—The beeswax medium of Egypt
not identical with the "encaustic" painting of the Greeks—Pigments
employed by Græco-Egyptian painters—Various nationalities depicted
in these portraits—Egyptian names of Greek and Roman settlers—Series of portraits of Greeks, Romans, Syrians, and Egyptians—Styles of
jewelry depicted — Diogenes, the flautist — The elderly Roman — The
lotus-bud necklace of Etruria an ancient Egyptian design—Antiquity of
the "Oxford pattern" frame—Inequality of artistic merit in the Fayûm
portraits—Singularly modern character of the heads—Close resemblance
of the ancient Greeks and Romans to the people of modern Europe and
America—Unchanged racial types of Egypt, Nubia, and Palestine—
Persistence of ancient Egyptian types...................Pages 70-112

IV.

THE ORIGIN OF PORTRAIT SCULPTURE, AND THE HISTORY OF THE KA.

Our interest in the past history of the human race—Great value of the art
of portraiture as preserved to us in the sculptures of Assyria, Babylon,
Susa, Persepolis, and ancient Egypt—Ancient Egyptian portraiture the
most ancient in the world — Funerary portrait-statues of the Ancient
Empire—Singular custom of immuring these statues—Ancient Egyptian notions regarding the nature of man—The Ka—Various definitions
of the Ka—Portraits for the benefit of the Ka—Tablet of Pepi-Na—
Tablet of Napu—Voracious appetite of the Ka—Funerary statues and
paintings fashioned for the benefit of the Ka—The Ka identified with
the life — The three names of the Pharaohs — Sculptured representations of the Ka—Remarkable tableaux of Amenhotep III. and his Ka
in the Great Temple of Luxor—Association of the Ka with the "ankh"
—Historical sculptures of Seti I. and his Ka on the walls of the Great
Temple of Karnak—Invariable inscription accompanying royal Kas—
Concrete mode of thought of the ancient Egyptians—Reasons why the
Ka needed food and drink offerings — Greek conception of life borrowed from Egyptian sources—The Hebrew notion of the "Khai," or

"life," identical with the Egyptian Ka—Extreme truth to nature of Egyptian Ka-statues—Egyptian funerary portrait-statues carefully studied from the life—The leading schools of Egyptian art—Great superiority of the earliest Egyptian school of portraiture—The oldest historical portrait-statue known—Group of Queen Mertetefs, her Ka, and private secretary, at Leyden—Semnefer and his wife—General Ra-hotep and Princess Nefert—The "Wooden Man" of Bûlak—Funerary statue of Ti—Admirable anatomical development of the "Cross-legged Scribe" —The Memphite School represents the finest period of Egyptian portraiture—Erroneous estimate commonly formed of the merits of Egyptian sculpture—Comparison of the sculptures of ancient Egypt with those of ancient Greece—The Twelfth Dynasty school—The Hyksôs school—The colossal sitting statues of Bubastis—The Eighteenth Dynasty school—Colossal head of Queen Hatasu—The Nineteenth and Twentieth dynasties register a new phase of Egyptian art—Semitic characteristics of this school—Remarkable family likeness of the Pharaohs of the two Ramesside dynasties—Art of portraiture in wood, as preserved in the mummy-cases of this time—Colossal mummy-case of Queen Ahmes Nefertari—Beautiful mask of Rameses II.—Probability that this mask may represent Her-Hor..................Pages 113-157

V.

EGYPT THE BIRTHPLACE OF GREEK DECORATIVE ART.

The irresistible fascination of Egyptology—Ancient Egyptian civilization the earliest known—Extent of the debt of the early Greeks to the ancient Egyptians—First mention of the Greeks upon the monuments of Egypt—The "Hanebu"—The Danæans in the time of Thothmes III.— The earliest portrait of a Greek in the world—Greeks of Thrace and Asia Minor, in alliance with the Syrian nations, invade Egypt in the time of Rameses II.—Armor of the Achæans—The Greek greave as an Egyptian hieroglyph—Carian and Ionian Greek troops of Psammetichus I. —Daphnæ of Pelusium, an early Greek settlement—Establishment of Greek traders at Naukratis—The æsthetic debt of Greece to Egypt— The earliest known examples of Greek architecture, sculpture, and decorative design copied from Egyptian sources—Wall and ceiling decoration of the rock-cut tombs of Beni-Hasan—Spiral ornament of Mycenæ—Spiral of Beni-Hasan—The *herz-blatt* and key patterns of Greece copied from Beni-Hasan designs—The ceiling pattern of the treasury of Minyas at Orchomenos—This pattern reproduces the cornice patterns of Beni-Hasan—"Proto-Doric" columns of the Beni-Hasan tombs—Comparison of these columns with Greek Doric—Egyptian origin of the Ionic capital—The Ionic capital derived from the lotus of the Nile—The lotus in nature and the lotus in art—The conventional lotus of Egyptian art—The earliest temple known to belong to the Ionic

order discovered by Mr. Petrie at Naukratis—Egyptian origin of the
Anthemion and Palmette—Egyptian origin of the "honeysuckle" pattern of the Greeks—Early Greek painted vases found at Daphnæ—
Florid development of Egyptian lotus pattern by Greek potters—The
lotus pattern in Greek goldsmith's work—Various religious conceptions
of the ancient Egyptians borrowed by the Greeks—The Egyptian soul,
or *Ba*, transformed into the harpy and syren of Greek art—Egyptian
character of early Greek statues........................Pages 158–192

VI.

THE LITERATURE AND RELIGION OF ANCIENT EGYPT.

Literary activity not a necessary result of the possession of an alphabet—
Importance of a material on which to write—Pastoral and literary ten-
dencies of the ancient Egyptians—Great antiquity of papyrus as a writing material—"The oldest book in the world"—Second dynasty tablet
at Oxford—Varied character of ancient Egyptian literature—Greek and
Roman papyri found in Egypt—Homer in Egypt—No contemporary
history of ancient Egypt yet discovered—The lost history of Manetho—
Peculiar characteristics of ancient Egyptian poetry—"Chant of Victory"
of Thothmes III.—The heroic poem of Pentaur—This poem composed in
commemoration of the victory of Rameses II. over the allied forces of
Syria and Asia Minor—Stratagem of the Hittites—Brilliant feat of arms
of Rameses II.—The battle of Kadesh—Poetic treatment of the facts by
Pentaur—Introduction of the *Deus ex machina*—Literary style of the
poem—Its reproduction on the walls of various great temples in Egypt—
A copy on papyrus in the British Museum—Great tableau of the battle
of Kadesh at Abû-Simbel—Curious incident of the drowning of the
Prince of Aleppo—The scientific literature of the ancient Egyptians—
Its value purely archæological—Astronomical observations of the ancient Egyptians—Their knowledge of the movement of the earth—Mathematical papyri—Medical papyri—The Ebers medical papyrus—Un-
pleasant character of ancient Egyptian pharmacopœia—The moral
philosophy of the ancient Egyptians—The maxims of Ptah-hotep—The
maxims of the scribe Ani—Romantic literature of the ancient Egyptians—Egyptian origin of Æsop's fables, and of various well-known
popular tales—The story of Rhodopis—The tale of the two brothers—
The taking of Joppa—The doomed prince—The shipwrecked mariner—
Historic characters introduced into ancient Egyptian fiction—Popular
poetry of the ancient Egyptians—A love song—Threshing song from
the tomb of Pahiri—The religion of ancient Egypt—Its obscurity and
diversity—Religions of various periods—Was monotheism the fundamental principle of the ancient Egyptian religion?—Theories of M.
Pierret and Dr. Brugsch—Barbaric origin of the ancient Egyptians—
The prehistoric Egyptians and the North American Indians—The "to-

tems " of the North American Indians — Importance of a tribal name among barbaric and semi-civilized communities — Totemism common to all quarters of the globe—Totemism the origin of animal worship—Totemism of the prehistoric Egyptians—Subsequent evolution of the Egyptian religion—Exalted pantheism of Ra-worship—Local character of the monotheism of the ancient Egyptians—Great local deities identified one with another—The ancient Egyptians the first people to recognize the immortality of the soul—" The negative confession "—Ancient Egyptian standard of morality........................Pages 193-233

VII.

THE HIEROGLYPHIC WRITING OF THE ANCIENT EGYPTIANS.

A new definition of the *genus homo* — The infancy of writing and the infancy of language—Limited vocabulary of prehistoric man—Writing a spontaneous growth—The beginnings of writing everywhere the same —Picture-writing — The picture-writing of the Hittites, Babylonians, Assyrians, and Chinese—The origin of picture-writing—Message of the Scythians to Darius—Object-writing the natural predecessor of picture-writing—Picture-writing of Mexico—The tribute-lists of the Mexican kings — General picture-written literature of the Mexicans — Picture-writing of the North American Indians—A petition of certain Indian chiefs—Incised sketches and bone drawings of prehistoric times—Prehistoric Egypt—The age of the " Horshesu " the probable age of Egyptian picture-writing—Successive stages of Egyptian writing—Ideography — Pictorial phonetism — Monosyllabic character of the earliest Egyptian vocabulary—Common objects of daily life the origin of hieroglyphic characters—Transition from pictorial phonetism to alphabetism —Immense antiquity of the ancient Egyptian alphabet—This alphabet the parent stock of all the alphabets of Europe—The way in which the alphabet was formed—The hieroglyphic alphabet as commonly in use —Conservatism of the ancient Egyptians—Egyptian spelling—Alphabetism in common with ideography—Determinating hieroglyphs — Determinatives of sound — Determinatives of sense—Generic determinatives—The great number and variety of hieroglyphic signs—Pictorial character of hieroglyphic signs—Their archæological and scientific value —Part played by the human figure in the hieroglyphic system—The study of hieroglyphs—Its facilities and difficulties—Perplexing simplicity of ancient Egyptian thought—Hieroglyphs relating to the sky, night, day, rain, and the like, with their esoteric meanings—The hieroglyph for " land," and its interpretation—Survival of ancient Egyptian words in European languages—Ancient name of Egypt in hieroglyphs — Hieroglyphic spellings of various words in common use — Other scripts in use by the ancient Egyptians—Necessity for a cursive writing—The hieratic script an abridgment of the hieroglyphic—Characteristics of the hieratic at various periods — The demotic script—The demotic script an abridgment of the hieratic — Great wealth of European museums in demotic documents—Classification of the three writings of the Egyptians — Obscure origin of the Egyptian language— The Egyptian language a member of the Khamitic family of tongues —The Khamitic and Semitic languages derived from a common prehistoric parent—The Egyptian verb as described by Mr. Le Page Renou ....Pages 234-260

VIII.

QUEEN HATASU, AND HER EXPEDITION TO THE LAND OF PUNT.

Queen Hatasu—Her birth and parentage—Important historical inscriptions at Karnak—Accession of Queen Hatasu during her father's lifetime— Throne-name of Hatasu—Her marriage to Thothmes II.—Recent discovery by M. Grébaut of the chapel of Prince Uatmes—The mothers of Thothmes II. and Thothmes III.—Incorrectness of the assumption that Hatasu was a usurper — Hatasu as Pharaoh — Profound peace during her reign—Her works of building and restoration—Obelisks of Hatasu at Karnak—Great temple of Hatasu on the western bank of the Nile— Novelty of its design—Sen-Maut the architect—Restoration of the temple of Dayr-el-Bahari by M. Brune—The chamber of the cow at Dayr-el-Bahari — Portrait of Queen Hatasu as a young prince — Hatasu despatches a maritime expedition to the land of Punt—This expedition depicted on the walls of her temple at Dayr-el-Bahari—Construction of the vessels built for this expedition—Strength of the expedition—Probable route taken by the exploring squadron—The ancient canal in the Wady Tûmilât probably constructed by Hatasu—Arrival of the squadron—Gifts of Queen Hatasu to the Prince of Punt — The Princess of Punt and her personal peculiarities — The odoriferous sycamores of Punt—Pliny's description of the myrrh-tree of "the land of the Troglodytes"—Identity of this tree with the "Ana-sycamore"—Landing of the Egyptian ships with sycamore saplings, ivory, ebony, and other products of Punt—Banquet offered to the Prince of Punt by the royal Envoy—Return of the squadron to Thebes—Processional subjects depicted in these tableaux: the procession from the ships, the procession of welcome, the procession of the Queen, sacrifice in the temple of Amen at Karnak, solemn visit of the naval expedition to the temple of Dayr-el-Bahari—Close of the reign of Hatasu wrapped in obscurity—Wholesale forgeries of Thothmes III.—Discovery of the tomb of Hatasu by Mr. Rhind — Extant relics of Queen Hatasu — Throne-chair of Queen Hatasu 261-300

LIST OF ILLUSTRATIONS.

           PAGE

Portrait—Miss Amelia B. Edwards . . . . *Frontispiece*

A Canal in the Delta. [From a photograph by Mr. W. M. F. Petrie.] . 3

Wig of Princess Nesikhonsu. [From a photograph.]. 5

Tell Nebesheh. [From a photograph by Mr. W. M. F. Petrie.] . . . 15

Tell-el-Yahûdieh. [From a photograph by Mr. W. M. F. Petrie.] . . 19

Tell Nebireh. [From a photograph by Mr. W. M. F. Petrie.] 21

Archaic Head (Cypriote type). [From a photograph.] 23

Plan of Naukratis. [From the plan made by Mr. W. M. F. Petrie.] . . 25

Foundation Deposits of Ptolemy Philadelphus (286–274 B.C.), Naukratis. [From a photograph by Mr. W. M. F. Petrie.] 27

Archaic Statuette, Naukratis. [From a photograph.]. 29

Terra-cotta Head of Aphrodite, Naukratis. [From a photograph.] . . 31

Votive Bowl, Naukratis. [From a photograph.] 33

Votive Bowl, Naukratis. [From a photograph.] 34

Gorgoneia, Naukratis. [From a photograph.] 35

Village of Sân (Tanis). [From a photograph by Mr. W. M. F. Petrie.] . 37

Plan of Pithom. [From the plan made by M. Naville.] 41

Tell-el-Maskhûtah. [From a photograph by Mr. W. M. F. Petrie.] . . 43

The Store-cellars of Pithom. [From a photograph by Mr. W. M. F. Petrie.]. 45

Colossal Statue of Mermashiu. [From a photograph by Mr. W. M. F. Petrie.]. 47

Plan of the Ruins of the Great Temple of Tanis. [From the plan made by Mr. W. M. F. Petrie.] 49

Shrine of Rameses II. (Tanis). [From a photograph by Mr. W. M. F. Petrie.]. 51

Toes of Great Colossus. [From a sketch.] 54

Group of Miscellaneous Objects (Tanis). [From a photograph.] . . 55

Objects from the House of Bakakhiu. [From a photograph.] . . . 59

Ruins of the Sanctuary (Tanis). [From a photograph by Mr. W. M. F. Petrie.]. 61

Tell Defenneh. [From a photograph by Mr. W. M. F. Petrie.] . . . 65

Cellar in the House of Bakakhiu. [From a drawing by Mr. Tristram Ellis.] 69

Ploughing Scene. [From an Egyptian bas-relief.] 70

PAGE

Tum 81

The Typical Syrian of Egyptian Art. [From a photograph by Mr. W.
M. F. Petrie.] 82

The Typical Libyan of Egyptian Art. [From a photograph by Mr.
W. M. F. Petrie.] 83

Procession of Ethiopians. [From a photograph by Mr. W. M. F. Petrie.] 85

The Typical Sardinian of Egyptian Art. [From a sketch.] 86

Greek Charioteer, archaic style. [From a proto-Homeric vase.] . . 87

Obsequies of a Greek Hero, archaic style. [From a proto-Homeric
vase.] 88

Greek Dancing-girl. [From a fragment of Daphniote ware.] . . . 89

Œdipus and the Sphinx. [From a fragment of Daphniote ware.] . . 90

Plate with Winged Sphinx. [From a photograph.] 91

Group of Etruscan Figures. [From a painted slab found at Cervetri.] 93

The Site of the Labyrinth. [From a photograph by Mr. W. M. F.
Petrie.] 95

Panel-portrait, a Young Greek. [From a photograph by Mr. W. M.
F. Petrie.] 97

Panel-portrait, an Egyptian Boy. [From a photograph by Mr. W. M.
F. Petrie.] 98

Panel-portrait, a Greek Lady. [From a photograph by Mr. W. M. F.
Petrie.] 99

Panel-portrait, an Egyptian Lady. [From a photograph by Mr. W.
M. F. Petrie.] 100

Panel-portrait, Diogenes the Flautist. [From a photograph by Mr.
W. M. F. Petrie.] 101

Panel-portrait, a Roman. [From a photograph by Mr. W. M. F. Petrie.] 102

Panel-portrait, a Young Greek. [From a photograph by Mr. W. M.
F. Pietrie.] 103

Panel-portrait, a Roman Lady. [From a photograph by Mr. W. M.
F. Petrie.] 104

Panel-portrait, a Romano-Egyptian Lady. [From a photograph by
Mr. W. M. F. Petrie.] 105

Panel-portrait, a Student. [From a photograph by Mr. W. M. F.
Petrie.] 106

Panel-portrait, a Gladiator. [From a photograph by Mr. W. M. F.
Petrie.] 107

Panel-portrait, a Young Lady. [From a photograph by Mr. W. M.
F. Petrie.] 109

Panel-portrait, a Young Boy. [From a photograph by Mr. W. M. F.
Petrie.] 111

The Great Sphinx. [From a photograph by Mr. W. M. F. Petrie.] . . 113

Funerary Offerings. [From an Egyptian wall-painting.] 121

Nemhotep. [From Maspero's *Archéologie Egyptienne*.] 132

Khufu-Ankh and Servants. [From a photograph by Mr. W. M. F.
Petrie.] 136

PAGE

Semnefer and Hotep-hers, his Wife. [From a photograph by Mr. W.
M. F. Petrie.] 137
Ra-hotep and Nefert. [From Edwards's *A Thousand Miles up the Nile.*] 138
Ra-em-ka ("The Wooden Man"). [From a photograph by Brugsch-
Bey.] 139
Ti. [From Maspero's *Archéologie Egyptienne.*] 141
The Kneeling Scribe 142
The Cross-legged Scribe. [From Perrot and Chipiez's *Egypte.*] . . . 143
Colossal Head of Amenemhat I. [From a photograph by Mr. W. M.
F. Petrie.] 144
Colossal Head of a Hyksôs King. [From a photograph by Mr. W. M.
F. Petrie.] 145
Hyksôs Sphinx (profile). [From a photograph by Mr. W. M. F. Petrie.] 146
Hyksôs Sphinxes of Tanis. [From a photograph by Mr. W. M. F.
Petrie.] 147
Colossal Head, Queen Hatasu. [From Perrot and Chipiez's *Egypte.*] . 148
Head of Rameses II. [From a photograph by Mr. W. M. F. Petrie.] . 149
Rameses II. (profile). [From a photograph by Mr. W. M. F. Petrie.] . 150
Seti II. (profile). [From a photograph by Mr. W. M. F. Petrie.] . . 151
Siptah (profile). [From a photograph by Mr. W. M. F. Petrie.] . . . 152
Rameses III. [From a photograph by Mr. W. M. F. Petrie.] 153
Mummy-case of Queen Ahmes Nefertari. [From a photograph by
Brugsch-Bey.] 154
Mask from Mummy-case of Rameses II. [From a photograph by
Brugsch-Bey.] 156
Ra-em-ka 157
Greek Potter modelling a Vase. [From a vase-painting.] 158
Profile of Hanebu Woman. [From a photograph by Mr. W. M. F.
Petrie.] 161
Egyptian Hieroglyph for a Greek Greave 164
Decorated Column, Mycenæ. [From Reber's *Ancient Art.*] 169
Spiral and Rosette Design. [From Mr. W. H. Goodyear's "The Ionic
Capital and the Origin of the Anthemion."] 170
Rosette and Key-pattern. [From Mr. W. H. Goodyear's "The Ionic
Capital and the Origin of the Anthemion."] 170
Examples of *Herz-blatt* Pattern. [From Mr. W. H. Goodyear's "The
Ionic Capital and the Origin of the Anthemion."] 171
Rosette, Spiral, and Lotus. [From Mr. W. H. Goodyear's "The Ionic
Capital and the Origin of the Anthemion."] 172
Cornice Designs (Beni-Hasan). [From Mr. W. H. Goodyear's "The
Ionic Capital and the Origin of the Anthemion."] 172
Proto-Doric Columns (Beni-Hasan). [From Maspero's *Archéologie
Egyptienne.*] 173
Examples of Doric Columns 174
Temple of Thothmes III. (Karnak). [From Maspero's *Archéologie
Egyptienne.*] 175

PAGE

Lotus Leaf Design. [From Mariette's *Mastabahs de l'Ancienne Empire*.] 176

Natural Lotus. [From Mr. W. H. Goodyear's "The Ionic Capital and the Origin of the Anthemion."] 177

Conventional Lotus of Egyptian Art. [From Mr. W. H. Goodyear's "The Ionic Capital and the Origin of the Anthemion."] 178

Example of Grecian Ionic. [From Ferguson's *History of Architecture*.] 179

Architectural Fragments from Archaic Temple of Apollo (Naukratis). [From a photograph by Mr. W. M. F. Petrie.] 181

Architectural Fragments from the Second Temple of Apollo (Naukratis). [From a drawing by Mr. W. M. F. Petrie.] 181

Egyptian Vase with Inverted Lotus Design. [From a drawing by Mr. W. M. F. Petrie.] 182

Archaic Græco-Egyptian Vase. [From a drawing by Mr. W. M. F. Petrie.] 182

Archaic Græco-Egyptian Vase. [From a drawing by Mr. W. M. F. Petrie.] 183

Example of Lotus and Bud (Naukratis). [From a drawing by Mr. W. M. F. Petrie.] 184

Gold Tray-handle (Defenneh). [From a drawing by Mr. W. M. F. Petrie.] 185

Mummy and "Ba." [Vignette from an Egyptian Ritual.] 187

Greek Harpy. [From a fragment of Daphniote painted ware.] . . . 188

Greek Harpy. [From a photograph of the Harpy-tomb of Xanthus.] 188

Odysseus and the Sirens. [From a vase-painting.] 189

The Archaic Apollo (Thera). [From a photograph.] 190

The Archaic Apollo of Naukratis. [From a photograph.] 191

Female Winged Sphinx of Greek Art. [From a drawing by Mr. W. M. F. Petrie.] 192

Head-piece 193

Camp of Rameses II. [After Rossellini.] 203

Syrian Spies Arrested and Bastinadoed. [After Rossellini.] 204

Pharaoh's War-chariot. [After Rossellini.] 206

Rameses Slaughtering the Hittites. [After Rossellini.] 207

The Battle of Kadesh. [After Rossellini.] 209

Brigade of Egyptian Infantry on the March. [After Rossellini.] . . 210

Egyptian Attack on Hittite Chariot. [After Rossellini.] 211

Fac-simile of the Opening Lines of the Poem of Pentaur 212

Mêlée of Chariots. [After Rossellini.] 213

War-chariots setting out. [After Rossellini.] 213

After the Battle. [After Rossellini.] 214

Rameses Enthroned. [After Rossellini.] 215

The Prince of Aleppo (Ramesseum). [From a photograph by Mr. W. M. F. Petrie.] 216

Ancient Egyptian Pen-drawing. [From a vignette in a funerary papyrus.] 233

Bas-relief Slab of Second Dynasty. [From a photograph.] 234

PAGE

Indian Petition. [From Sir J. Lubbock's *History of Civilization*.] . . 238

Prehistoric Bone-carving (The Mammoth). [From Sir J. Lubbock's *History of Civilization*.] 240

Ancient Egyptian Hoe, Adze-handle, and Sickle. [After drawings by Mr. W. M. F. Petrie.] 243

The Hieroglyphic Alphabet 245

Hieratic Papyrus of Princess Nesikhonsu. [From a photograph by Brugsch-Bey.] 257

Example of Demotic Writing. [From a funerary tablet.] 258

Thoth, the Egyptian God of Letters. [From an Egyptian bas-relief.] 260

Head-piece 261

Sitting Statue of Queen Hatasu. [From a photograph.] 265

Profile of Hatasu. [From the fallen Obelisk, Karnak.] 271

Temple of Hatasu (Dayr-el-Bahari). [From the restoration by M. Brune.] 272

Hathor-head Capital (Dayr-el-Bahari). [From a photograph by Mr. W. M. F. Petrie.] 273

Hatasu and Hathor (the Divine Cow). [From a photograph by Mr. W. M. F. Petrie.] 275

Ancient Egyptian Ship. [From Mariette's *Deir-el-Bahari*.] . . . 277

Map of Africa 279

A Village in Punt. [From Mariette's *Deir-el-Bahari*.] 282

Hatasu's Envoy. [From Mariette's *Deir-el-Bahari*.] 283

The Prince of Punt and his Family. [From Mariette's *Deir-el-Bahari*.] 284

A Chief of Punt (Karnak). [From a photograph by Mr. W. M. F. Petrie.] 286

Transport of "Ana" Saplings. [From Mariette's *Deir-el-Bahari*.] . 287

The Prince of Punt presenting Farewell Gifts to the Egyptian Envoy. [From Mariette's *Deir-el-Bahari*.] 289

Lading of the Egyptian Ships. [From Mariette's *Deir-el-Bahari*.] . 290

Tributaries of Punt Walking in Procession to the Temple of Amen. [From Mariette's *Deir-el-Bahari*.] 292

Procession of Hatasu. [From Mariette's *Deir-el-Bahari*.] 293

Hatasu's Throne-chair carried by Twelve Bearers. [From Mariette's *Deir-el-Bahari*.] 293

Hatasu Receiving her Troops. [From Mariette's *Deir-el-Bahari*.] . 294

Sacrifice in the Temple of Amen. [From Mariette's *Deir-el-Bahari*.] 294

Measuring the "Ana" of Punt. [From Mariette's *Deir-el-Bahari*.] . 295

Throne-chair of Queen Hatasu. [From a photograph of the original in the British Museum.] 298

Little Cabinet of Queen Hatasu. [From a photograph by Brugsch-Bey.] 300

PHARAOHS, FELLAHS, AND EXPLORERS.

I.

THE EXPLORER IN EGYPT.

IT may be said of some very old places, as of some very old books, that they are destined to be forever new. The nearer we approach them, the more remote they seem; the more we study them, the more we have yet to learn. Time augments rather than diminishes their everlasting novelty; and to our descendants of a thousand years hence it may safely be predicted that they will be even more fascinating than to ourselves. This is true of many ancient lands, but of no place is it so true as of Egypt. Our knowledge of how men lived and thought in the Valley of the Nile five or six thousand years before the Christian era is ever on the increase. It keeps pace with the march of discovery, and that march extends every year over a wider area. Each season beholds the exploration of new sites, and each explorer has some new thing to tell. What Mariette began thirty years ago, Maspero carried on and developed; and it was to Maspero's wise liberality that the Egypt Exploration Fund was indebted, in 1883, for liberty to pursue its work in the Delta. In that year the society despatched its first agent—M. Naville—upon its first expedition; and since 1883 the French in Upper Egypt, the English in Lower Egypt, have labored simultaneously to bring to light the buried wealth of the most ancient of nations. Thus the work of discovery goes on apace. Old truths receive unexpected corroboration; old histories are judged by the light of new readings; fresh wonders are disclosed wherever the spade of the digger strikes new ground. The interest never flags—the subject never palls upon us—the mine is never exhausted.

I will go yet further, and say that this mine is practically inexhaustible. Consider, for instance, the incredible number and riches of the tombs of ancient Egypt, and the immense population of the Nile Valley in the times of the Pharaohs. That immense population continued during a period of between four and five thousand years to embalm and secrete their dead, interring with them, according to the customs of successive epochs, funerary statues, vases, weapons, amulets, inscribed tablets, jewels, furniture, food, stuffs; articles of apparel, such as sandals, combs, hair-pins, and even wigs; implements, and written documents on papyrus, leather, and linen. Conceive, then, what must be the number of those sepulchres, of those mummies, of those buried treasures! The cemeteries of Thebes and Memphis and Abydos have enriched all the museums of Europe, and are not yet worked out. The unopened mounds of Middle and Lower Egypt, and the unexplored valleys of the Libyan range, undoubtedly conceal tens of thousands of tombs which yet await the scientific, or unscientific, plunderer.

The late Dr. Birch—a cautious man, and the last man in the world to exaggerate—estimated the number of corpses embalmed during two thousand seven hundred years at no less than 420,000,000. But recent discoveries(') compel us to assign 4700 instead of 2700 years for the observance of this rite; which, calculated after the same rate, brings us to a gigantic total of 731,000,000 of mummies. The majority of these were, of course, mere slaves and peasants, rudely embalmed and buried in common graves; but even so, we may be very certain that the time can never come when quarried rock and drifted sand shall have yielded all the noble and wealthy dead, and all their riches. The Greek, the Roman, the mediæval Arab, the modern Arab, the Copt, the Turk, and the European archæologist have ravaged the soil, but the harvest is still undiminished; and although "mummy was sold for balsam" in Sir Thomas Browne's day, and has been exported for manure in our own,(') there are probably

PRINCESS NESIKHONSU'S WIG.

This curious object, now in the National Egyptian Museum at Ghizeh, is one of several similar wigs buried with the mummy of Princess Nesikhonsu, a royal lady of the Twenty-first Dynasty, whose mortal remains and personal adornments were discovered in 1881, in the famous vault of the Priest Kings at Dayr-el-Bahari. Each wig was enclosed in a little hamper of plaited palm-fibre.

at this moment more ancient Egyptians under the soil of Egypt than there are living men and women above it.

It has been aptly said that all Egypt is but the façade of an immense sepulchre. This is literally true; for the terraced cliffs that hem in the Nile to east and west, and the rocky bed of the desert beneath our feet, are everywhere honey-combed with tombs. But this is not all. The very towns in which those vanished generations lived their busy lives, the houses in which they dwelt, the temples in which they worshipped, are as much entombed as their former inhabitants. What the ancient Egyptians did for their dead, Time has done for their cities. All who run and read have heard of the mounds of Memphis, of Bubastis, of Tanis, and of other famous capitals; but few have, perhaps, any very distinct idea of how these mounds came to be formed, or even of what they are like. To what shall I compare them? I can think of nothing which even distantly resembles them unless it be an ant-hill. These giant ant-hills are scattered all over the face of the country, and thickest of all in the Delta. They are the first objects that excite the traveller's curiosity when he turns his back upon Alexandria and his face towards Cairo. He looks out of the window of the railway carriage, and yonder, a mile or so off in the midst of the cotton-fields, he sees a huge, irregular brown tumulus, some fifty or sixty feet in height, perfectly bare of vegetation, which looks as if it might cover fifteen or twenty acres of ground. This strange apparition is no sooner left behind than two or three more, some smaller, some larger, come into sight; and so on all the way to Cairo. At first he can scarcely believe that each contains the dead bones of an ancient town. When he comes to travel farther and know the country better, he discovers that these mounds are to be reckoned not by scores but by hundreds. So numerous are they that many a district of the Delta, if modelled in relief, might be taken for a raised map of some volcanic centre, such as the chain of the Puy de Dôme, in Auvergne.

Some mounds are of great extent. The mounds of Tanis, for instance, cover no less than forty acres; but then Tanis (better known, perhaps, by its scriptural name, Zoan) was a very important city, and more than once was the chosen capital of the empire. Others are so small that they can scarcely represent anything but hamlets or fortified posts.

But why, it may be asked, have these places, instead of falling into heaps of ruin, become converted into mounds? For the simple reason that the material of which they were constructed was mere earth, and so to earth they have returned. Like the Arab fellah of the present day, the Egyptian of five or six thousand years ago built his house of mud bricks mixed with a little chopped straw, and dried in the sun. The houses of the rich—built of the same material—were plastered and stuccoed, the walls and ceilings being decorated with elaborate polychrome designs, and the exterior relieved by light wooden colonnades and balconies. The huts of the poor were much the same as they are now—mere beehives of brown clay, which crumble slowly away in dry weather, and melt if it rains. Easily built and easily replaced, they were constantly falling out of repair, being levelled to the ground, trodden down, and rebuilt. Thus, each new house rose upon the ruins of the old one; and every time the process was repeated, a higher elevation was obtained for the foundation. In a country subject to annual inundation this in itself was an important advantage; and so, in the course of ages, what was probably a mere rising ground when first the town was founded, became a lofty hill, visible for miles across the plain.

Rightly to understand what I will venture to call the geological strata of an Egyptian mound, it is, however, necessary to have some idea of the processes of its growth and decay. These processes were everywhere the same; and if I attempt to sketch the history of a typical site, it must at the same time be remembered that my description represents no one mound in particular, but that it applies, in a general sense, to all.

We will suppose our typical mound to be situate in the Delta—possibly in the old Land of Goshen—and we will in imagination go back to that distant time when as yet the site was a mere barren sand-hill rising some twenty feet above the level of the soil. These sand-hillocks are the last visible vestiges of the old ocean-bed which underlies the whole of the Delta, beginning at Kalyúb, about ten miles below Cairo, and widening out like a gigantic fan to Alexandria on the western coast, to Damietta on the east. Now, the entire Delta is one vast deposit of mud annually brought down by the inundation of the Nile, and in the course of ages this mud has driven the sea back inch by inch, foot by foot, for a distance of more than one hundred miles. These sand-hills, which were formerly under the sea, are called by the Arabs "Gezireh," or islands; and they were naturally resorted to by the earliest nomadic tribes as places of refuge for themselves and their flocks during the season of the inundation. For the same reason, they became the sites of the first settlements. Every ancient ruin, every mound, every modern town and village in the Delta rests on a sandy eminence which once upon a time was covered by the blue waters of the Mediterranean.

Here, then, on an irregular platform of yellow sand surrounded by rich pastures in winter and summer, and by turbid floods in autumn, a few half-barbarous shepherds erect their primitive huts of wattle and daub; and here they set up a rude altar, consisting probably of a single upright stone brought with much labor and difficulty from the nearest point of the eastern or western cliffs. By-and-by, they or their descendants enclose that altar in a little mud-built shrine roofed over with palm branches, and wall in a surrounding space of holy ground.

As the centuries roll on, this first rude sanctuary gives place to a more ambitious structure built of stone; and to this structure successive generations add court-yards, porticos, colonnades, gate-ways, obelisks, and statues in such number that by the time of the Nineteenth Dynasty—that is to say, about the time of the Oppression and the Exodus—the temple covers an area as large as St. Peter's at Rome. In the meanwhile, the level of the inhabited parts of the town has been steadily rising, and the crude-brick dwellings of the townsfolk—upraised like a coral-reef by the perpetual deposition of building-rubbish—have attained so great an elevation that the temple actually stands in a deep hollow in the middle of the city, as if erected in the crater of an extinct volcano. Such was the condition of the great Temple of Bubastis when visited by Herodotus in the fifth century before Christ; and such, to this day, is the condition of the magnifi-

cent Temple of Edfû, excavated twenty years ago by Mariette.
Here the mound has been cut away all round the building,
which stands on the paved level of the ancient city, forty feet
below the spot from which one first looks down upon it.

We have thus far traced the history of our typical mound
from its first rude beginnings to the apex of its prosperity.
As time goes on, however, and the last native Dynasties ex-
pire, the trade of the community languishes, the population
dwindles, and the temple falls out of repair. Then comes
the prosperous period of Greek rule. Commerce and letters
revive, and the Ptolemies repair the temple, or perhaps re-
build it. Next comes the Roman period, closely followed by
the introduction of Christianity; and by-and-by, when the
national religion is proscribed, a community of Coptic monks
take possession of the grand old building, converting its
chambers into cells, and its portico into a Christian church.
The town now overflows into what was once the sacred
area. Mud huts are plastered between sculptured walls and
painted columns, and the ground begins to rise in and
about the temple as formerly it had risen outside the enclosure. Ere long the monks, weary of living at the bottom of a pit, proceed to erect a new monastery in one of
the suburbs. The temple, therefore, is partly pulled down
for building material; and its desecrated ruins, which now
constitute the poorest and most crowded quarter of the city,
become gradually choked within and without. At last,
even the roof is converted into a maze of huts and stables
swarming with human beings, poultry, dogs, kine, asses,
pigeons, and vermin. Thus, in process of time, the whole
building becomes buried, and its very site is forgotten. A
few centuries later the town is devastated by some great
calamity of plague or war, and, after an existence of perhaps
five thousand years, is finally deserted. Then the crude-
brick shells of its latest habitations crumble away, and
what was once a busy city clustered round a splendid temple, ends by becoming a heap of desolate, unsightly mounds
strewn with innumerable potsherds.

Such are the constituent parts of my typical mound; and all the mounds of Egypt are but variations upon this one original theme.

A mound is a concrete piece of history; and, given the date of its first and last chapters, nothing is easier than to predict what may be found in it. Let us now excavate this typical mound, which began with prehistoric Egypt, and ended, probably, about Anno Domini 600. The explorer who should sink a vertical shaft through the heart of the mass would cut through the relics of one hundred and sixty-eight generations of men. It would not be one town which he would lay open; it would be an immense succession of towns, stratum above stratum, with a semi-barbarian settlement at the bottom and a Christian town at the top. Amid the caked dust and rubbish of that Christian town he would find little terra-cotta lamps of the old classical shape, stamped with the palm or cross. And he would find Roman coins, Gnostic gems, and potsherds scribbled over with Coptic, Greek, and demotic memoranda. Here, too—hidden away, perhaps, in an earthen jar, in the evil days of religious persecution — he might hope to find a copy of the earliest Coptic translation of the Scriptures, or a priceless second century codex of the New Testament.

Next below this, in strata of the Greek period, he would find coins of the Ptolemies, Greek and Egyptian inscriptions, Greek and Egyptian papyri, images of Greek and Egyptian gods, and works of art in the Græco - Egyptian and pure Greek styles. Among other possible treasures might be discovered a copy of Manetho's History of Egypt, or some of the lost masterpieces of the Greek poets. Still working downward, he would come upon evidences of various periods of foreign conquest, in the form of Persian and Assyrian tablets; and below these, in strata of the Saïte time, would be found exquisite works of art in bronze, sculpture, and personal ornaments. Even when so low down as the Nineteenth Dynasty—the grand epoch of Rameses the Great—we are not yet half through our mound. Under the débris of that sumptuous period we may find traces of the Hyksôs, or Shepherd Kings—those mysterious invaders of Mongolian type who ruled Egypt for five hundred years. Below this again, we come upon relics of the magnificent Twelfth Dynasty; and so on down to the time of the Pyramid Kings, when we should find scarabs of Pepi, Unas, Khafra, and Khufu, and perhaps even of Mena himself! Nor must the temple buried in the heart of our mound be forgotten — a temple of which, perhaps, no two stones are left standing the one upon the other, but which, nevertheless, is rich in broken statues of Kings and gods, and in fragmentary records of victories and treaties, calendars of feasts, and votive inscriptions.

This sketch, however, is a mere outline of possibilities. No mound would be likely to yield all these consecutive links of history. Some would be found in one mound, and some in another. There are mounds and mounds. Excavation is a lottery, and the prizes vary in number and value. Excepting, of course, the second century codex and the copy of Manetho's History, almost every object which I have named as likely to be discovered in my typical mound has, however, actually been found in different places and at different times. I have myself picked up terra-cotta lamps stamped with early Christian emblems on the mounds of Memphis, inscribed potsherds in Nubia, scraps of beautiful blue-glazed ware at Denderah, mummy-bandages in the tombs of Thebes, and fragments of exquisite alabaster cups and bowls in the shadow of the Great Sphinx at Ghizeh. The mountain-slopes of Siût are strewn with cerement wrappings, and the débris of mummies broken up for the sake of their funerary amulets by the predatory Arabs; and there is not an ancient burial-ground, or mound, or ruined temple in Egypt where the traveller who has patience enough to grub under the soil beneath his feet may not find relics of the dead and gone past.

The Valley of the Nile is, in short, one great museum, of which the contents are perhaps one-third or one-fourth part only above ground. The rest is all below the surface, waiting to be discovered. Whether you go up the great river, or strike off to east or west across the desert, your horizon is always bounded by mounds, or by ruins, or by ranges of mountains honey-combed with tombs. If you but stamp your foot upon the sands, you know that it probably awakens an echo in some dark vault or corridor, untrodden of man for three or four thousand years. The mummied generations are everywhere—in the bowels of the mountains, in the faces of the cliffs, in the rock-cut labyrinths which underlie the surface of the desert. Exploration in such a land as this is a kind of chase. You think that you have discovered a scent. You follow it; you lose it; you find it again. You go through every phase of suspense, excitement, hope, disappointment, exultation. The explorer has need of all his wits, and he learns to use them with the keenness of a North American Indian.

Here his quick eye notes a depression in the soil, and beneath the sandy surface he detects something like the vague outline of a vast chess-board. Do these indicate the foundations of a building? Farther on the ground is strewn with splinters of limestone. Do they mark the wreck of a tomb? Yonder the mountain-side is seamed with beds of calcareous deposit, layer above layer; but at one point the cliff is broken clear away, and this escarpment, whether natural or artificial, is marked by a pile of fallen blocks and débris. Is this an accident of nature, or does it mark the entrance to some hitherto undiscovered sepulchre? Here, again, is a mysterious sign cut on the face of a cliff, and here another, and another. What do these figures mean? Do they point the way to some cavern full of treasure hidden away thousands of years ago, and has the rock been "blazed," as the Canadian settler blazes the forest-trees, that he may know how to retrace his steps?

The slenderest clew may lead to good-fortune, and every inch of the way is full of vague suggestions.

At last, guided half by experience, half by instinct, the explorer decides on a spot and calls up his workmen. They come—perhaps a dozen half-naked Arabs and some fifteen or twenty children—the men armed with short picks, the children with baskets in which to carry away the rubbish. A hole is dug, the sand is cleared away, the stony bed of the desert is reached, and there, just below the feet of the diggers, a square opening is seen in the rock. There is a shout of rejoicing. More men are called up, and the work begins in earnest. The shaft, however, is choked with sand and mud. A little lower down, and it is filled with a sort of concrete composed of chips of limestone, pebbles, sand, and water, which is almost as compact as the native rock. The men get down to a depth of six, twelve, fifteen, twenty feet. The baskets are now loaded at the bottom and hauled up, generally spilling half their contents by the way.

At last the sun goes down; twilight comes up apace; and the bottom of the square black funnel seems as far off as ever. Then the men trudge off to their homes, followed by the tired children; and the explorer suddenly finds out that he has had nothing to eat since seven o'clock in the morning, and that he has a furious headache. He goes back, however, at the same hour next morning, and for as many next mornings as need be till the end is reached. That may not be for a week or a fortnight. Some tomb-pits are from a hundred to a hundred and fifty feet deep; and some pits lead to a subterraneous passage another hundred or hundred and fifty feet long, which has to be cleared before the sepulchral chamber can be entered. When that long - looked-for moment comes at last, the explorer trusts himself to the rope — a flimsy twist of palm fibre, which becomes visibly thinner from the strain—and goes down as if into a mine.

What will he find to reward him for time spent and patience wearied? Who shall say? Perhaps a great nobleman of the time of Thothmes III. or of Rameses the Great, lying in state, just as they left him there three thousand years ago, enclosed in three coffins gorgeous with gold and colors; his carven staff, his damascened battle-axe, his alabaster vases, his libation vessels, and his "funeral baked meats," all un-

touched and awaiting his resurrection.   For so lie the royal
and noble dead of those foregone days:

> " Cased in cedar and wrapped in a sacred gloom ;
>   Swathed in linen and precious unguents old ;
>   Painted with cinnabar and rich with gold.
>   Silent they rest in solemn salvatory,
>   Sealed from the moth and the owl and the flitter-mouse,
>   Each with his name on his breast."

Or perhaps the explorer may find only a broken coffin,
some fragments of mummy-cloth, and a handful of bones.
The Arabs or the Romans, the Greeks or the Persians, or
perhaps the ancient Egyptians themselves, have been there
before him, and all the buried treasures—the arms, the jewels, the amulets, the papyri—are gone.

Yet, even so, there may be an inscription carved on one of
the walls or passages which alone is worth all the cost of
opening the tomb. It may possibly be a new chapter of
" The Book of the Dead"; or a genealogical table of the
family of the deceased, restoring some lost link in a royal
Dynasty; or perhaps a few lines scratched by an ancient
Greek or Roman tourist who happened to be there when the
tomb was plundered in the days of the Ptolemies or the
Cæsars. The traveller of olden time was as fond of leaving
his autograph on the monuments as any Cook's tourist of
to-day, and an ancient traveller's *graffito* may be of great historical interest. The explorer who should find the autograph
of Herodotus or Plato would feel that he had made a discovery worth at least as much as a papyrus, and more than a
good many mummies.

Such an exploration as I have just described would belong
to Upper Egypt, where the ruins are all above ground, and
where the explorer's object is mainly to discover subterraneous tombs.* In Lower Egypt, his work assumes a quite dif-

* This description (from page 12 to page 14) of an exploration in Upper
Egypt is a free adaptation from a passage in Professor Maspero's address,
delivered to the pupils of the Lycée Henri Quatre in August, 1887.

ferent character. There he has to deal chiefly with mounds —huge rubbish-heaps from twenty to sixty or seventy feet in height—which extend over many acres, and mark the sites of deserted and forgotten cities. The labor here is all above the surface; but it is none the less difficult on that account, and none the less costly. The work of the Egypt Explora-

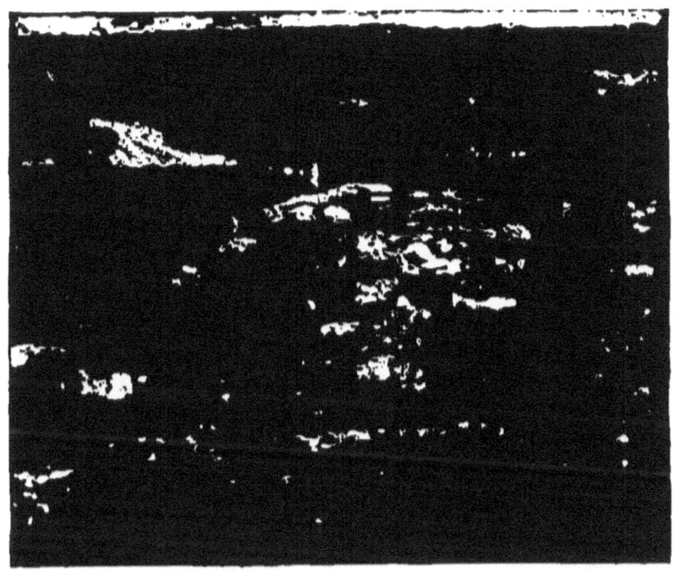

TELL NEBESHEH.

Tell Nebesheh is here shown as it appeared at the close of Mr. Petrie's excavations, the spot selected for excavation being the site of the great pylon gate-way in advance of the temple ruins. The black granite sphinx (headless) is seen in middle distance to left; and in the centre, on the edge of this group of ruins, lying upon its right side, may be detected the seated colossal statue of Rameses II.

tion Fund, for instance, has hitherto been restricted to the Delta, and its excavations have all been excavations of mounds. I know, therefore, only too well what unmanageable and expensive articles they are, and how heavily they tax the energies and health of the explorer.

A mound may be situate some fifteen or twenty miles

from the nearest railway station, market-town, or post-office. It may be in a district so thinly populated that the workmen have to be hired from a distance, and are obliged to camp out in the open desert. Long after the annual inundation has subsided south of Cairo a mound in the Delta may be surrounded by unwholesome swamps, and be unapproachable except by the higher order of amphibia, such as the explorer and his followers.

When Mr. Petrie and Mr. Griffith went to Tell Nebesheh in the month of February, 1886, they literally landed on an unknown island in the Eastern Delta, far from the Nile, far from the Mediterranean, and farther still from the Gulf of Suez. This statement, if unexplained, might well be received with polite incredulity; but it is literally true.

The winter floods were still out; the marshes were lakes; the desert was mud; the roads were under water. Mr. Petrie, coming from the westward by canal-boat, found himself put ashore, with three miles of swamp (including a canal, which he waded) between himself and his destination. Mr. Griffith, coming from the south-east, encountered worse swamps, and a canal both wider and deeper, which he was obliged to swim. To the southward, to the northward, it was all the same—water and sand, water and mud, water and marsh. On this dreary island the two explorers lived and labored for some eight or ten weeks, and it was not till the last month of their sojourn that the surrounding country became really dry. Nor could they be said, meanwhile, to have lived in the lap of luxury. They were lodged in a guest-chamber attached to the house of the Sheikh of Nebesheh, who rode into the room every evening on his donkey and paid them a visit of two hours. This room was of large size, with an earthen floor strongly impregnated with salt, and always damp. An earthen divan, under which the rats burrowed in legions, ran round the walls; and the ceiling was made of palm trunks, along which the said rats ran upsidedown with alarming activity from sunset till dawn.

Like many places in Egypt, modern as well as ancient, this

mound rejoiced in a variety of names, being known as Tell Nebesheh, *alias* Tell Bedawi, *alias* Tell Farûn. The first is the name of the modern village; the second means "the mound of the Bedouin"; the third (perpetuating, perhaps, an echo of old tradition) means "the mound of the Pharaoh." "The mound of graves" would be a better name than any of these, for the place proved to be a vast and very ancient cemetery, the level of which had been raised from age to age by successive strata of interments. Moreover, it was a large mound; so large that, besides the above-named cemetery, it contained the remains of two ancient towns and the site of a temple. The temple occupied the eastern extremity of the mound, and was formerly surrounded by a sacred enclosure about six hundred feet square.

Now this cemetery turned out to be a very curious place, quite unlike the cemeteries of Memphis, Abydos, and Thebes. It consisted of an immense number of small chambers, or isolated groups of chambers, scattered irregularly over a sandy plain. These were built of unbaked brick and roofed with barrel-vaulting. Some of the largest were cased (or lined, if subterranean) with limestone. These tomb-chambers dated from about the period of the Twentieth Dynasty. In later times—in the sixth century B.C., and after—large blocks of about a dozen chambers became frequent. These tombs had nearly all been pillaged in early times, so that in a hundred only half a dozen bodies were found; and not only had the chambers fallen to decay, but they had been levelled, and others built on them, so that three or four successive occupations of the same ground might be traced. In some of these vaults Mr. Petrie found quantities of bones indiscriminately piled, not as if they had been thrown in by spoilers or tomb-breakers, but as if they had been dug up *en masse* from some other site, and reinterred without ceremony.

In one of the earlier tombs no fewer than two hundred uninscribed funerary statuettes in green-glazed pottery were found; and in another some thirty thousand beads of glass, silver, and lapis lazuli. Bronze spear-heads, amulets,

2

scarabs, etc., were also turned up in considerable numbers. Last, but in point of interest certainly not least, came the discovery of two sets of masonic deposits under the corners of an unimportant building in the cemetery. These consisted of miniature mortars, corn-rubbers, and specimen plaques of materials used in the building, such as glazed-ware, various colored marbles, jasper, and the like.

A magnificent gray granite sarcophagus inscribed for a prince and priest of the Twenty-sixth Dynasty, and part of a limestone statue dedicated to Harpakhrat, the "child Horus," whose legendary birthplace was in these Delta marshlands, yielded the Egyptian name of this site, which represented all that remained of the ancient city of Am; while among other valuable monuments exhumed in the course of the excavations were a black granite altar of the reign of Amenemhat II., third Pharaoh of the great Twelfth Dynasty; two thrones in red sandstone, belonging to statues of royal personages of the same line; a colossal seated statue of Rameses II., in black granite; and, most interesting of all, a headless black granite sphinx,(') upon which successive Pharaohs had engraved their cartouches, or royal ovals, each in turn erasing the names and titles of his predecessors. The description of this granite palimpsest is best given in Mr. Petrie's own words, as written in his weekly report at the time of the discovery:

"Originally made under the Twelfth Dynasty, to judge by the style, it has erased cartouches on the chest, between the paws, on each shoulder, on the right flank (the left being broken away), and, sixthly, an erased inscription around the base. Besides these, two legible inscriptions remain—namely, the cartouche of Seti II. on the chest, and the cartouches of Set-nekht [Rameses I.] on the left shoulder."

If, however, statues and inscriptions and funerary treasures are the reward of the explorer, he pays amply for that reward in personal discomfort, and sometimes even in actual privation. At Tell Defenneh, where Mr. Petrie made his celebrated discovery of the ruins of "Pharaoh's House at Tah-

panhes," there were greater hardships to be borne than at
Tell Nebesheh. Here the mounds were hemmed in between
a barren desert and a brackish lake; there was no food pur-
chasable nearer than Zagazig, some fifteen miles distant,

TELL-EL-YAHÛDIEH.

This mound, excavated by M. Naville in 1887, gives an excellent idea of a mound
which has been cut and caved away by many generations of Arab husbandmen.
The whole mound was originally a homogeneous mass of the height of the nearest mass, which is scaled by the small human figures to the left of the picture.

and the water was barely drinkable. The diggers lived on
mere lentils, and in default of any shelter from the burning
sun of mid-day and the cold chills of midnight, they dug out
burrows for themselves in the sand-hillocks, and roofed them
over with tamarisk boughs. Mr. Petrie, of course, had his
tent; but in the matter of food he was not much better off
than his Arabs, having only biscuits and tinned vegetables
in his scanty larder.

When Mr. Petrie, Mr. Griffith, and Mr. Ernest Gardner

were working all three together at Naukratis they divided the work ; one superintending the excavation of the Temple of Aphrodite, another the excavation of the ancient town, and the third the excavation of the cemetery. Then arose a very important question—which should undertake the cooking, and which should do the washing-up? Now the work in the town was the heaviest, so he who took the heaviest task could not also be the cook. The cemetery, again, was a long way off, and the cook could not therefore go to and fro between the camp and the cemetery. The temple, though requiring great care and attention, was really the lightest work; so it was finally agreed that the town should take life easily when not on duty in the diggings, that the temple should do the cooking, and that the cemetery should do the washing-up.

The explorer, of all men, must "scorn delights and live laborious days." His day must begin at sunrise, when his workmen are due. First he must go round and assign to each worker his individual task, booking every man's name as he comes in: this takes perhaps one hour and a half. He then goes to his tent and has breakfast, and after breakfast he makes his second round. He now helps, perhaps, to move a huge block or two, stirs up the lazy digger, catches a pilferer in the act and dismisses him, separates gossips, copies inscriptions, or takes photographs, with the sun blazing overhead and the thermometer standing at 99° in the shade. In the evening he writes reports, journals, and letters; classifies and catalogues the objects discovered during the day ; draws plans, makes up his accounts, and so forth. At last he goes to bed, dead tired, and is kept awake half the night by predatory rats, mice, and other "small deer." At Tanis the mice were simply unbearable. Being field-mice, they would not walk into traps like civilized mice, so the explorer's only resource was to burn a night-light and shoot them. Now to lie in bed and shoot mice with a revolver is surely a form of sport exclusively reserved for the explorer in Egypt. Flies, of course, are legion, and the white ant is a perpetual plague of the first water. Besides a way they have of transporting biscuits, dates, coffee, sugar, and all sorts of portable provisions to their own private residences, these horrid insects have an abnormal appetite for paper, and consume reports, correspondence, and even hieroglyphic dictionaries as eagerly as young ladies devour novels and romances.

The great field of archæological exploration in Egypt is not by any means an easy field to cultivate. The ground has gone to waste for hundreds, perhaps thousands, of years, and become sheer wilderness; and he who would hope to

TELL NEBIREH.

Two of the great trenches cut by Mr. Petrie are visible in the illustration, one at the north end, the other at the south end of the mound. On the highest part to the left is an Arab cemetery.

reap a harvest from it must clear it, dig it, and put in a vast amount of that expensive patent manure called *brains.*

Few, very few, probably, of those who "sit at home at ease" have any clear notion of the qualifications which go to make an explorer of the right sort—still less of the kind of life he is wont to lead when engaged in the work of exploration. They know that he goes to Egypt just as our November fogs are coming on, and that he thereby escapes our miserable English winter. They also know that he lives in a tent, and that he spends his time in "discovering things." Now what can be more romantic than life in a tent? And what can possibly be more charming than "discovering things?" They may not be very clear as to the nature of the "things" in question; but they, at all events, conceive of his life as a series of delightful surprises, and of himself as the favorite of fortune, having but to dip his hand into a sort of archæological lottery-box, and take out nothing but prizes. Of the judgment, the patience, the skill which are needed in the mere selection of a site for excavation; of the vigilance which has to be exercised while the excavations are in progress; of the firm but good-humored authority requisite for the control of a large body of Oriental laborers; of the range of knowledge indispensable for the interpretation and classification of the objects which may be discovered, the outside public has no more conception than I have of the qualities and training necessary for the command of an iron-clad.

In the first place, the explorer in Egypt must have a fair knowledge of colloquial Arabic, no small share of diplomatic tact, a strong will, an equable temper, and a good constitution. It is important that he should be well acquainted with Egyptian, Biblical, Babylonian, Assyrian, Greek, and Roman history; for the annals of these nations continually overlap, or are dovetailed into one another, and the explorer is at any time likely to come upon cuneiform tablets such as have lately been found in large numbers at Tell el Amarna, in Upper Egypt; or upon relics of the Hebrews, such as the ancient Jewish cemetery discovered by M. Naville at Tell el Yahúdieh, in Lower Egypt, in 1887; or upon Greek documents, Greek pottery, and Greek terra-cottas, such as have rewarded the labors of Mr. Petrie, Mr. Griffith, and Mr.

Ernest Gardner at Naukratis, in the Eastern Delta. Fragments of Homer, Alcæus, Sappho, and other Greek poets have been found from time to time in Egypt during the present century, some scribbled on potsherds and some written on papyrus.(') It is not three years since Mr. Petrie found a complete copy of the Second Book of the "Iliad," written on papyrus in most beautiful uncial Greek by a scribe of the second century after Christ, and buried under the head of a woman in the Græco-Egyptian necropolis of Hawara, in the Fayûm. The woman had apparently been young and beautiful. Her teeth were small and regular, and her long, silky black hair had been cut off and laid in a thick coil upon her breast. Was she a

ARCHAIC HEAD OF CYPRIOTE TYPE.
Found in the ruins of Naukratis.

Greek, or was she an Egyptian lady learned in the language of the schools? We know not. There was no inscription to tell of her nationality or her name. We only know that she was young and fair, and that she so loved her Homer that it was buried with her in the grave. Her head and her beautiful black hair are now in the Ethnographical Department of the Natural History Museum at South Kensington, and her precious papyrus is in the Bodleian Library at Oxford.

To appreciate and report upon such a find as this, or upon the inscriptions discovered at Naukratis, the explorer must, of course, be a fairly competent Greek scholar.

Still more of course must he be sufficiently conversant with the ancient Egyptian language to translate any hieroglyphic inscriptions which he may discover. A knowledge of trigonometry, though not absolutely indispensable, is of value in surveying sites and determining ancient levels.

But, above all, the explorer must be a good "all-round" archæologist.

Now, does the world—meaning thereby the great body of
cultivated readers—at all realize what it is to be a good "all-
round" archæologist? It must be remembered, first of all,
what that science is, or rather that aggregate of sciences,
which goes by the name of Archæology. Were I asked
to define it, I should reply that archæology is that science
which enables us to register and classify our knowledge of
the sum of man's achievement in those arts and handicrafts
whereby he has, in time past, signalized his passage from
barbarism to civilization. The first chapter of this science
takes up the history of the human race at a date coeval with
the mammoth and other extinct mammalia; and its last
chapter, which must always be in a state of transition, may
be said to end for the present with about a hundred or a
hundred and fifty years ago.

Now archæology in Egypt begins later, and ends earlier,
than archæology in this broad and general sense. We have
never yet got far enough behind the first chapters of Egyptian history to discover any traces of a stone age.(ᵇ) The
stone age of the Nile Valley, if it ever existed, underlies
such a prodigious stratum of semi-barbaric civilization that
the spade of the excavator has not yet reached it. Also,
Egyptian archæology, properly so called, ends with the
last chapter of Egyptian history; that is to say, with the
abolition of the ancient religion in the latter half of the
fourth century of our era. Hence, our explorer in Egypt is
only called upon to be an "all-round" archæologist within
the field of the national history: namely, from the time
of Mena, the prototype of Egyptian royalty, who probably
reigned about five thousand years before Christ, down to
the time of the Emperor Theodosius, Anno Domini 379.
Yet even within that limit, he has to know a great deal
about a vast number of things. He must be familiar with
all the styles and periods of Egyptian architecture, sculpture,
and decoration; with the forms, patterns, and glazes of Egyp-

tian pottery; with the distinctive characteristics of the mummy - cases, sarcophagi, methods of embalmment and styles of bandaging peculiar to interments of various epochs; and with all phases of the art of writing, hieroglyphic, hieratic, and demotic. Nor is this all. He must know by the measurement of a mud brick, by the color of a glass bead, by the modelling of a porcelain statuette, by the pattern of

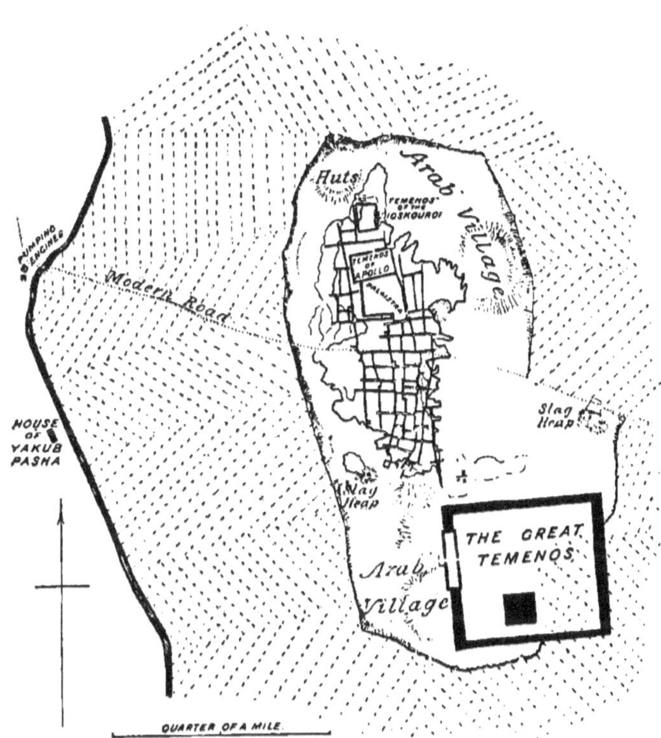

PLAN OF NAUKRATIS.

The plan is reduced from Mr. Petrie's large plate in "Naukratis," Part I., and shows the lines of the ancient streets, and the sites of such temples and public buildings as were discovered in the course of the first season's work, including the Great Temenos (Pan-Hellenion). The temples of Hera and Aphrodite were found the following year. The canal to left follows the course of the ancient canal which formed the famous "port" of the city.

an ear-ring, to what period each should be assigned. He must be conversant with all the types of all the gods; and last, not least, he must be able to recognize a forgery at first sight.

After this, it must I think be admitted that the explorer, like the poet, is "born, not made." The wonder perhaps is that he should ever be born at all. Fortunately, however, for the cause of knowledge, this phenomenal individual does from time to time make his appearance upon earth; and according to the form he assumes under his different *avatars*, he proceeds to excavate Troy, Curium, Halicarnassus, Nineveh, Bubastis, or Naukratis.

The discovery and excavation of the scanty ruins of this last site—the famous and long-lost city of Naukratis—was due to Mr. Petrie. Former travellers had, for the last fifty years, sought for it in vain, and given up the quest in despair. Ebers looked for it at Dessûk, and Mariette at Salhadscher, in the neighborhood of Saïs. Mr. Petrie found it, almost by accident, in the course of an archæological tramp undertaken at the commencement of his working season in 1884. He was tracking the western frontier-line of the Delta, and thus came across a large mound some three thousand feet in length by fifteen hundred feet in width, the surface of which was so thickly strewn with fragments of fine Greek figured ware that it was impossible to walk upon it in any direction without crushing these beautiful potsherds at every step. It was, in fact, to quote his own words, "like walking through the smashings of the vase-room of the British Museum." It was to this place that he returned in 1885, when he made one of the most important historical and archæological discoveries which have ever rewarded the labors of the explorer in Egypt.

The local name of the mound and of the adjacent village (for which it is vain to look in any guide-book maps) is Nebireh. The place lies about equidistant between Alexandria and Cairo, and about six miles west-north-west of Tell el Barûd. When Mr. Petrie first found his way thither, he

FOUNDATION DEPOSITS OF PTOLEMY PHILADELPHUS, B.C. 286–274.

The model mortar is the most distant object in the group, which consists of seven ranks. In the second rank are the corn-rubbers, *i.e.* two pieces of red granite, the one concave, the other convex. Rank 3, two libation vases in green glazed ware. Rank 4, four libation cups in same ware. Rank 5, bronze trowels and chisels, and two pegs of alabaster. Rank 6, bronze hatchet, chisels, sacrificial knife, and two pegs of alabaster. Rank 7, specimens of materials, mud brick; plaque of glazed ware; ingots of gold, silver, lead, copper, and iron; fragments of lapis lazuli, agate, jasper, turquoise, and obsidian. This set of masonic deposits, as also those discovered by M. Naville at Tell Qarmus, are in the British Museum.

was the first European traveller who had set foot in that secluded hamlet; and when he applied for permission to excavate the mound, he found the place unknown, even by name, to the official world at Bûlak. The painted potsherds with which the place was strewn, literally " thick as leaves in Vallombrosa," proved on examination to be even more beautiful and various than he had at first supposed. Here were cup-handles with men's heads modelled in relief;

fragments of archaic vases painted in black and crimson on a buff ground with figures of griffins, hogs, and the like; fragments of light brown ware with archaic animals in black and red, the ground *parsemé* with flowers; others of the finest work, with figures of horses, goddesses, and so forth, left in the brown body on a black ground; and a great abundance of all the common sorts of red pottery with raised patterns of lines and balls, brown with red fretwork, black on bronze picked out with chocolate and white, and many more varieties than I have space to enumerate. With these he also found fragments of Greek and Cypriote statuettes in limestone and alabaster; pottery and limestone whorls (some notched where worn by the thread); stamped amphora-handles, Greek and Egyptian weights, beads, terracotta statuettes, and small objects of various kinds in green glazed ware.

Strangely enough, Mr. Petrie seems to have had no suspicion of the truth, and when, on the fourth day after his arrival at Nebireh, he discovered a limestone slab engraved with an inscription in honor of one Heliodorus, a citizen of Naukratis, he was utterly taken by surprise. "I almost jumped," he said, " when I read these words :*

> "'The City of Naukratis [honors]
> Heliodorus, son of Dorion Philo . . .
> Priest of Athena for life . . .
> Keeper of The Records for virtue and good-will.'"

So, here was Naukratis—that ancient and famous mart where Greek and Egyptian first dwelt and traded together on equal terms; Naukratis, founded, as it is believed, by Milesian colonists; granted, with special privileges and charters, to the Hellenic tribes by Amasis II. of the Twen-

* Η ΠΟΛΙΣ Η ΝΑΥΚΡΑΤ Η . . .
ΗΛΙΟΔΩ ΡΟΝ ΔΩΡΙΩΝΟΣ ΦΙΛΘ . . .
ΤΟΝ . . . ΕΑΤΗΣ ΑΘΗΝΑΣ ΔΙΑΒΙΟΝ . . .
ΣΥΙ . . . ΡΑΦΟΦΥΛΑ ΑΡΕΤΣΚΑ . . .
ΕΝΕΚΤΗΣ ΕΙΣ ΑΥΤΗΝ . . .

ty-sixth Egyptian Dynasty; and renowned in the times of Athenæus and Herodotus for the skill of its potters and the taste of its florists! And now discovery followed fast upon discovery, every day's work bringing more and more corroborative evidence to light. Inscriptions, coins, sculptures, bronzes, terra-cottas turned up in astonishing profusion, and among other treasures a fine slab engraved with the dedication of a palæstra, or public wrestling-school, for the youth of the city. As the trenching and clearing progressed, yet more important results were obtained. The sites, ruins, and sacred enclosures of two temples dedicated to Apollo — the one erected upon the débris of the other —were first brought to light.

The earlier structure was built of limestone, and, to judge by the style of columns and cornice, dates from about B.C. 700 to B.C. 600. The later (*circa* B.C. 400) was of white marble, and exquisitely decorated. Close outside the temenos-wall of one of these temples Mr. Petrie came upon a great deposit of magnificent libation-bowls, accidentally broken in the service of the temple, and thrown out as useless. Most of them are inscribed with votive dedications by pious Milesians, Teans, and others. Later on, the remains of the famous Pan-Hellenion, and the ruins of the temples of Hera, Zeus, and Aphrodite were discovered, all of them mentioned by Herodotus and Athenæus. These discoveries were the work of two successive seasons, the first season's explorations being conducted by Mr. Petrie, and the second by Mr. Ernest A. Gardner, now Director of the English School of Archæology at Athens. The

ARCHAIC STATUETTE OF A HUNTER.

Found in the ruins of the Temple of Aphrodite at Naukratis. —British Museum, Greek department.

lines of the streets of the ancient city were yet traceable; the "potters' quarter" was identified; and not only were several of the potters' kilns found intact, but also the ruins of a potter's factory. This potter, whomsoever he may have been, did a great trade in scarabs. He made all sorts of things—miscellaneous amulets, toys, gods, beads, and so forth—but scarabs were his specialty. The Egyptian scarab is now so familiar an object in all museums and private collections that I need hardly describe how these tiny amulets are made in the shape of a beetle—the backs exactly imitated from nature, but the undersides engraved, like seals, with an immense variety of devices, such as mottoes, sacred emblems, figures of gods and kings, scrolls, animals, fish, flowers, and the like.(') In the ruins of this old artist's workshops Mr. Petrie found hundreds of scarabs, finished and unfinished, hundreds of clay moulds for casting the same, lumps of various pigments for coloring the scarabs, and other appliances of the trade. The scarab-maker's business came somehow to an untimely end about five hundred and seventy years before Christ; for the place had evidently been suddenly deserted, all the good man's stock in trade being left behind. As the Greek colonists fought at that time on the side of Apries, the legitimate Pharaoh, when Amasis revolted and usurped the throne, we may fairly conclude that Naukratis suffered for the loyalty of her inhabitants, and that our scarab-maker was ruined with the rest of his fellow-citizens.

In another part of the town Mr. Petrie came upon the remains of a jeweller's workshop, containing a quantity of lump silver, and a large store of beautiful archaic Greek coins, fresh from the mint of Athens. These coins had never been in circulation, and they were doubtless intended to be made up into necklaces and ear-rings, after a fashion much admired by the fair ladies of Hellas, and recently revived by the jewellers of modern Europe.

Most important, also, is the evidence here brought to bear upon the origin and growth of the ceramic arts of Greece. Patterns which we had long believed to be purely Greek are now traced back, step by step, to Egyptian originals. The well-known "Greek honeysuckle" pattern, for instance, is found to be neither Greek nor honeysuckle. The Naukratis pottery furnishes specimens of this design in all its stages.

In its most archaic form, it is neither more nor less than the stock "lotus pattern" of the Egyptian potters.(') Taken in hand by the Greek, it becomes expanded, lightened, and transformed. Yet more important is the light thrown upon the origin and development of Greek art. We have long known that the early Greek, when emerging from prehistoric barbarism, must have gone to school to the Delta and the Valley of the Nile, not only for his first lessons in letters and science, but also for his earliest notions of architecture and the arts. Now, however, for the first time, we are placed in possession of direct evidence of these facts. We see the process of teaching

HEAD OF APHRODITE.

From the ruins of the Temple of Aphrodite, Naukratis. Alexandrian period. This head is in the British Museum, Greek department.

on the part of the elder nation, and of learning on the part of the younger. Every link in the chain which connects the ceramic art of Greece with the ceramic art of Egypt is displayed before our eyes in the potsherds of Naukratis.

More novel and curious than all, however, was a series of discoveries of ceremonial deposits buried under the four corners of a building adjoining the Pan-Hellenion.(")

The enclosure wall of the Pan-Hellenion was fifty feet thick and forty feet high, and it was built about six hundred or six hundred and fifty years before the Christian era. Within this enclosure were clustered not only the temples of the gods, but the treasury and storehouses of the citizens, who were essentially a trading and manufacturing community. In a later age Ptolemy Philadelphus appears to have filled up a breach in this wall with a great building and gate-way, and it was under the four corners of this gateway that the masonic deposits of the royal builder were found. Under each corner, upon the dark clay of the soil, had been laid a little bed of white sand; and in this bed of white sand, which Mr. Petrie scraped away with his own hands, he found a whole series of diminutive models laid in a specially prepared hole, upon which sand had afterwards been poured in such wise as completely to cover the objects beneath.

These objects were of three kinds; namely, models of tools, models of materials, and models commemorative of the ceremony performed in laying the foundations. There was, for instance, a model hoe for digging out the ground; a model rake, such as those used for making mortar; a model adze; a model chisel; a tiny trowel for spreading the mortar; a model hatchet for shaping the beams; and four little alabaster pegs —models of those used to mark out the four corners of the building. These were the models of tools.

Then came models of articles used in the masonic ceremony: a model mortar and pair of corn-rubbers, a pair of model libation-vases, and four model cups in glazed pottery. These, probably, had reference to some rite in which offerings of bread, oil, and wine were made. Also, there was found with them a model sacrificial knife and axe, such as might be used for the slaying of victims. These were the ceremonial objects.

Finally, there were samples of materials: a model brick of Nile clay; a tiny plaque of glazed-ware; other plaques of lapis lazuli, agate, jasper, turquoise, and obsidian; a Liliputian ingot of iron; and other ingots of copper, silver, lead, and gold. The largest of these are less than a domino, and the majority are less than half that size. Last of all—last and lowest—so firmly attached by a bed of rust to the handle of a second miniature bronze trowel that it could not be removed without danger of breakage, was found a little plaque of oval lapis lazuli in the form of a royal cartouche, engraved with the names and titles of Ptolemy Philadelphus. The model clay brick shows the material of the mass of the building; the plaque of glazed-ware represents the tile-facings and general surface decoration; while the plaques of precious stones show the more costly substances used for inlaying. These objects are now in the British Museum. They are most beautifully wrought, in perfect preservation, and so small that they would all lie upon a sheet of letter-paper. This was the first discovery of masonic deposits ever made in Egypt, and it marks an entirely new departure in the field of exploration. It is impossible, indeed, to over-estimate the historical value of a discovery which thus places in our hands for future use a key to the age and date of every important building in Egypt.

This discovery was made five years ago, and it has already borne abundant fruit. Masonic deposits were found by Mr. Petrie in 1886, at Tell Nebesheh, under the substructions of a temple built by Amasis II. in the ancient Egyptian city of

VOTIVE BOWL

(mended) discovered in the great trench of the Temple of Aphrodite, Naukratis.
British Museum.

(mended) discovered in the great trench of the Temple of Aphrodite, Naukratis.
British Museum.

Am; and again under the substructions of a ruined temple
at Tell Gemayemi, during the same year, by Mr. Griffith.
At Tell Qarmus, in 1887, M. Naville also discovered a series of ceremonial deposits of the time of Philip Arrhideus.
Explorers, in short, now make systematic search for foundation deposits, and up to the present time, with but one exception, they have invariably found them.

No large works of sculpture were found in the ruins of
Naukratis, with the exception of two much-damaged sphinxes and the remains of a headless colossal ram in white marble. Hands, feet, and other fragments of life-size statues
were, however, turned up in the precincts of the various temples, besides a large number of smaller heads ·and torsos of
marble, limestone, and terra-cotta. Some of these represent

the deities worshipped in these temples, while others are fashioned in the likeness of their votaries. Some, again, date
from the rude archaic beginnings of the Greek school of
Naukratis, and others carry us on to the finest period of
Alexandrian art. Very interesting as an example of the
earlier school is this statuette of a man carrying a hare over
each shoulder, and a knife in his girdle. It has been supposed to represent Apollo as the hunter god; but as it was
found in the ruins of the Temple of Aphrodite, it is more
probably a votive offering on the part of a sportsman who
thus dedicates himself to the service of the goddess. The
treatment of the head and hair is distinctly Cypriote in
style, while the rigidity of the pose, and the "hieratic" position of the feet and arms, are as distinctly Egyptian. A
much-defaced votive inscription in archaic Greek characters
is engraved on the right leg. Found on the same site, but
widely separate in date, is the beautiful terra-cotta head of
Aphrodite, here reproduced as an example of the high degree
of perfection to which the Greek
artists of Naukratis had attained
before the decadence of the city,
when superseded by Alexandria.

The excavation of the Temple
of Aphrodite proved to be ex-
traordinarily rich in fragments of
painted and inscribed Greek ware.
A huge trench appears to have
been dug round the temple platform in ancient times, and into
this trench must have been thrown
an immense store of bowls, vases,
cups, and figurines—the ceramic
treasures of the temple. The clearing of this mine of precious fragments occupied Mr. Gardner for
several weeks, six or seven basketfuls being the result of each day's

GORGONEIA.

(From the cemetery, Naukratis.)
The Greeks of the later period
at Naukratis were interred for
the most part in wooden coffins
ornamented with rosettes, gry-
phons, and gorgoneia in terra-cotta, painted and gilded.
These gorgoneia are moulded
in the classic type of the Alexandrian period.

work. One week alone—the week ending on February 13, 1886 — yielded no less than thirty-five large basketfuls of these exquisite potsherds, making, at a rough computation, about four hundred and fifty pounds in weight, or a total number of twenty-five thousand fragments. The sorting and classifying of the fragments consumed more than a year of Mr. Gardner's time; and about twenty or twenty-five vases, bowls, and other objects have been put together more or less completely. Two of these mended bowls, described by Mr. Ernest A. Gardner as among "the most magnificent examples of ancient pottery found at Naukratis," are here reproduced. These bowls have each two triple handles terminating in a human face at each end; while midway between the handles on each side is a boss with two faces back to back. A frieze of gazelles browsing on a ground parsemé with floral and other emblems, runs round the outside; the inside being decorated with a central star-shaped ornament surrounded by a frieze of lions, geese, sphinxes, etc.(*) Some of these votive offerings, as shown by the *graffiti* of the donors, were given by citizens of Teos, and others by Milesians.

Taken chronologically, these Naukratis fragments—for they are mostly fragments—constitute not only a series of valuable finds, but an "object-lesson" of the highest interest on the history of the ceramic arts of Greece. We first of all detect the Milesian colonist trying his "'prentice hand" at scarab-making, and producing at best but a blundering imitation of that popular product of his adopted home. Next we find him taking to pottery, properly so called; and, with the vivacious fancy of his race, adapting, varying, and playing with the old stock subjects of Egyptian ornament. Presently he casts aside the trammels of tradition and launches out into a style of his own—a style as purely Hellenic, and as original, as if his first lessons had never been learned in an Oriental school.

II.

THE BURIED CITIES OF ANCIENT EGYPT.

IF as a rule the busy American, no less than the busy Eng·lishman, knows less about Egypt both ancient and modern than about many less interesting lands, we may assume that his apparent indifference is mainly due to the remoteness of the place and the subject. From the port of New York to the harbor of Alexandria, as the crow flies, may be roughly estimated at between five and six thousand miles; while for those who are not crows the transit, even at high pressure, would scarcely be accomplished under three weeks.

But if modern Egypt is so far away that it takes three weeks to get there, ancient Egypt is infinitely more distant. The traveller who would visit the court of Memphis in the days of the earliest Egyptian monarchy must undertake a journey of some six or seven thousand years. He must not only go up the Nile; he must ascend the great River of Time and trace the stream of History to its source.

Do we realize how far distant is his goal, or how many familiar landmarks he must leave behind? We are accustomed to think of the days of Plato and Pericles, of Horace and the Cæsars, as "ancient times." But Egypt was old and outworn when Athens and Rome were founded; the great

Assyrian Empire was a creation of yesterday as compared with that of the Pharaohs; the middle point of Egyptian history was long past when Moses received his education at the court of Rameses II.; and the Pyramids were already hoary with antiquity when Abraham journeyed into the land of Egypt.

Where, then, it may be asked, are we to place the starting-point of Egyptian history? That is a very difficult question to answer. The dawn is long past when we catch our first glimpse of that far-distant epoch when Mena, Prince of Thinis, became chief of the chieftains of the primitive clans, and founded the first monarchy. That earliest landmark—dimly seen down the vista of ages—carries us back to about five thousand years before the Christian era; and even Mena, who is undoubtedly an historical personage, has a background of tradition behind him. That background of tradition represents prehistoric Egypt; and of prehistoric Egypt we at all events know that it was subdivided into a number of principalities which subsequently became the "Nomes," or Provinces, of United Egypt.

The rulers of these earliest petty states were remembered by the Egyptians of after ages as the *Horshesu*, or "Followers of Horus." They occupied, in fact, much the same place in Egyptian history and tradition which the demi-gods occupied in the history and tradition of Hellas; but with this great difference—the demi-gods were purely mythical heroes, whereas the *Horshesu* were human rulers, living in a land where political boundaries were already sharply defined. It is possible—we may even go so far as to say it is probable—that a gigantic work of art belonging to that inconceivably remote age survives to this day in the great Sphinx of Ghizeh.([10]) Hence it may be seen that even in prehistoric Egypt we are as far as ever from the beginnings of civilization; and beyond this, all is impenetrable night.

The existence of Egypt as a nation begins with Mena, the first king of the First Dynasty, and ends with Cleopatra. These two names are the preface and finis of Egyptian history.

Between them lies a space of 4790 years, comprising thirty-three royal dynasties and many hundreds of kings. Those kings were not all native to the soil. Egypt, during the long centuries of her slow decadence, was often ruled by princes of alien blood. But it was not till Cleopatra's galley turned and fled at the fatal sea-fight in which Mark Antony was defeated that the empire of the Pharaohs ceased to be a nation, and became a Roman province. So fell the most ancient of monarchies, the parent of all our arts and all our sciences, bequeathing to later ages a history so long that, compared with the history of other nations, it is almost like a geological period.

It was during these 4790 years of national existence that all those temples were erected, all those pyramids, obelisks, and colossal statues, of which the shattered remains are to this day the marvel and admiration of travellers.

Now, Egypt is unapproachably rich in building material. From Cairo to the first cataract—a stretch of five hundred and eighty-two miles—the Nile flows between a double range of cliffs which sometimes dip sheer down to the water's edge, and sometimes recede to a considerable distance from the bed of the river. For the first five hundred and fifteen miles —that is, from Cairo to Edfû—these cliffs are of fine white limestone; then, for a distance of sixty-five miles, the limestone is superseded by a rich yellow sandstone; and this again is succeeded, some sixty-seven miles higher up, by the red granite and black basalt of Assûan.

With such resources within easy reach, and with the great river for a means of transport, it is no wonder that the Egyptians became a nation of builders. In no country ancient or modern were there so many cities, so many temples, so many tombs. The cities have become rubbish-mounds. The tombs have been plundered for ages, and are being plundered every day. The temples have been ravaged by the Persian, the Assyrian, and the Mohammedan invader, defaced by the Christian iconoclast, and smashed up for the limekiln by the modern Arab. Hundreds, probably thou-

sands, have been utterly destroyed; and yet we stand amazed
before the splendor and number of the wrecks which remain.

In Upper Egypt, those wrecks are noble ruins open to the
cloudless sky, and touched with the gold of dawn and the
crimson of sunset; but in Lower Egypt, and especially in
the Delta where there is no desert, but only one vast plain
of rich alluvial soil, those ruins are buried under the rubbish
of ages, thus forming those gigantic mounds which are so
striking a feature of the scenery between Alexandria and
Cairo. Nothing in Egypt so excites the curiosity of the
newly landed traveller as these gigantic graves, some of
which are identified with cities famous in the history of the
ancient world, while others are problems only to be solved
at the edge of the spade. He sees mounds everywhere; not
only in the Delta, but in Middle Egypt, in Upper Egypt, and
even in Nubia. And wherever he sees a mound, there, but
too surely, he sees the native husbandmen digging it away
piecemeal for brick-dust manure.

It was in order to rescue at least a part of the historical
treasures entombed in these neglected mounds, and especially in the mounds of the Delta and the district of the old
Land of Goshen, that the society known as the Egypt Exploration Fund was founded in 1883, under the presidency
of the late Sir Erasmus Wilson. An influential committee
was formed in London, a subscription list was opened in
England and America, and the work of scientific exploration
was immediately begun.

From that time to this, the Egypt Exploration Fund has
sent out explorers every season, having sometimes two, and
even three, simultaneously at work in different parts of the
Delta. Each year has been fruitful in discoveries. Ancient
geographical boundaries have been traced; the sites of famous cities have been identified; sculptures, inscriptions,
arms, papyri, jewellery, painted pottery, beautiful objects in
glass, porcelain, bronze, gold, silver, and even textile fabrics,
have been found; a flood of unexpected light has been cast
upon the Biblical history of the Hebrews; the early stages

of the route of the Exodus have been defined; an important chapter in the history of Greek art and Greek epigraphy has been recovered from oblivion; and an archæological survey of the Delta has been made, nearly all the larger mounds having been measured and mapped. This survey is now about to be carried out on a much extended scale, covering the whole of Egypt, and including copies of inscriptions, photographs of monuments, triangulations, careful descriptions of the condition of the ruins, etc., etc. For this important work two specially trained archæologists will be despatched every season by the Fund.

It was, as I have said, in 1883 that the Egypt Exploration Fund began its labors in the Delta, the first explorer sent out by the society being the eminent Egpytologist, M. Naville, of Geneva. M. Naville selected as the scene of his first excavation a celebrated mound in the Wady Tùmilât, between Zagazig and Ismaïlia; a mound which Lepsius had conjecturally identified with "Raamses," one of the twin "treasure-cities" built by the forced labor of the Hebrew colonists in the time of the Great Oppression. Of these it is said in the first chapter of Exodus that "they built for Pharaoh treasure-cities, Pithom and Raamses"; by "treasure - cities" meaning fortified magazines, such as the Egyptians were wont to erect for the safe custody of grain and military stores.

Now, the South-eastern Delta was for some five hundred years as much the father-land of the descendants of Jacob as modern Egypt is now the father-land of the descendants of Amr's Arab hordes. The pleasant pastures of Goshen were theirs by right of gift and settlement. There they increased and multiplied, and there for centuries they dwelt, a favored and a

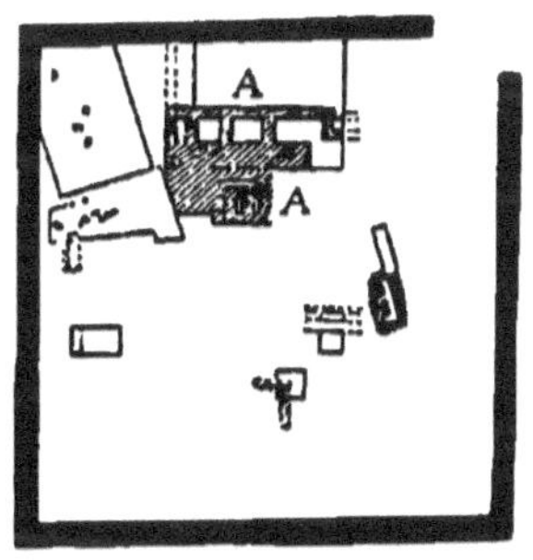

PLAN OF THE "TREASURE-CITY"
OF PITHOM.

A, A: Excavated store-chambers.

prosperous race. All this time, while they were happy, they had no history. It was only when much fighting and building had drained Egypt of men and treasure that the Hebrews began to be oppressed; and it is with their oppression that their history as a nation may be said to commence. No part of the Bible is more dramatically interesting, or more circumstantially related, than those chapters which tell of their sufferings, their flight, and their escape. Egyptologists, Hebraists, geographers, and travellers have exhausted speculation as to the road by which they went out, the places at which they halted, and the point at which they forded the great water. That they must have started by way of Wady Tûmilât is admitted by the majority of Exodus theorists. Then, as now, that famous valley was by far the shortest and most direct route from the old Land of Goshen to the desert. Then, as now, it was watered by a navigable canal, which in all probability the Hebrew settlers themselves helped to keep in repair, or possibly to excavate, and which may yet be traced for a considerable distance. Forty years ago Lepsius identified Tell Abû Suleiman at the westward mouth of the valley, and Tell-el-Maskhûtah near the eastward end, with the twin treasure-cities built for Pharaoh by the persecuted Israelites; and so unhesitatingly were his identifications accepted that these two places have ever since been entered in maps and guide-books as "Pithom" and "Raamses." Even the little railway station erected by the French engineers on the line of the Fresh-water Canal in 1860 was called "Ramses," and is so called to this day. It is unnecessary to recapitulate the argument upon which Lepsius based his identification; but it was, at all events, universally accepted. M. Naville went, therefore, to prove the correctness of this argument; and it was very much to his own surprise, and to the surprise of all concerned in his expedition, that he discovered it to be erroneous.

What M. Naville actually found under the mounds of Maskhûtah was a peribolos wall, the site of a temple, a dromos, a camp, some ruins of a city, and a series of most curious subterraneous structures, entirely unlike any architectural remains ever discovered in Egypt or elsewhere. The peribolos wall, twenty-four feet in thickness, enclosed

TELL-EL-MASKHÛTAH.

a quadrangular space of about fifty-five thousand square yards. The temple, which occupied one corner, though small, was originally surrounded by an outer wall of brickwork, the inner walls being of fine Tûrah limestone. Both temple and city proved to have been founded by Rameses II., the names and titles of that Pharaoh being the earliest recorded in the inscriptions discovered. Statues, bas-relief sculptures, and hieroglyphic texts of various kings, priests, and officials of subsequent periods were also found upon the spot. Among these must be especially noted part of a dedicatory tablet of Sheshonk I., the Biblical Shishak, and a broken colossus of Osorkon II., both of the Twenty-second Dynasty; two statues of functionaries, engraved with important inscriptions; some remains of an admirably sculptured and fully gilt wall-screen and pillar of Nectanebo I. (Thirtieth Dynasty); and a magnificent granite stela of Ptolemy Philadelphus, which is not only the largest Ptolemaic tablet known, but is also historically the most interesting. All the foregoing kings appear to have embellished the temple. Besides readable inscriptions of various periods, an immense quantity of minute fragments, some yet showing a hieroglyph or two, were found built into walls or reduced to gravel chips. This barbarism was the work of the Romans, who, being the last occupants of the site, appear to have smashed up any available material in order to level the ground for their camp. Thus the history of the place begins with Rameses II., the Pharaoh of the Great Oppression, about 1400 B.C., and ends with a Roman milestone of Galerius Maximian and Severus, about A.D. 306 or 307.

The temple was dedicated to Tum, (") the god of the setting sun; Tum being the patron deity of the town and the surrounding district. Now, as this place was not only a store-fort but a sanctuary, so also it had a secular name and a sacred name; like our own venerable English abbey-town of Verulam, which is also called St. Albans. Its secular name proved to be "Thukut" or "Sukut,"(") and its sacred name "Pa-Tum." These particulars we learn from inscriptions found upon the spot.

Engraved, for instance, on a black granite statue of a deceased prince and high-priest named Aak, we find a prayer in which he implores "all the priests who go into the sacred abode of Tum, the great god of Sukut," to pronounce a certain funerary formula for his benefit; while a fragment of another statue is inscribed with the names and titles of one Pames Isis, who was an "official of Tum of Sukut and governor of the storehouse." In these two inscriptions (to say nothing of several others) three important facts are recorded: namely, that the place was a "storehouse," that its sacred name was Pa-Tum; and that its secular name, also the name of the surrounding district, was Sukut.

Now, "Pa-Tum" means the House, or Abode, of Tum; "Pa" being the Egyptian word for house, or abode.   Thus, the temple gave its name to the city, just as " Pa-Bast "—the Abode of Bast—gave its name to the city which the Greeks called Bubastis.   But as the Greeks, according to the Greek method of transcription, rendered "Pa" by "Bu," and "Bast" by "Bastis," so the Hebrews, according to the Hebrew method of transcription, rendered "Pa" by "Pi," and "Bast" by "Beseth."   Thus it is as "Pi-Beseth" that we read of Bubastis in the Bible.   And so, in like manner, the Hebrews changed "Pa" into "Pi," and "Tum" into "Thom," when dealing with "Pa-Tum," of which they made "Pi-Thom."   Accordingly, it is of this very store-fort, "Pa-Tum," that we read in the pas-

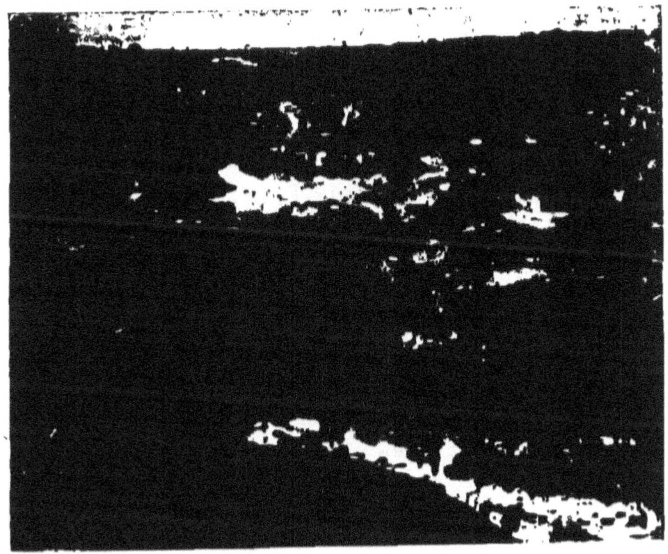

THE STORE-CELLARS OF PITHOM.

sage which I have already quoted from the first chapter of Exodus: "And they built for Pharaoh treasure-cities, Pithom and Raamses."

So, although Lepsius was mistaken in identifying Tell-el-Maskhûtah with "Raamses," he was not so very far wrong after all. The place was not "Raamses," but it was "Pithom."

But this town had also a secular name—Sukut. Now "Pa-Tum of Sukut" had been known to Egyptologists for many years in certain geographical lists of temples and local festivals sculptured on the walls of various temples in Upper Egypt; and Dr. Brugsch, our greatest authority on ancient Egyptian topography, had long ago identified it with "Pithom of Succoth." But till M. Naville excavated Tell-el-Maskhûtah, Pithom of Succoth was but a name and a theory. Now Pithom is a fact, and Sukut is a fact; and when it is remembered that the departing Hebrews "journeyed from Raamses to Succoth" on their way to Etham and Pihahiroth, it at once becomes evident that we have not only found one of the "treasure-cities" built by their hands, but that we have identified the district in which that great mixed multitude first halted to rest by the way. Identifying this district, we also identify the route of the Exodus. We know, in fact, that they went out by way of Wady Tûmilât in the direction of the modern town of Ismaïlia, a few miles north of the old Bitter Lakes which, according to the majority of geologists, now occupy what was originally the head of the Gulf of Suez. They crossed, in all probability, near Shalûf; but for clearer insight into this matter we must wait for further explorations and "more light."

But our "treasure-city" had yet another name—a name by which it was known in later times, under the Ptolemies and under the Romans; and this more recent name was Heroöpolis. A rude *graffito*, scratched apparently by a Roman soldier, on one of the uprights of a limestone door-way, when the place had been converted into a Roman camp, gives us this name under the form of "Ero Castra"; and it is as "Heroöpolis" that we read of Pithom in the Septuagint translation, where it is said, in the forty-sixth chapter of Genesis, that Joseph "made ready his chariot, and went up to

FALLEN COLOSSUS OF MERMASHIU. (THIRTEENTH DYNASTY.)

This magnificent colossal statue is one of a pair which yet lie prostrate in the ruins of the great Temple of Tanis. It represents a king of whom history has preserved no record, and who would be unknown but for these twin memorials. The statues, if raised from the ground, would sit twelve feet high without counting the plinths. The modelling and anatomy are admirable, and the polished surfaces are as lustrous to this day as when first executed.

Heroöpolis to meet Jacob his father." This, however, was a verbal anachronism on the part of the Septuagint; for there was neither a Pithom nor a Heroöpolis in the time of Joseph, but only a "Land of Goshen," as correctly given in the Hebrew original. The anachronism is, however, valuable, since it shows that Pithom was already known as Heroöpolis in the time of Ptolemy Philadelphus.([13]) As for the historical tablet of Ptolemy Philadelphus, it is of great importance.

It records how this king "rebuilt the Abode of Tum," and how one of his generals "captured elephants for his Majesty" on the east coast of Africa, and brought them hither in transport ships by way of the canal. That canal was the ancient Pharaonic canal, the bed of which is yet distinctly traceable, following the same direction as the present Sweet-water Canal in the Wady Tûmilât. This tablet also mentions a place called "Pikerehet," beyond Pithom and nearer to the Red Sea, which seems to be identical with Pihahiroth, where the Israelites encamped between Migdol and the sea.

The mounds of Maskhûtah, as shown in our illustration, may be described as a series of undulating sand hillocks. In the distance is seen the little railway station, now disused; and here and there a dark pit excavated in the middle distance marks one of the store-chambers, or cellars, opened by M. Naville. Not only these cellars, but also the great wall of circuit twenty-four feet in thickness, were probably the work of the oppressed Hebrews.

These subterraneous store-chambers, magazines, granaries, or whatever it may please us to call them, are solidly built square chambers of various sizes, divided by massive partition walls about ten feet in thickness, without doors or any kind of communication, evidently destined to be filled and emptied from the top by means of trap-doors and ladders. Except the corner occupied by the temple, the whole area of the great walled enclosure is honey-combed with these cellars.

They are, as I have said, well and solidly built. The bricks are large, and are made of Nile mud pressed in a wooden mould and dried in the sun. Also they are bedded in with mortar, which is not common, the ordinary method being to bed them with mud, which dries immediately, and holds almost as tenaciously as mortar. And this reminds us that Pharaoh's overseers "made the children of Israel to serve with rigor, and made their lives bitter with hard bondage in mortar and in brick." We remember all the details of that pitiful story—how the straw became exhausted; how the

poor souls were driven forth to gather in stubble for mixing
with their clay; and yet how they were required to give
in as large a tale of bricks at the end of each day's work as
if the straw had been duly provided.

Now, it is a very curious and interesting fact that the
Pithom bricks are of three qualities. In the lower courses
of these massive cellar walls they are mixed with chopped
straw; higher up, when the straw may be supposed to have

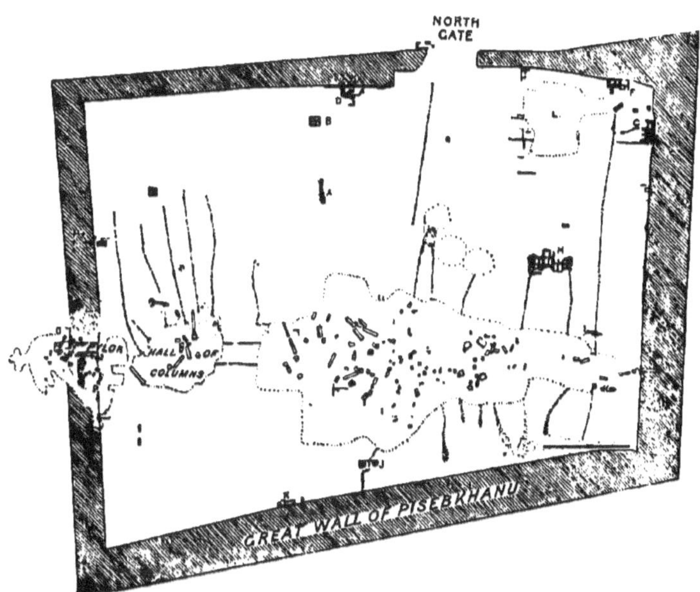

PLAN OF THE RUINS OF THE GREAT TEMPLE OF TANIS.

The above is reduced from Mr. Petrie's large plan in "Tanis," Part I., showing the
position of the ruins within the enclosure wall, the obelisks being figured as they
lie. The private houses of Roman date are marked in thicker lines than the ruins
of the temple; and the dotted lines show the course of Mr. Petrie's trenches,
which were thirty-five in number, from seven to twenty-four feet in depth, and
from fifty to four hundred feet in length. The main entrance-pylon, where a few
blocks yet stand in situ, is at the west end of the great enclosure wall, the north
gate being a later opening cut in Roman times. The length of the temple was
one thousand feet, by seven hundred feet in breadth; and the great enclosure
wall added by Pisebkhanu, an obscure king of the Twenty-first Dynasty, is no less
than eighty feet thick on the south side. The avenue (necessarily omitted in our
illustration) was three hundred and seventy-five feet in length.

4

run short, the clay is found to be mixed with reeds—the same kind of reeds which grow to this day in the bed of the old Pharaonic canal, and which are translated as "stubble" in the Bible. Finally, when the last reeds were used up, the bricks of the uppermost courses consist of mere Nile mud, with no binding substance whatever.

So here we have the whole pathetic Bible narrative surviving in solid evidence to the present time. We go down to the bottom of one of these cellars. We see the good bricks for which the straw was provided. Some few feet higher we see those for which the wretched Hebrews had to seek reeds, or stubble. We hear them cry aloud, "Can we make bricks without straw?"

Lastly, we see the bricks which they had to make, and did make, without straw, while their hands were bleeding and their hearts were breaking. Shakespeare, in one of his most familiar passages, tells us of "sermons in stones;" but here we have a sermon in *bricks*, and not only a sermon, but a practical historical commentary of the highest importance and interest.

The discovery of Pithom in 1883 was followed in 1884 by Mr. Petrie's excavations at Tanis; again by his discovery of Naukratis in 1885, and of the palace-fort of Daphnæ in 1886. Then followed, in 1887, M. Naville's discovery of the Jewish cemetery in which were interred the followers of the high-priest Onias, who fled from Syria, according to Josephus, during the reign of Ptolemy Philometer;(") and, at the latter end of the same season, came the discovery of the great temple of Bubastis.

It was, then, in 1884 that Mr. Petrie worked for the Egypt Exploration Fund on the site of that famous city called in Egyptian Ta-an, or Tsàn; transcribed as "Tanis" by the Greeks, and rendered in the Hebrew as "Zoan." It yet preserves an echo of these ancient names as the Arab village of "Sàn." This site, historically and Biblically the most interesting in Egypt, is the least known to visitors. It enjoys an evil reputation for rain, east winds, and fever; it is very difficult of access; and it is entirely without resources for the accommodation of travellers. Not many tourists care to encounter a dreary railway trip followed by eight or ten hours in a

SHRINE OF RAMESES II. IN THE RUINS OF TANIS. (SANDSTONE.)

The shrine shown in this illustration is one of a pair placed on opposite sides of the great avenue of statues, sphinxes, and obelisks which led to the Temple. These shrines are of quartzite sandstone, each being cut in a single block. The surface is most delicately sculptured with groups of figures and hieroglyphic texts; while inside, enthroned at the upper end, is a triad of deities. The companion shrine to the above has been smashed to pieces.

small row-boat, with no inn and no prospect of anything but salt fish to eat at the end of the journey. The daring few take tents and provisions with them; and those few are mostly sportsmen, attracted less by the antiquities of Sân-el-Hagar than by the aquatic birds which frequent the adjacent lake. Mr. Petrie went to this desolate spot provided not only with a sufficient store of canned soups, meats, and vegetables, jams, biscuits, and the like, but also with scientific instru-

ments, carpenters' tools, and a large quantity of iron roofing
for the mud-brick dwelling which he had to build for himself
and his overseer. The great temple of Tanis-Zoan was one
of the largest and most splendid in Egypt. It dated apparently from the Pyramid Period, the earliest royal name
found in the ruins being that of Pepi Merira of the Sixth Dynasty. It was, however, rebuilt by Amenembat I. and his
successors of the Twelfth and Thirteenth dynasties, many of
whom have left evidences of their work in the shape of colossal
statues, obelisks, and the like. Next came Rameses II., who
seems to have pulled the whole temple to pieces, in order to
reconstruct it according to the style of the Nineteenth Dynasty; covering its architraves with huge hieroglyphic inscriptions, and adorning it with a forest of obelisks and an
army of colossal portrait statues of himself. It now strews
the ground, an utter wreck, covering a space of one thousand
feet from end to end.

Mr. Petrie turned, cleaned, and planned every stone in this
immense ruin, and copied every hieroglyphic inscription
sculptured upon the surfaces of those fallen blocks, obelisks,
cornices, and statues. In the course of this laborious task he
brought to light an extraordinary number of reworked stones
of all periods, each stone a fragment torn from a page of history. Obelisks, statues, and historical tablets prove to have
been cut up into lengths, dressed down, and built in with as
little ceremony as though they were blocks fresh from the
quarry. Some of these destroyed obelisks are palimpsests in
stone. They date from the important times of the Eleventh
and Twelfth dynasties, and were originally covered from top
to bottom on all four sides with inscriptions elaborately engraved in small hieroglyphs about one inch in length. These
inscriptions prove to have been effaced by Rameses II., who
re-engraved the surfaces with his own titles and cartouches,
cut on a large scale. Finally, some three centuries later, a
Sheshonk, or an Osorkon, with a sacrilegious recklessness worthy of a Turkish pasha, hewed them in pieces to build a wall
and a gate-way. The historical stelæ, apparently a uniform

series of large size, were found in halves, none of which match,
but their legends seem to have been already corroded and illegible when they were thus utilized. The other halves must either have been destroyed or are yet imbedded in the structure.

Here also Mr. Petrie discovered the remains of the largest
colossus ever sculptured by the hand of man. This huge
figure represented Rameses II. in that position known as
"the hieratic attitude;" that is to say, with the arms straightened to the sides, and the left foot advanced in the act of
walking. It had been cut up by Osorkon II., of the Twenty-
second Dynasty, to build a pylon gate-way; and it was from
the fallen blocks of this gate-way that Mr. Petrie recognized
what it had originally been. Among these fragments were
found an ear, part of a foot, pieces of an arm, part of the pi-
laster which supported the statue up the back, and part of
the breast, on which are carved the royal ovals. *Ex pede
Herculem.* These fragments (mere chips of a few tons each),
although they represent but a very small portion of the
whole, enabled Mr. Petrie to measure, describe, and weigh the
shattered giant with absolute certainty. He proved to have
been the most stupendous colossus known. Those statues
which approach nearest to him in size are the colossi of Abú-
Simbel, the torso of the Ramesseum, and the colossi of the
Plain. These, however, are all seated figures, and, with the
exception of the torso, are executed in comparatively soft
materials. But the Rameses of Tanis was not only sculptured in the obdurate red granite of Assúan, and designed
upon a larger scale than any of these, but he stood erect
and crowned, ninety-two feet high from top to toe, or one
hundred and twenty-five feet high, including his pedestal.
This is nearly fifty feet higher than the obelisk in Central
Park, New York, or than its fellow, the British obelisk on
the Thames embankment. The minimum weight of the
whole mass is calculated by Mr. Petrie at twelve hundred
tons, this being three hundred and thirteen tons more than
the estimated weight of the colossus of the Ramesseum, when
entire. We ask ourselves with amazement how so huge a

monolith was extracted unbroken from the quarry; how it was floated from Assûan to Tanis; how it was raised into its place when it reached its destination. "The effect," wrote Mr. Flinders Petrie, "when there were no high mounds here, must have been astounding. The temple was probably not more than fifty feet high, and the tallest Tanis obelisks were less than fifty feet high. The statue must, therefore, have towered some sixty-five feet above all its surroundings, and have been visible for many miles across the plain."([16]) These measurements are calculated from the foot, one large block having the toes of the right foot nearly complete.

We have here an outline of the toes drawn to scale. They

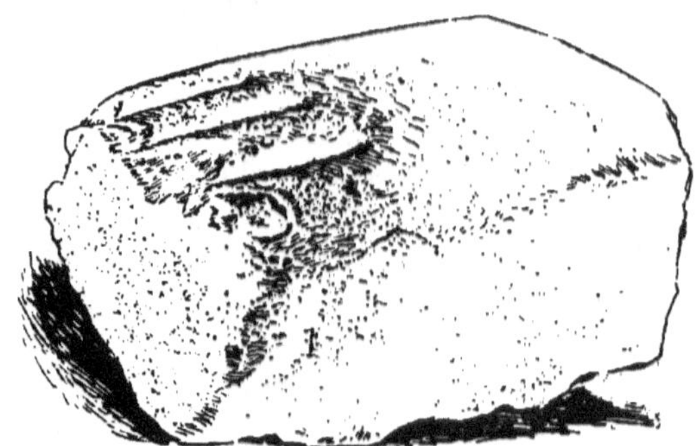

OUTLINE OF TOES OF COLOSSUS.

have been cut across the ends of the nails, and shaved up the sides by the saw of the mason. The great toe measured fourteen inches and seven-eighths, the second toe twelve inches and five-eighths, the third toe ten inches and four-eighths, the fourth toe eleven inches and two-eighths, and the little toe eight inches and four-eighths. The whole foot, when perfect, was fifty-seven inches and two-eighths in length. Although it is impossible now to prove that this gigantic statue was cut from a single block, there cannot be any reasonable doubt of the fact. Every known colossal statue in Egypt is monolithic, and it is inconceivable that the great Tanis colossus should have been an exception to this universal rule.

Desert Hare.   Piece of Porcelain Sceptre.   Isis and Infant Horus.   Shu;
Kohl Pot.   Alabaster Capital.   Ram;   Knum.   Tsur.—(Pottery.)
Apis Amulet.—(Pottery.)   Bowl. (Greenstone ware.)
Infant Horus.—(Bronze.)   Calyx Capital.—(Bronze.)   Ceramic Jar.   Calyx Capital. (Bronze.)   Tahuti (Thoth). (Green bone-ware.)

GROUP OF OBJECTS DISCOVERED IN A PRIVATE HOUSE AT TANIS (PERIOD, THIRTIETH DYNASTY).

Many very precious things were found by Mr. Petrie in the course of his work at Tanis. In the cellars of some large private mansions which perished in the great conflagration by which the city was destroyed in the time of the Emperor Diocletian, were discovered a mass of very interesting domestic relics, such as small household deities in bronze, alabaster, and glazed ware; mortars, moulds, works of art in sculpture and terra-cotta, and a great abundance of pottery, both coarse and fine. The house of one Bakakhiu contained a remarkable portrait statuette of himself; and in that of his next-door neighbor was found a zodiac painted in gold and colors upon a sheet of thin glass, this being the only known example of ancient glass-painting. From this house came the most important discovery of all; namely, seven ancient waste-paper baskets full of letters, deeds, memoranda, and other MSS. Some were on papyrus, and some on parchment; some were written in Greek, and some in the old Egyptian language, these last being penned in the hieroglyphic, hieratic, and demotic scripts. These priceless documents were alone worth the whole cost of the expedition. One proves to be a mathematical treatise; another is an almanac; and another is a syllabary. The first is in the hands of Professor Revillout, of the Louvre, who has offered to translate it. The second has been translated by Mr. Petrie, and the third by Mr. Frank Llewellyn Griffith. The two latter have been quite recently published as an extra volume by the Committee of the Egypt Exploration Fund; and the society hopes in time to publish fac-similes and translations of the entire collection.

Some very interesting work was done by M. Naville in the course of the same season in the Eastern Delta, where, at a place called Saft el - Henneh, he excavated the ruins of a black basalt temple of Rameses II., and discovered the remains of a beautiful monolithic shrine erected by Nectanebo II., the last of the native Pharaohs. What the inscription of Heliodorus was to Mr. Petrie at Naukratis, these fragments of the granite shrine were to M. Naville at Saft el-

4—2

Henneh. For centuries they had lain neglected in an open field, where for half the year they were covered by the waters of the inundation; yet all this time they held a secret as precious in its way as that of Naukratis—the secret of the ancient city buried in the neighboring mound. That city was none other than Goshen, the capital town of that Land of Goshen which was the special home of Israel in Egypt. I may add that, although M. Naville hesitates to positively identify the site of the ancient city of "Kes," or Goshen, with that of "Raamses," there is very strong reason for believing that Rameses II. rebuilt the place, and gave it his own name, and that in "Kes," "Goshen" (now Saft el-Henneh), we have the site of that other "treasure-city" built by the Hebrews at the time of the Great Oppression. (¹⁰)

The traveller who should turn his back upon Saft el-Henneh and journey northward as far as the shores of Lake Menzaleh, would there find himself upon the scene of Mr. Petrie's work in 1886, and at the foot of Tell Defenneh. Now, Tell Defenneh is a large mound, or group of mounds, situate close to Lake Menzaleh, at the extreme north-eastern corner of the Delta; and the name of this group of mounds, "Defenneh," is a corrupt Arab version of "Daphnæ," the "Daphnæ of Pelusium" of the Greek historians. The identity of Defenneh and Daphnæ has never been questioned by scholars, and the identity of both with the Biblical Tahpanhes has also been admitted by the majority of Bible commentators.

The history of Daphnæ begins with Psammetichus I., Prince of Saïs and Memphis, who fought his way to the throne by the aid of Carian and Ionian mercenary troops, and founded the Twenty-sixth Egyptian Dynasty. This event dates from about 665 B.C. Here Psammetichus constructed two large camps for the permanent accommodation of his foreign soldiers, one on each bank of the Pelusiac branch of the Nile; and here they founded a large military colony. In course of time, a Greek town sprang up in the neighboring plain. This was the earliest legalized

GROUP OF OBJECTS CHIEFLY FOUND IN THE HOUSE OF BAKAKHIU.

Portrait statuette of Bakakhiu in Roman costume; large statuette of Thoth; group of four smaller gods; basalt mortar, cups, stone mould, grotesque jar, three Apis ,tablets, bas-relief sculpture of winged sphinx with mural crown, emblematic of the city of Tantis, statuete of an unnamed king in Pharaonic costume, etc., etc.

settlement of Greeks in Egypt—a settlement ninety years earlier than that of Naukratis.

The foreigners continued to occupy Daphnæ for nearly a century, till King Amasis, the fourth successor of Psammeti-

THE RUINS OF THE SANCTUARY.   (GREAT TEMPLE OF TANIS.)

chus, removed them to Memphis. Now, the immediate predecessor of Amasis was Uabra, called by the Greek "Apries," and in the Bible "Hophra." It was during the reign of Apries, about 585 B.C., that Jerusalem was besieged by Nebuchadnezzar, who took King Zedekiah captive, put out his eyes, and bore him away, with the bulk of the Jewish citizens, to Babylon. But Zedekiah's daughters were left behind in Jerusalem, then occupied by a Chaldean garrison under a Chaldean governor. It was a time of plot and strife and disorder; and finally Johanan, the son of Kareah, acting as the guardian and adviser of the forlorn princesses, conveyed them for safety to Egypt. Their flight may be described as a later Exodus—an Exodus from Syria to Egypt, instead of from Egypt to Syria; for with them went "all the remnant of Judah, and all the captains of the forces;" a mixed multitude, in fact, consisting mainly of old men, women, and children, and such of the citizens as the sword and chains of the conqueror had spared. Convinced of the impolicy of rousing the wrath of Nebuchadnezzar, Jeremiah vehemently opposed the project of Johanan, and prophesied against it, saying:

"And now therefore hear the word of the Lord, ye remnant of Judah; Thus saith the Lord of hosts, the God of Israel; If ye wholly set your faces to enter into Egypt, and go to sojourn there;

"Then shall it come to pass, that the sword, which ye feared, shall overtake you there in the land of Egypt; and the famine, whereof ye were afraid, shall follow close after you there in Egypt; and there ye shall die.

"So shall it be with all the men that set their faces to go into Egypt to sojourn there; they shall die by the sword, by the famine, and by the pestilence: and none of them shall remain or escape from the evil that I will bring upon them."*

Johanan refused, however, to listen to Jeremiah, who, sorely against his will, threw in his lot with that of his brethren, and went across the frontier. Meanwhile Apries, with royal hospitality, placed his palace of Daphnæ at the disposal of the fugitive princesses, and granted a large tract of land to their followers. But Jeremiah continued to prophesy the pursuit of the Babylonian host, and lifted up his warning voice upon the very threshold of the palace of Pharaoh. The whole scene is thus related in the forty-third chapter of the Book of Jeremiah, the seventh, eighth, ninth, tenth, and eleventh verses:

"So they came into the land of Egypt; for they obeyed

* Jeremiah, chap. xlii., verses 15 and 16.

not the voice of the Lord.   Thus came they, even unto Tahpanhes.

"Then came the word of the Lord unto Jeremiah in Tahpanhes, saying,

"Take great stones in thine hand, and hide them in mortar, in the brickwork which is at the entry of Pharaoh's
house in Tahpanhes, in the sight of the men of Judah;

"And say unto them, Thus saith the Lord of hosts, the
God of Israel; Behold, I will send and take Nebuchadrezzar
the King of Babylon, my servant, and will set his throne
upon these stones that I have hid; and he shall spread his
royal pavilion over them.

"And he shall come, and shall smite the land of Egypt;
such as are for death shall be given to death, and such as are
for captivity to captivity, and such as are for the sword to
the sword."

I quote from the Revised Version; and it must be particularly noted that there is an alternative reading given in the
margin, where the "brick-work" which is at the entry of
Pharaoh's House is rendered as the "pavement" or "square."

Upon what happened after this, the Bible is silent; and
beyond the scant record of this brief chronicle, we only know
that Tahpanhes and Daphnæ were one and the same, and that
Tell Defenneh marks this interesting meeting-point of Egyptian, Greek, Assyrian, and Hebrew history.   Mr. Petrie went
therefore to Tell Defenneh to prove or disprove an accepted
identification.   There, in the midst of an arid waste, half
marsh, half desert—far from roads, villages, or cultivated soil
—in view of an horizon bounded by the heron-haunted lagoons
of Lake Menzaleh and the mud-swamps of the plain of Pelusium—he found three groups of mounds.   These groups lay
from half a mile to a mile apart, the intermediate flat being
covered with stone chips, potsherds, and the remains of brick
foundations.   These chips, potsherds, and foundations marked the site of an important city, in which the lines of the
streets and the boundaries of two or three large enclosures
were yet visible.   Two of the mounds were apparently mere

rubbish-heaps of the ordinary type; the third being entirely composed of the burned and blackened ruins of a huge pile of brick buildings, visible, like a lesser Birs Nimroud, for a great distance across the plain. Arriving at his destination towards evening, foot-sore and weary, Mr. Petrie beheld this singular object standing high against a lurid sky, and reddened by a fiery sunset. His Arabs hastened to tell him its local name; and he may be envied the delightful surprise with which he learned that it was known far and near as " El Kasr el Bint el Yahûdi "—the "Castle of the Jew's Daughter."

Setting to work with some forty or fifty laborers, he soon discovered that he had to do with the calcined ruins of a structure which was both a fort and a palace. It consisted of one enormous square tower containing sixteen rooms on each floor; while, built up against its outer walls, were a variety of later structures, such as might have been added for guard-rooms, offices, and the accommodation of a court. There was every evidence that the place had been taken by assault, plundered, and burned, the upper stories of the tower having fallen in and buried the basements. Layer by layer, Mr. Petrie cleared away these masses of burned rubbish— each layer a chapter in the history of the place. The royal apartments had once been lined with fine limestone slabs exquisitely sculptured and painted; but these had been literally mashed to pieces before the place was fired, and lay in splintered heaps among the débris of charred beams and blackened bricks. That this stronghold was actually built, as Herodotus states, by Psammetichus I. was proved by the discovery of that king's foundation deposits under the four corners of the building. These deposits consisted of libation vessels, corn-rubbers, specimens of ores, model bricks, the bones of a sacrificial ox and of a small bird, and a series of little tablets in gold, silver, lapis lazuli, porcelain, carnelian, and jasper, engraved with the names and titles of the royal founder.

Under this mountain of rubbish, the basement chambers,

strange to say, were found absolutely uninjured. The kitchen was intact—a big room with recesses in the walls which served for dressers, in which fourteen large jars and two large flat dishes were yet standing in their places. Here also were found weights for weighing the meat, spits, knives, plates, cups, and saucers in abundance. Another room contained hundreds of amphora lids and plaster jar-sealings, some stamped with the royal ovals of Psammetichus; some with those of Neko, his son; and some with those of Apries. This was the room in which the wine-jars were opened; in other words, the butler's pantry. In an adjoining chamber were

TELL DEFENNEH. ("EL KASR EL BINT EL YAHÚDI.")

found a vast number of empty wine-jars, some perfect, some broken; while in others of the ground-floor rooms were piled large numbers of early Greek vases ranging in date from 550 B.C. to 600 B.C., some finely painted with scenes of gigantomachia, chimeras, harpies, sphinxes, processions of damsels, dancers, chariots, and the like — all broken, it is true, but many in a mendable condition.

Most curious of all, however, was a little room containing a bench, recesses, and a sink formed of one huge jar with the bottom knocked out. This was the scullery! The bench was to stand the things on while being washed; the recesses were to receive them when washed; and the jar sink, which opened into a drain formed of a succession of bottomless jars going down to the clean sand below the foundation, was found to be filled with potsherds placed on edge—these potsherds being coated with organic matter and clogged with fish-bones. All this is doubtless very prosaic; but to have discovered Pharaoh's kitchen, scullery, and butler's pantry is really more curious and far more novel, than would have been the discovery of his throne-room.

A great variety of objects from the royal apartments were found in the fallen rubbish above the level of the servants' offices—such as bronze and silver rings, amulets, beads, seals, small brass vessels, draughtmen, a grand sword-handle with a curved guard, and a quantity of burned and rusted scale-armor. The great camp, in the midst of which the palace-fort was built, also yielded a harvest of military relics. This camp (the camp founded by Psammetichus for the Carian and Ionian troops to whose valor he owed his crown) measured 2000 feet in length by 1000 feet in breadth; and though Mr. Petrie excavated but a corner of it, he found hundreds of objects belonging to these ancient Greek soldiers —arrow-heads in bronze and iron, horses' bits, fragments of chain-work, iron bars, blacksmith's tools, and the like. He also excavated part of the Greek town in the plain, where large quantities of beautiful carnelian, onyx, garnet, and other beads were found; scraps of gold-work, indicating a large trade in articles of personal adornment; and an immense number of very small weights, such as could only be used by jewellers and dealers in precious stones.

A massive gold handle, apparently the handle of a tray,

was also found buried in a corner of the camp, where doubtless it had been hidden by some plunderer when the place
was sacked and burned. This undoubtedly formed part of
Hophra's service of gold plate (that service of gold plate
which he would, of course, have placed at the disposal of his
royal Jewish guests), and it is, with one exception, the only
piece of gold plate ever found in Egypt.

To return, however, to Jeremiah and his famous prophecy—to that day when he took "great stones in his hand,
and placed them with mortar in the brick-work which was
at the entry of Pharaoh's House in Tahpanhes." In illustration of this passage, I may here quote a few lines from Mr.
Petrie's private report addressed to the Honorary Secretary and Executive Committee of the Egypt Exploration
Fund, during the month of April, 1886:

" This 'brickwork, or pavement' at the entry of Pharaoh's
House has always been a puzzle to translators; but as soon
as we began to uncover the plan of the palace, the exactness
of the description was manifest; for here, outside the buildings adjoining the central tower, I found by repeated trench-
ings an area of continuous brickwork resting on sand, and
measuring about 100 feet by 60 feet, facing the entrance to
the buildings at the east corner.

" The roadway ran up a recess between the buildings, and
this platform, which has no traces of superstructures, was
evidently an open-air place for loading and unloading goods,
or sitting out in the air, or transacting business, or convers-
ing—just such a place, in fact, as is made by the Egyptians
to this day in front of their houses, where they drink coffee,
and smoke in the cool of the afternoon, and receive their
visitors.

" Such seems to have been the object of this large platform, which was evidently a place to meet persons who
would not be admitted into the palace or fort; to assemble
guards; to hold large levées; to receive tribute and stores;
to unlade goods; and to transact the multifarious business
which, in so hot a climate, is done in the open air. This

platform is therefore, *unmistakably*, the brickwork, or pavement, which is at the 'entry of Pharaoh's House in Tahpanhes.' The rains have washed away this area and denuded the surface, so that, although it is two or three feet thick near the palace, it is reduced in greater part to a few inches, and is altogether gone at the north-west corner."

Now, the Arabic name for a platform of this kind is " Balât;" and that we have in this " Balât" the brickwork referred to in the Bible is scarcely to be doubted by the most determined sceptic. And it is to be noted that in the alternative reading above mentioned, "the brickwork which is at the entry of Pharaoh's house" is rendered as "the pavement or square."

Here, therefore, the ceremony described by Jeremiah must have been performed, and it was upon this spot that Nebuchadnezzar was to spread his royal pavilion. It will be asked, perhaps, if Mr. Petrie actually found the stones which Jeremiah laid with mortar in the thickness of that pavement. He looked for them, of course, turning up the brickwork in every part; and he did find some large stones lying loosely on the surface. But these had probably rolled down from the wreck of the palace. At all events, it was impossible to identify them.

Meanwhile, we turn in vain to the pages of sacred and secular history for some record of the fate of those hapless princesses—the last, the very last—of the ancient and noble royal line of Judah, who were recognized as royal. What fate befell them and their followers? Did the Assyrian pursue them with fire and sword? And was the conqueror's pavilion actually spread upon the spot marked out by the prophet? The Bible tells us no more; but certain Egyptian inscriptions state that Nebuchadnezzar again invaded Egypt, and was defeated by Apries—Pharaoh Hophra; while on the other hand, certain Babylonian inscriptions give the victory to Nebuchadnezzar. Which are we to believe? For my own part, I unhesitatingly accept the impartial evidence of that burned and blackened pile, " The Castle of the Jew's

Daughter;" and I do not doubt that the invincible Assyrian wrought his uttermost vengeance upon the "remnant of
Judah."

Nor must we forget the additional testimony of three
clay cylinders of Nebuchadnezzar, inscribed in cuneiform
characters, and now in the National Egyptian Museum.
Some seven or eight years ago these cylinders were sold to
Professor Maspero by an Arab who found them, as we have
every reason to believe, upon this very spot; and such cylinders were precisely the memorials which Nebuchadnezzar
would have left buried beneath the spot where he spread
his pavilion, and planted his royal standard, in the hour of
victory.

POTTERY IN THE CELLAR OF HOUSE OF BAKAKHU.

PLOUGHING SCENE.

III.

PORTRAIT-PAINTING IN ANCIENT EGYPT.

THE oldest sculptures and the oldest paintings which have come down to our time are the work of ancient Egyptian artists who lived some four thousand years before the Christian era. This would look as though sculpture and painting were twins—twins born of the fruitful Nile, and therefore of parallel antiquity. But the art of painting implies first the art of drawing; and the art of drawing is infinitely more ancient than that of sculpture. It is more ancient than the immemorial civilization of Egypt. It is almost as old as man himself.

The child by the sea-shore tracing rude figures of men and animals upon the wet sands, and the cave-dweller in the ages before history outlining the forms of the mammoth and the mastodon on a fragment of polished bone, are obeying the same imitative bent, and that imitative bent is due to one of the primary instincts of our race. An incised outline upon bone is not sculpture. It is drawing—drawing with a point. It precedes the attempt to model in clay, or to carve images in wood or stone. In a word, it is the earliest form of fine art in the world.

From the prehistoric cave-dweller we pass at one step to

the ancient Egyptian draughtsman.   In the history of art, all is blank between them.   We cannot measure the abyss of time which separates the one from the other.   We only know that in the meanwhile there had been changes of many kinds —upheavals and subsidences of land and water; disappearances of certain forms of animal and vegetable life; and the like.   We do not know—we cannot even guess—how long it had taken the ancient Egyptian to work his way up from primitive barbarism to that stage of advanced culture at which he had arrived when we first make his acquaintance on his native soil.   This is about the time of the building of the Great Pyramid, or nearly six thousand years ago, counting to this year of grace, 1890.   Already he was a consummate builder, geometrician, and mathematician.   Already he was in possession of a religious literature of great antiquity.   He was master of a highly complicated system of writing; he had carried the art of sculpture, in the most obdurate materials, to as high a degree of perfection as was possible with the tools at his command; and he drew the human figure better —far better—than he did in those later days when Herodotus and Plato and Strabo visited the Valley of the Nile.

The earliest Egyptian paintings to which it is possible to assign a date, are executed in *tempera* upon the walls of certain tombs made for the noble personages who were contemporary with King Khufu (better known as Cheops), the builder of the Great Pyramid.   In these paintings we see herdsmen driving herds of goats, oxen, and asses; vintagers working the wine-press; scenes of ploughing, feasting, dancing, boating, and so forth.   There is no attempt at scenery or background. The heads are given in profile, but the eyes are given as if seen frontwise.

The head being in profile, one would expect to see the body in profile; but this was not in accordance with ancient Egyptian notions.   The artist desired to make as much of his sitter as possible—to give him full credit for the breadth of his chest and the width of his shoulders, and to show that he had the customary allowance of arms and legs; so he represented the body in front view. But he thus landed him-self in a grave difficulty. To draw a pair of legs and feet in front view is by no means easy. It requires a knowledge of foreshortening, and the Egyptian artist was as ignorant of foreshortening as of perspective. He, however, met this dif-ficulty by boldly returning to the point from which he first started, and drawing the legs and feet in profile, like the face. Nor was this all. Having no idea of perspective, he placed every part of his subject on the same plane; that is to say, a man walking or standing has the one foot planted so exactly in front of the other that a line drawn from the middle toe of the front foot would precisely intersect the soles of both. I have sometimes wondered whether it ever occurred to an ancient Egyptian artist to try to place him-self in the attitude in which he elected to represent his fel-low-creatures—namely, with his body at a right angle to his legs and his profile. He would have found it extremely un-comfortable, not to say impossible. Yet in this preposterous fashion he depicted princes and peasants, priests and kings, and even armies on the march. Strange to say, the effect is neither so ugly nor so ridiculous as it sounds. The outline is drawn with such freedom, and the forms, taken separate-ly, are so graceful that, despite our better judgment, we accept the conventional deformity, and even forget that it is deformity.

When the ancient Egyptian artist had drawn the face and figure of his sitter, he proceeded to fill up the outline with color. It it were the portrait of a man, he covered the face, body, arms, and legs with a flat wash of dark, reddish-brown; if it were the portrait of a woman, he substituted a yellow-ish-buff. Not that the men were in reality red-brown or the women yellow, but because these were the conventional tints employed to distinguish the complexions of the two sexes. He next indicated the eyebrow by a black line of uniform thickness; and for the eye, he painted a black disk on a white ground. The garments and the border-patterns of the gar-ments, the necklaces, the bracelets, the rich belts, the elaborate head-dresses, were all treated with exquisite minuteness, and in the same flat tints.

Such being his system of color, it was of course impossible for our Egyptian to represent light and shadow, or the texture of stuffs, or the flow of drapery. His art, in fact, cannot be described as painting, in our sense of the term. He did not paint; he illuminated. (") Inasmuch, therefore, as he excelled in the methods of illumination, he was a singularly skilful craftsman; but inasmuch as he has never been surpassed for purity and precision and sweep of outline, or for the fidelity with which here produced the racial characteristics of foreign nations, or for the truth and spirit with which he depicted all varieties of animal life, he was undoubtedly and unquestionably an artist. Drawing only in profile, and painting only in flat washes, he could not, and did not, attempt to show the changing expression of the human face in joy or grief or anger. The widow wailing over the mummy of her husband, the Pharaoh slaying his thousands on the field of battle, looks out into space with the smiling serenity of a cherub on a tombstone. But let Rameses return to Thebes after a victorious campaign in Ethiopia or Asia Minor, bringing a string of foreign captives bound to his chariot-wheels, and see then what our Egyptian artist can do! With nothing but his reed-pen and his whole-colored washes, he produces a series of portraits of Syrians, Libyans, negroes, and Asiatic Greeks which no English or French or American artist could surpass for living and speaking individuality, and which probably none of them could do half so well if compelled to employ the same methods.

There is, however, one point upon which it is necessary to insist in this connection. Among even those who care much and know much about art, there prevails an impression that the art of the Egyptians was phenomenally rigid and incorrect, and that Egyptian painters committed more glaring errors in their treatment of the "human form divine" than the early artists of other nations. This is a grave misconception. The beginnings of pictorial art in all nations,

at all periods, are curiously alike. The archaic tyro tries his
"'prentice hand" on the same subjects; he encounters the
same difficulties; he meets those difficulties in the same way;
he commits the same blunders. Egyptian, Assyrian, Etruscan, Greek, repeat one another. They all draw the face in
profile, and the eye as if seen from the front. They all represent the feet planted on precisely the same line. They all
color in flat tints, and are alike ignorant of light and shade,
of foreshortening and perspective.

Greek painting—the whole body of Greek painting, from
its earliest to its latest phase, with the one exception of the
art of painted vases—is irrecoverably lost. Of the masterpieces of Greek sculpture, some few priceless relics have survived the general wreck; but of the famous creations of the
great Greek painters there remains but an echo in the pages
of Pausanias and Pliny. The walls enriched with their immortal frescos, the panels on which they painted their in-
comparable easel pictures, have long since become dust. But,
like the glow that streams up from the west after the sun has
gone down, the splendor of their fame yet lights the horizon
and is reflected on the hills of Athens.

Strange to say, despite the ruin which has overtaken their
works, we know almost as much about those dead and gone
painters of between two and three thousand years ago as we
know about the artists of our own day. We have elaborate
descriptions of their pictures, notes on their methods, criticisms on their styles, and abundance of anecdotes of their
sayings and doings. We know that Polygnotus, who excelled
in battle-pieces, was called the "most ethical of painters;"
that Xeuxis carried realism to the point of actual illusion;
that Protogenes (an earlier Albert Dürer) finished his pictures with microscopic minuteness; and that Apelles excelled
all the rest in ideal beauty and grace.

The prices which these artists received for their pictures
were by no means contemptible. Nikias, it is said, refused to
sell one of his works to Ptolemy Lagus for sixty talents, a sum
equivalent to sixty thousand dollars, or twelve thousand

pounds sterling. Aristides, when commissioned to paint a battle-piece containing one hundred figures, bargained for two hundred dollars, or forty pounds sterling, per figure ; and Alexander, for his own portrait in the character of Zeus hurling a thunder-bolt, gave Apelles no less than twenty talents of gold—that is to say, fifty thousand pounds sterling, or two hundred and fifty thousand dollars. As for the painters who commanded these extraordinary prices, they rivalled each other in ostentation and vanity. They robed themselves in the purple of royalty ; they wore golden wreaths upon their heads and golden clasps upon their sandals; and they squandered their wealth with both hands.(")

Yet the art which rose to this height of renown started from beginnings more humble than anything which has come down to us in the shape of ancient Egyptian painting. The paintings of the Greeks, as I have said, are lost, and only their vase-paintings remain. But as the vase-paintings of the finest period reflect the art of the finest period, so the vase-paintings of the archaic period reflect the art of the archaic period; and they show with what a childish hand the first attempts of the Greek draughtsman were traced. Nothing in the way of drawing which has yet been discovered in Egypt is so ludicrously feeble as the drawing upon the so-called Proto-Homeric vases found at Athens. These vases are supposed to date from the tenth century before our era, and are therefore contemporaneous with the Twentieth Egyptian Dynasty—the dynasty of Rameses III. and his successors.

But the Twentieth Egyptian Dynasty, if it registers the beginnings of art in the very core of Hellas, marks its old age and decadence in Egypt. Pliny laughed the Egyptians to scorn, when they claimed their priority as painters.

"Concerning the first origin of the painter's art," he says, "I am not ignorant that the Egyptians do vaunt thereof. avouching that it was devised by them. and practised sixe hundred years before there was any talke or knowledge thereof in Greece, a vaine brag and ostentation of theirs. as all the world may see."(") But the incredulity of Pliny was the incredulity of ignorance. Himself living in an age when the Egyptians spoke only Coptic or Greek, and when the secret of the old Egyptian writing was lost, neither he nor his contemporaries, nor the Coptic Egyptians themselves, had any standard left by which to measure the history of the great African province. It was not a priority of six hundred years that the Egyptians should have claimed in this controversy, but a priority of more than three thousand. The painted tombs of the Pyramid plateau were already close upon four thousand years old in the time of Pliny.

But there is yet another fact bearing on this question—a fact which none of us suspected till the mysterious records sculptured on stone and written on papyrus were deciphered —namely, that the so-called Pelasgic Greeks, the very early Greeks of the Archipelago and the coast of Asia Minor, had been known to the Egyptians, and fought by them, and vanquished by them, and brought as captives to Thebes, as early as the time of King Sankhara of the Eleventh Dynasty. Of this king it is recorded in a contemporary rock-cut inscription in the Valley of Hamamat, that "he broke down the power of the Hanebu." As I explain in Chapter V. of this volume, "Hanebu" is the name by which the Greeks were first known to the Egyptians. Later on, in inscriptions of the time of Thothmes III. of the Eighteenth Dynasty, we meet with them as the Danæans; and later still, under the Pharaohs of the three following dynasties, they appear with their distinctive names as Achæans, Lycians, Dardanians, Mycians, Teucrians, Ionians, and Carians.

It has, however, been supposed up to the present time that these early Greeks knew Egypt only as miserable captives toiling in the mines and quarries, and that the land of the Pharaohs was jealously closed against them until they settled at Daphnæ as a military colony under Psammetichus I., and at Naukratis as a trading colony under Amasis II. But so recently as the spring-time of 1889 a strange new light dawned upon the horizon eastward of Hellas. In two little ruined towns situate within a few miles of each other

on the borders of the Fayûm, Mr. Petrie discovered traces
of two separate colonies of foreigners, the one colony dating
from the reign of Usertesen II. of the Twelfth Dynasty,
about three thousand years before our era; and the other
dating from the reign of Thothmes III. of the Eighteenth
Dynasty, about fifteen hundred years later. The earlier
mound is locally known as Tell Kahun, and the more recent
as Tell Gurob. In both have been found innumerable fragments of pottery of Cypriote and archaic Greek styles; and
hundreds of these potsherds are inscribed with characters,
some of which may be Phœnician, or that earliest derivative
of Phœnician known as Cadmæan Greek; while others belong to the Cypriote, Græco-Asiatic, and Italic alphabets.
Nor is this all. The cemetery belonging to one of these
towns has given up its dead, who prove to have been a fair
and golden-haired race, like the "Golden-tressed Achæans"
of Homer.

The ancient settlers who lived and died at Tell Gurob
were mummified like the native Egyptians, having apparently
adopted the religion of the country; and on the mummy-case
of one, we read that its occupant's name was An-Tursha, and
that he was "Governor of the Palace." Now, in its etymolo-
gy, An-Tursha is a very remarkable name—for the man who
bore it must have belonged to a foreign people called the
Tursha, who allied themselves with the Libyans and Sardinians in an attack upon Egypt during the reign of Seti I.,
and were signally defeated. About a century later, in the reign
of Rameses III. of the Twentieth Dynasty, they again ventured across the sea in their "hollow ships," allied this time
with the Danæans, Sicilians, Lycians, and others. Descending upon the Egyptian coast near Pelusium, they were encountered by the whole naval and military force of Rameses III., and wellnigh annihilated. Who, then, were these
Tursha that come before us first in company with the Sardinians, and next with the Sardinians and Sicilians—both
nations from the northern waters of the Mediterranean?
The Tursha are none other than the primitive rulers of

Latium, the mysterious Etruscans, whose identification has been convincingly established by François Lenormant.([19]) And it was on the potsherds of Tell Gurob, a settlement which was inhabited by the fair-haired foreigners precisely during the reign of Seti I. and his immediate successors (the settlement in which the man An-Tursha lived and died) that those especial signs were found which are unquestionably identical with certain letters of the Etruscan alphabet. Without venturing to draw any conclusion from these facts, I desire to call attention very particularly to the sequel in which they follow each other.

About 3000 B.C. Sankhara subdues the tribes of the Greek Archipelago. Some three generations later, in the reign of Usertesen II., a colony of foreign workmen, who were probably employed in transporting the stone of which that Pharaoh's pyramid was built, settle close beside it, on the edge of the desert. They decorate their domestic pottery with patterns unknown to Egyptian potters, and they inscribe them with characters closely resembling the archaic alphabets of Phœnicia and Cyprus. Is it not allowable to ask whether these foreigners might not be descendants of the captives brought home by Sankhara?

Fifteen hundred years later, Thothmes III. celebrates his victories over the Dardani—Dardani being here used, as by Homer, to designate the Asiatic Greeks generally. And it is in the reign of Thothmes III. that another alien colony is established, perhaps not altogether by chance, within a few miles of the deserted site occupied fifteen centuries before by the earlier settlers. The new town, Tell Gurob, continues to be inhabited for nearly one hundred years, and is then deserted, like its predecessor. In the course of that century Egypt is again and again attacked, not only by the Greeks of Asia Minor and the Ægean, but by the coast-folk and islanders of the Tyrrhene Sea. It is significant that the signs inscribed on the potsherds of the new colony comprise letters belonging to the archaic alphabets of those very tribes which hurled themselves in vain against the trained battalions of Seti I. and Rameses II.; namely, the Leku, or Lycians; the Aiuna, or Ionians; the Akaiusha, or Achæans; and the Tursha or Etruscans.(²¹) It is to this later colony that the man An-Tursha belonged. It is on the pottery of this colony that we find the Etruscan letters; and it is in the cemetery belonging to this colony that the yellow-haired mummies have been found.

Now, these facts, take them from what point of view we may, are most extraordinary. Mr. Petrie has brought to light the earliest Greek alphabetical signs yet discovered; for the most ancient specimens of Greek writing previously known are the rock-cut and lava-cut inscriptions found in the very ancient cemeteries of Santorin and Thera, and the famous Greek inscription cut upon the leg of one of the colossi at Abû-Simbel. The Abû-Simbel inscription is contemporaneous with the Forty-seventh Olympiad, and Lenormant attributes the oldest of the Theran inscriptions to the ninth century before Christ. But the potsherds found by Mr. Petrie in the Fayûm carry back the history of the alphabet to a period earlier than the date of the Exodus, and six centuries earlier than any Greek inscriptions known.

But if they throw a new and surprising light upon the history of writing and of language, they throw no less valuable a light upon the history of art. By revealing the astonishing fact that Egypt contained settlements of early Greek and Italian tribes at a date long anterior to the earliest date at which those people had any history or monuments of their own, they show in what school of art those nations studied. And thus the marked Egyptian character of the archaic painting and sculpture of Greece and Etruria is at once explained.

It is not, however, to be for one moment supposed that it was the settlers in those two little towns in the Fayûm who handed on the arts of Egypt to their barbarian brethren over the sea. The results of the excavation of these sites are samples—mere samples—of what the minor mounds of Egypt hold in store for the explorer. There are probably hundreds of such sites in Egypt—sites so insignificant in appearance that no one supposes them to be worth the trouble of excavation. The Pharaohs drafted immense numbers of prisoners into Egypt. They needed men for their gigantic public works, which could only be carried on by means of a reckless sacrifice of human life. It was for this purpose, quite as much as for mere booty, that they made their incessant raids upon Ethiopia and Syria. When, therefore, the barbarian hordes of southern Europe and Asia Minor attacked Egypt by land or sea, they rushed, not merely upon defeat and death, but upon slavery. There must have been tens of thousands, perhaps hundreds of thousands, of these foreigners in Egypt during the Nineteenth and Twentieth dynasties; for again and again during the reigns of Rameses II. and Rameses III., they came upon the same desperate errand, and with the same result. Vast numbers were sent to the mines and the quarries, and, like the Children of Israel, to the brick-fields. But to such as were skilled in handicrafts, a less intolerable lot would be assigned. These would be employed as artisans rather than as beasts of burden. The Greek characters traced on the backs of certain encaustic tiles found in the ruins of a building erected by Rameses III. at Tell el-Yahudieh may well be the work of some of these prisoners of war. The foreigners would naturally herd together close against the pyramid or temple or canal where the taskmasters kept them at work; and it is in the little nameless, unnoticed mounds scattered up and down the Nile Valley that relics of their presence will be found.

This discovery of Mr. Petrie's throws an entirely new light upon the synchronous history of Egypt, Cyprus, Asia Minor, and Etruria. It carries back the literary history of these nations to a date hitherto undreamed of by the classic historians or by ourselves, and it promises to clear up a host of very obscure problems concerning the origin and development of Greek and Etruscan art.([22])

And now it will be interesting to examine in detail the

principles upon which the human figure was drawn by the
artists of ancient Egypt; to note the skill with which they
seized upon and delineated the ethnic characteristics of foreign nations; and to trace the influence of Egypt upon the
schools of Assyria, Etruria, and Greece. The accompanying
illustration represents one of the great
gods of Heliopolis—the Biblical "On."
His name is rendered as Tum, Tumu,
or Atmu. He typified the setting sun.
The figure is drawn in pure line, and
presents all the peculiar characteristics
of the Egyptian school. The head and
face are shown in profile, and the shoulders are set squarely frontwise. But
from below the waist, the point of view
changes back to profile, the legs and
feet being shown sidewise, like the face.
The feet are placed in line, the heel of
the one foot being exactly in front of
the toes of the other. It is an impossible position, yet the figure is so boldly
and so simply drawn that we do not
realize how impossible it is. The eye
is shown as if seen in the full face.
The hieroglyphic inscription contains
the name and titles of the god: Tum,
or Tumu, Lord of the Two Lands, i. e.,
of Upper and Lower Egypt, (") Great
God of On, Ruler of the Gods. In this
figure we have an admirable example
of ancient Egyptian figure-drawing in
pure line. A portrait of a god is, how-

TUM.

Also called Tumu and
Atmu. He wears the
"pschent," or double
crown, signifying his
domination over Upper
and Lower Egypt. The
hieroglyphic inscription
recounts his name and ti-
tles: "Tumu, Lord of the
Two Lands, Great God of
On, Divine Ruler of the
Substance of the Gods."

ever, necessarily an ideal portrait; if, therefore, we would
form a just notion of the fidelity with which the artists of
Pharaonic times painted the portraits of living men and
women, we cannot do better than turn to the tomb-paintings of the Theban Period, and above all to the famous

typical groups known as "the four races" in the great rock-cut sepulchres of the kings of the Nineteenth and Twentieth dynasties. These groups represent the conven-

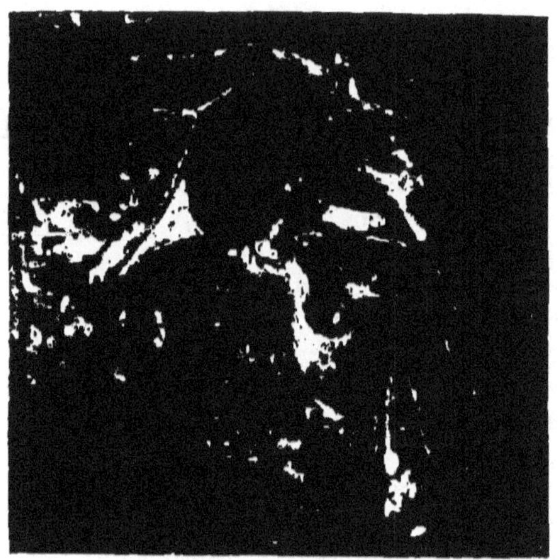

THE TYPICAL SYRIAN OF EGYPTIAN ART.
From a photograph by Mr. W. M. Flinders Petrie.

tional "four races" of the ancient world, as classified by the Egyptians; namely, the Egyptians themselves (arrogantly ranked as "mankind" *par excellence*), the Asiatics, the Libyans, and the Ethiopians; or, more comprehensively, the browns, the yellows, the whites, and the blacks.

This spirited head of a Syrian chief was photographed by Mr. Petrie from a wall-painting in the tomb of Rameses III. It dates, therefore, from about 1100 B.C. The wall is damaged and the plaster has scaled off in places, but the head is fortunately uninjured. The Asiatic type is admirably caught. This man was probably a Canaanite. He has all the ethnic characteristics of the race. The eye, as usual, is falsely drawn, but it is set at the Semitic angle, and the face has a vivid look that speaks of actual portraiture. He wears a head-gear of some spotted material, bound with the Syrian fillet yet in use. The fringed and patterned robe, the cap and fillet, are all true to the Syrian costume of three thousand years ago.([24])

Very different in type is the typical Egyptian as we see him represented in the portraits of Ra-hotep, Khufu-Ankh, Semnefer, and Ra-em-ka.* The flesh-tints of Egyptians are rendered of a reddish-brown, and the hair coal-black. The facial angle is quite different from the facial angle of the Asiatics. It is the facial angle of the European races, and it has therefore a certain affinity with that of the typical

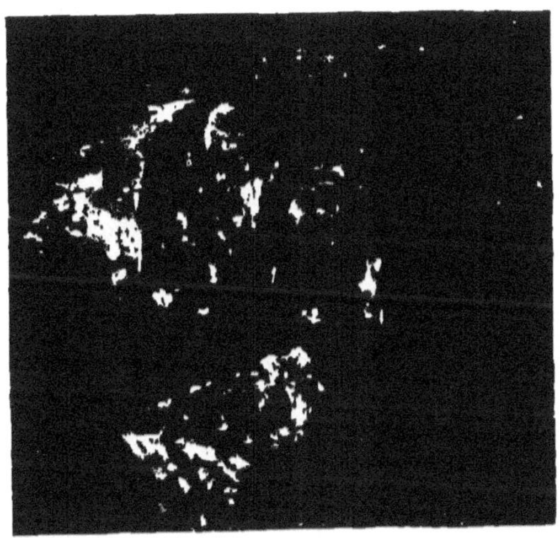

THE TYPICAL LIBYAN OF EGYPTIAN ART.
From a photograph by Mr. W. M. Flinders Petrie.

Libyan. Now, the typical Libyans of ancient Egyptian art were a fair-skinned, red-haired, and blue-eyed race, whose descendants survive to this day eastward of Algeria. We

* See illustrations to chap. iv.

find them to be invariably distinguished by the massive side-lock shown in the illustration. A piece of the wall-plaster has unfortunately been knocked out of the cheek, but otherwise the face is perfect. It is a very interesting face, gentle and intelligent, and drawn, one would say, from the life. These fair Libyans were doubtless emigrants from Europe or Asia, and were most probably of Pelasgic origin. The side-lock was a fashion peculiar to the Libyans and Mashuasha outside Egypt; and it is stated by Herodotus that the Maxyans (who are in all probability identical with the Mashuasha of Egyptian inscriptions), allowed their hair to grow in a long lock on the right side of the head, but shaved it on the left.(**) The side-lock was also a special fashion observed by Egyptian princes in childhood and youth, and it is worn to this day by little boys in Egypt and Nubia.

The " blameless Ethiopian " was a very familiar figure in the land of the Pharaohs, and it is therefore no wonder that Egyptian artists excelled in depicting his homely characteristics. The illustration on page 85 is from Mr. Petrie's series of photographs of wall-paintings in the tomb of a Theban noble named Hui, who was governor of Ethiopia under one of the Pharaohs of the Eighteenth Dynasty. The painted tombs of Egypt have suffered deplorably at the hands of tourists and Arabs, and the tomb of Hui has not escaped injury. Yet, when it is possible, illustrations direct from damaged originals are preferable to copies made fifty or sixty years ago, when the paintings were comparatively perfect. The copy, though more pleasing, may err; but the photograph is a faithful witness. In the present subject, we see a procession of Ethiopian chiefs, one of whom is accompanied by his wife and children. The negro types are admirably given, but it must be admitted that the dark lady who brings up the rear is not beautiful. She wears a richly patterned garment of many colors, and she carries her youngest child in a funnel-shaped bag over her shoulder.

Last in the procession (for which we have not space here, as it covers a large wall-space in the tomb) comes the Ethiopian queen herself, in a chariot drawn by spotted oxen. Her face is wofully damaged, and the head of the groom-boy who stands before the oxen has been cut out from the wall by some unscrupulous traveller; but her Majesty's charioteer and her attendant chiefs are in excellent preservation. The Queen's arms are loaded with bracelets, and round her neck she wears a splendid necklace, consisting of many rows

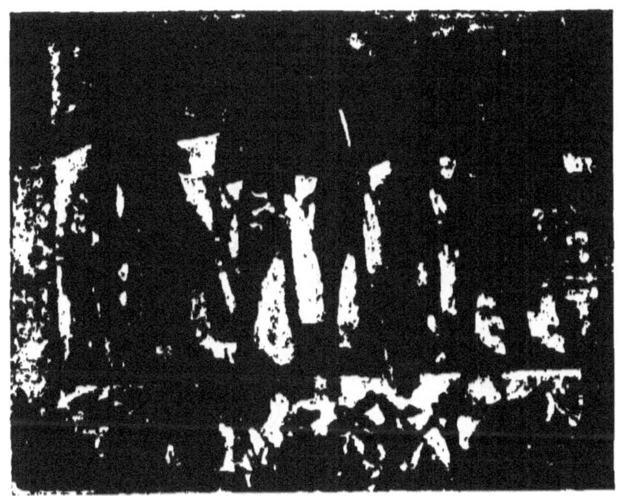

PROCESSION OF NEGROES.

From a wall-painting in the tomb of Hui at El Kab, reproduced from a photograph
by Mr. W. M. Flinders Petrie.

of beads and pendants. Her head-dress is a stupendous work of art, consisting of a framework decorated with ostrich plumes mounted on a golden crown. Plumed negroes carrying trays piled with gold rings and bags of gold dust, and others bearing tribute of elephant tusks, logs of ebony, and other products of the Soudan, bring up the rear.[*]

Although the ancient Egyptian artist was naturally most

[*] See Mr. Petrie's series of photographs of "Racial Types."

familiar with the characteristics of the traditional "four races," he was no less skilful when called upon to deal with the unaccustomed European type. In the heads of the Sardinian body-guard of Rameses II., as we see them depicted in the famous battle-subject on the north wall of the Great Temple of Abû-Simbel, we find these fair-skinned, blue-eyed, and small-featured islanders represented with a freshness and vivacity which seem to point to the delight of the draughtsman in a new subject.

THE SARDINIAN OF EGYPTIAN ART.

The ethnic characteristics of these ancient Sardinians are very unlike those of the Sardinians of to-day. The type is almost that of the modern Englishman, a resemblance which is heightened by the neatly trimmed whiskers of the royal body-guard. Curiously enough, however, the Sardinian chieftain represented on the pavilion pylon of Rameses III. at Medinet - Habû is of a distinctly Semitic type. This would look as though Sardinia, in the time of the Twentieth Dynasty, had fallen under the rule of foreign conquerors; or as if the native Sardinian troops were officered at that time by Semites. In the foregoing head, as in the heads of all the Sardinian body-guard of Rameses II. in the great Abû-Simbel tableau, we have, at all events, a purely European type:

and this type, it is to be remembered, dates from about eighty years earlier than the sculptures of Medinet-Habû.

We will now pass on to Greece. As it has already been said, the only specimens of the graphic arts of Greece which time has spared are found on painted vases, the earliest being the so-called " pre-Homeric " vases of Athens, which cannot

GREEK CHARIOTEER.
From a " pre-Homeric " vase.

be less ancient than 1000 B.C., and may be yet older. The designs are absurdly archaic; but they at all events show us how barbarous were the beginnings of Greek art when isolated from foreign influences.

Here we have an example of the earliest Greek draughtsmanship which has come down to our time. The subject is taken from a " pre-Homeric " vase figured in Woltmann's *History of Painting*, vol. i. The subject is a charioteer driving a pair of animals, which may be horses, or giraffes, or both. The early Greek had, of course, no notion of perspective; therefore the chariot-wheels, though intended to be one on each side of the chariot, are placed in line. Neither have the chariot-pole and wheels any connection with the body of the chariot. As for the expressive countenance and classic draperies of the noble Athenian, it need scarcely be pointed out that they are immeasurably inferior to the poorest known specimens of Egyptian figure-drawing, being paralleled only by the dot-and-line performances of our childhood.

The following funerary scene is also from a vase of pre-Homeric type, of which an illustration is given in Collignon's *Archéologie Grecque*. In the figure-drawing of this fragment there is a marked improvement, which would seem to be traceable to the study of Egyptian models. These personages have faces, or, at all events, noses and chins; also, they have legs which are very substantially developed. As in Egyptian paintings, their bodies, from the waist upward, are shown frontwise, and their legs and faces in profile. The feet also are placed in line. The central object is a bier, upon which lies the body of a dead hero, covered with a pall. Two mourners strew it with palm branches; the rest clasp their hands above their heads in token of grief. The women sit on the floor beside the bier, in attitudes of lamentation. Of perspective, the artist had not the faintest perception. The bier stands on four stout legs, which are placed in a row like ninepins. The figures stand on a single line. It is a scene from a world of but two dimensions, in which all things have length and breadth, but no thickness.

OBSEQUIES OF A HERO.

A fragment of archaic painted ware found by Mr. Petrie in the ruins of the palace-fort of Psammetichus I. at Daphnæ, in the Eastern Delta, is decorated with the following figure of a Greek dancing-girl. Now, Daphnæ was founded by this Pharaoh for the accommodation of his Carian and Ionian mercenary troops about the middle of the seventh century before our era, and the place was abandoned ninety years later, in the reign of Amasis II. We have therefore a sufficiently accurate date for this design of a dancing-woman ; that is to say, we may take it for granted that the Greek colonists who settled in the neighborhood of the camp would scarcely have built their town, and devel-

oped their trades as potters and goldsmiths, until at least a decade had elapsed. Consequently, this product of their industry would fall within the strict limit of eighty years. Our Greeks had by this time much improved in their treatment of the human figure. But for the old false drawing of the frontwise eye in the profile face, the features are naturally given. And it is a thoroughly Greek face, which is very interesting. The fillet, the ear-ring, and the long side-curl are all characteristic of archaic Greek costume. The

GREEK DANCING-GIRL.

From a fragment of an archaic Greek vase found at Daphnæ.

figure has, however, all the Egyptian conventionalities grossly exaggerated, the body being shown frontwise to the waist, while the legs and feet are placed sidewise, the breadth of the shoulders and the length of the arms being ludicrously out of proportion.

On another fragment of the same date and from the same place, we have next a stock subject of the Greek vase-painters; namely, Œdipus and the Sphinx. It is probably the earliest example of the subject extant. This, again, is better drawn than the last design. But for the portentous length of his hair and the amazing curve of his beard, Œdipus is a very respectable-looking personage. The Egyptian element is here unmistakable. The sphinx is a purely Egyptian monster and of immemorial antiquity, the Great Sphinx of Ghizeh being probably the oldest monument in Egypt.

The true Egyptian sphinx, however, has the head of a bearded man crowned with the double crown of the Pharaohs.
But the Greeks, when they borrowed the sphinx (as they
borrowed so much else) from Egypt, added wings to the
lion body, and changed the bearded head of the god into
the filleted and ringleted head of a Greek woman. In
doing thus, they lost sight of the old Egyptian myth which
identified the sphinx with Horus in one of his transforma-
tions, and they adapted the conception to one of their
own national legends. This fragment of painted ware from
Daphnæ marks, therefore, a starting-point in the history of
Greek art. Henceforth the sphinx became one of the most
familiar of Greek decorative subjects, not only in painting,
but in sculpture and metal-work. Sphinxes were represented as supporting
the arms of the throne
of Zeus; and a sphinx-
crest surmounted the
helmet of Athena.

A great advance in
freedom of drawing
characterizes our next
subject, a fine painted
plate discovered by
Mr. Petrie in the ruins
of Naukratis. This is
really a plaque-paint-
ing, two small holes
pierced through the
rim of the plate show-
ing that it was intend-

ŒDIPUS AND THE SPHINX.

From a fragment of an archaic Greek vase
found at Daphnæ.

ed for suspension on the wall. The lotus ornament at the
bottom is, like the sphinx, borrowed from Egyptian models.
The work of the vase-painter is executed with singular delicacy and freedom, only four colors being employed, namely.
yellow, brown, purple, and white—the typical four colors of
the earliest school of Greek painting. These were the four

colors of the palette of Polygnotus and his contemporaries; and from the harmony with which they are used in this charming plaque-painting, which has been aptly compared (*) with the panel-painting of the early Greek artists, we may form some idea of the style and treatment of the earliest masters.   As an example of the technique of a lost

PAINTED PLATE WITH WINGED SPHINX, FOUND AT NAUKRATIS.

school of art, this Naukratis plate is invaluable.   It is certainly not later than 500 B.C., and it is more probably as early as 600 B. C.*

Having considered these few examples of the dominant Egyptian influence in early Greek painting, we will next observe how that influence affected the arts of Etruria.

The Etrurians are the most mysterious people of antiquity.

* See chap. v. on "Egypt the Birthplace of Greek Decorative Art."

We meet with them in the sculptured chronicles of ancient Egypt as the Tursha, and in the pages of the earliest Greek writers as the Tyrrhenes, or Turseni.(") According to ancient tradition, they came from Lydia in prehistoric times, and colonized Latium. Certain details of their costumes and customs appear to be identical with those of Lydia, and the legend is probably based upon fact. But until the inscriptions of Etruria can be read, we are not likely to solve this problem. The Etruscan characters closely resemble the archaic alphabets of Asia Minor; but no scholar has yet succeeded in identifying more than proper names. and the names of deities.

The rock-cut sepulchres of Etruria are singularly Egyptian in style, and the wall-paintings with which they are decorated bear the unmistakable impress of Egyptian teaching. A very interesting series of Etruscan paintings on terra-cotta slabs, from a tomb discovered at Cervetri, were purchased by the British Museum in 1889. Two of these slabs are painted with fantastic sphinxes, winged like those of Daphnæ and Naukratis, and purely decorative. These sphinx slabs were placed apparently on either side of the entrance of the tomb. The others contain figures walking, as it would seem, in a funerary procession. Some carry lotus plants with drooping lotus buds, and one bears a kind of covered vase, or perfume-jar. The women wear buskins and the men greaves, and both are long-haired. The eyes are set, as in the Egyptian paintings, frontwise in the profile face; and the feet, as usual, are placed the one precisely in advance of the other.

The accompanying example is reproduced from a chromolithographed plate in the *Journal of Hellenic Studies*, 1890.

The men are colored red, as in the Egyptian school, and they wear pointed beards, like the Œdipus of the Daphnæ potsherd. The flesh-tints of the woman are white. The bull-crested standard borne by the middle figure is purely Egyptian, and we have numberless examples of the type in Egyptian paintings and bas-reliefs from the Eighteenth Dynasty downward. This Etruscan tomb was evidently the tomb of a hero. The woman carries his spear and wreath of victory ; the first man, who wears a white tunic, carries his standard or sceptre ; the second man, who seems to be in the act of declaiming, has a palm branch to lay upon the bier. The Egyptian influence in this whole series of painted slabs is quite unmistakable.

The Egyptian military standard was generally surmounted by the figure of a lion in gilded bronze, the lion being sometimes surmounted by a fan-shaped ornament. Now, if the Etruscans borrowed their military insignia from Egypt, the Romans, we know, borrowed their insignia of triumph and of

ETRUSCAN PAINTED SLAB, FOUND AT CERVETRI.

royalty from Etruria, an ivory standard, or long-stemmed sceptre surmounted by an eagle, being invariably carried in their triumphal processions. Thus, the eagles borrowed by the first Napoleon from the classic Cæsars, are to this day the lineal representatives of the insignia of Rome, of Etruria, and of ancient Egypt.

We have now cast a rapid glance at some few examples of the three earliest schools of painting—the Egyptian, the Greek, and the Etruscan; we have traced the influence of Egyptian teaching upon the two younger nations; and we have seen how the pupils began by reproducing and even exaggerating the conventional errors of their masters. Unlike the Egyptians, however, they did not go on perpetuating those errors from age to age, from cycle to cycle. They learned to look at nature with their own eyes, and to paint, not what they had been taught, but what they actually saw. They discovered, for instance, that objects diminish with distance; that grass in sunshine is not the same color as grass in shadow; that a man's nose, because it projects, catches the light. They discovered that it was possible, merely by imitating the natural effects of light and shadow, to obtain a semblance of relief upon a perfectly flat surface. In a word, they discovered the laws of chiaroscuro, and with them the art of foreshortening, which is, in fact, perspective applied to the human figure.

Greek tradition ascribes these great discoveries to an Athenian named Apollodorus,(²⁰) who flourished about four hundred and thirty years before our era; and it is from this date that the true art of painting may be said to begin. How rapidly the great Greek school developed, and to what a height of splendor it ultimately attained, we have already seen.

The Egyptians, meanwhile, went on in the old grooves for a few centuries longer. But even the Egyptians were converted at last; and the evidence of their conversion comes, strangely enough, from the cemetery of what was once a fifth-rate town in the Fayûm. The town occupied one corner of an immense quadrangular platform artificially raised

THE SITE OF THE LABYRINTH.

From a photograph by Mr. W. M. Flinders Petrie. In the foreground is seen the level sand of the desert and the vast platform of chips marking the position of the building. The brick foundations on the surface of the platform show the lines of the streets of the Graeco-Roman town.

above the level of the desert. This platform, which measures one thousand feet in length by eight hundred in breadth, represents the site of the Labyrinth—that famous building of which it was said by Herodotus that it was "larger than all the temples of Greece put together, and more wonderful than the pyramids." The Labyrinth was utterly destroyed by order of the Roman Government some seventeen or eighteen centuries ago, and all that remains of its former magnificence is this platform, heaped six feet deep with thousands and tens of thousands of tons of limestone and granite chips. This tremendous destruction was undoubtedly wrought by order of the Roman Government, and the people who smashed up and quarried out the most splendid building of the ancient world lived in that little town on the south-west corner of the platform. As they went on clearing the site they made use of it for a cemetery; and so, in course of time, the last vestiges of the Labyrinth disappeared, and the place thereof became a city of the dead. It was this cemetery which Mr. Petrie explored during the seasons of 1887–88 and 1888–89; and it was here that he discovered the extraordinary series of portraits, some of which are here reproduced from his original photographs.([20])

The town appears to have contained a mixed population consisting of Egyptians, Greeks, Syrians, and Romans, the Egyptians being for the most part small tradesfolk, artisans, servants, and slaves; whereas the naturalized foreigners— some of whom were resident Roman officials, and others the descendants of Ptolemaic Greeks — represented the aristocracy of the place. Such, at all events, is the story told by their graves; the rich mummy-cases covered with gilding being mainly inscribed with Greek and Roman names, as Artemidorus, Demetrius, Titus, and the like.

The town continued to be inhabited, and the cemetery to be used, for several generations, during which time the burial customs of these people underwent many alterations. They seem, in fact, to have changed their fashions for the dead almost as often as we change our fashions for the living. At one time they wrapped them in elaborate bandages, and enclosed their heads and feet in a kind of piece-armor of stiffened linen, stuccoed, painted, and gilded. This piece-armor consisted of a head-piece, breastplate, and foot-case, the head-piece having a carefully modelled face representing the features of the deceased. Later on, they gave up gilding the faces and substituted color, at the same time inserting artificial eyes, and even imitating the hair, as it was black or brown, wavy or curly. When realistic treatment in modelled stucco had been carried as far as it could be carried, the fashion changed again, and a portrait painted on flexible canvas was laid over the face of the mummy. A certain degree of actual relief was thus obtained by the prominence of the bandaged features beneath.

From the flexible canvas it was but one bold, last step to portraiture on a flat panel, the semblance of relief being given by light, shadow, and foreshortening. This bold, last step marks the first appearance of the art of true painting in Egypt. It signalizes the transition from the Eastern to the Western school; it signs the death-warrant of the old conventional Egyptian system; and it coincides in point of time with the Emperor Hadrian's visit to Egypt in the year A.D. 130. That visit brought Western culture and Western art to the very gates of Thebes. Thus, three hundred years after Apollodorus had, as Pliny said, "opened that door by which all the great Greek painters entered," Egypt—better late than never —crossed the magic threshold. Fettered as the Egyptians had been by the traditions of their schools, they would scarcely have recognized the properties

YOUNG GREEK.

of light and shadow, or the value of color in transition, unless their eyes had been opened by teachers from without. Greece, however, could well afford to pay this one instalment of her enormous debt to Egypt; and Egypt could afford to accept this gift from Greece, who owed her all the rest.

A few specimens of the Græco-Egyptian school of panel-portraiture have been found from time to time within the last quarter of a century, and those few have been classed among the choicest treasures of our European museums; but it was not until 1887 that any considerable number were brought to light.   One series was discovered by Arab diggers at a place called Rubaiyat, in the Fayûm.   These were purchased by Herr Graff, an Austrian gentleman, and have been made the subject of a pamphlet by Dr. Ebers. The other series was discovered about the same time by Mr. Petrie in the cemetery of this Græco-Roman town on the Labyrinth plateau.

The mummies adorned by these portraits were enclosed in fine cases solidly stuccoed and brilliantly painted, an oval space being left over the face of the mummy, in which the panel was inserted.   In one instance the panel, instead of being laid over the dead face, was found enclosed in a

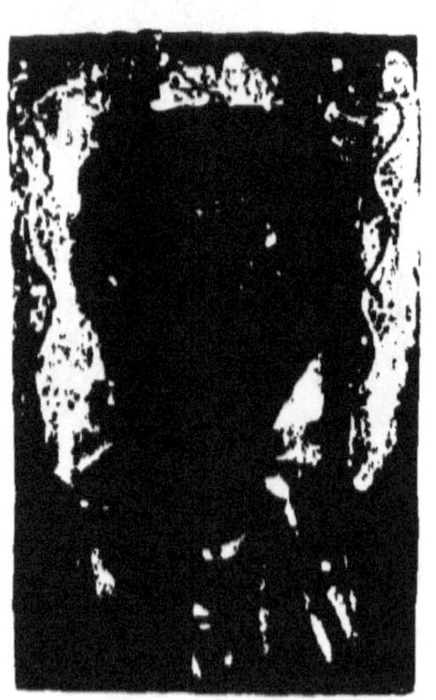

frame of the modern "Oxford pattern," and deposited beside the mummy in his tomb.   It had evidently hung in his house during the lifetime of the sitter, the cord by which it was anciently suspended being yet knotted round the corners.

The heads are painted of life size, on thin cedar panels measuring about seventeen inches by nine inches, and varying from one-sixteenth to a quarter of an inch in thickness. In the earliest specimens the panel is found to have been first covered with a thin coat of stucco, on which the portrait is painted in *tempera ;* but this process was dry and brittle, and the color flaked off, which caused it soon to be abandoned in favor of a medium of melted beeswax.   The colors, being in powder, mixed readily with the wax, and were laid on with a stiff reed-brush fuzzed out at the end, such as had been used by the old Egyptian painters from time immemorial. The panel was first covered with a priming of distemper. Then came the ground color, which was generally laid in of a leaden tint for the background, and of a flesh tint for the face and neck. The next step was to outline the features with the brush — this being generally done in a purple hue—and the last was to work in the surface color, or painting proper, the hot sun of Egypt sufficing to keep the wax in a creamy and manageable condition. This method, as practised in Egypt, cannot have been identical with what is commonly called the "encaustic painting of the ancients." That was a difficult and laborious process, the colors being fused on the picture by means of a red-hot implement described by Pliny as "a punching-iron." No artificial heat was needed in Egypt, and the colors were undoubtedly applied with the reed-brush, the fibres of which are clearly traceable in these Fayûm

GREEK LADY.

portraits. Also, the encaustic was a slow process, whereas these bold and sketchy heads evince the utmost rapidity of execution.

As for the pigments employed, it would have been impossible to analyze them without destroying a picture, but for the fortunate discovery of the grave of an artist, whose paint-saucers were laid beside his head—six in number, piled one upon the other. They prove to contain:

1. *Dark red*, made from oxide of iron, with a small admixture of sand, making a good sienna color. 2. *Yellow*, made from ochre and oxide of iron, and a little alumina. 3. *White*, made from sulphate of lime and gypsum. 4. *Red*, made from minium and oxide of lead, and apparently some

alumina. 5. *Blue*, made of glass colored by copper, and ground to a blue powder. 6. *Pink*, made with sulphate of lime colored with some organic substance, which is almost certainly madder.

One question connected with these ancient and remarkable portraits can never be satisfactorily resolved; namely, to what extent they represent the work of native Egyptian artists. Some, and probably the best, will almost certainly have been executed by Greek and Roman painters settled in Egypt; others will be the work of Egyptians who had studied in the Greek schools. We may perhaps, with more or less accuracy, guess which are due to the alien, and which to the native hand; but such guessing is necessarily inconclusive. With far more certainty is it possible to trace the nationality of these various personages, some of whom are identified by the names inscribed on their bandages and mummy-cases, while others, who are anonymous, are as surely identified by their racial characteristics. Some are unmistakably Roman; others are unmistakably Greek; while in others again we recognize Egyptian, Nubian, and Semitic types.

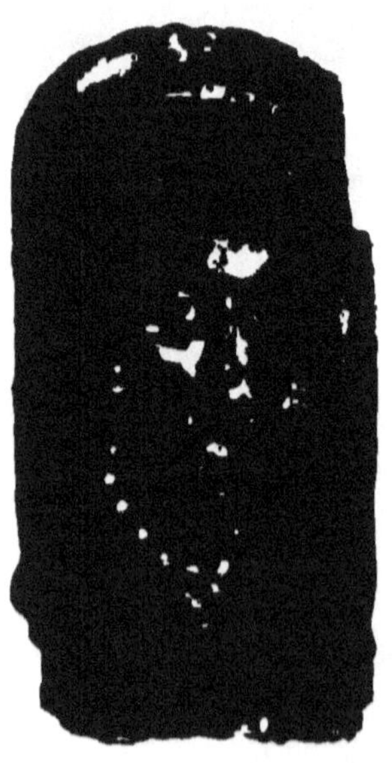

EGYPTIAN LADY

Neither is it difficult to classify the paintings in something like chronological order. The costumes, the style of wearing the hair, and even the fashions of the jewellery as depicted in the likenesses of women, afford valuable data for comparison with the portrait-sculptures of the Romans, and with the wall-paintings of Latium and Campania. Coins have also been occasionally found with the mummies; and the testimony of coins is in-valuable.   Lastly, there is the evidence of technique and ex-ecution, as shown by the rejection of *tempera* in favor of beeswax, and the progressive mastery of materials and effects on the part of the painters. That so many of the heads should be portraits of Greeks and Romans is no more than we might expect. Egypt had been flooded with Greeks during the two hundred and seventy-four years of Mace-donian rule, and the descendants of these friendly invaders long continued to form a large pro-portion of the population. Mean-while the Romans, as actual ru-lers of the country, administered the civil and military govern-ment, and were everywhere in force from Alexandria to Syene, and from Syene to Ibrim. The inevitable result followed. Ar-tists and artisans, embroiderers,

DIOGENES THE FLUTE-PLAYER.

jewellers, house-decorators and portrait-painters found their best patrons among these Greek settlers and Roman auto-crats, in whose hands the wealth of the country, as well as the power, was practically vested. It was for them that the richest stuffs were woven, the finest houses built, the costliest ear-rings, necklaces, and fibulæ designed. It was also for them that the most gorgeous mummy-cases were ex-ecuted. Engrafting upon their own religion certain of the beliefs and rites yet current in the Valley of the Nile, these aristocratic Greeks and Romans embalmed their dead "after the manner of the Egyptians," and even adopted names com-posed with the names of Egyptian deities. The Lady Isa-rous, whose name is painted in Greek characters on either side of her neck, and whose features are distinctly Greek, was a votary of Isis, Isarous being a somewhat clumsy transcription of *Isi-ari-s*, or *Ast-ari-s*—a name which is found in its original Egyptian form upon a funerary tablet in the Museum of the Louvre, and which signifies "Isis made her." Another name composed with that of Isis is "Isiön;" and another, evidently derived from *Ari-n-Amen* ("made by Amen"), is "Ammonarin." "Sarapis" (misspelled, of course, for "Serapis") was written on the breast of one of the finest of these portrait-mummies, both mummy and portrait being now in the national Egyptian collection. It is interesting to note how Isis and Amen were always the Egyptian deities most in favor with the Greeks and Romans, and how they identified Apis, under the name of "Serapis," with Zeus and Jupiter. "Ta-Ast," an Egyptian name signifying the "gift of Isis," became a favorite Greek and Roman name under the form of "Isidora," and it survives to this day in the French "Isidore."

ROMAN HEAD.

Some of the panel portraits found on these Hawara mummies are surrounded by a decorative border of gilt stucco, representing vine-tendrils and grapes. This bordering, as a rule, is modelled on the panel, though in some instances it is found to be moulded on a canvas ground and laid round the picture. The portraits thus decorated are among the earliest in date, beginning, that is to say, about 130 B.C. In our two first examples, a young Greek gentleman and a plebeian-looking boy (pp. 97, 98), in whose saucy eyes, open nostrils, thick lips, and swarthy skin I cannot but recognize the prototype of the native Egyptian donkey-boy of our own time,* we have excellent specimens of the Hawara school of portraiture at the beginning of its career. The light and shadow in the Greek head is very forcible, and the spirit and character conveyed in the other are quite remarkable. The Greek wears a white chiton with a purple stripe on the right shoulder, and the boy a yellow chiton with a narrow purple stripe, and a yellow himation over the left shoulder.

The Greek lady on page 99 is very gayly attired in a scarlet chiton bordered by a broad band of black edged with gold, and she wears a black himation over the left shoulder. Her ear-rings consist of a large ball suspended from a smaller ball; the jewellery being modelled on the panel in stucco, and gilt with gold leaf. These ball ear-rings appear to have been es-

YOUNG GREEK WITH GILT OLIVE-WREATH.

pecially fashionable about the time of Hadrian—that is to say, during the early period of the Hawara school of portraiture—and the ball or disk covered with small clustered balls, as in this portrait, is but a variation upon a more simple design. This lady is clearly a Greek. The nose and forehead are in one unbroken line, the eyes are well spaced and well opened, and the mouth is prettily drawn. She wears her hair in a style which is familiar to us in Roman

---

* Neither of these mummies bore any indication of name or nationality. Mr. Cecil Smith conjecturally describes the boy as Roman, but it seems to me that his Egyptian type (of the plebeian class) is unmistakable.

portrait-busts of this age: and the bands of open-work which pass under the bodice of her dress and over each shoulder are very probably of knotted thread, like the caps and head-scarfs found by Mr. Petrie in many of these Hawara graves.([30])

For a lavish display of jewellery, however, and a curious variety of patterns, the native Egyptian lady reproduced on page 100 surpasses all her compeers. On her head, she wears a gold wreath fashioned in imitation of the victor's wreath of laurel leaves: in her ears, elaborate ear-rings con-

ROMAN LADY.

sisting of a pearl drop, from which hangs a crossbar of gold with three pendant pearls; and round her neck, two necklaces— the upper one a string of alternate pearls and garnets, and the lower one a gold chain with a small crescent-shaped pendant. Her features are moulded in the unmistakable Egyptian type. The eyes are long and heavy-lidded, the nostrils wide, the lips full and prominent. The complexion is swarthy, with a dull reddish blush under the skin, and the whole expression of the face is that of Oriental languor. We may conclude that this lady belonged to one of the few wealthy native families yet remaining in the Fayûm. Unfortunately, there is no record of her name. The portrait is well but somewhat coarsely painted, and it looks as though it were a successful likeness.

Finer by far, as a work of art, is the portrait of a young man named Diogenes (p. 101). He was apparently a professional musician. A small wooden label found with the mummy-case calls him " Diogenes of the Flute of Arsinoe:" while a second inscription, written in ink upon one of the mummy-wrappings, describes him as " Diogenes who abode at the Harp when he was alive." From these it is evident that he was a flautist, born in the city of Arsinoe, and that when he came to live at Hawara, he lodged at the sign of the Harp. The panel, like too many others, is badly cracked; but the head is so characteristic, and the expression so fine, that not even this blemish mars its effect. There is a set look in the face, as of some solemn purpose to be fulfilled; and the eyes arrest us, like the eyes of a living man. The hair is very thick and curly, and the features are distinctly Jewish in type. That he should be a Jew would be quite in accordance with his profession for the gift of music has ever been an inheritance of the children of Israel.

ROMANO-EGYPTIAN LADY.

Finer than even the Diogenes, though in a different way, is an admirable character-study of a shrewd-looking, hard-featured Roman (p. 102). The man is somewhat on the wrong side of fifty. His face is deeply furrowed, probably by business cares, and he looks straight out from the panel with the alert and resolute air of one who is intent on a profitable bargain. The artist has not flattered him. His nose is bent, as if from a blow, and about the lines of the mouth there is a hint of humor, grim and caustic, which has been caught with evident fidelity. Unlike the rest of the portraits, this head is a detached study thrown upon the upper part of the panel, with no attempt at drapery or finish. When Sir Frederick Burton, Director of the English National Gallery, saw this series of heads on exhibition at the Egyptian Hall, Piccadilly, in 1888, a few weeks after they had been discovered, he pronounced our elderly Roman to be " worth all the rest put together"—not, of course, as "a thing of beauty," but for force, character, and mastery of the painter's craft. On hearing this verdict, the owner of the picture, who had intended it for his private collection, generously presented it, with two others, to the National Gallery.

THE STUDENT

There is not only individuality but spirit in the head of a young Greek reproduced on page 103. The eyes are bright and translucent; the nose is well shaped; the chin is disproportionately long. Dashed off in hot haste, the effect is brilliant but sketchy, as if done at one sitting. The hair is apparently unfinished; the background is flung upon the panel with a few strokes of a broad brush, every fibre of which is traceable; and the artist, content to get in the effect of the white chiton, has not even carried it down to the bottom of the picture. Our young Greek was probably somewhat of a *petit-maitre*, for the olive wreath on his head is gilded. This reminds us of the golden wreaths and golden sandal-clasps of Xeuxis, and other painter-princes of the golden age of Hellenic art, and it is interesting to find this special piece of dandyism surviving down to the time of Hadrian.

There is no lack of expression in the dejected countenance of the Roman lady who follows on page 104. Her features wear the stamp of long-continued ill-health; her complexion is "sicklied o'er" with suffering; and her eyes are encircled by heavy purple rings. One would say that she knew but too well, while sitting for this portrait, that it would erelong be transferred from the picture-frame to her coffin. She wears her black hair in a curiously modern fash- ion, gathered up in a thick coil at the back, parted down the middle, and laid in plain bands. Her gown is purple, with a square-cut bodice trimmed with a broad black and gold braid; and over her shoulders is cast a purple himation. The necklace consists of large pale-green opaque stones, cut in the form of oblong parallelograms, con- nected by slender gold wires. Mr. Cecil Smith takes them for green beryls; but they are, I think, more probably intended to represent the so-called "mother- of-emerald," a stone which was popular in Egypt under the Ro- mans, and has frequently been found in graves of this period.

THE GLADIATOR.

In the head of the next lady (p. 105) it is impossible not to recognize a portrait which is not only a portrait but a likeness. She is probably of Romano-Egyptian parentage. The eye- brows and eyelashes are singularly thick and dark; the eyes long, and of Oriental depth and blackness; and the swarthi- ness of the complexion is emphasized by the dark down on the upper lip. It is a passionate, intense-looking face—the face of a woman with a history. She wears her black hair cut in a short fringe round the brow, and laid in two long roll-curls, like the hair of the Greek. Her ear-rings consist of a single pearl from which is suspended a horizontal bar of gold, while from this bar hang two more pearls, each terminated by a pyramidal cluster of three small gold balls. The necklace is particularly interesting, being the only representation of an elaborate Egyptian collarette in the whole series. It is three rows deep, the two upper rows being apparently of chain-work, while the lowest row consists of lotus-bud pendants, colored red to represent carnelian. Necklaces of these carnelian lotus-bud pendants are frequently found with mummies of the Roman period, and many fine specimens enrich the glass-cases of the principal European museums. The design is of remote antiquity, and the lotus pendant in glass and porcelain is found in graves of Pharaonic times in Upper Egypt. The Etruscans copied it at an early date, changing the lotus-bud, either intentionally or by mistake, into the amphora, which it resembles in form ; and it is this very lotus-bud pendant of Egypt which we find reproduced in the delicate and elegant gold amphora necklaces of Etruria. Revived by Signor Castellani of Rome, this exquisite design again became popular during the later half of the present century.

The young Greek who comes next (p. 106) has a modern type of face, good features, and a grave preoccupied expression, such as might become a student of philosophy or science. The brows are slightly knitted, as if from habitual meditation; the head is well posed and well balanced; and the hair is remarkably free and well put in. He wears a dull green chiton with a purple stripe on the right shoulder, and a himation of the same color. The panel is slightly cracked in several places.

In going through this series of paintings, one curious and interesting question inevitably suggests itself; namely, the immediate object with which these portraits were executed. Were they painted for the pleasure of the sitter and his family, and for the adornment of private houses? Or were they painted expressly for the decoration of mummy-cases, and in commemoration of the dead? If the former, then they were, of course, done from the life ; if the latter. is it possible that they were painted after death ?

These are questions which have been discussed by several competent authorities, but which, from their nature, cannot be satisfactorily settled. The fact that one framed portrait was found laid up against the mummy-case in the grave, and that the cord by which it had once been suspended was yet knotted round the transverse bars at the corners of that frame, gives conclusive proof that the people of this town loved portraiture for itself, and hung their portraits in their rooms, as we do now. Such portraits, as a rule, would probably be copied on smaller panels for funerary purposes. and this would account for their bright and life-like expression. Where no previous portrait existed. it may reasonably be supposed that an artist would be summoned, and a sketchy like-

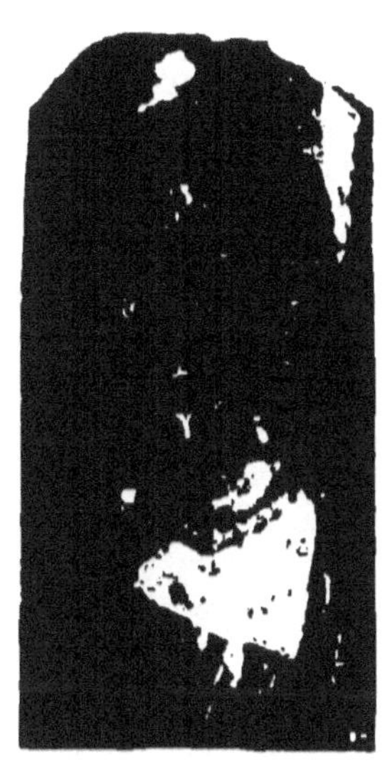

YOUNG LADY IN PURPLE CHITON.

ness would be hastily painted on a panel of the required size, immediately after death. If we compare the heads reproduced in these pages, it is not difficult to conjecture which are studies from the life, and which are studies after death. Some of the least expressive faces may very possibly owe their passive vacuity to the fact that "life and thought had gone away" before the artist came with his saucers of powdered colors, his reed-brushes, and his pot of melted beeswax. to transfer their pallid features to that narrow panel which was destined to adorn the mummy-case when the prescribed seventy days of embalmment should have expired. In these portraits, and some others. the eyes are represented unnaturally large. and with a fixed stare, such as might be given by an artist who had never seen his subject while living, and who added the eyes from his imagination.   The head of a coarse-featured, plebeian-looking Roman (p. 107), who should certainly be a prize-fighter or a gladiator, is a case in point.   There is no "speculation" in his eyes, which are much too large : the whole effect being that of a rapid sketch after death.   The head of Diogenes the flute-player (p. 101), the young Greek with the meditative brow (p. 98), the vivacious youth with the gilt olive wreath (p. 103), the intense-looking Romano-Egyptian dame with the dark eyebrows (p. 105), and one or two others, bear the direct impress of vitality, and cannot possibly be anything but studies, or copies of studies, from the living sitter.

So, too, I think, is the sweet and gracious portrait of a fair-skinned girl (p. 109), with chestnut hair, and soft brown eyes, and a mouth every curve of which is drawn with exquisite delicacy and truth.   Was she a Greek?   Or was she not, more probably, of Græco-Asiatic parentage?   Her complexion is of that creamy-olive tint which bespeaks a touch of Oriental blood ; and in the crisp waviness of her hair, the languorous tenderness of her eyes, and the arched black eyebrows, I think I detect traces of her Cypriote or Lycian ancestry.   Her purple chiton is gathered in classic folds across her bosom, and on her shoulders she wears a mantle of the same color.   In her ears are hoop ear-rings, each set with three emeralds, and round her neck she wears two necklaces—the upper one of gold beads and emeralds alternately, the lower a string of garnets with a centre ornament of one large emerald and two pendant pearls.   This is a charming portrait, well and carefully painted, and in excellent preservation.   Equally well preserved, and perhaps even more interesting, is the beautiful and touching head of a young boy (p. 111) with which our little portrait-gallery ends.   He, too, is of mixed descent—probably Græco-Egyptian, or Græco-Asiatic.   The complexion is of a clear dark olive : the eyes are large, black, luminous, and informed by a gentle melancholy, as if he had some presentiment of early death. The hair is black, curling, and abundant, and on the upper lip we note the soft black down of an incipient mustache. The mouth repeats the sweet and delicate curves which are so charming in the mouth of the young girl just gone before. There is, in fact, a certain likeness between the two faces. Not only the mouths are alike, but the eyes, and the peculiar curvature of the dark eyebrows. The names of both are unknown to us, but the resemblance is just what we might expect to find between a sister and brother. The age of this boy was about twelve or thirteen, and the size of the mummy corresponds with the age indicated by the portrait—both portrait and mummy being now in the British Museum. The mummy is very beautifully and elaborately bandaged, five or six strips of saffron-colored linen being used in successive layers, and so disposed, layer above layer, as to form a diamond-shaped, recessed

YOUNG BOY

pattern, sunken in the centre, and terminating in a kind of knob, or button, at the bottom.

These are but a few examples selected from Mr. Petrie's splendid series of funerary portraits; but they suffice to show that there was not only a school of art, but an art-market, in this obscure little provincial town during the second and third centuries of our era. The demand for portraiture being very considerable, the supply naturally varied in quality to suit the means of all comers. Hence the inequality of the painter's work. Those who could afford to pay for the best art commanded the best art, while those who were less wealthy, or more thrifty, patronized the sign-board school. Remembering the fabulous prices which Zeuxis and Apelles, and the rest, received for their pictures a few centuries earlier, one would like to know after what rate the Fayûm painters were paid; and it is always possible that among the hundreds of fragmentary papyri found by Mr. Petrie on this spot, some may prove to contain entries of payments made or received on account of one of these very portraits.

One very striking feature of the Fayûm portraits is the modern character of the heads. There is not a face in the whole series which we might not meet any day in the streets of London or New York. There is nothing to surprise us in this fact; and yet, so accustomed are we to think of the men and women of the far past as the *dramatis personæ* of ancient history, and as belonging to another age, that it is with a shock of something like incredulous astonishment that we find them so precisely like ourselves. The truth probably is that as regards features, stature, and complexion, the ancient Egyptians differed very little, if at all, from the Copts of the present day; and that the Greeks and Romans of the classic period were actually more like the people of northern Europe than are their modern descendants. Hadrian, Marcus Aurelius, Lucius Verus, and many another noble Roman who yet lives in marble and bronze, far more nearly resembles the type of the modern Englishman than that of the modern Italian. Seneca, Germanicus, and Julius Cæsar might pass for typical Americans. Past or present, we are in truth but members of one great family; and as we look through this ancient and interesting portrait-gallery, we cannot but recognize our kinship with these men and women, these youths and maidens, who lived and loved and died nearly two thousand years ago. Yet even these are but things of yesterday compared with the Ethiopian subjects in the tomb of Hui at El Kab, or with the paintings of the four races of men in the tombs of the kings at Thebes. And in these we see depicted racial types which survive unchanged to the present day in Nubia and Palestine.

IV.

THE ORIGIN OF PORTRAIT SCULPTURE,

AND THE HISTORY OF THE "KA."

It has been said by a celebrated poet that "the proper study of mankind is man." This sweeping proposition was accepted as an axiom by the contemporaries of the ingenious Mr. Pope; but to our nineteenth century ears it sounds, perhaps, too much like an epigram. We should, I think, prefer to say that the most *interesting* study of mankind is man. Certain it is, that whatsoever concerned man in the past concerns and interests ourselves in the present. Hence the eagerness with which we track his footsteps down the path of the centuries. From that far-distant age when we catch our first glimpse of the prehistoric cave-dweller chipping flint arrow-heads wherewith to wage war against the hyena and the mammoth, down to the pleasant "teacup time" of the day before yesterday, when Adam carried a clouded cane

8

and Eve wore hoops and patches, we are always eagerly curious to know what our forefathers were like, how they lived, and wherewithal they were clothed. This is why the art of portraiture touches us more nearly than any other. It brings us literally face to face with those who lived and loved and died "in the old time before us." It preserves for us the features, the expression, the costumes of Pharaohs and Cæsars discrowned, of orators long silent, of beauties long faded, of heroes whose swords are rust, of poets whose lutes are dust, and who, but for the accidental preservation of a bas-relief, a bust, a coin, or a painting, would have passed away like shadows and been no more seen.

By the extent of our wealth in the possession of certain portraits we may estimate what our poverty would have been without them. We can scarcely realize, for instance, the difference it would have made to us had we possessed no likeness of Shakespeare. We are as familiar with his honest English face and massive head as if the man himself were yet among the living. But could we have felt the same personal affection for him, or even quite the same personal pride in him, if there had been no bust at Stratford-on-Avon, and no Dreyschout engraving to the folio of 1623? Dante, again —Chaucer, Albert Dürer, Raphael, Michael Angelo, and a hundred others whom we could name in a breath—think what our loss would be if their faces were a blank to us! As for history, what would history be without the personality of those kings and captains who have moulded the destinies of nations from Alexander to Wellington?

But the interest of portraiture is not merely historical; it is also ethnographical. The sculptures of Assyria and Babylon, of Susa and Persepolis, record racial characteristics, and enable us to trace the origin, and sometimes to track the migrations, of peoples and tribes.

Lastly, there is the human interest—that interest which we take in the counterfeit presentment of our fellow-man simply because he *was* our fellow-man, and because the portrait is stamped with his individuality. He may have lived fifty or five thousand years ago; his very name may be unknown to us; but if the ancient artist was a master of his craft, and if he has handed down to us a face instinct with power or furrowed by thought, that face arrests us and holds us like the face of a living man. So long, indeed, as such a likeness survives, the man, in a sense, retains his hold upon our sympathies and his place among the living. One could almost say that he is not altogether dead.

All portraiture is in its origin funerary—that is to say, the earliest known specimens of portraiture are found in tombs, and represent the dead. The oldest tombs, I need hardly say, are the tombs of ancient Egypt; and the oldest known specimens of portraiture, whether in sculpture or painting, represent ancient Egyptians.

When saying, however, that all portraiture is in its origin funerary, I must not be understood to mean that such portraiture is of a memorial character. To adorn the last homes of the honored dead with sculptured effigies seems to ourselves a natural expression of respect. We desire that their likenesses as well as their memories shall be handed down to posterity; and we even derive some consolation from the knowledge that our remote descendants will know them as we have known them. But the ancient Egyptians buried their funerary effigies in the darkness and secrecy of the tomb itself. No people were so lavish of statues, of statuettes, of wall-sculptures and wall-paintings, representing the tenant of the tomb, his wife, and his family; yet no people were ever at such pains to hide those works of art from every eye. In the oldest time of all—that is, in the time of the First Empire, when every king had his pyramid, and every great man his stone-built tomb—portrait-statues were invariably buried with the dead. Strange as this custom seems, it is not half so strange as the fact that the Egyptians were wont to bury, not one statue, but several statues, all of the one man and all precisely alike. The average number of portrait-statues found in tombs of the first period is from three to seven; but as many as twenty duplicate statues of heroic size have actually been taken from a single tomb. Our astonishment culminates, however, when we learn that a hiding-place without inlet or outlet was constructed for the accommodation of these statues in the thickness of the wall of the tomb. Thus they were doubly buried, in a sepulchre within a sepulchre.

Here, no matter how admirable they might be as works of art—and some are indeed admirable—they were immured, as it was hoped and intended, forever. The National Egyptian Museum of Ghizeh, near Cairo, is rich in statues of this class, all found within the last twenty-five years, and all found in hiding-places such as I have described. The tombs which contain these recesses are peculiar to the great burial-fields of Ghizeh, Sakkarah, and Meydûm, and they belong to the time of the Pyramid Kings of the Fourth, Fifth, and Sixth dynasties—that is to say, from about four thousand to three thousand five hundred years before our era. They had all been plundered, who shall say how many centuries before Mariette and Maspero explored them? The mummies and their funerary belongings had long since been scattered to the winds; but the statues, secure and unsuspected, yet stood erect inside their narrow prisons. And they are, to this day, as perfect, and the colors with which they are painted are as fresh, as if they had left the hand of the ancient artist but a month ago.(³¹)

But it may be asked, What possessed this people that they should produce elaborate works of art, merely to hide them forever? Why not have erected them where they might have been seen by the descendants of those whom they commemorated? The answer, however, is that they were not memorial statues. They were not intended to "commemorate" the dead, as our dead are commemorated in modern churches and cemeteries. The ancient Egyptians were actuated by motives altogether different from our motives—by motives arising out of one of the most curious beliefs which ever influenced the mind of man at any period in the history of religious thought.

If, therefore, we are rightly to apprehend the place which ancient Egyptian portraiture holds in relation to the art of portraiture in other and later civilizations, it is necessary that we should know what that belief was, and in what way it affected the actions of those who entertained it.

Man, emerging from barbarism, is like an intelligent child, full of curiosity about himself. He is puzzled by the mystery of his own existence; and, according to his limited experience, he seeks to account for that mystery. Now, the ancient inhabitant of the Nile Valley accounted for himself in a very elaborate and philosophical fashion. He conceived of man as a composite being, consisting of at least six parts; namely, a body, "Khat"; a soul, "Ba"; an intelligence, "Khou"; a shadow, "Khaïbit"; a name, "Ren"; and another element, called in Egyptian a "Ka." To these six parts, as enumerated by Maspero,* Dr. Wiedemann adds two more—the heart, "Ab," and the "Sahu," which has hitherto been translated as the mummy, but is now defined by Dr. Wiedemann† as "the husk," which is, in fact, the same thing; a mummy from which all the internal organs have been removed, being really only the outer shell of the man. Now, the co-operation of these several parts as one harmonious whole constituted the living man; but they were dissociated by death, and could only be reunited after a long probation. When so reunited, it was forever. The man attained immortality, and became as one of the gods. Meanwhile, being dead, the Body lay inert in the depths of the tomb; the Soul performed a perilous pilgrimage through a demon-haunted Valley of Shades; the Intelligence, freed from mortal encumbrance, wandered through space; the Name, the Shadow, and the Heart awaited the arrival of the

---

* See Maspero's "Bulletin Critique de la Religion Égyptienne," in the *Revue de l'Histoire des Religions*, vol. xiii.   † *Die Unsterblichkeit der Seele nach altägyptischer Lehre.*—Von A. Wiedemann.

[The *Sahu*, considered as only the "husk," may from this point of view be regarded as somewhat differing from the *Khat*, or body, which is the whole corporeal being.—A. B. E.]

Soul when its pilgrimage should be accomplished; and the Ka dwelt with the mummy in the sepulchre.

Now, the Ka is a very interesting personage. He is designated in the Egyptian writing by a special hieroglyph representing a pair of hands and arms upraised as if in adoration.

Such is the pictorial symbol of which the phonetic reading is "*Ka.*" This name, or rather the conception represented by this name, has been variously interpreted by European Egyptologists. Dr. Brugsch, in his Hieroglyphic Dictionary, explains it as "the person, the individuality, the being." Professor Maspero, recognizing its incorporeal character, calls it "the double." Mr. Le Page Renouf (") likens it to the "eidolon" of the Greeks, the "genius" of the Romans; and Dr. Wiedemann has lately written an interesting paper to show that it was not the person, but what he calls "the personality" or "individuality" of the deceased—meaning thereby that which distinguished him in life from other men; in other words, the mental impression which was evoked when his name was mentioned.

Widely as these definitions differ, their authors agree as to the shadowy nature of the Ka itself. They recognize that it was a Spectral Something, apart from the man's body, inseparable from him during life, surviving him after death, and destined to be reunited to him hereafter. So much is proved by a multitude of inscriptions—chiefly of a funerary character; for, although the Ka occasionally figures in historical texts, and with reference to living persons, he is *invariably* met with in memorial inscriptions, from the old Pyramid Period down to the comparatively recent time when the ancient religion was superseded by Christianity. Throughout that long time (namely, from about four thousand years before Christ to the reign of the Emperor Theodosius I., three hundred and seventy-nine years after Christ), one special formula, graven on funerary tablets, remained almost word for word the same. That formula was neither more nor less than an invocation addressed by the deceased to all who might visit or pass by his tomb, imploring them to offer up a prayer on his account to Osiris, the god of the dead. This sounds curiously modern, reminding us of a similar prayer which we have all seen many a time in little village church-yards on the continent of Europe. The resemblance, however, does not go very far.

Jacques Bonhomme petitions you to say a *Pater-noster* for the repose of his soul; but the ancient Egyptian appealed to passers-by on behalf, not of his Soul, which was performing its pilgrimage in Hades, but of his Ka, which was the companion of his mummy in the tomb.

And what may we suppose he wanted for his Ka? Peace, after the battle of life? Loving remembrance on the part of those who survived him?

Not at all. His supplication was of a far more material character. It was literally for the good things of this world —in a word, for what is expressively termed "a square meal." Take, for example, the literal translation of one of these *post-mortem* petitions from the funerary tablet of one Pepi-Na, who lived in the early part of the Sixth Dynasty, some three thousand five hundred years before our era.

FUNERARY TABLET OF PEPI-NA.([33])

(Sixth Dynasty.)

"O ye who live upon the earth!
Ye who come hither and are servants of the Gods!
Oh, say these words:
"Grant thousands of loaves, thousands of jars of wine, thousands of jars of beer, thousands of beeves, thousands of geese, to the Ka of the Royal Friend Pepi-Na, Superintendent of the Royal Household, and Superior of the Priests of the Pyramid of King Pepi!"

This is a very early specimen. We will now take a great leap of nearly three thousand years, to the Saïte Period—the period of Psammetichus and his dynasty—and turn to the tablet of one Napu, a priest of Thebes who lived and died about two thousand four hundred years ago.

(Twenty-sixth Dynasty.)

Adoration to Osiris,
The Great God,
Lord of Abydos!

"May he grant sepulchral meals, beeves, geese, burnt incense, wine, beer, linen vestments, vegetables, and all good, pure, and sweet things to the Ka of the Holy Priest of Maut, Napu, Son of the Holy Priest of Maut, Asi, and of the Lady Mautemhatmest."

To multiply examples would be easy. Such funerary tablets are accumulated by hundreds in European museums. Some are elaborately carved in granite and basalt; some are painted on panels of acacia-wood. Some are from five to seven feet in height; others are about the size of an ordinary octavo volume. Few travellers come back from Egypt without one of these smaller tablets, and few private collections are without a specimen. But from the earliest to the latest, in the largest as well as in the smallest, the one most remarkable feature of the formula is the voracious appetite of the Ka. He is invariably clamoring for "beeves and geese, wine and beer," fruits, bread, and the like. And the proportions of his bill of fare put the most stupendous of civic banquets to shame. He asks for "thousands" of all these good things. An ox roasted whole would be of no more account to him than a beef-lozenge to an alderman. And it is yet more extraordinary that the Ka actually got what he asked for; though not, perhaps, to the full extent of his demands. The four oxen who dragged the funeral sledge to the tomb on the day of burial were slaughtered and cut up on the spot; gazelles and geese were also slain; and these, together with great sheaves of onions and cucumbers, and basket-loads of bread, corn, dates, nuts, and other eatables, as well as a number of large jars filled with wine, milk, water, and barley beer, were deposited in the sepulchral chamber, and there walled up with the mummy.

Now this, it is to be remembered, was not by way of a

sacrifice to the gods, nor yet for the benefit of the mummy. It was for the sustenance of the Ka.   The mummy, in fact. is a very secondary personage in comparison with the Ka. The tomb itself is called the " House of the Ka"—not the house of the mummy.   The food-offerings thus buried were

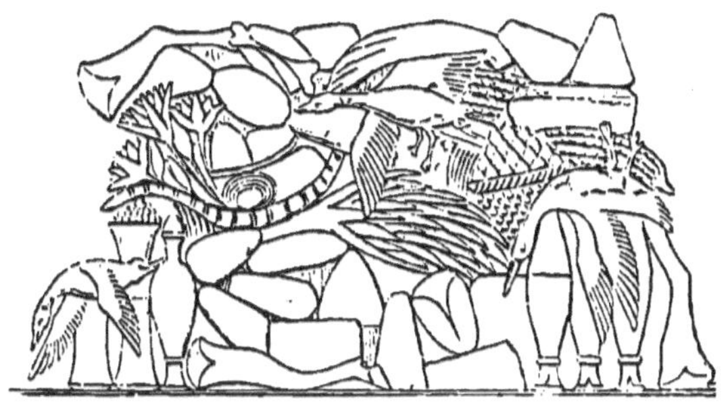

FUNERARY OFFERINGS.
From a tomb of the Fifth Dynasty.

·not supposed, however, to last the Ka for very long.   They had to be periodically renewed.   This was sometimes done by the descendants of the dead, who at stated dates deposited food and drink in the votive chapel attached to the tomb. But the wealthy Egyptian more commonly provided for the future of his Ka by bequeathing a portion of his estate to the priesthood, in prepayment for sepulchral meals in perpetuity.   There are inscriptions in the Museum of Naples, and in the Louvre, which prove that these endowed offerings were kept up for many centuries.

Supposing, however, that unforeseen circumstances caused the endowment to lapse, the Ka had still a last resource in the piety of strangers.   Such was the magical power of the formula engraved upon his funerary tablet that its mere repetition by a passer-by sufficed to insure a supply of ideal beeves and geese, ideal jars of wine and beer, ideal onions and cucumbers for the nourishment of the hungry Ka.   By simply reading aloud the invocations of Pepi-Na and Napu we may therefore at any moment replenish the larders of that worthy pair—a piece of good-fortune which has probably not befallen either of them for a considerable time.

And now a very curious question suggests itself, namely, why should the immaterial Ka stand in need of material meats and drinks? It may, perhaps, be asked in return what that question has to do with the subject of ancient Egyptian portraiture?

It has everything to do with it. It has to do with the portrait-statues immured in the walls of the tomb. It has to do with the portraits sculptured in bas-relief, or painted in distemper, on the inner chambers and passages of the tomb. It lies at the bottom of the whole history of portraiture.

Those statues and paintings, as it has already been said, were not memorial. When once the tomb was closed, they were never again to be seen by mortal eyes. With what object, then, were they fashioned?

They were fashioned for the purpose of providing an artificial body for the Ka.

Opinions may differ as to the nature of the Ka itself—one regarding it as a ghost, another as a double, another as an "eidolon" or genius; but no Egyptologist doubts that all forms of portraiture in ancient Egypt were funerary, or that they were expressly designed for the accommodation of the Ka.

The Ka and the Body were inseparable till death dissolved their partnership. Once dead and mummified, the body was exposed to many dangers. The tomb might be broken open; the mummy might be burned, and scattered to the four winds of heaven; but so long as the statues remained intact in their hiding-places—so long as the painted portraits on the walls were not utterly defaced—the Ka had still a body to depend upon. Professor Maspero, conceiving of the Ka as a "double," supposed this double to need a material support on which to extend itself—as a glove, for instance, is extended on a wooden hand in a glove-maker's shop. But I have recently ventured to suggest another explanation of the nature of the Ka, which seems to me not only more satisfactory from a metaphysical point of view, but which also places in our hands a key to the interpretation of many texts which till now have been hopelessly obscure.

I believe that the Ka stood, not for the genius or double, but for *the life*—in other words, for the vital principle. I have been led to this conclusion by the evidence of certain sculptures and inscriptions of which the exact sense seems, from my point of view, to have escaped observation. If, however, the nature of this evidence is to be explained, no matter how popularly and briefly, it becomes necessary to enter into a few preliminary details.

I must first point out that every reigning Pharaoh had three names: (1) his personal, or family name, being the same by which he was known when but a prince; (2) his "throne-name," or "solar-name," assumed on his accession, and indicating his divine descent from the god Ra; (3) his "banner-name," or "standard-name," so called because enclosed in an upright rectangular frame, like a banner, decorated with a margin of vertical strokes at the lower end, somewhat resembling a fringe. Now, Mr. Petrie* has recently shown that this misnamed "standard" is neither more nor less than an abridged representation of the "false door" of a tomb—such a door as was sculptured, or painted, on the walls of the upper chamber in which funerary food-offerings were deposited. These fictitious doors were supposed to lead to the equally fictitious apartment of the Ka; and it was through them that he passed to and fro to feed upon the "beeves and geese" and other good things provided for his sustenance.† Mr. Petrie has conclusively demonstrated the accuracy of his interpretation by numerous examples from monuments of all periods, some of these "standards" actually showing the hinges, bolts, and bars of the imitation

* *A Season in Egypt.* By W. M. Flinders Petrie. Chap. iv. 1888.
† See *Egyptian Archæology.* By G. Maspero. Chap. iii., p. 125. 1880.

door. The so-called "standard" being the abridged representation of the door supposed to give access to the imaginary chamber of the Ka. Mr. Petrie was at once led to the further discovery that the standard-name was in reality the Ka-name of the King. Hence it followed that each sovereign, on succeeding to the throne, not only assumed a throne-name, but took also a name for his Ka. The throne-name was enclosed in a royal oval, or cartouche, like the family-name; but the Ka-name was represented as if inscribed above the false door-way, just where the name of a deceased person would be inscribed above the actual door of his sepulchre. It may seem strange, perhaps, that a living Pharaoh should emblazon part of the decoration of his tomb among the insignia of his royalty; but that tomb, it is to be remembered, was the destined abode, not only of his mummy, but of his Ka. Consequently, no better device could be employed by way of substitute for a royal oval than the rectangular framework enclosing a representation of the false door inscribed with the Ka-name. The tomb itself, as already stated, is known in funerary texts as the "House of the Ka"; and as each king on his accession began immediately to build his pyramid or excavate his rock-cut sepulchre, it followed that he was as much interested in providing for the future accommodation of his Ka as in providing for the future accommodation of his mummy. Many texts point, however, to the fact that Ka-houses were erected by the Egyptians for the worship and service of their Kas, independently of their tombs;* so that, after all, the false door represented in a royal Ka-name may as probably stand for the false door of a Ka-chamber in a royal votive chapel, as for the false door of a Ka-chamber in the sepulchre. It would seem, from the absence of any record to the contrary, that the Kas of private persons were either nameless, or called by the names of those persons; and that the King alone was

---

* Khnumhotep, in the great Beni-Hassan inscription, states that he built chapels for the Ka of his father.

entitled to a special and separate name for his Ka. Some
Pharaohs, indeed, took more than one Ka-name, Amenhotep III. indulging in no less than seven.

Now, as I have already said, the Ka occasionally figures
in historical texts, and with reference to living persons. This
is especially true of royal persons, the King or Queen being
frequently represented as attended by his or her Ka, which
is sometimes shown as a duplicate, or *alter ego*, of the individual, and sometimes as a male figure with the Ka-arms,
and Ka-name on its head. In the Museum of Leyden, for
instance, there is a group of three figures, representing Queen
Mertetefs,* her Ka, and her secretary, the Queen and her
Ka being in all respects duplicate statues. At Dayr el-Bahari, on the other hand, Queen Hatasu† is shown in Pharaonic costume, her Ka standing behind her in the guise of
a small bearded man crowned with the Ka-arms and Ka-
name of the Queen. He grasps the *ankh* and feather of
Ma in his right hand, and a human-headed staff in his left.
The features of the Ka, and of the head upon his staff, are
identical with the features of the Queen. In a very curious
series of tableaux sculptured on the walls of one of the inner
halls of the Great Temple of Luxor, we find, however, the
most interesting and instructive of all these royal Ka subjects. They relate to the birth and bringing-up of Amenhotep III., the founder of the temple, and they date, consequently, from the latter half of the Eighteenth Dynasty. In
the first of these bas-reliefs we see the Queen-mother Mante-
mua kneeling on a kind of dais, having just given birth to
the royal infant. Hathor kneels facing her, with the babe
in her arms, and a second Hathor, with a second babe in
her arms, kneels behind the first. This second babe is the
Ka of the first babe. Over the head of the first (the actual

* A queen of the Third and Fourth dynasties. She was wife of Seneferu, the last king of the Third Dynasty, and wife of Khufu (Cheops), the
first king of the Fourth Dynasty, builder of the Great Pyramid.

† See Mariette's *Deïr el-Bahari*. Plate 6. The details of the false door
are, however, omitted in Mariette's plate.

Amenhotep) are engraved his two royal ovals, while the space above the head of the infant-Ka is left vacant. Most curious of all, however, is the Ka of the Queen-mother, represented as a kneeling female figure with the Ka-arms on its head; while from each of these Ka-arms is suspended an *ankh*, or symbol of life. The meaning here is obvious. The child is but just born, and the maternal Ka presides over the lives of both mother and child. Below the dais we see the child Amenhotep and the child-Ka, both in the act of being suckled by Hathor, in the shape of the divine cow.*

In the next subject, the two Hathors present the two children to the goddess Safekh, the patron deity of libraries, who dips her reed-pen in an inkpot, preparatory to recording the name of the Ka-infant in the royal archives; the names of the actual prince being already inscribed above his head in two ovals. The Ka-child, meanwhile, carries his name-frame on his head, but the field is vacant.† Lastly, the child-prince and the child-Ka are presented by Ra to Amen-Ra, the great god of Thebes; while behind Ra stands the god Nilus, also carying the child-prince and the child-Ka, the former with his two royal ovals above his head, and the latter crowned with the Ka-stand and Ka-name. Behind this Nilus advances yet another Nilus, carrying three "ankhs" tied together in his right hand—an "ankh," evidently, for each of the royal names, *i.e.*, the family-name, throne-name, and Ka-name of the infant Amenhotep.‡

Now, in these tableaux it is to be observed that there is a close and significant association of the Ka with the "ankh;" the "ankh" figured thus, ☥ , being the current hieroglyph for "life."

If we next turn to the storied walls of the Great Temple of Karnak, and examine some of the famous battle-pieces illustrating the career of Seti I., about a century later, we

---

* See Rossellini, *Monumenti Storici.* Plate xxxviii.
† Idem.   Plate xxxix.   ‡ Idem.

find this connection between the Ka and the ankh yet more distinctly emphasized.

In these elaborate chronicles in stone, we see the hero attacking fortresses, charging the enemy, trampling the vanquished under his chariot-wheels, and slaughtering all before him. The goddess Maut, in the form of a vulture, and the "hut," or disk of Horus, hover above his head; while behind him, floating apparently in mid-air, we see the "ankh" and Ka conjoined, the Ka-arms grasping a lotus-staff surmounted by an ostrich feather.* In some scenes, the united "ankh" and Ka become the head and arms of a tiny figure which holds a parasol or feather - fan outstretched towards the King.† Now, the "hut" (which is the sun-disk flanked on either side by the uræi, or royal basilisks) is the emblem of Horus the Victor, and it symbolizes the triumph of the King; while Maut, the

mother - goddess, protects the royal warrior with her outspread wings. What, then, is the meaning of the fantastic little figure which waves a feather-fan, or holds a parasol? As I take it, the meaning is very obvious.

The Ka no longer carries the "ankh," as before, but is identified and made one with it, thus standing for the life of the King. The flabellum or parasol, frequently represented as carried over the King's head in processional subjects, is not only used in religious texts to symbolize the Shade or Shadow ‡ (one of the essential and immortal parts of the man),

* Rossellini, *Monumenti Storici.* Plate xlviii.

† Idem. Plates liv. and lv.

‡ "On the Shade or Shadow of the Dead." By S. Birch, D.C.L., LL.D., etc. *Transactions of the Society of Biblical Archæology.* Vol. viii. Part 3. 1885.

but it also signifies protection, defence, shelter, etc.* Held
thus in the arms of the Ka, it means protection to his life
in the peril of battle—such protection as is also symbolized
by the out-spread wings of the vulture-goddess above.

There is yet another class of monuments, connected with
neither birth nor peril of death, in which the Ka figures
very conspicuously: namely, in scenes of worship. In these,
the Ka appears as if in attendance upon the King, and always with the "ankh" in one or both hands. Also—and this
is a point of great importance—he has generally a short inscription over his head. In this inscription he is expressly
designated as " Suten Ka, Ankh Neb Taui;" *i. e.*, " Royal Ka,
Life [of the] Lord of the Two Lands "—an inscription of
which the meaning is absolutely clear, and which is of itself,
I venture to think, a positive testimony to the correctness of
my interpretation. Thus, in a bas-relief group in the Great
Temple of Luxor,† Amenhotep III., followed by his Ka, is
depicted in the act of advancing towards the god Khem
with a libation-vase in each hand, his Ka standing behind
him in human form, with the Ka-name on his head, surmounted by the pschent-crowned hawk, emblem of Horus.
The Ka-figure carries the "ankh" in one hand, and in the
other, the customary staff terminating in a bust of the King.
Over his head is graven the above-named formula: "The
Royal Ka, Life of the Lord of the Two Lands." So also at
Dayr el-Bahari, the Ka-figure standing behind Queen Hatasu ‡ bears the Ka-name on his head, the " ankh " in his right
hand, and the staff surmounted by the royal bust in his left
hand. Above him is engraved the self-same inscription:
"The Royal Ka, Life of the Lord of the Two Lands."

In addition to this close and invariable association of the
Ka and the " ankh," there is yet another corroborative point
to be noted, namely, the persistent recurrence of the bull

* S. Levi, *Vocabolario Geroglifico*. Vol. vi., p. 141.
† Rossellini, *Monumenti Storici*. Plate cli.
‡ *Deïr el-Bahari*. Par Mariette-Bey. Planche 7.

(also called Ka, and expressive of vital energy) in royal Ka-names, beginning with the Ka-name of Thothmes I., and continuing to be incorporated in the Ka-name of almost every succeeding Pharaoh of the Eighteenth and Nineteenth dynasties.*

The evidence is abundant and uniform. The Ka-figure always carries the "ankh;" the bull (Ka) figures significantly in a large number of royal Ka-names; and the Ka-figure in the titular inscription by which it is invariably accompanied, is expressly defined as the "life" of the King. The words of this inscription are of elementary simplicity, and admit of no other interpretation.

It is for these reasons—supported by many more illustrations than can be crowded into this volume—that I have ventured to define the Ka as the life, or vital principle. In other words, I mean that transmitted energy which must undoubtedly have descended from the primal source of life to all who live, or have lived, upon earth.

Seeing how subtly the ancient Egyptians resolved the living man into what may be called his constituent parts, it would be strange if they had omitted that informing principle which alone makes of those constituent parts a co-ordinate whole. And if the Ka is not the life, then the Egyptians altogether omitted the life from their careful analysis, which is inconceivable.

---

* "Life," as the translation of Ka, makes sense of a passage in *The Book of the Dead* (chap. xxx.), the obscurity of which was long since pointed out by Mr. Le Page Renouf. The deceased, addressing the heart-scarab, says, "Entuk Ka em Khat-a," which is currently rendered by, "Thou art a Ka in my body"—a phrase devoid of meaning if Ka be translated as "double" or "genius," but which is perfectly intelligible if read as, "Thou art life in my body," the heart being the most essentially vital of organs, and the heart-scarab being placed inside the chest of the mummy as a substitute for the actual heart. This scarab is invariably engraved with a special formula (chap. xxx., *Book of the Dead*) beginning, "Oh, my heart, which came to me from my mother! my heart, which was mine upon earth," etc. The transmission of the life from mother to child points clearly to the true meaning of the above phrase, "Entuk Ka em Khat-a."

It has, however, been said, and with truth, by Dr. Wiedemann that the ancient Egyptian was incapable of conceiving abstract ideas; hence it follows that he necessarily conceived of vitality as a separate entity. We ourselves speak figuratively of the life as "going out of the body" at the moment of death; but the Egyptians believed not only that it went out, but that it thenceforth led an independent existence. They knew that the living man nourished his life—his Ka—with meats and drinks; and they naturally and naïvely concluded, from their concrete point of view, that meats and drinks were necessary to the existence of the Ka when its partnership with the body should be dissolved. It was, in fact, because the Ka was the life that it required nourishment; and because it was of divine origin that it survived the death of the body. The starvation of the Ka was therefore a more grievous calamity than the destruction of the body. The body could be replaced by a statue, or even by a painting; but the extinction of the Ka meant the extinction of the divine spark—the annihilation of the dead man's prospects of ultimate reunion with his Ka. In a word, it meant the loss of immortality.

Translate Ka, then, as "life," and the Ka-statue becomes more intelligible than heretofore. The life needed a body in which to abide, just as it needed bread, meats, fruit, wine, and milk for its sustenance. The Ka informed the statue, dwelt within it, felt through it, just as the life informs, dwells in, and feels through the living body. Lacking funerary offerings, it suffered all the pangs of starvation; and it was to guard against this dreaded possibility that the Egyptians provided for its material nourishment by means of pious foundations in perpetuity.

The astonishing way in which these foundations were maintained from age to age, from dynasty to dynasty, is proved by the funerary inscriptions of priestly personages who officiated for kings of by-gone periods. The Museum of the Louvre, for instance, contains the tablet of one Psammetichus of the Twenty-sixth Dynasty, who flourished about 600 B.C., and held the office of Priest of Khufu, the builder of the Great Pyramid; Khufu having reigned and died at least two thousand six hundred years before.

Now, it is a most remarkable and interesting truth that the ancient Egyptians were the first, the very first, people of antiquity who believed in the immortality of the soul. That is a cardinal fact which we must never omit to place to their credit. But they believed also in the immortality of the rest of the man — in the literal resurrection of the body, and in the ultimate reunion of Body, Soul, Intelligence, Name, Shadow, and Ka — which last I venture to call the Life. What they conceived the life to be, I cannot say.

We ourselves, with all our science, have never yet solved the physical problem of vitality. The Greeks conceived of it as a spark of divine fire, stolen by Prometheus from heaven. Probably the Egyptians believed it to be an emanation from Ra, the great solar god, from whom their Pharaohs claimed direct descent. It may be that the Greeks borrowed this "vital spark," as they borrowed so much else, from the Egyptians; and I do not doubt that the Hebrews—who carried away even more intellectual spoils than spoil of silver and gold and raiment out of the Land of Bondage—were indebted to their taskmasters for their doctrine of the "Khai," or life. They in fact borrowed not only the notion but the word, for "Kha" and "Khai" are surely one and the same.

One of the most solemn judicial oaths which an Egyptian could take was by the Ka of the Pharaoh; and to take that oath lightly was punishable by death. Seeing that the Ka was the life, and that the King's life was from Ra, the greatest of the solar gods, the tremendous character of this oath is easily understood. It was in this sense, and the more to impress his brethren with the extent of his power, that Joseph twice invoked the life of the King his master; and for my own part, I have not the slightest doubt that what he actually said was, "By the Ka of Pharaoh, surely ye are spies!"* If I appear to dwell at too much length upon this sermon on the text of the Ka, I at all events hope to show that it explains much which would otherwise be inexplicable in the origin of the art of portraiture. It explains, for instance, the reason why Egyptian portrait sculpture differs in its primary conception from the portrait sculpture of all other nations. Elsewhere, men began by making images of their gods that they might fall down and worship them. The earliest works of Chaldean and Assyrian art represent deities and demons. The archaic sculptors of Phœnicia, Cyprus, and Greece first tried their 'prentice hands on gods, demigods and deified heroes. But the fine art of the first period of Egyptian history—the period of the Pyramid Kings—is exclusively funerary; and it reproduces, with extraordinary fidelity, the men and women of that age.

In order that the Ka should feel at home in his new body of stone or wood, the statue was bound to be as exactly like the man as the sculptor's art could make it. If the man was ugly, the statue must also be ugly. If he had any personal defect, the statue must faithfully reproduce it; as, for

NEMHOTEP.

* "Send one of you, and let him fetch your brother, and ye shall be kept in prison, that your words may be proved, whether there be any truth in you: or else by the life of Pharaoh surely ye are spies."— *Genesis*, xlii., 16. See also verse 15.

instance, in this funerary statue of Nemhotep, a deformed dwarf who held a high office at court under a Pharaoh of the Sixth Dynasty. The sculptor of a Ka-statue dared not flatter. He might not model the best side of the sitter's face, and then make the other side to match it, like our fashionable artists. That is not nature's way of working. Put the loveliest woman in the world before a looking-glass, peep over her shoulder, and you will see that one eye is larger than the other; or that her nose, or her mouth, is a little to one side. Our powers of observation are, however, so blunted, that without the looking-glass we should not find this out. But those old Egyptian artists lived while the world was yet young. Their eyes were not vitiated by custom, and their sitters (actuated by a motive in which personal vanity had no part) were not anxious to be flattered. The welfare of the Ka was at stake; and the portrait was destined, not for the annual exhibition of a Memphite Royal Academy, but for the tomb.

That these early funerary portrait-statues were studied from the life, admits of no doubt. The technical treatment proves that point. And it is this certainty—the certainty that the living man sat to the artist for his likeness—which makes the unique value of the early Memphite school. Later on, when Asiatic influences were at work in Egypt, an element of Asiatic conventionality makes itself felt in Egyptian portraiture. But the singular skill with which Egyptian artists of all periods seized upon, and reproduced, the ethnic types of foreign races has never been surpassed. It shows that however they may have been influenced by fashion in their treatment of historical portraiture, their power of literal portraiture remained unimpaired.

The leading schools of Egyptian art are classified under the heads of either dynasties or capitals, a change of dynasty generally involving a change of capital. It thus followed that Memphis was at one time the centre of government; at another time Tanis; at another time Thebes, Bubastis, and so on. Thus we have the Memphite school of art, which was the earliest; the Twelfth Dynasty school, the Theban school, the Saïte school, and some minor schools of less note. The rise and fall of these various schools mark a succession of decadences and renaissances of art, each renaissance being distinguished by its own special characteristics. All these schools, all these renaissances, had, nevertheless, one essential principle in common: they were primarily exponents of the religious idea. In the hands of the sculptor and the painter, the gods were made manifest to the eyes of their worshippers; the terrors of Hades and the delights of Elysium were depicted with curious minuteness of detail; and the art of portraiture continued to be, from first to last, the concrete expression of one of the most singular, obscure, and fantastic religious beliefs which was ever inculcated by a priesthood, or by which the mind of a people was influenced. For every sculptured statue, every painted portrait, whether of a living person or of a dead person, was regarded as *a supplementary body dedicated to the service of the Ka.*

And this strange dogma which we have traced from its earliest known beginnings, four thousand years before the Christian era, retained its hold upon the minds of the Egyptians, and continued to be enforced as a cardinal article of faith by the Egyptian priesthood, till the abolition of the ancient national religion by the edict of Theodosius, A.D. 379.

One of the most surprising facts by which we are confronted when beginning the study of ancient Egyptian portrait sculpture is the immense superiority of the earliest school, when compared with the schools of later periods. It is in this respect that the history of art in the Valley of the Nile differs most strikingly from the history of art in any other country of the ancient world. When we speak, for instance, of an archaic Greek statue, we mean by implication a stiff figure with a vacant expression of face, eyes set aslant, a meaningless smile, rigid limbs, and muscles abnormally developed. But when we speak of an Egyptian statue of the time of the Ancient Empire—that is to say, of the most ar-

chaic period known—we refer to a figure modelled direct
from the life, and treated on ultra-naturalistic lines. We
now know why the art of the Memphite school was so essentially realistic. We now know that these statues are, one
and all, Ka-statues, and that the sculptors who produced
them were governed by the necessity of providing a faithful likeness for the benefit of the Ka. But the marvel
of their execution remains the same. We in vain ask how
long a period of foregone civilization must have elapsed before the art can have attained to this high degree of excellence. We only know that the earliest work of Egyptian
sculpture to which it is possible to put an approximate date
is a funerary tablet in bas-relief belonging to the remote
period of the Second Dynasty,* and that it is not inferior to
similar works executed under the Fourth Dynasty. It is
impossible even to conjecture the length of time during
which the Egyptians must have been gradually working
their way upward through higher and higher levels of civilization, in order to arrive at these results. When we first
become acquainted with them as sculptors and builders, they
are already adults; and as yet we have found no relics of
their infancy.

The oldest historical portrait-statue yet discovered is that
of Queen Mertetefs,† wife of Seneferu, the last king of the
Third Dynasty, and wife, by her second marriage, to Khufu,
the first king of the Fourth Dynasty, who was no less famous a personage than the builder of the Great Pyramid.
The statue is one of a limestone group of three figures, representing Queen Mertetefs, her Ka, and a priest named Ken-
nu, who was her private secretary. The Queen and her Ka

---

* This tablet was found in the Necropolis of Sakkara, brought from
Egypt by J. Greaves, an Oxford professor, about the middle of the seventeenth century, and presented to the Ashmolean Museum in 1683 by the
Rev. R. Huntington. It is of the time of Senta, the thirteenth Pharaoh of
the Second Dynasty.

† This statue, or rather the group of which it forms part, is among the
Egyptian treasures of the Museum of Antiquities at Leyden.

sit side by side, and are exactly alike, the flesh-tints being painted buff, and the hair black.   Queen Mertetefs survived her second husband, and lived to hold three important offices under her nephew Khafra, who was the second king of the

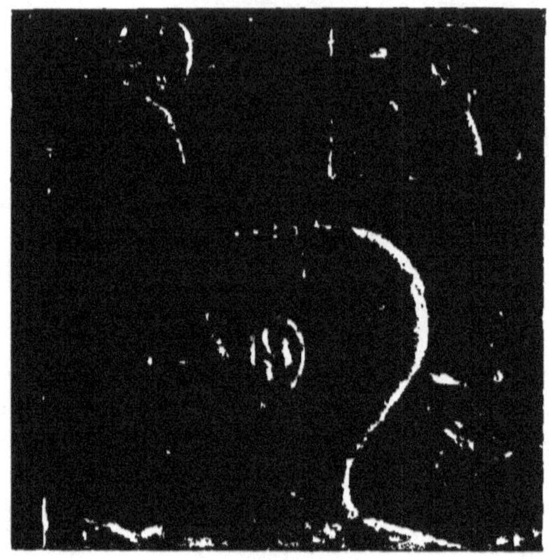

KHUFU-ANKH AND HIS SERVANTS.

From a bas-relief sculpture in his tomb at Ghizeh.   Photographed by Mr. W. M. Flinders Petrie.

Fourth Dynasty, and builder of the second pyramid of Ghizeh.   She was "Administrator of the Great Hall of the Palace, Mistress of the Royal Wardrobe, and Superintendent of the Chamber of Wigs and Head-dresses."   Her name, Mertetefs, signifies "beloved of her father."

Contemporary with Queen Mertetefs was Khufu-Ankh, a great nobleman of the time of Khufu, whose tomb is in the shadow of the Great Pyramid, and whose magnificent sarcophagus is preserved in the Museum of Ghizeh.   Khufu-Ankh was Keeper of the Royal Seal; and he is represented in the bas-relief sculptures on the walls of his tomb attended

by his servants.   Later in point of date, but on the same
plane as regards *technique*, is the example below of bas-relief
sculpture from the tomb of one Semnefer, also in the Necropolis of Ghizeh.   Semnefer lived about two hundred and
fifty years later than Queen Mertetefs; and we have here the
profile portraits of himself and his wife, the Lady Hotep-hers.
The heads of all these Fourth Dynasty personages are marked
by that child-like simplicity which distinguishes the archaic
school, and they place before us with much fidelity the ethnological type of the earliest Egyptians.   There is not a

SEMNEFER AND HIS WIFE HOTEP-HERS.

From a bas-relief sculpture in the tomb of Semnefer at Ghizeh.   Photographed by
Mr. W. M. Flinders Petrie.

drop of negro blood in this race.   Their noses are slightly
arched; their lips are full and well turned; their chins are
short; their jaws are delicate; their heads high, and well
rounded.

To about the same date belong the statues of General Ra-
hotep and his wife, Princess Nefert, on the following page.

This old-world couple have been largely popularized of late
years in various illustrated books treating of ancient Egyptian
art: but they cannot be spared from any typical series of

GENERAL RA-HOTEP AND PRINCESS NEFERT.

Painted limestone statues, life-size, discovered at Meydûm, and attributed by Mariette to the time of Seneferu, Third Dynasty. Professor Maspero assigns them,
however, to a later period.

the Memphite school. In General Ra-hotep we behold a
stalwart, square-cut, sturdy man of the same racial type as
Semnefer. The brow is well developed; the nose is sharply
cut and slightly arched; the cheek-bones are high; the lips
are full; the chin is small; the brain-case is of ample size.
He was a man, one would say, of strong common-sense and
determination of character.

The features of his wife, Princess Nefert, though cast in
a more delicate and aristocratic mould, are marked by the

same physiological traits; and it is evident, from these and other examples of the same period, that the Egyptians of the Ancient Empire were a strongly built, massive-headed race, with well-defined noses, high cheek-bones, and full lips.

These statues are carved in fine limestone, seated, and colored. The flesh-tints of Nefert are buff, and those of Ra-hotep reddish-brown; the buff representing the fairer complexion of the woman, while the darker hue of the man is intended to convey the results of exposure to the sun. The eyes of both are inserted, the whites being of opaque white quartz, and the iris of transparent crystal. A small silver nail fixed behind the iris receives and reflects the light, thus imitating the shifting light of the living orb.

The famous statue known as the "Wooden Man of Bû-lak" is about half life-size. It represents a stout, commonplace, elderly Egyptian named Ra-em-ka, who was an overseer of public works in the time of the Fourth Dynasty. He must have witnessed the building of one or other of the great pyramids of Ghizeh, and he probably superintended the workmen at their toil.

RA-EM-KA.

Called "The Wooden Man of Bûlak."

It is a good-natured, contented face, carefully studied from the life; and the eyes, like those of Ra-hotep and Nefert, are inserted.

Long admixture with Asiatic blood has so thinned down the race that a fat native is now one of the rarest of Egyptian curiosities; but elderly men of very comfortable proportions are frequently represented in the sculptures of the early school. The treatment of this admirable head is so masterly that one scarcely notices how the wood is split in every direction; but that it should be thus split is not wonderful if we remember that the tree which was felled to make this statue, and the man who sat for it, flourished nearly six thousand years ago.

In marked contrast to the plebeian type of Ra-em-ka is the limestone statue of one Ti, a courtly gentleman of the Fifth Dynasty. No less than nineteen statues of Ti were found immured in the substance of the walls of his tomb, which is one of the most beautiful in Egypt. The figure stands about seven feet high, the flesh-tints being of a pale brick-dust color, and the wig yellow. The pose of the head is spirited, and the expression of the face is open and life-like. Ti's shoulders are very square, his arms long, his body slender; this being the characteristic type of the well-grown fellah of the present day. The muscles of the arms and thorax are excellently rendered. With the statues of the master were frequently buried statues of his servants, that they might continue to wait upon him and work for him in the world beyond the tomb.(³⁵) These statues generally represent the servant as engaged in his or her daily work— making bread, carrying burdens, washing out wine-jars, and the like. Our next example was found in the tomb of a gentleman of the Fifth Dynasty, and it represents a household scribe. This humble dependant kneels with crossed hands, as though awaiting his lord's instructions. His vacant and deprecating smile expresses the patient resignation of a life of servitude. He has no will, and no opinions of his own. His back is well acquainted with the time-honored "stick," and he is so well trained in the virtues of obedience and submission that he not only takes his punishment without a murmur, but is ready to kiss the hand by which it is administered.

The "Cross-legged Scribe" (p. 143) belongs to the same class and the same period. He is a man of about forty years of age, plain-featured, intelligent, a little more fleshy and less muscular than one who has lived the life of the fields, yet hardly and active. He is writing to dictation, and he waits, pen in hand, till the next sentence shall fall from the lips of his employer. The face is instinct with attention. The eyes are inserted. The hands, the knees, the muscles of the arms and body are sculptured with minute anatomical exactness. This is one of the most celebrated of ancient Egyptian statues, and, fortunately, the original of our illustration can be seen without a journey to Cairo, for it is in the Museum of the Louvre.

With the Memphite school we bid good-bye to the first, and in some respects the finest, period of Egyptian portraiture. It was, *par excellence*, the one great realistic school of the ancient world, and it owed its inspiration to that extraordinary dogma which necessitated the making of an artificial body for the Ka. This dogma, as I have said, continued in force as long as the Egyptian religion lasted; but its influence upon the art of the sculptor is more manifest in the time of the Ancient Empire than at any subsequent period. Seeing how marvellously life-like these earliest Ka-statues are, one would almost be tempted to say that the faith which inspired

STATUE OF TI.
In the Museum of Ghizeh.

their makers was more vivid than the faith of later times. They are, as it were, informed with something of that vitality which they were supposed to enshrine. When Mariette's

Arabs opened the tomb in which the statues of Nefert and Ra-hotep were discovered, they first drew back in terror; and then, believing them to be inhabited by demons, were with difficulty restrained from smashing them. Their alarm was natural enough. Looking into the eyes of this wonderful pair, and seeing how the light shifts in their liquid depths, it is difficult not to believe that they look at us, even as we look at them, and that their gaze is not following us as we move from group to group in the hall of the museum where they sit enthroned. But how strangely and luridly those eyes of quartz and crystal must have gleamed from the depths of that dark sepulchre of Meydûm into which no ray of daylight had found its way for nearly six thousand years!

Up to the time when Mariette discovered the secret Ka-chambers in the massive walls of the tombs of the Ancient Empire, there had prevailed an entirely erroneous notion as to the characteristics of Egyptian sculpture. It was believed to be wholly conventional, stiff, and unnatural; and this sweeping condemnation was applied without distinction to the art of all periods. It, however, needs but a glance at one of the masterpieces of

THE KNEELING SCRIBE.
Limestone statue, Fifth Dynasty. In the Museum of Ghizeh.

the early Memphite school—or even at the foregoing illustrations—to dispel that prejudice. Yet we must be careful
not to claim too much for even the sculptors of the "Cross-
legged Scribe" or the "Wooden Man." Their skill was in

THE CROSS LEGGED SCRIBE.
Limestone statue, colored, half life-size. In the Museum of the Louvre.

many respects quite marvellous; but it had its limitations.
If I might venture somewhat to paraphrase one of Sir
Charles Newton's happiest definitions,([20]) I would say that
the sculptors of ancient Egypt never grappled with some of
the most difficult problems which were solved by the sculptors of ancient Greece. They lacked that fine insight which
enabled a Praxiteles and a Phidias to detect the whole internal organism beneath the bodily surface. They never
succeeded, perhaps, in thoroughly expressing the relation be-

tween those muscles which are the sources of motive power, and the bones which supply leverage. Neither did they attempt to represent the texture and elasticity of the skin, which clothes, yet does not hide, the structure beneath the surface. But they did perceive, and they did correctly reproduce, the general effect and proportions of the human form. They indicated with remarkable skill all its most salient features, such as the muscles of the legs, arms, and thorax, and the modelling of the knees; yet, strange to say,

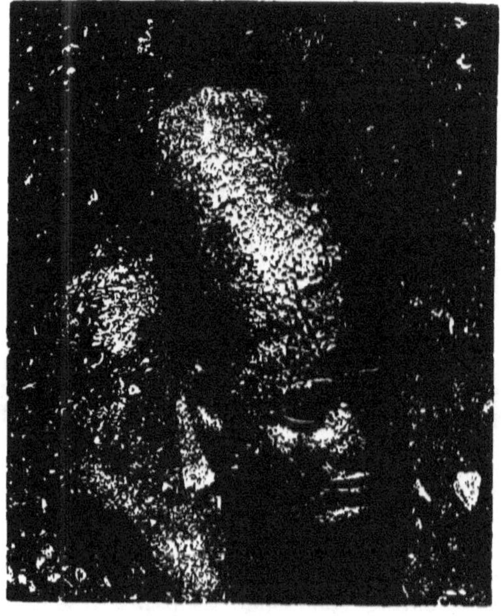

AMENEMHAT I. (TWELFTH DYNASTY.)

Colossal head in red granite, from the ruins of the Great Temple of Tanis.
Photographed by Mr. W. M. F. Petrie.

they never attained to even a moderate degree of success in their treatment of the hands and feet. These are always wooden and ill-proportioned. Take them, however, with all their shortcomings, the old Memphite sculptors were of that stuff of which the early Florentine school was made some fifty-five centuries later. As for portraiture, properly so

COLOSSAL HEAD OF A HYKSÔS KING.

(Supposed to be Salatis.) Sculptured in black granite, and discovered by Mariette at Tell Mokhdam, in the Fayûm.

called, namely, heads, faces, expression, and that indescribable something which indicates *character*—or in other words, the outward modifications wrought upon the features by the workings of the mind—no artists of any age have therein excelled the sculptors of the Ancient Empire.

The next great school of Egyptian portrait sculpture is that of the Middle Empire, which culminated under the Twelfth Dynasty.

The sculptors of this age excelled in the skill with which they cut and polished the hardest stones, such as basalt, diorite, and granite. A vast crowd of Twelfth Dynasty Pharaohs, their queens and families, carved in these obdu-

10

rate materials have been found in the ruins of the great temples of Tanis and Bubastis. Unfortunately, most of them have been usurped by the kings of later periods, who have erased the names of the originals and substituted their

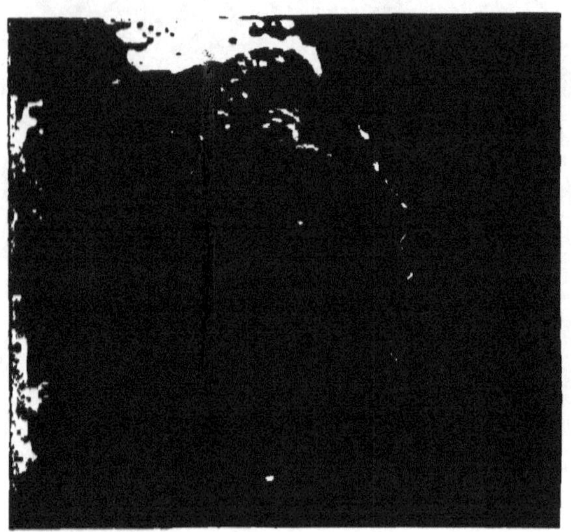

HYKSÔS SPHINX, IN PROFILE.

From the ruins of the Great Temple of Tanis, and now in the Museum of Ghizeh. Black granite. Photographed by Mr. W. M. F. Petrie.

own. These grand statues are chiefly of colossal size, and are almost invariably mutilated. A royal portrait-statue of the Twelfth or Thirteenth Dynasty with its royal nose intact is a *rara avis*.

During the interval which elapsed between the Thirteenth and Seventeenth dynasties, Egypt was overrun by a barbarian host from beyond the Eastern border, and so lost her liberty for nearly five hundred years. This dark interval is known as the Hyksôs Period, or the time of the Shepherd Kings. The invaders were a mixed multitude of warlike tribes from Mesopotamia, Syria, Arabia, and that vast dis-

trict known in a later age as the two Scythias.   These
hungry hordes were led by a race of Turanian type who
founded the so-called Hyksôs dynasties, and portraits of
certain of their kings have been preserved to us in Egyptian sculptures of that period.   They were a race of hard-
featured warriors, with wide and high cheek-bones, open
nostrils, and mouths curved sternly downward at the corners.

We have on page 145 a full-face view of a colossal fragment
found in the Fayûm.   It is believed to be a portrait of Salatis, the first king of the Hyksôs line.   His heavy plaited wig
is quite unlike the wig worn by the Egyptians, and he wears
uncouth ornaments of barbaric style.   Battered though it

HYKSÔS SPHINXES (TANIS.)

The broken fragments of several of these sphinxes yet strew the ruins of the Great
Temple of Tanis.   They are all duplicates of the one in the Museum of Gizeh.   In
the above illustration we see the fore part of two, and beyond them the broken
halves of a red granite obelisk of Rameses II.   Photographed by Mr. W. M. F.
Petrie.

is, this rugged face is thoroughly representative.   The high
cheek-bones, the saturnine expression, and the curious muscular bosses at the corners of the mouth are especially characteristic of the Hyksôs race.

The same racial characteristics are strongly marked in
this profile of a human-
headed sphinx found in the
ruins of the Great Temple
of Tanis. The type is distinctly Mongolian, and the
skill with which the Egyptian sculptor has seized
upon and reproduced it
shows that the portrait
sculptors of this period
were in nowise inferior to
their Memphite predeces-
sors. It is probably a portrait of Apepi, the last
and most celebrated of the
Hyksôs usurpers.

By far the finest piece
of portrait sculpture of the
Hyksôs school is, however,
the colossal sitting statue
of a Hyksôs king discov-
ered in 1888 by M. Na-
ville, in the course of his
excavations on the site of
the Great Temple of Bu-

QUEEN HATASU.

Colossal head in limestone, discovered in
the ruins of the Great Temple of Karnak and preserved in the Museum of
Ghizeh. From the drawing by Bourgoin
in Perrot and Chipiez's *Egypte*.

bastis. This superb work of ancient art is one of a pair
which were placed on either side of the great gate-way
through which the Temple was approached; and as the
names and titles of Apepi were sculptured on a door-jamb
of that gate-way, close by the spot where the broken colossi
were found, there would seem to be good reason for the
assumption that we have in one or other of these statues, if

not in both a portrait of the famous tyrant of the First
Sallier Papyrus. ([37]) The features of the pair are, however,
very different; the one whose head is reproduced in the
illustration on page 146 being the likeness of a man some
twenty years the junior of his fellow. Which of the Hyksôs
usurpers that elder figure may represent we cannot even
guess; but the face of the younger is identical with the
faces of the human-headed sphinxes of Tanis; and to them,

RAMESES II., SURNAMED "THE GREAT."
From a group in red granite. Tanis. Photographed by Mr. W. M. F. Petrie.

as to him, in the absence of any evidence to the contrary,
we may provisionally assign the name of Apepi. ([38])

The Theban princes rose at last, expelled the alien ty-
rants, and restored the descendants of the old Twelfth-Dy-

nasty Pharaohs.   Then followed the glorious days of the
Eighteenth Dynasty—a line of builder and warrior kings, in
whose roll are numbered the great names of Thothmes III.,
Amenhotep III., and the renowned Queen Hatasu.   In pre-

RAMESES II.

Bas-relief, from the Great Temple of Karnak.   Photographed by Mr. W. M. F.
Petrie.

senting this beautiful head as a portrait of Hatasu, it must
be premised that it has already been attributed by Mariette
to Queen Tii, the wife of Amenhotep III., and by Maspero
to the wife of Horemheb. Seen in profile, however, this
face is identical in outline with the profile of Queen Hatasu as sculptured upon one of the fragments of her broken
obelisk at Karnak.   Even the dimple in the chin, which is so
conspicuous in the front face, is represented by a slight depression in the profile chin of the obelisk portrait.*   I have

* See Profile of Hatasu, chap. viii.

been furthermore informed that the above fragment was
discovered under the débris of a small chamber at the back
of one of Hatasu's obelisks in the ruins of the Great Temple
of Karnak; and it is for these reasons that I venture to think
that it can represent none other than the great queen herself.   The rest of the statue is lost; but this precious fragment is one of the masterpieces of Egyptian art.   The eyes
laugh; the lips all but speak; and every feature is alive with

SETI II.

Bas-relief, from his sepulchre in the Valley of the Tombs of the Kings at Thebes.
From a photograph by Mr. W. M. F. Petrie.

a vivacious charm, which is ever the rarest achievement in
sculpture.   The size is colossal, and the material a fine, mar-
ble-like limestone.

When we pass from the Eighteenth to the Nineteenth and
Twentieth dynasties, we enter upon an entirely new phase
of Egyptian art.   Rameses I., the founder of the former line,

was of Semitic birth ; and although his son, Seti I., wedded an Egyptian princess of the old royal line, the Pharaohs of his dynasty retained a marked Semitic type which affected the sculptors and figure-painters of the time in a very curious manner. Because Seti I. and Rameses II. had long noses, long heads, long bodies, and long legs, the artists of the Nineteenth Dynasty gave long noses, long heads, long bodies, and long legs to all their sitters ; thus falsifying the

SIPTAH.

Bas-relief, from his sepulchre in the Valley of the Tombs of the Kings, Thebes.
From a photograph by Mr. W. M. F. Petrie.

national type, and introducing an element of great monotony into the art of the period.

The history of portraiture, like the history of nations, repeats itself. In times comparatively recent, court beauties set the fashion in features, and court painters adapted all fair faces to the prescribed pattern. It was so in the days of Charles II. and Louis XIV., and it was so in the far-off days of the Pharaohs.

The hereditary characteristics of the two Ramesside lines

RAMESES III. (TWENTIETH DYNASTY).

From a bas-relief in his sepulchre in the Valley of the Tombs of the Kings at Thebes. Photographed by Mr. W. M. F. Petrie.

are nowhere more strikingly shown than in the numerous bas-relief portraits of royal personages sculptured on the walls of the great temples of Karnak and Medinet-Habû, and in the famous sepulchres of the Valley of the Tombs of the Kings. Of these, a few examples will suffice.

On page 149 is shown a head of Rameses the Great, from a group in red granite. This fine head (unfortunately mutilated) yet lies amid the ruins of Tanis. The nose being gone, we lose the Semitic profile, which, however, is well seen in our illustration on page 150, taken from a beautiful bas-relief sculpture in the Great Temple of Karnak. In the first of these portraits the great Pharaoh wears the *khepersch*, or war-helmet, adorned in front with the uræus of royalty. This head-dress is sometimes represented in colored bas-reliefs as covered with panther-hide; and sometimes it is shown of a brilliant cobalt-blue, the surface studded with small yellow rings. This, perhaps, is intended to reproduce the effect of a copper helmet artificially colored by being plunged, when in a heated condition, into a sulphur spring, thus converting the surface into copper sulphide. This, if covered with amulets of gold, would have a beautiful effect. It is possible that copper thus colored was the Homeric *kuanos*.

In the second portrait Rameses wears a wig of close-laid curls, and on his brow the golden uræus. In both these sculptures the great Pharoah is represented at about eighteen years of age.

Our illustration on page 151 reproduces the features of Seti II., grandson of Rameses II., from his tomb in the same valley. This charming profile closely resembles the profile of his grandfather Rameses the Great. The reign of this prince was apparently long and un-

MUMMY CASE OF QUEEN AHMES NEFERTARI.

eventful. Several of his colossal portrait-statues are preserved in the museums of Europe, and his fine tomb in the Valley of the Tombs of the Kings at Thebes, yet contains his granite sarcophagus, carved on the lid with his full-length figure in bas-relief. But by far the most interesting monument of his reign is a fragile papyrus in the British Museum, containing the celebrated "Tale of the Two Brothers." This tale consists of two parts of different date, the first half being evidently very ancient, and the second showing by unmistakable internal evidence that it was composed under the Nineteenth Dynasty. According to the colophon, this papyrus was written by the hand of the royal librarian by order of the Chief of the Treasury, and it was apparently the King's own copy, being twice endorsed with his name on the back of the document. As the handwriting differs from that of the manuscript, these may be Seti's own autographs.

The family likeness of the Ramessides is perpetuated in a marked degree in the portrait of Siptah on page 152, a prince whose history is obscure, but who seems to have been a son of Seti II., and great-grandson of Rameses the Great. Siptah and his queen, contrary to the custom of Egyptian royalty, were buried in one grave.

With Rameses III., we enter upon the Twentieth Dynasty. Descended through his father from the Pharaohs of the preceding line, Rameses III. inherited not only the same Semitic type, but the same warlike tastes and the same passion for building. He was the last of the fighting Pharaohs, and with him the glory of Egypt expired. The first naval battle known to history was fought in his reign, and is pictured on the walls of his great temple in western Thebes. His tomb is one of the finest in the Valley of the Tombs of the Kings; his funerary papyrus, ninety feet long, is in the British Museum; and his mummy is in the National Egyptian Museum at Ghizeh. He was succeeded by nine kings of the name of Rameses. Several of these were his sons, and they seem to have followed each other with ominous ra-

pidity.   The portrait is from the walls of his great temple
at Medinet-Habû.

There was yet another variety of portrait sculpture which
cannot be passed over in silence, and which was peculiarly
an Egyptian art: namely, the portrait-masks carved in wood,
with which the mummy-cases of this extraordinary people
were decorated.   Many of the portrait-masks are evidently
carefully studied likenesses, and reproduce the features of
the deceased with as much fidelity as do the portrait-statues
and bas-relief subjects found in his tomb.   One of the largest

MASK FROM MUMMY-CASE OF RAMESES II.

and most magnificent mummy-cases ever discovered is that
of Queen Ahmes Nefertari, now in the Museum of Ghizeh.
It is of colossal size, and it represents this celebrated royal
lady as holding the "ankh" in each hand, while on her head
she wears the helmet and plumes of Amen.   The material
of the mummy-case is the usual "cartonnage," consisting of

many layers of linen hardened together by glue, and coated outside with stucco. This cartonnage is impressed all over the arms, shoulders and head-dress, with a reticulated sexagonal pattern, which gives the surface the appearance of being honey-combed. Each little sexagonal hollow is painted blue, the groundwork being of a vivid yellow. The face, hands, and necklace are also painted blue.

This mask of Rameses II., from the lid of his wooden sarcophagus, is in the Museum of Ghizeh. The head, however, is not a contemporary portrait; neither does it faithfully reproduce the features of Rameses II.; but it is a very beautiful specimen of portrait sculpture in wood of the time of the Twenty-first Dynasty. The sarcophagus adorned with this wood-sculpture appears to have been made to receive the mummy of Rameses II., in the sixth year of the rule of Her-Hor Se-Amen, of the Twenty-first Dynasty, when the tombs of the earlier Pharaohs were visited by Government inspectors, and when (according to the entries inscribed on their coffins) the "funerary appointments" of Seti I. and Rameses II. were renewed by order of Her-Hor, then High-Priest of Amen, and afterwards king.([18])

RA-EM KA.

The features of this mask bear, however, a curious resemblance to the features of the little pen-portraits of Her-Hor in the great funerary papyrus of his mother, Queen Notem-Maut; and this furnishes us, perhaps, with a clue to its unwritten history. To give up his own tomb in favor of another, has ever been a distinguished mark of honor among the nations of the East;([19]) and it is quite possible that Her-Hor may have given up to his illustrious predecessor the beautiful mummy-case made for his own mortal remains, when he too should be summoned to traverse the Valley of the Shadow of Death.

V.

EGYPT THE BIRTHPLACE OF GREEK DECORATIVE ART.

A SCHOLAR of no less distinction than the late Sir Richard Burton wrote the other day of Egypt as "the inventor of the alphabet, the cradle of letters, the preacher of animism and metempsychosis, and, generally, the source of all human civilization." This is a broad statement; but it is literally true. Hence the irresistible fascination of Egyptology — a fascination which is quite unintelligible to those who are ignorant of the subject. I have sometimes been asked, for instance, how it happens that I — erewhile a novelist, and therefore a professed student of men and manners as they are—can take so lively an interest in the men and manners of five or six thousand years ago. But it is precisely because these men of five or six thousand years ago had manners, a written language, a literature, a school of art, and a settled government that we find them so interesting. Ourselves the creatures of a day, we delight in studies which help us to realize that we stand between the eternity of the past and the eternity of the future. Hence the charm of those sciences which unfold to us, page by page, the unwritten records of the world we live in. Hence the eagerness with which we listen to the Story of Creation as told by the geologist and the paleontologist.

But the history of Man, and especially of civilized man, concerns us yet more nearly; and the earliest civilized man of whom we know anything is the ancient Egyptian.

From the moment when he emerges—a shadowy figure—from the mists of the dawn of history, he is seen to have a philosophical religion, a hierarchy, and a social system. How many centuries, or tens of centuries, it took him to achieve that result we know not. Of the time when he was yet a savage we detect no trace. His faintest, farthest footprint on the sands of Time bears the impress of a sandal.

To this nation which first translated sounds into signs, and made use of those signs to transmit the memory of its deeds to future generations, we naturally turn for the earliest information of other races; nor do we so turn in vain.

Before they have any writing or any history of their own, we meet with the Ethiopians, the Libyans, the Phœnicians, the Babylonians, the Assyrians, in the hieroglyphic inscriptions of ancient Egypt. And in these inscriptions, graven on the storied walls of temples and pylons older by a thousand years than the opening chapters of classical history, we also find the first—the very first—mention of the people of Greece and Italy.

It would be difficult to find a more interesting subject of inquiry than the relations of prehistoric Greece to Egypt, or than to measure, as far as possible, the extent of that debt which the early Greeks owed to the teaching and example of the ancient Egyptians.

The history of Greece and the Greeks, as told by themselves, may be said to begin with the first recorded Olympiad, seven hundred and seventy-six years before the Christian era. It is at this point that we begin to draw the line between fable and fact. But the first mention of the Greeks upon the monuments of Egypt goes back some seventeen centuries earlier, to a rock-cut tablet of the time of Sankhara, a Theban King of the Eleventh Dynasty who reigned about two thousand five hundred years before Christ. They appear in this memorable inscription as the "Hanebu"—

that is to say, "the people of all coasts and islands;" thereby meaning the coast-folk of Greece and Asia Minor, and the islanders of the Ægean. Now, it is a very interesting fact that "Hanebu," as a generic name for these same tribes, is exactly paralleled by the Hebrew "*îyê haggôîm*," which is used not only by the prophets, but earlier still in the Mosaic books, where it is said of the sons of Yavan,(") in the tenth chapter of Genesis, "Of these were the isles of the nations divided in their lands." The Revised Version, here quoted, gives an alternative reading of "coastlands" for islands; "Hanebu" and "*îyê haggôîm*" being strictly capable of both interpretations. After this, we hear no more of the early Greeks in Egypt till they reappear as the Danai or Danæans, some twelve or thirteen hundred years later, in the reign of Thothmes III. Now, Thothmes III. was the Alexander of ancient Egyptian history. He conquered the known world of his day; he carved the names of six hundred and twenty-eight vanquished nations and captured cities on the walls of Karnak; and he set up a tablet of Victory in the Great Temple. It is in this famous tablet, engraved with the oldest heroic poem known to science, that we find the Greeks mentioned for the second time in Egyptian history.

"I came!" says the Great God Amen, addressing the King, who is represented at the top of the tablet in an attitude of worship, "I came! I gave thee might to fell those who dwell in their islands. Those also who live in the midst of the sea hear thy war-cry and tremble! *The isles of the Danai are in the power of thy will!*"

That they are now called Danai, or descendants of Danaos, the traditional King of Argolis, is a point to be noted; for it shows that these barbarian Greeks had already a legendary lore of their own. And it does more than this. It shows that in the time of Thothmes III., although we are still distant some eight hundred years from the presumed date of the "Iliad," the name of Danæans (like that of Achæans somewhat later) was already applied in the Homeric sense to the whole Hellenic race. According to no other interpretation could the Danai, who were originally but a small tribe settled on the mainland in Argolis, be described as "those who dwell in their islands."   Danai, however, which is a transcription from the Greek, did not supersede "Hanebu," which is pure Egyptian.   We accordingly find "Hanebu" again employed about two hundred years later in a colossal bas-relief group of Pharaoh Horemheb and his prisoners of war, among whom may be seen a gang of captive "Hanebu"—men and women —with their race-name inscribed against them.   The heads of the men are defaced, but the profile of one woman is yet per-

fect; and that profile is the earliest portrait of a Greek in the world. The eye is defaced; but the delicate out-line of the features is yet uninjured. She wears one long ring-let (presumably one on each side); and this ringlet is a character-istic feature of female heads in archaic Greek art. It may therefore be assumed that it was a national fashion from the earliest period. I may as well add that the word "Hanebu," as a generic term for the Hellenes, whether Asiatic or European, survived till the time

HEAD OF HANEBU WOMAN.

Bas-relief from the Pylon of Horemheb, at Karnak.   From a photograph by Mr. W. M. Flinders Petrie.

of the Ptolemies, when the Greeks ruled in Egypt.   Native Egyptian scribes of that comparatively modern age used it to denote the governing race, just as their remote fore-fathers had used it to denote Greek barbarians taken in battle.

11

From Horemheb to Rameses II. carries us a hundred years farther along the stream of time. In Rameses II. we are fain to recognize the Pharaoh of the Great Oppression, and in Meneptah, his son and successor, the probable Pharaoh of the Exodus. Under both these kings, and again under Rameses III. some fifty or sixty years later still, the Greeks of the main-land, the Greeks of the islands, the Greeks of Asia Minor, come thronging in quick succession upon the stage of history.

Leagued with the Hittites under the command of a Hittite prince, they invade the Syrian provinces of Egypt in the fifth year of Rameses II. Pharaoh himself goes forth against them, and being cut off from the main body of his forces, is waylaid under the walls of Kadesh, a fortified place on the Orontes. Thus surprised, with only his body-guard to defend him, the hero charges them in his chariot, hews them down, puts them to flight, and defeats them utterly. Six times, says a contemporary poet, he rushed upon the foe. " Six times he trampled them like straw beneath his horse's hoofs. Six times he dispersed them single-handed, like a god. Two thousand five hundred chariots were there, and he overthrew them; one hundred thousand armed warriors, and he scattered them. Those that he slew not with his hand, he pursued unto the water's edge, causing them to leap to destruction as leaps the crocodile !"

So said Pentaur, the poet-laureate of his day, in an epic which it is no exaggeration to describe as the "Iliad" of ancient Egyptian literature. It may be that Pentaur's version of the facts is somewhat florid. I fear that we must accept his statistics with some reserve; but laureates are privileged, and Pentaur scarcely abused that privilege more than Dryden and his successors.

In this poem, which is sculptured at full length on four great temples and written on a precious papyrus in the British Museum, we find a list of the allies of the Hittites. Among them are five Hellenic nations—namely, the " *Masu*," or Mysians; the "*Leku*," or Lycians; the "*Akerit*," or Carians; the

"*Aiuna*," or Ionians; the "*Dardani*" or Dardanians. Four of these — the Lycians, Mysians, Carians, and Ionians—are dwellers on the coast of Asia Minor, and near neighbors of the Hittites. The fifth is from Thrace, on the European main-land, where their name, the Dardanians, survives to this day in the Dardanelles.

The Greeks disappear for the remainder of the long reign of Rameses II.; but in the fifth year of his successor, as we learn from an inscription at Karnak, the Libyans, in alliance with a host of barbarians from over the sea, invade Egypt from the westward. The battle-roll of this new coalition is in truth the first page of the first chapter of European history. The Etruscans, Sardinians, and Sicilians, the Lycians and Achæans, are in the ranks of the enemy. This event marks the earliest entry of the Achæans upon the world's great stage, as it also marks the entry of the Latin races. They come into momentary contact with Egyptian civilization, and in the record of their defeat receive for the first time a name and a place in the annals of the ancient East.

Of these new-comers the most interesting to us, by far, are the Achæans. That they should have crossed from the Peloponessus to the coast of Libya, shows that they were already skilled to speed their hollow ships along the wine-colored sea. But what of the men themselves? Were they fair, long-haired, and stalwart, as became the forerunners of the comrades of Achilles? We know not; for the wall on which this inscription is carved is in a ruinous state, and the part which was once occupied by the bas-relief sculptures is unfortunately gone. But for this accident, Egypt might have preserved for us a portrait-group of prehistoric Achæans. We do know, however, that they were clad in brass, like the heroes of Homer; for in the catalogue of booty seized by the victorious Egyptians, we find a list of three thousand one hundred and seventy-five swords, poignards, cuirasses, and even greaves—the distinctive armor of "the well-greaved Achæans."

For cuirasses the Egyptian language had a special term,

'*Tarena;* but for "greaves," wearing no leg-armor themselves, they had no synonym. They therefore represented the greave pictorially, and made of it an ideographic hieroglyph. (")

This figure, accurately representing a Greek greave, even to the strap by which it was buckled on the inner side of the knee, is clearly cut in the inscription. It is followed, moreover, by the hieroglyph for "copper," and by the generic ideograph which stands in Egyptian for "metals;" thus indicating that the Achæan armor was of brass, which the scribe probably mistook for copper.

EGYPTIAN HIEROGLYPH FOR A GREEK GREAVE.

And now, for the space of a century there is peace, till again, about twelve hundred years before our era, the barbarian flood pours southward. Foremost among the foe are the Danæans and the Lycians. First in alliance with the Syrians, next with the Libyans, they attack Egypt by land and sea; and each time they are signally routed.

It may be that at last they had learned to look upon the Egyptians as invincible; or it may be that they found the balmy climate and fertile soil of Southern Europe more attractive; but the tide of invasion, at all events, set henceforth in a north-westerly direction; nor do we again encounter the Greek on Egyptian soil till some five hundred and thirty-four years later, when Psammetichus, Prince of Säis and Memphis, defeats his colleagues of the Dodecarchy by the aid of an army of Carian and Ionian mercenaries, and founds the Twenty-sixth Egyptian Dynasty.

Too wise to part from the weapon which his own hand had forged, too politic to irritate his subjects by a display of foreign force, Psammetichus established his Greeks in two large camps, one on each side of the Pelusiac branch of the Nile. There, within a few miles of the Syrian frontier, he granted them lands and a permanent settlement. Here, too, he built a royal stronghold, or "palace-fort," for the occasional accommodation of himself and his court. Soon a busy town sprang up in the shelter of the camps and the castle, and more Greek settlers came from over the sea — potters and metal-workers, shipwrights, jewellers, and the like.   And docks were built; and the place became a port, and a centre of Greek industry; and it was known far and near as Daphnæ of Pelusium.   This also is the town which in the Bible is called "Tahpanhes;" and this same palace-fort, founded by Psammetichus six hundred and sixty-six years before Christ, is the royal residence which Hophra, a later Pharaoh of the same dynasty, assigned for a refuge to the daughters of Zedekiah, when they fled from Jerusalem into "the land of Egypt."   The Egyptian name for that ancient castle is unknown to us; but we read of it in the forty-third chapter of the Book of the Prophet Jeremiah as "Pharaoh's house at Tahpanhes."

Now, according to Herodotus, these fortified camps at Daphnæ and the town adjoining formed the site of "the first settlement of a foreign-speaking people in Egypt;" and Herodotus was probably so far right that Daphnæ was the first legally established colony of aliens in conservative Egypt. Mr. Flinders Petrie's explorations in 1889 having, however, brought to light traces of two much earlier Greek settlements, we are fain to rectify, in some degree, this statement of Herodotus.*

That the Greeks, who were the most active, imitative, quick-witted, and ingenious people of antiquity, did settle in Egypt, no matter how early or how late, is the really important fact—a fact of primary significance in the history of the arts.

Daphnæ of Pelusium was destined to be eventually superseded by Naukratis.   It flourished for about one hundred years, till Amasis, the last of the Saïte Kings, removed the Greek garrison to Memphis, and made over the city of Naukratis to the Greek traders.   He thus transferred the Egyptian centre of Greek commerce from the Eastern to the

* See chap. iii. on "Portrait-Painting in Ancient Egypt."

Western Delta.   Daphnæ from this time seems to have been completely abandoned; for Herodotus, who writes as if he had seen the place with his own eyes, states that "the docks where the Greek vessels were laid up, and the ruins of the houses in which the Greek citizens of Daphnæ once dwelt," were yet visible in his time.

At Daphnæ first, and then at Naukratis, the Greeks thus found a permanent and ·recognized footing in Egypt. No longer as undisciplined and semi-civilized hordes hurling themselves in vain against the trained battalions of the Pharaohs, no longer as miserable captives haled through the streets of Thebes behind the chariot wheels of a conqueror do they now come before us; but as hardy soldiers, as busy citizens, as thriving merchants. The native Egyptians despise them, mistrust them, and will neither eat nor wed with them, nor do anything but trade with them. But the strangers are quick to learn and skilful to imitate; and ere long they rival their masters as artists and craftsmen, disputing many a market in which the Egyptians have for ages enjoyed an immemorial monopoly. At Daphnæ, the Ionians and Carians, and at Naukratis the Milesians, rapidly become famous as potters, reproducing and improving upon the time-honored designs of Egypt. They even make scarabs, and amulets, and images of the Egyptian gods for the Egyptian bazaars.

I am drawing no imaginary picture. The sites of Daphnæ and Naukratis have been excavated within the last four years by Mr. Flinders Petrie, and it is not too much to say that the direct and indirect results of these explorations have completely settled that interesting question which has been so often debated and so long unanswered—namely, the question of the nature and extent of the æsthetic debt of Greece to Egypt.

That debt, in so far as it was in their power to estimate it, was freely admitted by the later Greeks themselves. Solon, Thales, Pythagoras, Eudoxus, Eratosthenes, Plato, and a host of others, were proud to sit at the feet of the most ancient of nations; but they were wholly ignorant of the fact that they owed the first elements of civilization and those greatest of all gifts, the alphabet and the art of writing, to the wisdom of the Egyptians.

We now know what the Greeks themselves never knew. We know that their prehistoric ancestors ventured their desperate fortunes against the might of the Pharaohs at a date so remote that they must have beheld the dawn, as well as the splendor, of Thebes; and, knowing this, we also know what they saw in Egypt, and what they must certainly have learned there.

It is not, of course, to be supposed that these coastmen and islanders of the Ægean were without some rudimentary notions of art of their own. In the time of Thothmes III., there were already Cypriote settlers making Cypriote pottery, and inscribing their pots with Cypriote characters at Tell Gurob. In the time of Meneptah, the Lycians and Carians and Achæans were ship-builders and workers in bronze; and we may take it for granted that they fashioned rude Cyclopean temples, like the primitive temple discovered a few years ago in Delos, with probably an upright stone for a god. But architecture, sculpture, and original decorative art, we may be sure they had none.

And the proof that they had none is found in the fact that the earliest known vestiges of Greek architecture, Greek sculpture, and Greek decorative art are copied from Egyptian sources.

It is not at all strange that the Greeks should have borrowed their first notions of architecture and decoration from Egypt, the parent of the arts; but that they should have borrowed architectural decoration before they borrowed architecture itself, sounds paradoxical enough. Yet such is the fact; and it is a fact for which it is easy to account.

The most ancient remains of buildings in Greece are of Cyclopean, or, as some have it, of Pelasgic origin; and the most famous of these Cyclopean works are two subterraneous structures known as the Treasury of Atreus and the Treasury of Minyas—the former at Mycenæ, in Argolis, the latter at Orchomenos, in Bœotia. Both are built after the one plan, being huge dome-shaped constructions formed of horizontal layers of dressed stones, each layer projecting over the one next below, till the top was closed by a single block. The whole was then covered in with earth, and so buried. Such structures scarcely come under the head of architecture, in the accepted sense of the word.

Now, whether the Pelasgi were the rude forefathers of the Aryan Hellenes, or whether they were a distinct race of Turanian origin settled in Greece before Hellas began, is a disputed question which I cannot pretend to decide; but what we do know is, that the prehistoric ruins of Mycenæ and Orchomenos are four hundred, if not five hundred, years older than the oldest remains of the historic school. Of all that happened during the dark interval which separated the prehistoric from the historic, we are absolutely ignorant.

If, however, the builders of Mycenæ and Orchomenos were Pelasgians, and if the builders of the earliest historic temples were Hellenes, it is, at all events, certain that the Pelasgians went to Egypt for their surface decoration, and the Hellenes for their architectural models. Moreover—and this is very curious—they both appear to have gone to school to the same place. That place is on the confines of Middle and Upper Egypt, about one hundred and seventy miles above Cairo, and its modern name is Beni-Hasan.

The rock-cut sepulchres of Beni-Hasan are among the famous sights of the Nile. They are excavated in terraces at a great height above the river, and they were made for the great feudal princes who governed this province under the Pharaohs of the Twelfth Dynasty. Their walls are covered with paintings of the highest interest; their ceilings are rich in polychromatic decoration; and many are adorned with pillared porches cut in the solid rock.([9])

It is to be remembered that the foundation of the Twelfth Egyptian Dynasty—the great dynasty of the Usertesens and Amenemhats—dates from about 3000 to 2500 years before

Christ. These Beni-Hasan sepulchres are therefore older by many centuries than the so-called "Treasuries" of Orchomenos and Mycenæ.

Now, at Mycenæ, near the entrance to the Treasury of Atreus, there stands the base and part of the shaft of a column decorated with a spiral ornament, which here makes its first appearance on Greek soil. This spiral (though it never achieved the universal popularity of the meander, or "key pattern," or of the misnamed "honeysuckle pattern") became in historic times a stock motive of Hellenic design; and all three patterns—the spiral, the meander, and the honeysuckle — have long been regarded as purely Greek inventions. But they were all painted on the ceilings of the Beni-Hasan tombs full twelve hundred years before a stone of the Treasuries of Mycenæ or Orchomenos was cut from the quarry. The spiral, either in its simplest form, or in combination with

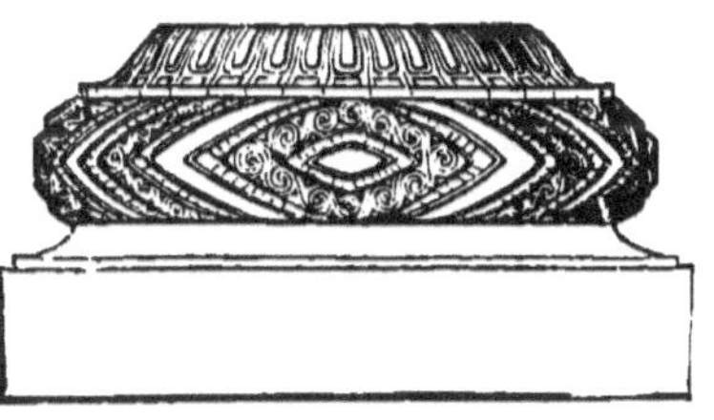

DECORATED COLUMN AT MYCENÆ.

the rosette or the lotus, is an Egyptian design. The rosette is Egyptian; and the honeysuckle, which Mr. Petrie has identified as a florid variety of the lotus pattern,(") is also distinctly Egyptian.

The spiral in combination with the rosette is first found, as a decorative design, on a ceiling in one of the tombs at Beni-Hasan, as in the following illustration; and in another ceiling decoration from the same rich mine of early design, we have the key pattern—the canonical Greek key pattern—combined also with the rosette.

The identity of these and other Beni-Hasan designs with the classic motives of Greek decorative art was first pointed out by Mr. W. H. Goodyear in his remarkable paper on the "Egyptian Origin of the Ionic Capital and of the Anthemion," contributed to the *American Journal of Archæology* in 1888. To the same chain of demonstrations belongs the next illustration, representing, side by side, a specimen of Beni-Hasan decoration and a fragment of prehistoric painted pottery found by Dr. Schliemann in the course of his excavations at Mycenæ—a fragment coeval, apparently, with the Treasury and the pillar.

SPIRAL AND ROSETTE DESIGN.
Beni-Hasan ceiling, Twelfth Dynasty.

This pattern is known as the heart-shaped, or *herz-blatt*, pattern. It has always been accepted as of Greek origin; but beside it is given an example of the same design, more ornately treated, from another of the Beni-Hasan ceilings.

The foregoing illustrations of Greek design being derived from Mycenæan sources, we will next turn to Orchomenos. It was here that Dr. Schliemann, in 1880, discovered in the Treasury of Minyas a small and hitherto unsuspected chamber, which had originally been decorated

ROSETTE AND KEY-PATTERN.
Beni-Hasan ceiling, Twelfth Dynasty.

with a stone ceiling consisting of four large slabs elaborately carved.(") These slabs had fallen, and were lying on the floor; and Dr. Schliemann was thus enabled to take paper casts of the design, which consists of an outer border of small squares, an inner border of rosettes, and a centre which he describes as "spirals interwoven with palm-leaves, between which a long bud shoots forth."

Dr. Schliemann then goes on to say that the same sort of spiral is found at Troy and at Mycenæ, and that rosettes (which he designates as "palmettes") also occur at the latter place; but he claims that the *composition* of the Orcho-

TWO EXAMPLES OF HERZ-BLATT PATTERN.

1. Potsherd from Mycenæ.   2. Beni-Hasan ceiling.

menos design is "perfectly new."   He further adds that Professor Ziller believed this decoration to have been "the motive of a carpet, from which it was copied on the ceiling;" while, according to Professor Sayce, the rosettes were "originally Babylonian, and passed over into Phœnician art, which they characterize."(")

But these eminent archæologists, when they lent the weight of their authority to these views, were for once in error.   The carpet theory is, of course, below criticism.   The Pelasgians, or Prehistoric Greeks, may have spread their floors with skins, the spoils of the chase; but it needs some imagination to conceive of them as weavers of carpets and rugs.   The rosettes were Egyptian before they were ever Babylonian or Phœnician.   And as for the composition of the Orchomenos pattern, so far from being "perfectly new," it is found as a cornice design at Beni-Hasan, where it decorates tombs older by at least twelve centuries than the Treasury of Minyas.

EXAMPLE OF ROSETTE BORDER AND CENTRAL DESIGN OF SPIRAL AND LOTUS.

From a ceiling pattern at Orchomenos. Prehistoric Greek.

The illustration reproduces two cornice patterns from Beni-Hasan. The first example gives the spiral in combination with a fan-like ornament, which is but a simplified variation on the lotus pattern. In the second example the rosette is substituted for the inner curves of the spiral, and the intermediate space is filled in with the true lotus motive. The Orchomenos design is palpably an adaptation from these two Egyptian originals. The spiral is the spiral of No. 1; the rosettes are taken out of the spirals of No. 2, and transferred to the border; while Dr. Schliemann's "long bud" is simply an elongation of the centre petal of the lotus. As for the so-called "palmette," it is neither more nor less than a variation of the lotus. It should be added that all these Beni-Hasan patterns are to be found in Rosellini's volume of *Monumenti Civili;* and that Mr. W. H. Goodyear's further researches into the Lotus origin of these and other motives of decorative design, not only in

CORNICE PATTERNS FROM BENI-HASAN TOMBS.

1. Spiral and Lotus. 2. Spiral, Lotus, and Rosette.

Greece, but in many other lands of the ancient world, will shortly be given to the public in his forthcoming work, entitled *The Grammar of the Lotus.*

The identity of these patterns being demonstrated, and the priority of the Egyptian originals being beyond dispute, it remains to be asked whether it is possible to regard the Greek reproductions as mere fortuitous coincidences.

Let us for a moment suppose that we know nothing of the presence of prehistoric Greeks in Egypt. Let us grant that the triumphal chant of Thothmes III., and the epic of Pentaur, and the annals of Meneptah and Rameses III. had never been translated. Could we, even so, have gone through this series of designs without recognizing that some must be originals and others copies? We might not, it is true, have known whether the Greek sat at the feet of the Egyptian, or the Egyptian at the feet of the Greek ; but we

FAÇADE OF TOMB AT BENI-HASAN.

should surely have seen that one must be the pupil, and the other the master.

The historic school of Greek architecture begins at Corinth with the remains of a Doric temple dating from about 650

B.C.; and this ruin is believed to be the oldest in Greece. In its extreme simplicity of style and the inelegant strength of its proportions, it is impossible not to recognize a close but clumsy relationship to Egyptian models. Ferguson boldly asserts, indeed, that this structure is "indubitably copied" from the pillared porches of Beni-Hasan.(")

The columns of these pillared porches have sixteen flutings, a plain abacus, and no plinth. They also support a plain entablature. This is the "proto-Doric" type about which archæologists have disputed so long and so hotly.

It is important to compare this so-called "proto-Doric" with the Greek Doric, of which we here have three examples, showing the development of the order at three periods.

The first is from the early temple at Corinth; the second is from the Parthenon, dating, therefore, from the age of Pericles; the third and latest is from a temple at Delos, of the time of Philip of Macedon.

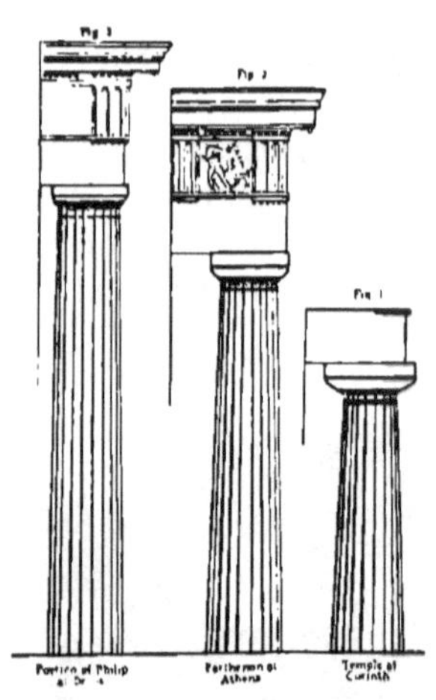

EXAMPLES OF DORIC COLUMNS.

1. From Corinth   2. From the Parthenon   3. From Delos.

The column of the Corinth temple is identical in design and proportions with the columns of Beni-Hasan; the Parthenon column is loftier, and of admirable grace; while in the Delian example we have yet more height, no gradation, and no grace.

But whether loftier or lower, plain or decorated, the essential principle of the Doric order is Egyptian to the last.

The Corinth column, however, was not necessarily copied from Beni-Hasan. It may, with equal probability, have been studied from the Temple of Thothmes III. at Karnak—the finest example of this style in Egypt.

M. Perrot in the first volume of his *Histoire de l'Art dans l'Antiquité*, has urged, among other objections, that this style was already archaic in Egypt when the Corinth temple was built; and that, "not being *archæologists*," the Greeks, had they borrowed from Egypt, would surely have borrowed from the more ornate and modern school. But this is a fallacious

TEMPLE OF THOTHMES III. AT KARNAK.
Eighteenth Dynasty.

argument. Younger nations, when they borrow from older civilizations, invariably take those things which suit their special needs; and in the proto-Doric column of Egypt, the Greek instinctively recognized not only the easiest model upon which to try his "'prentice hand," but that which especially embodied those principles of simplicity and grace which were most in harmony with his taste and his climate.

From the Egyptian origin of the Doric order, we pass on

to the Egyptian origin of the Ionic. In order to prove this point, I must draw upon Mr. W. H. Goodyear's essay in the *American Journal of Archæology*, already referred to, and briefly sketch the part played by the lotus in Egyptian art —a part much more considerable than has hitherto been suspected.

To the modern traveller who ascends the Nile from Cairo to Assûan without seeing a single specimen of this famous lily, it would almost seem as if the lotus had become extinct with the people who in olden time associated it with all the pleasures of their social life, and with all the ceremonies of their religion. This, however, is not the case. Of the three varieties which flourished abundantly in the time of Herodotus — the white, the blue, and the rose lotus—only the last (the *Nelumbium speciosa*) has disappeared. The white and the blue *Nenuphar** yet star the unfrequented water-ways of the Delta, and grow with rank luxuriance in the ditches and stagnant pools which abound in the neighborhood of Rosetta and Damietta. Here the children of the fellaheen still pluck the pods and eat the seeds, as the Egyptians plucked and ate them in the days of the Pharaohs. Beautiful as it was, the rose lotus was not the dominant lotus of Egyptian decorative art. The architect, the potter, the bronze-worker turned rather to the blue or white variety, preferring the flat and floating leaf of these species to the bell-shaped leaf of the *Nelumbium speciosa*. This floating leaf slightly curved at the edge and divided at its point of junction with the stem, furnished the architects of the Ancient Empire with a

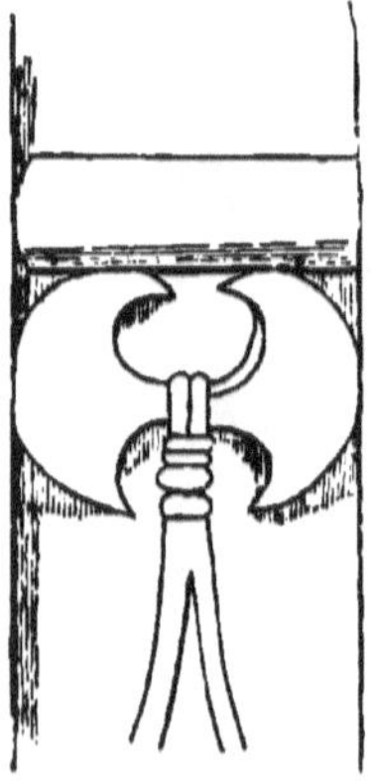

LOTUS LEAF DESIGN.

From a tomb of the Ancient Empire, Sakkarah. From a sketch by Mariette-Pasha, in *Les Mastabas de l'ancienne Empire.*

* The *Nymphæa Alba* and the *Nymphæa Cærulea.*

noble and simple model for decorative purposes. Very slightly conventionalized, it enriches the severe façades of tombs
of the Fourth, Fifth, and Sixth dynasties, which thus pre-
serve for us one of the earliest motives of symmetrical design in the history of ornament.

In the next illustration* we have the blossom and leaf of

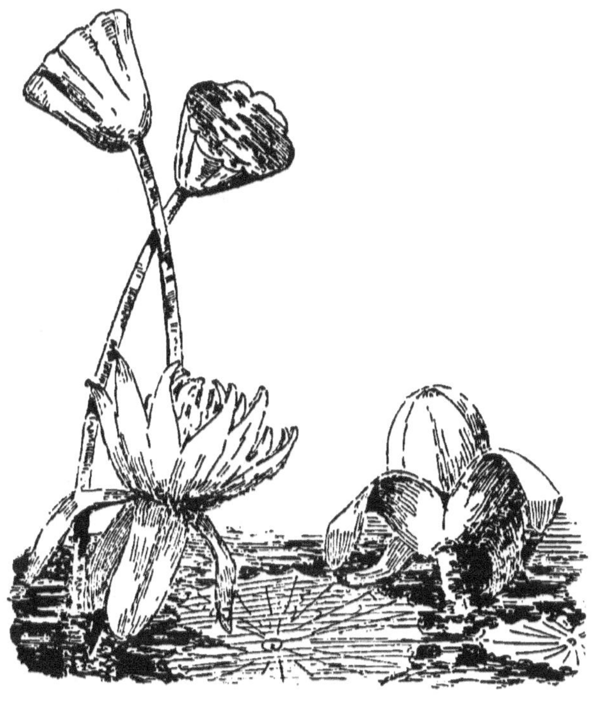

NATURAL LOTUS IN BUD, BLOSSOM, AND SEED-POD.

the blue lotus, and two seed-pods of the pink lotus. The
blossom is full-blown, and the calyx-leaves, which closely

* Abridged from an illustration to Mr. W. H. Goodyear's article in the
American Journal of Archæology.   Vol. iii.

12

enfold it in its earlier stages, separate from the fully-opened flower. Thus separating, they droop over, and assume a variety of graceful curves. These drooping calyx-leaves play a very important part in the history of architecture; for from these—and these only—were derived the volutes of the Ionic capital.

We now pass from the lotus in nature to the lotus in art. Of the Egyptian treatment of the lotus in decoration, we next have three examples.

1. First in order comes the conventional lotus of the Egyptian school of flower-painting—that lotus with upright calyx-leaves and ordered petals which we know so well from the illustrations to Wilkinson and Ebers. As an offering upon the altar, as an oblation to the *manes* of the dead, wreathed as a chaplet, strung as a necklace, carried as a bouquet, we meet with it at every turn in the tombs and temples of Egypt.

THREE EXAMPLES OF CONVENTIONALIZED LOTUS.

1. From a wall-painting.   2. Wooden capital, from a wall-painting.   3. Bas-relief on square limestone column.

2. The next example, from a Theban wall-painting, represents the capital of a wooden column. Here we have three lotus lilies, one large blossom and two smaller blossoms, issu-

ing from a conventionalized base of drooping calyx-leaves. A bud on each side of the calyx repeats the symmetrical arrangement of the smaller lotuses above. Fantastic though it is, and overcharged with detail, this capital gives a good example of the curvature of the calyx-leaf in architectural design.

3. The third example reproduces a bas-relief decoration upon a square granite column of Thothmes III. at Karnak. Here we have the calyx without the flower; and at this stage of the design we are but one remove from the Ionic capital. Suppose a flat stone to be placed on the top of those curved calyx-leaves, let the weight of the stone press them downwards and outwards, and we have the Ionic capital of Greece.

Of the earliest known example of true Ionic it is not possible to give an illustration; yet that earliest example was in existence only six years ago. It belonged to the archaic Temple of Apollo, at Naukratis.

It was in 1885 that Mr. Petrie identified the site of that long-lost city with a large mound situate about half-way between Alexandria and Cairo, in the Western Delta. The modern Arab name for this mound is Tell Nebireh. It is rather more

EXAMPLE OF GRECIAN IONIC.

than half a mile in length by a quarter of a mile in breadth : and the canal along which, in olden days, the Greek merchant-galleys sailed to and fro between Naukratis and the sea yet skirts one side of the mound. Now, Herodotus says of Naukratis that Amasis assigned it to the Greek traders, and therewith granted them special privileges ; hence it has always been taken for granted that they then first settled in that place. But Mr. Petrie's excavations show them to have been in possession of the city from a much earlier period—earlier, perhaps, than the dynasty to which Amasis belonged. What Amasis actually did for the Greeks of Naukratis must, therefore, have been to confirm them in their occupation of that site, and to grant them an exclusive charter whereby they should be entitled to hold it in perpetuity.

The beginnings of Naukratis seem to have been humble enough, the earliest town having been built of wood and burned to the ground, we know not when nor by whom. Its ashes underlie the ruins of the second town, which dates from about the time of Psammetichus I., the founder of Daphnæ.*

To this period—that is, from about 666 B.C. to 640 B.C.—belong the remains of that first temple to Apollo which is the very earliest of which it can be said with certainty that it belonged to the Ionic order.

It was a primitive little structure built of mud-bricks faced with stucco, and finished with decorations and columns of limestone. All that remained of it when discovered were a few fragments of sculptured decoration, the piece of fluted column figured on the following page, and a single volute. That volute — the oldest Ionic volute known — was seen by Mr. Petrie at the moment when it was turned up by the spade of the digger. He hastened to fetch his camera that he might photograph the fragments as they lay; but before he could return to the spot, the volute had been smashed up and carried to the nearest lime-kiln. The rest of the fragments are now in the British Museum.

Like the Beni-Hasan columns, the flutings on this fragment of shaft are sixteen in number, and meet edge to edge, without any flat between.

The first Temple of Apollo seems to have been destroyed about 440 B.C., to make way for a second and a larger structure, adorned with columns and architraves of fine white marble.

* See chap. i., "The Buried Cities of Ancient Egypt."

The only relics of this second temple are here reproduced from a photograph by Mr. Petrie.   Scant though they are,
they at all events show to what skill the Greeks of Naukratis had by this time attained in the art of decorative sculpture. Among these fragments we note an anthemion, some bits of the so-called Oriental palmette, and a few scraps of lotus pattern, naturalistically treated. That the anthemion and the palmette are

FRAGMENTS OF SHAFT, ETC., FROM THE ARCHAIC
TEMPLE OF APOLLO, NAUKRATIS.

lotus motives conventionally treated has been conclusively demonstrated by Mr. W. H. Goodyear in a series of examples from Egyptian, Cypriote, Greek, and Græco-Roman

FRAGMENTS FROM THE SECOND TEMPLE OF APOLLO,
NAUKRATIS.

monuments, which trace the evolution of these forms step by step, and leave no room for debate.([8])

It is impossible in the course of a few pages to do more than touch upon some of the more striking instances of the influence of the lotus upon Greek decorative art. The subject, as a whole, is too complicated and too extensive for summary treatment. It will, however, be interesting to glance at two or three more examples of lotus designs, beginning

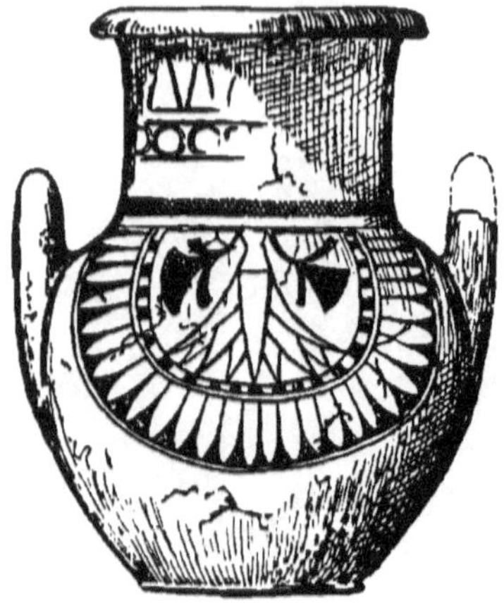

EGYPTIAN VASE WITH INVERTED LOTUS
DESIGN.
From a drawing by Mr. W. M. F. Petrie.

with the conventional treatment of Egypt, and leading up to what is erroneously called the "honeysuckle pattern of the Greeks."

In this illustration we have an alabaster vase of pure Egyptian style and workmanship, found by Mr. Petrie at Tell Nebesheh in a tomb of the time of the Twentieth Dynasty. The lotus design engraved on the shoulder of this vase is identical in treatment with the conventional lotus of the Egyptian flower-painters, as shown in the previous illustration. This is easily demonstrable by reversing the page, and looking at the vase upsidedown.

This next vase is more modern by six hundred years. It was found at Tell Defenneh (Daphnæ of Pelusium) in the ruins of the palace-fort of Psammetichus I. As an example of very early Greek painted ware, reproducing the stock motives of Egyptian decoration and dominated by Egyptian influences, this beautiful vase is most instructive. The friezes of birds and animals are Greek, and re-

ARCHAIC GRÆCO-EGYPTIAN VASE.
(Tell Defenneh.)
From a drawing by Mr. W. M. F. Petrie.

mind us of the Rhodian and Cypriote schools. The enriched
"key pattern" between the two friezes, and the simpler "key
pattern" below, are Egyptian. We have already seen them
in the Beni-Hasan designs; while the floral subjects in the
two lower bands mark the first appearance of the misnamed "honeysuckle" pattern, which is neither more nor
less than a Greek variation upon the old familiar lotus and
scroll of the Beni-Hasan cornice patterns. The form of the
vase is restored in dotted lines where broken.

The vase next reproduced from a drawing by Mr. Petrie is
also from Tell Defenneh. The lotus and scroll are treated
with yet more playful freedom and grace, and the artist has
even ventured to combine
some dancing figures with
his design. In the lowest
register we observe, how-
ever, a return to the old
conventional forms — a se-
verely simplified lotus of
the Egyptian type alternat-
ing with an upright bud.

This simplified lotus-and-
bud pattern, which is much
more nearly related to the
Egyptian school of design
than to the Greek, was by
no means monopolized by
the potters of Daphnæ. It
speedily became the com-
mon property of both architects and vase-painters in
all the schools of Hellas. It

ARCHAIC GRÆCO-EGYPTIAN VASE.
(Tell Defenneh.)
From a drawing by Mr. W. M. F. Petrie.*

appears for the first time as an architectural decoration in a
fragment of sculptured necking from the archaic Temple of

* For these three illustrations of vases, see Plates i., xxvii., and xxviii.,
Tanis, Part II., by W. M. Flinders Petrie, Trubuer, 1887.

Apollo at Naukratis, which is dated by Mr. Petrie at 666 B.C. to 640 B.C.

In this piece of necking, which belonged to one of the limestone columns, we at once recognize the lotus-and-bud pattern of the second Defennch vase, which may be ascribed to about 650 B.C. or 640 B.C. The vase and the temple, if not actually contemporaneous, fall, therefore, within about ten years of the same date; and both are decorated with a design directly borrowed from the lotus pattern of Egyptian art. This design is none other than the so-called "egg-and-dart" pattern of Greek architecture.

SKETCH OF LOTUS-AND-BUD PATTERN

(*i. e.* "Egg-and-Dart"), from a fragment of necking from archaic Temple of Apollo, Naukratis.

I will cite but one more instance of the uses to which Greek craftsmen adapted this well-worn subject. At Daphnæ there would seem to have been a busy trade in jewellery as well as in pottery, and the jewellers were no less ready than the potters to seize upon the national flower-subject. Innumerable scraps of fine goldsmiths' work, such as amulets and parts of ear-rings, chains, and the like, were found by Mr. Petrie's Arabs in the ruins of the town; but by far the most striking object of this class was discovered in a corner of the great camp, where it had probably been buried when the palace-fort was sacked and burned. This very precious and beautiful relic is a tray-handle in solid gold, showing a new variety of lotus pattern, the petals being arranged in an elongated form, issuing from voluted calyx-leaves.   Here we identify the original of the supposed "palmette" motive.   It is also important to note the identity of these voluted calyx-leaves with the bas-relief calyx capitals from Karnak which gave the derivation of the Ionic volute.*   This exquisite handle was originally inlaid with colored glass, or stones; the body of the lotus being cast, and the dividing ribs for holding the inlaying being soldered on.

This very brief and inadequate sketch may serve to convey a general idea of the important part played by the Egyptian lotus in Greek decorative art, from its first appearance on the Orchomenos ceiling down to the time when the Greeks obtained a permanent footing in the Delta. Thenceforth, whether issuing from the workshops of Naukratis or multiplied in the studios of Hellas, the time-honored lily of the Nile not only continued to be the stock motive of all floral decoration upon Greek vases, but held its place as a leading motive for architectural ornament.   It was repro-

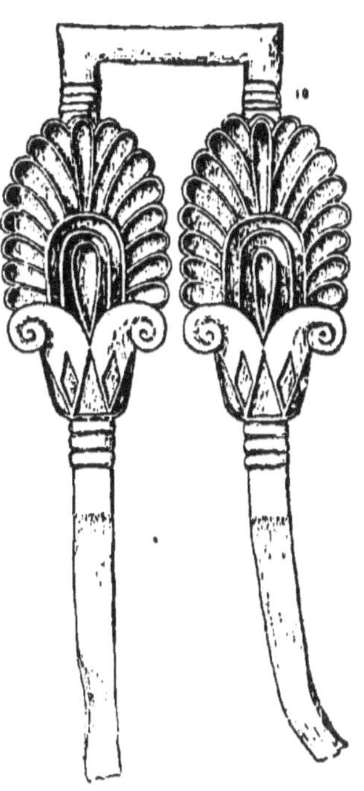

GOLD HANDLE OF A TRAY.

Found in the ruins of the Greek camp at Tell Defenneh.   The two pendant straps, which passed under the tray, are also of solid gold.   From the three bands out of which the calyx springs to the top of the handle measures 2.95 inches (.075 metres).

---

* See third example in illustration of "The Conventional Lotus in Egyptian Art."

duced in the painted vases of Rhodes and Cyprus; it blossomed in ordered beauty along the entablature of the Erectheum; as an anthemion, it crowned the pediment of the Parthenon; and it enriched the prize vases awarded to victors in the Panathenaic games. Professor Alan Marquand, whose voice in matters of Greek archæology is second in authority to none, is even of opinion that the Corinthian capital is of lotus derivation.

As regards the exclusive employment of the lotus motive in Greek ceramic art, we marvel at the ingenuity with which the Hellenic vase-painter varied, played with, and adapted this one subject; but far more extraordinary is the poverty of invention which allowed him to remain forever content to execute only variations, however ingenious, upon the one invariable theme.

The Greeks borrowed many things from Egypt besides the lotus. From the Fields of "*Aahlu*" in the realm of Osiris, where the pure-souled Egyptian steered his papyrus bark amid the sunny islands of a waveless sea, the Greeks borrowed their Elysian Fields and their Islands of the Blest.

The child-god Horus, son of Osiris and Isis, depicted as an infant with his finger in his mouth, became the Greek God of Silence, with his finger on his lip; and "*Hor-pa-khroti*," "Hor-the-child," was transformed into Harpocrates.

It would be easy to multiply such instances, were it not that my present inquiry is directed to the sources of Greek art, and not to the sources of Greek religious thought. Sometimes, however, the one conception involves the other; and when this is the case, the Greek, as a rule, entirely misunderstands the Egyptian idea.

According to old Egyptian belief, for instance, the living man consisted of a Body, a Soul, an Intelligence, a Name, a Shadow, and a Ka, which last I have elsewhere ventured to interpret as the Vital Principle.* He died, and each of these

* See chap. iv., "The Origin of Portrait Sculpture and the History of the Ka."

component parts fulfilled a different destiny. The Body was embalmed; the Ka dwelt with the mummy in the sepulchre; the Intelligence fled back to the immortal source of light and life; the Name and the Shadow awaited reunion with the Body in a state of final immortality; and the Soul, or "*Ba*," represented as a human-headed hawk, fluttered to and fro between this world and the next, occasionally visiting and comforting the mummy in its tomb. These visits of the Soul to the Body are frequently represented in Egyptian tomb-paintings, and in illustrations to the *Book of the Dead;* as, for example, in this vignette to the eighty-ninth chapter of that famous collection of prayers and invocations which has been called—not too correctly—the ancient Egyptian Bible.

The mummy lies on the bier, attended by Anubis, the jackal-headed god of embalmment. The Soul, grasping in one hand a little sail, the emblem of breath, in the other hand the "*ankh*," or emblem of

THE MUMMY AND THE "BA."
From a vignette in "The Book of the Dead."

Life, hovers over the face of the corpse. Now this Soul, this "*Ba*," is a loving visitant to the dead man. It brings a breath of the sweet north wind, and the cheering hope of immortality in the sunny Fields of Aahlu. The Greeks, however, misapprehending its nature and functions, conceived of it as a malevolent emissary of the gods, and converted it into the Harpy. We have next the Greek conception of a Harpy, from a fragment of early Greek painted ware found at Daphnæ. But we have a still finer example in the illustration reproduced from the famous Harpy-Tomb in the British

GREEK HARPY.
From a fragment of painted ware.   Tell Defenneh.   650 B.C.

Museum. The Harpy is carrying off one of the daughters of Pandarus. She wears a fillet and pendant curls, and besides the claws of a bird, she has human arms like the Egyptian " *Ba*," wherewith to clasp her prey. The monument from which this group is copied was discovered by Sir Charles Fellows at Xanthus, in Lycia, and it dates from about five hundred and forty years before our era. It is more recent, that is to say, by about a century, than the painted potsherd of the preceding illustration.

Not less interesting than the self-evident connection between the Greek Harpy and the Egyptian " *Ba* " is the fact that this Harpy-tomb is the work of Lycian artists; for the Lycians, or " Leku," as we have already seen, had been brought into close contact with Egypt as early as the time of the Nineteenth Dynasty, having been among those very nations which allied themselves with the Hittites against Rameses II. and with the Libyans against Meneptah.

Not content to convert

HARPY.
From the Harpy-Tomb of Xanthus.

the gentle bird-soul of the Egyptians into a Harpy, the later Greeks went yet further, and transformed it into a Siren.

The illustration is from a vase in the British Museum, and it may be about one hundred, or one hundred and twenty years later than the Xanthian tomb.   The scene shows Odysseus

ODYSSEUS AND THE SIRENS.
From a vase in the British Museum.

passing the Sirens.   He is bound to the mast of his galley, which glides between two rocks, on each of which perches a Siren.   A third Siren hovers over the rowers.   All three wear the fillet and pendant curl of the Harpy of the Lycian tomb—that same pendant curl which is worn by the " Hanc-bu" woman, sculptured nearly a thousand years before on the pylon of Pharaoh Horemheb at Karnak.*

The question of archaic Greek figure-sculpture, and its unquestioned derivation from Egyptian sources, is so wide and far-reaching that it would demand, not a chapter, but a volume.   It is far too complex for a rapid survey.   The Egyptian character of all very early Greek statuary may,

* See Page 161.

however, be at once recognized by any observant visitor to the British Museum, the Louvre, the Berlin Museum, or the Glyptotheca of Munich. He needs but to walk from the galleries containing the Egyptian collections into the galleries assigned to the archaic Greek marbles, and the evidence will be before his eyes. In the Museum of Athens he will see the archaic Apollo of Thera; in the British Museum, the Strangford Apollo, and in the Glyptotheca of Munich the Apollo of Tenea, to say nothing of other examples in which the general proportions and treatment are distinctly Egyptian. The Strangford Apollo, the Apollo of Thera, and the Apollo of Tenea, are even represented in the canonical, or "hieratic" attitude, with clenched hands, and arms straightened to the sides, which stamps all Egyptian figure-sculpture in stone.

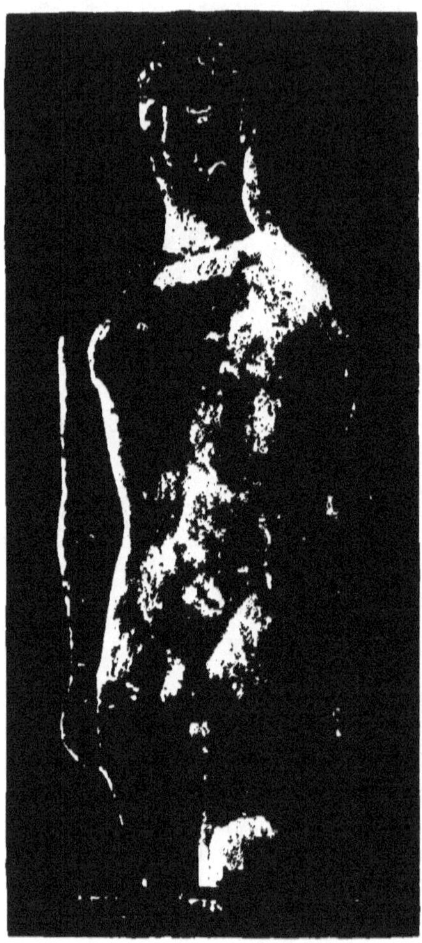

THE ARCHAIC APOLLO OF THERA.
In the National Museum, Athens.

I should add that, among the numerous fragments of votive sculpture discovered by Mr. Petrie in the ruins of the second temple of Apollo at Naukratis, there was found a well-executed torso of an archaic Apollo* in this attitude; thus demonstrating the starting-point of Græco-Egyptian figure-sculpture on Egyptian soil.

We have now followed the footsteps of our prehistoric Greek from the moment when he first emerges from primeval darkness, to the hour of his entry upon the stage of history. That is to say, from a period some seventeen centuries earlier than the accepted date of the "Iliad," to a time when that immortal poem had been current for more than a hundred and fifty years. We have traced the Dardaneans to the reign of Thothmes III., thus proving the existence of at least one important Hellenic tradition at an epoch eight hundred years earlier than its first appearance in Homer. And, further, we have identified those "shining savages,"

THE ARCHAIC APOLLO OF
NAUKRATIS.

the well-greaved Achæans, with the armored warriors of the West who fought and fell with the Libyan host but a few years, probably, before the Children of Israel went forth out of the House of Bondage. Thus far, our facts are drawn from Egyptian sources. Passing on thence to Greek sources, and to the tangible results of recent explorations, we have beheld the colonization of Daphnæ and Naukratis, and followed the evolution of Greek from Egyptian art. We have traced the Doric shaft, and the elaborate ceiling pattern of Orchomenos to the tombs of Beni-Hasan; and we have indentified the Ionic capital, the familiar honeysuckle pattern, and *all* the

---

* This important fragment is now in the Museum of Fine Arts, Boston, United States of America, and its close relationship to the Strangford, Tenean, and Theran Apollos, has been recognized by Mr. Robinson (curator), in his very interesting and able report to the Trustees for the year 1889.

floral decorative motives of Greek ceramic art with the lotus of the Nile.

It is such results as these which unite the Orientalist and the Classical scholar in a bond of brotherhood which had not even begun to exist a few years ago, and which I believe and hope will never, and can never, be dissolved.

FEMALE WINGED SPHINX OF GREEK ART.
(From a fragment of Daphnæan pottery.)

VI.

THE LITERATURE AND RELIGION OF ANCIENT EGYPT.

That the first people who possessed letters in the literal sense should also be the first people to possess letters in the literary sense, is no more than we should expect. Not, indeed, that the possession of an alphabet necessarily implies literary activity on the part of those who possess it. The Romans engraved their codes on tablets of stone and brass, and sculptured inscriptions on their public buildings, for centuries before they wrote histories and dramas, odes and satires. The Oscans, the Etruscans, and other early nations of Italy, never, so far as we know, got beyond mere inscriptions. Even the Greeks of the Ægean, as we are now just beginning to find out, were in possession of the Cadmæan alphabet some five or six centuries before the time of Homer; and yet we have no evidence that the Iliad was committed to writing earlier than some four hundred years after the death of the poet. Literature is, in fact, the fruit of leisure. Nations which are going through the struggle for existence call for soldiers, not scribes. The bard, the rhapsodist, the extemporaneous singer of war-chants and dirges, is the only representative of literature at that early stage in the history of a people; and it is not till the arts of peace have taken their place side by side with the arts of war, that poems are written, not sung—that histories are recorded with the pen, not carved out by the sword.

13

But when we are dealing with the origin and evolution of national literatures, there is yet another factor to be taken into the account; namely, the possession of a cheap and convenient material upon which to write. This is a very commonplace and vulgar necessity; yet it is one of paramount importance. So long as stone and metal are the only available substances, so long will they be used for inscriptions and state documents only. It is not till papyrus, and parchment, and finally paper, become current articles of commerce, that writing as a career or a recreation is even possible. Without papyrus or parchment, we should never have had a literature of Egypt, Greece, or Rome. Without paper, we could never have had the magnificent literary efflorescence of the Renaissance. Fancy Anacreon and Sappho, Martial and Horace, laboriously scratching their poems on tablets of limestone, or plates of bronze! How the perfume of the roses and the sting of the epigrams and the aroma of the Sabine wine would have evaporated under such a process!

So far as we know, the people of ancient Egypt had to make no struggle for existence at the outset of their career. Hemmed in between two vast and pathless deserts, their fertile valley was so strongly fortified by nature herself that they had little cause to fear danger from without. It is not, in fact, till thirteen royal dynasties, comprising about two hundred kings, have passed in shadowy succession across the stage of Egyptian history, that we hear of the Hyksôs invasion.

The Egyptians of the first twelve dynasties, and, indeed, the bulk of the nation at all times, were a pastoral and peaceful people, well content with their lot in this life, and much occupied with preparations for the next. They were naturally averse to soldiering, and the armies of the great military Pharaohs of the Nineteenth and Twentieth dynasties were largely composed of foreign auxiliaries. What the native-born Egyptian most dearly loved was to cultivate his paternal acres, to meditate on morals and religion, and to prepare a splendid tomb for his mummy when the inevitable summons should come.

And he not only loved meditation, but he loved to record his meditations in writing, for the benefit of posterity.

How early the Egyptians began to cut and press the stalks of the papyrus plant in order to make a material for the use of the scribe, it is impossible to say. But we know that material to have been already employed for literary purposes in the time of the Third Dynasty; that is to say, some three thousand eight hundred years before the Christian era. There is at this present time, in the archives of the Bibliothèque Nationale of Paris, a papyrus written by a scribe of the Eleventh Dynasty, which contains copies of two much more ancient documents, one dating from the Third, and one from the Sixth Dynasty. This most precious document (known as the Prisse Papyrus) is the only Eleventh Dynasty papyrus yet discovered. It has been well styled "the oldest book in the world;"(") and it is, at all events, the oldest papyrus known.

When I say that it is the oldest papyrus known, it is not to be inferred that the Prisse Papyrus is the oldest specimen of Egyptian writing yet discovered. If we turn to inscriptions cut in stone—as, for instance, to the Fourth Dynasty tombs of Ghizeh, which are contemporary with the Great Pyramid, or to the famous Second Dynasty tablet of the Ashmolean Museum in Oxford—we can point to inscriptions dating from 4000 B.C. and 4200 B.C. But stone-cut inscriptions, even when they run to a considerable length, are not what we naturally classify under the head of literature. When we speak of the literature of a nation, we are not thinking of inscriptions graven on obelisks and triumphal arches. We mean such literature as may be stored in a library and possessed by individuals. In a word, we mean *books*—books, whether in the form of clay cylinders, of papyrus rolls, or any other portable material.

The Egyptians were the first people of the ancient world who had a literature of this kind: who wrote books, and read books; who possessed books, and loved them. And their literature, which grew, and flourished, and decayed with

the language in which it was written, was of the most varied character, scientific, secular, and religious.   It comprised
moral and educational treatises; state-papers; works on geometry, medicine, astronomy, and magic; travels, tales, fables,
heroic poems, love-songs, and essays in the form of letters;
,hymns, dirges, rituals; and last, not least, that extraordinary
collection of prayers, invocations, and religious formulæ
known as *The Book of the Dead*.   Some of these writings
are older than the pyramids; some are as recent as the time
when Egypt had fallen from her high estate and become a
Roman province.   Between these two extremes lie more than
five thousand years.   Of this immense body of literature we
possess only the scattered wrecks—mere "flotsam and jet-
sam," left stranded on the shores of Time.   Even these *dis-
jecta membra*, though they represent so small a proportion
of the whole, far exceed in mere bulk all that remains to us
of the literature of the Greeks.   Every year, moreover, adds
to our wealth.   No less than a dozen papyri of the remote
Twelfth Dynasty period were found by Mr. Petrie in the
season of 1888–1889 among the ruins of an obscure little
town in the Fayûm.   How precious these documents are
may be judged from the fact that only three or four papyri
of that period were previously known; and that Abraham's
visit to Egypt is believed to have taken place during the
reign of a Pharaoh of this line.   In the course of the same
season, and of the previous season, Mr. Petrie discovered at
least as many papyri of later dynasties, besides hundreds of
fragments of Greek papyri of Ptolemaic and Roman times.
These consist chiefly of accounts, deeds, royal edicts, and the
like, not forgetting a magnificent fragment containing nearly the whole of the Second Book of the Iliad.   Nor is
this the first time that Homer has been found in Egypt.
The three oldest Homeric texts previously known come from
the land of the Pharaohs.   To those three Mr. Petrie has
now added a fourth.([80])   Other papyri found within the present century contain fragments of Sappho, Anacreon, Thespis,
Pindar, Alcæus, and Timotheus; and all, without exception,

come from graves. The great Homer Papyrus of 1889 was
rolled up as a pillow for the head of its former owner; and
its former owner was a young and apparently a beautiful
woman, with little ivory teeth, and long, silky black hair.
The inscription on her coffin was illegible, and we are alike ignorant of her name, her nationality, and her history. She may
have been an Egyptian, but she was more probably a Greek.
We only know that she was young and fair, and she so loved
her Homer that those who laid her in her last resting-place
buried her precious papyrus in her grave. That papyrus is now
among the treasures of the Bodleian Library at Oxford, and
all that is preserved of its possessor—her skull and her lovely
hair—are now in the South Kensington Museum, London.

But we are not now concerned with the transcripts of foreign classics which have been found on Egyptian soil. Our
subject is the native literature of that ancient and wonderful
people whose immemorial home was the Valley of the Nile.

The two most important subjects in the literature of a nation are, undoubtedly, its history and its religion ; and up to
the present time nothing in the shape of an Egyptian history
of Egypt has been found. We have historical tablets, historical poems, chronicles of campaigns, lists of conquered cities,
and records of public works sculptured on stelæ, written on
papyrus, and carved on the walls of temples and tombs. But
these are the materials of history—the bricks and blocks
and beams with which the historian builds up his structure.
Brugsch, in his *Geschichte Aegyptens Unter Den Pharaonen*,
has brought together all such documents as were known at the
time when he wrote it; but no one can read that excellent
work without perceiving that it is but a collection of inscriptions, and not a consecutive narrative. Whole reigns are sometimes represented by only a name or a date ; whole dynasties
are occasionally blank. This is no fault of the learned author.
It simply means that no monuments of those times have
been discovered. Yet we cannot doubt that histories of
Egypt were written at various periods by qualified scholars.
We know of one only—the work of Manetho, who was High

Priest of Ra, and Keeper of the Archives in the Great Temple of Heliopolis, in the time of Ptolemy Philadelphus, some two hundred and fifty years before our era. Manetho, though a true-born Egyptian, wrote his history in Greek, which was the native tongue of the Ptolemies and the language of the court. He wrote it, moreover, by the royal command. Now, the Sacred College of Heliopolis was the most ancient home of learning in Egypt. Its foundation dated back to the ages before history; the oldest fragments embedded in *The Book of the Dead* being of Heliopolitan origin. Manetho had, therefore, the most venerable, and probably the largest, library in Egypt at his command; and whatever histories may have been written before his time, we may be very certain that his was the latest and the best. But of that precious work, not a single copy has come down to our time. A few invaluable fragments are preserved in the form of quotations by later writers—by Josephus, for instance, in his *Antiquities of the Jews*, by George the Syncellus, by Eusebius—and by various chronologers; but the work itself has perished with the libraries in which it was treasured and the scholars by whom it was studied.

Still, there is always room for hope in Egypt; and it may yet be reserved for some fortunate explorer to discover the grave of a long-forgotten scribe whose head shall be pillowed, not on a transcript of Homer, but upon a copy of the lost History of Manetho.

Of the numerous historic documents which remain to us, the three most interesting are perhaps the celebrated "Chant of Victory" of King Thothmes III., the "Epic of Pentaur," and the great international treaty between Rameses II. and the allied Princes of Syria.

The first of these is engraved on a large black granite tablet found in the Great Temple of Karnak, at Thebes. It records the conquests of Thothmes III.; and Thothmes III. was the Alexander of ancient Egypt. He was possessed by the same insatiable thirst for conquest, by the same storm-driven restlessness. Ever on the march and ever victorious,

he conquered the known world of his time. It was his magnificent boast that he planted the frontiers of Egypt where
he pleased; and he did so. Southward as far, apparently, as
the great equatorial lakes which have been rediscovered in
our time; northward to the islands of the Ægean and the
upper waters of the Euphrates; over Syria and Sinai, Mesopotamia and Arabia in the east; over Libya and the North
African coast as far as Scherschell in Algeria on the west, he
carried fire and sword, and the terror of the Egyptian name.
He was by far the greatest warrior-king of Egyptian history,
and his "Chant of Victory," though rhapsodical and Oriental
in style, does not exaggerate the facts. This chant, written
by the laureate of the day, is one of the finest example extant of the poetry of ancient Egypt. For the Egyptians, notwithstanding the poverty of their grammar and the cumbrous structure of their language, had poetry, and poetry of
a very high order. It was not like our poetry. It had
neither rhyme nor metre; but it had rhythm. Like the
chants of the Troubadours and Trouvères, it was largely al-
literative, cadenced, symmetrical. It abounded in imagery,
in antithesis, in parallelisms. The same word, or the same
phrase, was repeated at measured intervals. In short, it had
style and music; and although the old Egyptian language is
far more literally dead than the languages of Greece and
Rome, that music is still faintly audible to the ears of such
as care to listen to its distant echo.

A two-fold bas-relief group at the top of the tablet of
Thothmes III. represents the King in adoration before Amen-
Ra; and the context shows the poem to have been composed
in commemoration of the opening of the Hall of Columns
added by this Pharaoh to the Temple of Amen at Karnak.
It is the god who speaks. He begins with a few lines of
prose; thus:

THE DISCOURSE OF AMEN-RA,

LORD OF THRONES.

"Come unto me! Tremble thou with joy, Oh my Son,

my avenger, Ra-men-Kheper, endowed with life everlasting! I am resplendent through thy love, and my heart is dilated on beholding thy joyous entrance into my Temple. My hands have endowed thy limbs with living strength; thy perfections are pleasant in my sight. I am established in my Abode. I give thee victory and power over all the nations. I have spread the fear of thee throughout all lands, and thy terror unto the limits of the four props of heaven. It is I who magnify the dread of thy name, and the echo of thy war-cry in the breasts of the outer barbarians. I stretch forth my arm, and I seize the people of Nubia in myriads, and the nations of the North in millions, and I bind them for thee in sheaves! I have cast thine enemies under thy sandals, and thou hast trampled their chiefs under thine heel. By my command, the world in its length and its breadth, from East to West is thy throne! Joyful of heart, thou dost traverse the lands of all the nations, none daring to oppose thee. Thou hast sailed the waters of the great sea,* and thou hast scoured Mesopotamia in victory and power. I have made the nations to hear thy war-cry in the depths of their caves, and I have cut off the breath of life from their nostrils. I made their hearts to turn back before thy victories. My glory was on thy brow, dazzling them, leading them captive, burning them to ashes in their settlements. Thou hast struck off the heads of the Asiatics, and their children cannot escape from thee. Every land illuminated by thy diadem is encircled by thy might; and in all the zone of the heavens there is not a rebel to rise up against thee. The enemy bring in their tribute on their backs, prostrating themselves before thee, their limbs trembling and their hearts burned up within them."

And now the god breaks suddenly into rhythmic verse:

"1. I came! I gave thee might to fell the princes of Taha.†

---

* Literally " the great circuit "—*i.e.*, the Mediterranean basin.

† *Taha*; *i.e.*, Gaza, according to Birch; but, according to De Rougé, the coast-land of Syria between Lebanon and the sea.

I cast them beneath thy feet, marching across their territories. I made them to behold thy Majesty as a Lord of Light, shining in their faces, even in my own likeness!

"2. I came! I gave thee might to fell the nations of Asia. Thou hast reduced to captivity the chiefs of the Rotennu.* I made them to behold thy Majesty in the splendor of thy panoply of war, wielding thy weapons and combating in thy war-chariot.

"3. I came! I gave thee might to fell the people of the far East! Thou hast traversed the provinces of the Land of the Gods.† I made them to behold thee like unto the Star of Morning, shedding radiance and showering dew!

"4. I came! I gave thee might to fell the nations of the West! Phœnicia and Cyprus have thee in terror. I made them to behold thy Majesty even as a young Bull, bold of heart, horned, and unconquerable!

"5. I came! I gave thee might to fell the dwellers in the harbors of the coast-lands! The shores of Maten‡ tremble before thee. I made them to behold thy Majesty even as the Crocodile, the Lord of Terror of the water, whom none dare to encounter.

"6. I came! I gave thee might to fell those who dwell in their islands! Those who live in the midst of the great deep hear thy war-cry and tremble. I made them to behold thy Majesty as an avenger who bestrides the back of his victim.

"7. I came! I gave thee might to fell the people of Libya! The isles of the Danæans are under the power of thy will. I made them to behold thy Majesty as a furious Lion, crouching over their corpses and stalking through their valleys.

"8. I came! I gave thee might to fell those beyond the limits of the sea! The circuit of the great waters lies within

---

* *Rotennu*, a powerful nation of North Syria.

† The Land of the Gods (*Tanuter*); a district identical, or conterminous, with *Punt*, on the east coast of Africa.

‡ *Maten*, identified by Maspero with Cilicia, and by Lenormant with Midian.

thy grasp. I made them to behold thy Majesty as the Hawk which hovers on high, beholding all things at his pleasure.

"9. I came! I gave thee might to fell the tribes of the marsh-lands,* and to bind in captivity the Herusha,† lords of the desert sands. I made them to behold thy Majesty as the Jackal of the South, Lord of Swiftness, who scours the plains of the upper and lower country.

"10. I came! I gave thee might to fell the nations of Nubia, even to the barbarians of Pat! I made them to behold thy Majesty like unto thy two brothers, Horus and Set, whose arms I have united to give thee power and strength."

The poem concludes with a few lines of peroration in measured prose, in which the god approves the additions which Thothmes had made to his temple. "Longer is it and wider," he says, "than it has ever been till now. Great is its gateway. I bade thee make it, and thou hast made it. I am content."

Mariette wrote of this ancient Hymn of Praise as being "redolent with the perfume of Oriental poetry;" while Brugsch ranks it with the heroic poem of Pentaur and a few other similar compositions, as destined for ever to remain one of the representative specimens of ancient Egyptian literature at its finest period.

The poem of Pentaur, which is sometimes called the Egyptian Iliad, is in a quite different style. It is much longer than the chant of Thothmes. It is full of incident and dialogue, and it recites, not a mere catalogue of victories, but the events of a single campaign and the deeds of a single hero. That hero is Rameses II., and the campaign thus celebrated was undertaken in the fifth year of his reign, against the allied forces of Syria and Asia Minor. The coalition thus formed included the vassal princes of Karkhemish, Kadesh,

* By the marsh-lands is meant the swampy regions of the Eastern Delta, lying between the Phatnitic and Pelusiac mouths of the Nile.

† The *Herusha;* i. e., the desert tribes.

Aradus, and Kati, all tributaries of Egypt, headed by the prince of the Kheta, or Hittites, with a large Hittite army, and an immense following of the predatory and warlike Græco-Asiatic tribes of Mysia, Lydia, Pedasos, and the Troad.

Rameses took the field in person with the flower of the Egyptian army, traversing the Land of Canaan, which still remained loyal, and establishing his Syrian headquarters at Shabtûn, a fortified town in a small valley a short distance to the south-west of Kadesh. Here he remained stationary for a few days, reconnoitring the surrounding country, and

CAMP OF RAMESES II. AT SHABTÛN.

From the Great Tableau in the Temple of Abû-Simbel.

The rectangular space enclosed on three sides by a row of shields represents the royal camp. The oblong structure to the right of the centre is the pavilion of Rameses; five attendants kneel before the entrance to an inner apartment, surmounted by a royal oval watched over by winged genii. This represents the sleeping-place of the King. The pavilion appears to be a movable structure raised on arches; it was probably of wood, and was constructed in such wise as to be easily taken to pieces and put together again. To the left, the horses of the charioteers are feeding in mangers and attended by grooms. Bags of fodder lie on the ground. A blacksmith with his brazier prepares to shoe a horse near the middle of the camp. Elsewhere we see charioteers dragging away empty chariots, a soldier mending a hoe, a man carrying a pair of water-buckets suspended at each end of a pole across his shoulders; infantry and charioteers arriving in camp; soldiers squatting round a bowl at their supper; officers chastising lazy or recalcitrant subordinates, and the like. Close above and behind the royal pavilion there is a brawl among the king's officers, one of whom is in the act of being stabbed. Just below this group a horse prepares to lie down, bending its fore-legs with a remarkably natural action; while in the foreground to the right, we see the two Syrian spies being soundly bastinadoed, in order to force the truth from them. All the busy life of a great camp is depicted in this wonderful section of the largest battle-subject in the history of art.

endeavoring, but without success, to learn the whereabouts of the enemy. The latter, meanwhile, had their spies out in all directions, and knew every movement of the Egyptian host. Two of these spies, being previously instructed, allowed themselves to be taken by the King's scouts. Introduced into the royal presence, they prostrated themselves before Pharaoh, declaring that they were messengers from certain of the Syrian chiefs, their brothers, who desired to break their pact with the Kheta, and to serve the great King of Egypt. They further added that the Khetan host, dreading the approach of the Egyptian army, had retreated to beyond Aleppo, forty leagues to the northward. Rameses, believing their story, then pushed confidently onward, escorted only by his body-guard. The bulk of his forces, consisting of the brigade of Amen, the brigade of Ptah, and the brigade of Ra, followed at some little distance; the brigade of Sutekh, which apparently formed the reserve, lingering far behind on the Amorite frontier.

Meanwhile two more spies were seized, and the suspicions of the Egyptian officers were aroused. Being well bastinadoed, the Syrians confessed to the near neighborhood of the

From the Great Tableau in the Temple of Abû-Simbel.

allied armies, and Rameses, summoning a hasty council of war, despatched a messenger to hurry up the brigade of Amen. At this critical juncture the enemy emerged from his ambush, and by a well-executed flank movement interposed between Pharaoh and his army. Thus surrounded,

Rameses, with right royal and desperate valor, charged the Hittite war-chariots. Six times, with only his household troops at his back, he broke their lines, spreading disorder and terror and driving many into the river. Then, just at the right moment, one of his tardy brigades came hurrying up, and forced the enemy to retreat. A pitched battle was fought the next day, which the Egyptians claimed for a great victory.

Such would appear to be the plain, unvarnished facts. The poet, however, takes some liberties with the facts, as poets are apt to do even now. He abolishes the household troops, and leaves Rameses to fight the whole field single-handed. Nor is the *Deus ex machina* wanting — that stock device which the Greek dramatists borrowed from Egpytian models. Amen himself comes to the aid of Pharaoh, just as the gods of Olympus do battle for their favorite heroes on the field of Troy.

This poem is certainly the most celebrated masterpiece of Egyptian literature; I therefore make no apology for quoting at some length from the original. We will take up the narrative at that critical point where the Hittites are about to execute their flank movement, and so isolate Rameses from his army.

"Now had the vile Prince of Kheta, and the many nations which were leagued with him, hidden themselves at the north-west of the city of Kadesh. His Majesty was alone; none else was beside him. The brigade of Amen was advancing behind. The brigade of Ra followed the watercourse which lies to the west of the town of Shabtûn. The brigade of Ptah marched in the centre, and the brigade of Sutekh took the way bordering on the land of the Amorites.*

"Then the vile Prince of Kheta sent forth his bowmen and his horsemen and his chariots, and they were as many as the

---

* The translated extracts here given are in part from the French of De Rougé and Maspero, and in part from the English version of Professor Lushington.

grains of sand on the sea-shore. Three men were they on each chariot; and with them were all the bravest of the fighting-men of the Kheta, well armed with all weapons for the combat.

"They marched out on the side of the south of Kadesh, and they charged the brigade of Ra; and foot and horse of King Rameses gave way before them.

"Then came messengers to his Majesty with tidings of defeat. And the King arose, and grasped his weapons and donned his armor, like unto Baal, the war-god, in his hour of wrath. And the great horses of his Majesty came forth from their stables, and he put them to their speed, and he rushed upon the ranks of the Kheta.

THE ROYAL CHARIOT AND GREAT HORSES OF RAMESES ARE BROUGHT ROUND FROM THE STABLES.

Four of the King's spearsmen and two of his Sardinian body-guard await his approach. From the Great Temple of Abû-Simbel.

"Alone he went—none other was beside him. And lo! he was surrounded by two thousand five hundred chariots; his retreat cut off by all the fighting-men of Aradus, of Mysia, of Aleppo, of Caria, of Kadesh, and of Lycia. They were three on each chariot, and massed in one solid phalanx."

Here the form changes, and Rameses breaks forth into an impassioned appeal to Amen.

"None of my princes are with me," he cries. "Not one of my generals—not one of my captains of bowmen or chariots. My soldiers have abandoned me—my horsemen have

fled—there are none to combat beside me! Where art thou,
oh Amen, my father? Hath the father forgotten his son?
Behold! have I done aught without thee? Have I not
walked in thy ways, and waited on thy words? Have I
not built thee temples of enduring stone? Have I not dedicated to thee sacrifices of tens of thousands of oxen, and of
every rare and sweet-scented wood? Have I not given thee
the whole world in tribute? I call upon thee, oh Amen, my
father! I invoke thee! Behold, I am alone, and all the nations of the earth are leagued against me! My foot-soldiers
and my chariot-men have abandoned me! I call, and none
hear my voice! But Amen is more than millions of archers
—more than hundreds of thousands of cavalry! The might
of men is as nothing—Amen is greater than all!"

Then, suddenly, Rameses becomes aware that Amen has
heard his cry—is near him—is leading him to victory.

RAMESES II. SLAYING THE ASIATICS BEFORE RA, THE TUTELARY DEITY OF THE
GREAT TEMPLE OF ABÙ-SIMBEL.

"Lo! my voice hath resounded as far as Hermonthis! Amen comes to my call. He gives me his hand—I shout aloud for joy, hearing his voice behind me!"

And now the god speaks.

"Oh, Rameses, I am here! It is I, thy father! My hand is with thee, and I am more to thee than hundreds of thousands. I am the Lord of Might, who loves valor. I know thy dauntless heart, and I am content with thee. Now, be my will accomplished."

Then Rameses, inspired with the strength of a god, bends his terrible bow and rushes upon the enemy. His appeal for divine aid is changed to a shout of triumph.

"Like Menthu, I let fly my arrows to right and left, and mine enemies go down! I am as Baal in his wrath! The two thousand five hundred chariots which encompass me are dashed to pieces under the hoofs of my horses. Not one of their warriors has raised his hand to smite me. Their hearts die in their breasts—their limbs fail—they can neither hurl the javelin, nor wield the spear. Headlong I drive them to the water's edge! Headlong they plunge, as plunges the crocodile! They fall upon their faces, one above the other, and I slay them in the mass! No time have they to turn back—no time to look behind them! He who falls, falls never to rise again!"

Then the Kheta, and the Kadeshites, and the warriors of Karkhemish and Aleppo, and the princes of Mysia, and Ilion, and Lycia, and Dardania turned and fled, crying aloud:

"It is no man who is in the midst of us! It is Sutekh the glorious! It is Baal in the flesh! Alone—alone, he slays hundreds of thousands! Let us fly for our lives!"

"And they fled; and the King pursued them, as he were a flame of fire!"

The rest of the poem is necessarily somewhat of an ante-climax. It tells how the Egyptian brigades come up towards evening, and are filled with wonder as they wade through the blood of the slain, and behold the field strewn with dead

THE BATTLE OF KADESH.
From the Great Temple of Abû-Simbel.

This sculptured tableau is divided horizontally by the river Orontes, represented by zigzag lines. The fortified city of Kadesh occupies a projecting tongue of land, almost surrounded by the great bend of the river. To the right, where there is apparently a ford, some Egyptian chariots are dashing across in pursuit of a Khetan chariot, in which are seen three warriors. Other Khetan chariots are shown in the lower register, to right, all containing three warriors. The Egyptian chariots are distinguished from those of the Kheta by containing only two. In the top register, to right, an aide-de-camp on horseback gallops off with orders for the tardy rear-guard, and we see a horse running away with an empty chariot. To the left Rameses (depicted of colossal size) pursues the flying foe to the water's edge. Some lie trampled under his chariot-wheels, and some are drowning in the river. A drowning chief is dragged to shore by a soldier of the garrison. Forming a frieze round the end of the tableau to left is a squadron of Egyptian chariots in single file.

and dying. They exalt the prowess of the King, who overwhelms them with reproaches.

"What will the whole world say," he asks, "when it is known that you left your King alone, with none to second him?—that not a prince, not a charioteer, not a bowman was there to join his hand with mine? I fought alone! Alone, I overthrew millions! It was only my good horses who obeyed my hand, when I found myself alone in the midst of the foe. Verily, they shall henceforth eat their corn before

BRIGADE OF INFANTRY ON THE MARCH, PROTECTED BY CAVALRY.
From the great Abû-Simbel Tableau.

me daily in my royal palace, for they alone were with me in the hour of danger."

The next day at sunrise Rameses assembles his forces, and, according to the chronicler, achieves a signal victory, followed by the submission of the Prince of Kheta and the conclusion of a treaty of peace. This treaty was shortly confirmed by the marriage of Rameses with a Khetan princess; and the friendship thus cemented continued unbroken throughout the rest of his long reign.

The foregoing passages are much abridged, but they fairly represent the fervent diction and the dramatic action of this celebrated poem. The style is singularly capricious, narrative and dialogue succeeding each other according to the exigencies of the situation. These changes are unmarked by any of those devices whereby the modern writer assists his reader; they must therefore have been emphasized by the reciter.

To use a very modern word in connection with a very ancient composition, one might say that Rameses "published" this poem in a most costly manner, with magnificent illustra-

EGYPTIAN ATTACK ON HITTITE CHARIOT.
From the great Abû-Simbel Tableau.

tions. And he did so upon a scale which puts our modern publishing houses to shame. His imperial edition was issued on sculptured stone, and illustrated with bas-relief subjects gorgeously colored by hand. Four more or less perfect copies of this edition have survived the wreck of ages, and we know not how many have perished. These four are carved on the pylon walls of the Great Temples of Luxor and the Ramesseum at Thebes, on a wall of the Great Temple of Abydos, and in the main hall of the great rock-cut Temple of Abû-Simbel in Nubia. One of the tableaux in this hall is fifty feet in length by about forty feet in height, and it contains many thousands of figures. A fifth copy is also graven

without illustrations on a side-wall of the Great Temple of
Karnak; and some remains of a great battle-scene with defaced inscriptions appear to belong to another copy, on one
of the walls of the Temple of Derr, in Nubia. In these
temple-copies, the poem is sculptured in hieroglyphs.

But there were also popular editions of this immortal poem
—copies written on papyrus by professional scribes; and one
of these copies is in the British Museum, a fragment of the
beginning of the same copy being in the Museum of the
Louvre. The British Museum document contains one hundred and twelve lines of very fine hieratic writing, and the
last page ends with a formal statement that it was " written
in the year VII., the month Payni, in the reign of King Rameses Mer-Amen, Giver of Life eternal like unto Ra, his father. For the chief librarian of the royal archives . . . by the
Royal Scribe, Pentaur."

Whether this Pentaur was, as it is generally supposed, the

FAC-SIMILE OF THE OPENING LINES OF THE POEM OF PENTAUR.
From the original Hieratic papyrus in the British Museum.

author of the poem, or but a copyist in the employment of
the King's principal librarian, is perhaps an open question.
As, however, the colophon is unmistakably clear as to date,
and as that date is but two years subsequent to the events
narrated in the poem,
we may at least as-
sume that the papy-
rus is a contemporary
document.([51])

It is from the huge
battle-piece sculpt-
ured on the north wall
of the great hall at
Abû-Simbel that we
derive many minor
details not recorded
by the poet.   In this
elaborate composition
the events of the first
and second engage-
ments are combined
in a single subject. In
one place we see Ra-
meses, single-handed,

THE MÉLÉE OF CHARIOTS.
From the great Abû-Simbel Tableau.

rushing upon the foe in his chariot, and driving them headlong into the river; in another we behold the pitched battle
of the following morning.   Every circumstance of that momentous fight is shown with the most painstaking fidelity.
The chariots start first, an officer of bowmen leading the
way on foot.

WAR-CHARIOTS SETTING OUT.
From the great Abû-Simbel Tableau.

Next follow the infantry, marching in a solid square, and protected, van, flank, and rear, by a force of chariots. The infantry are armed with only spear and shield. This is a very interesting section of the great tableau, as it shows us the Egyptian order of battle.

Next comes the encounter with the enemy—the shock of chariots—the overthrow of the Hittite warriors. Part of this fight is arbitrarily introduced into that section of the subject where Rameses is performing his great feat of arms on the

AFTER THE BATTLE.

From the great Abû-Simbel Tableau. In this section of the great tableau the Egyptian artist depicts the incidents of the battle-field after the victory is won. We see the charioteers and infantry returning in order, and the enemy's cattle being driven to the camp. Long files of prisoners are brought along, some tied together by the neck, others with their arms bound behind their backs. In the lowest register a captain of archers brings in a string of eight captives, and is greeted by his comrades with acclamations. In the second register, to the right, Rameses sits in his chariot with his back to the horses and witnesses the counting of the hands of the slain, while three scribes enter the numbers on their tablets.

preceding day; but merely to fill the spaces with figures. In some of these minor episodes we see the Egyptian warriors descending from their chariots and attacking the enemy on foot. The Hittite chariots are clumsily built, the wheels being cut from a solid block of wood, like millstones, and working on a central pivot. The Khetan soldiers wear a scalp-lock, and are three in a chariot.

Finally, the field is fought—the battle is won; and the King, seated in his chariot with his back to the horses, witnesses the bringing in of the prisoners and the counting of the hands of the slain. Three officers cast the severed hands in a heap before the feet of the conqueror, while the captives, strung together by the neck, are brought into his presence with their arms fast bound behind their backs.

In the last scene of all, Rameses, depicted of colossal size, sits enthroned, and receives the congratulations of his great officers of state. His fan - bearer and his bow-bearer stand behind his chair, and his chariot and horses are taken back with honor to the royal stables.

It is evident that the artists who designed the sculptured illustrations at Abû-

RAMESES, ENTHRONED, RECEIVING THE CONGRATULATIONS OF HIS OFFICERS AFTER THE VICTORY.

From the great Abû-Simbel Tableau.

Simbel and Thebes were not dependent on only the text of the poem for the subject-matter of their battle-scenes. They were familiar with incidents of which the poet takes no note, and of which we could know nothing had they not been recorded by the chisel of the sculptor and the brush of the painter. In that spirited scene where Ramóses, Phœbus-like, stands erect in his chariot, bending his great bow and

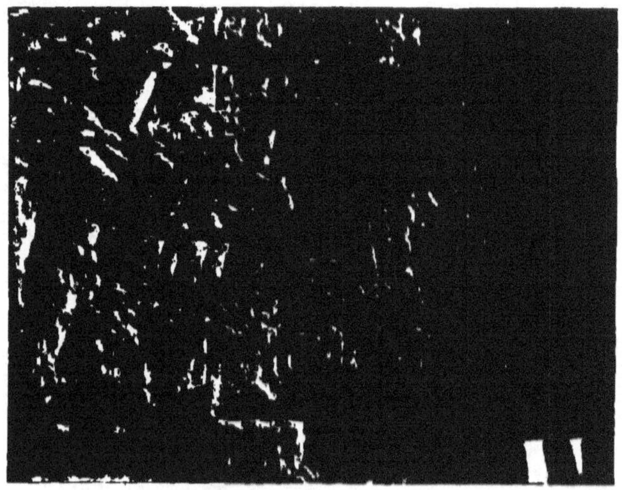

THE PRINCE OF ALEPPO HELD UPSIDEDOWN AFTER DROWNING.
From the Pylon of the Ramesseum, Thebes.   Photographed by Mr. W. M. F. Petrie.

chasing the enemy into the water (page 209), we see, for instance, a half-drowned chieftain being dragged to land by one of the Hittite garrison, and we learn that he was no less a personage than the Prince of Aleppo. A hieroglyphic inscription engraved over the head of the rescued man in the Abú-Simbel tableau runs thus: "The Great of Aleppo. His warriors lift him up after the King has flung him into the water." Now, it is certain that this is no merely fanciful episode designed by the artist in order to heighten the effect of his tableau, for the same incident is depicted in the version sculptured on the great pylon of the Ramesseum at Thebes. The artist of the Ramesseum, however, chooses a later phase of the catastrophe, when the unlucky prince has been dragged ashore, and is held up head downwards, in order to let the water run out of his mouth—a method by no means to be recommended under the circumstances. The color is yet preserved on this part of the subject, and it shows the Prince of Aleppo to have been of the race of fair Syrians, his eyes being painted blue, and his hair and beard light red. We also learn from one of these battle-subjects that "the writer of books of the vile Hittite" (that is to say, the official scribe of the Hittite leader) accompanied the Syrian host. Rameses, without doubt, had also his following of royal scribes, and one of them was in all probability the author of this poem. How highly it gratified the vanity of Rameses may be gathered from the frequency with which he caused it to be reproduced upon the walls of temples and pylons during his long reign.([42])

The scientific literature of the Egyptians is extremely interesting, inasmuch as it illustrates that eager spirit of inquiry which is the mainspring of intellectual effort, and without which there can be no intellectual progress. But its value to us is, of course, purely archæological. We have nothing to learn from these earliest pioneers of astronomy, of mathematics, of medicine. We smile at their childlike and fanciful speculations; but we are sometimes amazed to find how near they were to grasping many truths which we have been wont to regard as the hard-won prizes of modern research.

This is especially true of ancient Egyptian astronomy. Their observations were singularly exact. They understood perfectly well the difference between the fixed stars and the planets; the first being "the genii which never move," and the last "the genii which never rest." They even knew that our own earth forms part of the planetary system, and is subject to the same law of motion. In a hieratic inscription of the Pyramid Period, for instance, it is said that "the earth navigates the celestial ocean in like manner with the sun and the stars."([63]) Again, in a remarkable passage of the Great Harris Papyrus, we read how Ptah, the primordial god, "moulded man, created the gods, made the sky, and formed the earth *revolving in space*." Unhappily, no papyrus treating of astronomy has yet been discovered; but zodiacs, calendars, and astronomical tables, showing the divisions of the year, the phases of the moon, and the dates and hours of the rising and setting of certain planets, abound on the walls of temples and tombs.

Two mathematical papyri have been found. One was discovered by Mr. Petrie in the ruins of a buried house in Tanis. This papyrus is the property of the Egypt Exploration Fund, and Prof. Eugène Revillout, of the Egyptian Department of the Louvre, has undertaken to translate it. The other mathematical papyrus was found by Mr. Rhind at Thebes. It belongs to the British Museum, and has been translated by Dr. August Eisenlohr, of Heidelberg. This curious document treats of plane trigonometry and the measurement of solids; and it contains not only a system of reckoning by decimals, but a series of problems for solution by the student. Of the practical geometry of the Egyptians, we have a magnificent example in the Pyramids, which could never have been erected by builders who were not thoroughly conversant with the art of measuring surfaces and calculating the bulk and weight of materials.

Works on medicine abounded in Egypt from the remotest times, and the great medical library of Memphis, which was of immemorial antiquity, was yet in existence in the second century before our era, when Galen visited the Valley of the Nile. The Egyptians seem, indeed, to have especially prided themselves on their skill as physicians, and the art of healing was held in such high esteem that even kings made it their study. Ateta, third king of the First Dynasty, is the reputed author of a treatise on anatomy. He also covered himself with glory by the invention of an infallible hair-wash, which, like a dutiful son, he is said to have prepared especially for the benefit of his mother.

No less than five medical papyri have come down to our time, the finest being the celebrated Ebers papyrus, bought at Thebes by Dr. Ebers in 1874. This papyrus contains one hundred and ten pages, each page consisting of about twenty-two lines of bold hieratic writing. It may be described as an Encyclopædia of Medicine as known and practised by the Egyptians of the Eighteenth Dynasty; and it contains prescriptions for all kinds of diseases—some borrowed from Syrian medical lore, and some of such great antiquity that they are ascribed to the mythologic ages, when the gods yet reigned personally upon earth. Among others, we are given the recipe for an application whereby Osiris cured Ra of the headache.

The Egyptians attached great importance to these ancient medical works, which were regarded as final. The physician who faithfully followed their rules of treatment might kill or cure with impunity; but if he ventured to treat the patient according to his own notions, and if that patient died, he paid for the experiment with his life. Seeing, however, what the canonical remedies were, the marvel is that anybody ever recovered from anything. Raw meat; horrible mixtures of nitre, beer, milk, and blood, boiled up and swallowed hot; the bile of certain fishes; and the bones, fat, and skins of all kinds of unsavory creatures, such as vultures, bats, lizards, and crocodiles, were among their choicest remedies. What we suffer at the hands of the faculty in this nineteenth century is bad enough; but we may rejoice that we have escaped the learned practitioners of Memphis and Thebes.

The moral philosophy of the ancient Egyptians is peculiarly interesting to us of a later age. It is not a profound philosophy. On the contrary, it is simple, practical, and very much to the point. We have several papyri containing collections of moral precepts, and most of them are written in the form of aphorisms on the conduct of life, addressed by a father to his son. Such are the Maxims of the Scribe Ani, the Maxims of Ptah-hotep, and others. The Maxims of Ptah-hotep are contained in the famous Prisse Papyrus, which has been styled "The Oldest Book in the World." This papyrus dates from the Twelfth Dynasty, and is copied from a yet more ancient document of the Fifth Dynasty, written some three thousand eight hundred years before our era. It is one of the treasures of the Bibliothèque Nationale, in Paris.

"Be not proud because of thy learning," saith Ptah-hotep. "Converse with the ignorant as freely as with the scholar, *for the gates of knowledge should never be closed.*"

"If thou art exalted after having been low, if thou art rich after having been needy, harden not thy heart because of thy elevation. Thou hast but become a steward of the good things belonging to the gods."

"If thou wouldst be of good conduct and dwell apart from evil, beware of bad temper; for it contains the germs of all wickedness. When a man takes Justice for his guide and walks in her ways, there is no room in his soul for bad temper."

"If thou art a leader doing those things which are according to thy will, do for the best, which shall be remembered in time to come, so that the word which flatters, or feeds pride, or makes for vainglory, shall not weigh with thee."

"Treat well thy people, as it behooves thee; this is the duty of those whom the gods favor."

"Do not disturb a great man; do not distract the attention of the busy man. His care is to accomplish his task. Love for the work they have to do brings men nearer to the gods."

"Do not repeat the violent words [of others]. Do not listen to them. They have escaped a heated soul. If they are repeated in thy hearing, look on the ground and be silent."

"Take care of those who are faithful to thee, even when thine own estate is in evil case. So shall thy merit be greater than the honors which are done to thee." ("")

These, taken at random, are some of the wise words written by Ptah-hotep when, as he himself tells us, he had reached the patriarchal age of one hundred and ten years.

The Scribe Ani, who lived about one thousand years later, preaches the same just and gentle gospel. He says:

"Beware of giving pain by the words of thy mouth, and make not thyself to be feared."

"He who speaks evil, reaps evil."

"Work for thyself. Do not count upon the wealth of others; it will not enter thy dwelling-place."

"Do not eat bread in the presence of one who stands and waits, without putting forth thine hand towards the loaf for him."

"Enter not into a crowd if thou art there in the beginnings of a quarrel."

Good manners are the minor morality of life, and Ani was not only a sage but a man of the world. He has something to say on the subject of etiquette:

"Be not discourteous to the stranger who is in thy house. He is thy guest."

"Do not remain sitting when thy elder, or thy superior, is standing."

"If a deaf man is present, do not multiply words; it is better thou keep silent."

A demotic papyrus ("") of comparatively recent date (in the Louvre collection) contains a series of maxims of much the same character as those propounded by Ptah-hotep in the time of the Ancient Empire, and by the Scribe Ani under the New Empire; thus proving that the moral code of the Egyptians remained in all essential points the same, from the earliest to the latest chapter of their national history.

"Associate not thyself with the evil-doer," says this last moralist.

"Ill-treat not thine inferior; respect the aged."

"Ill-treat not thy wife, whose strength is less than thine. Be thou her protector."

"Save not thine own life at the expense of the life of another."

It is such brief and simple sayings as these which bring us nearest to the hearts of the old Egyptian people. We see them "as in a glass." and we see them at their best: a gentle, kindly, law-abiding race, anxious to cultivate peace and good-will, and to inculcate those rules of good conduct whereby their own lives had been guided. Their philosophy was not profound. They were not tormented by "the burden and the mystery of all this unintelligible world." They made no attempt to formulate or to solve those deeper problems which have perplexed the students of humanity since their time. To live happily, to live long, to deserve the favor of their superiors, to train their children in sane thinking and right-doing, to be respected in life and honorably remembered by posterity, represented the sum of their desires. It is a philosophy of utility and good-will, in which the ideal has no part.

The ancient Egyptians would have been unlike all other Orientals if they had not loved stories and songs; yet it was not till the first ancient Egyptian romance was discovered that any one dreamed of a popular literature of the days of the Pharaohs. We had, I suppose, been so accustomed to think of the ancient Egyptians as mummies that we scarcely remembered they were men. Those mummies, it is true, had once been alive in a solemn, leathery, unsympathetic way, as became a people who were destined to be spiced, bandaged, and ultimately consigned to glass-cases in modern museums. But as for an ancient Egyptian in love, chanting a sonnet to his mistress's eyebrow and accompanying himself on the lute—we should have blushed to think of him in connection with so trivial an occupation!

And yet, within the last five-and-thirty years, no less than fifteen or sixteen romantic stories, and almost as many love-songs, have been brought to light.(") Some had been lying undeciphered in the learned dust of various museums. Others were found in graves—buried, strange to say, with the mummies of their former owners. Some are as old as the Twelfth Dynasty; others are as recent as the time of Alexander and the Ptolemies. In some we recognize stories familiar to us from childhood as old nursery tales, and as stories first read in the *Arabian Nights Entertainments;* in others we discover the originals of legends which Herodotus, with a credulity peculiar to the learned, accepted for history. Even some of the fables attributed to Æsop are drawn from Egyptian sources older by eight hundred years than the famous dwarf who is supposed to have invented them. The fable of "The Lion and the Mouse" was discovered by Dr. Brugsch in an Egyptian papyrus a few years ago. "The Dispute of the Stomach and the Members" has yet more recently been identified by Professor Maspero with an ancient Egyptian original.(") When we remember, however, that tradition associates the name of Æsop with that of Rhodopis, who lived at Naukratis in the time of Amasis, we seem to be within touch of the actual connection between Æsop and Egypt.

Of this same Rhodopis it is said, in an ancient Egyptian story repeated by Herodotus, that an eagle flew away with her sandal while she was bathing, and dropped it at the feet of the Egyptian King, at Memphis. Struck by its beauty, he sent out his messengers in all directions to find the owner of this little sandal; and when they had found her, he made her his queen. In another Egyptian story, called "The Tale of the Two Brothers," a lock of hair from the head of a beautiful damsel is carried to Egypt by the river, and its perfume is so ravishing that the King despatches his scouts throughout the length and breadth of the land, that they may bring to him the owner of this lock of hair. She is found, of course, and she becomes his bride. In these tales we have apparently the germ of Cinderella.

In another story, called "The Taking of Joppa," we meet with what is unquestionably the original source of the leading incident in the familiar story of "Ali Baba and the Forty Thieves." One Tahuti, a general of Thothmes III., who is sent to lay siege to the city of Joppa, conceals two hundred of his soldiers in two hundred big jars, fills three hundred other jars with cords and fetters, loads five hundred other soldiers with these five hundred jars, and sends them into the city in the character of captives. Once inside the gates, the bearers liberate and arm their comrades, take the place, and make all the inhabitants prisoners. Now, although the King and the General are both historical personages, and although Joppa figures in the lists of cities conquered by Thothmes III., the story itself is evidently pure romance. As. for the big jars with their human cargoes, they are clearly the forefathers of the jars which housed the "Forty Thieves."

We turn to another story, called "The Doomed Prince," and we are at once reminded of the story of "Prince Agib and the Lodestone Mountain." After years of hope deferred, a king and queen are blessed with a beautiful son. The seven Hathors, who play the part of fairy godmothers in these old Egyptian stories, predict that the prince will die from the bite of a crocodile, a serpent, or a dog. The King accordingly builds a castle on the top of a lofty mountain, and there makes a state-prisoner of his son. His precautions are, of course, in vain. The young man escapes from durance vile, and becomes the husband of a lovely princess and the master of a faithful dog. The princess kills the serpent; the dog kills the crocodile; and, although the end of the story is unfortunately lost, it is evident that the dog, by some fatal accident, will fulfil his master's doom, just as the doom of Agib is fulfilled by his friend.

Another tale of extreme antiquity, entitled "The Shipwrecked Mariner," tells of a seaman cast on the shores of a desolate island abounding in delicious fruits, and inhabited by a limited population of seventy-five amiable and intelligent serpents. The head of this charming family was thirty cubits long. His body was incrusted with gold and *lapis lazuli*, and nature had adorned him with a magnificent beard. He talks like a book; treats the seaman with distinguished hospitality; and when a ship comes that way, dismisses his guest with gifts of perfumes, incense, rare woods, elephant-tusks, baboons, and all kinds of precious things. Here is probably the starting-point of our dear old friend, "Sindbad the Sailor," who was also cast among a population of serpents.

In others of these ancient fictions, King Khufu, the builder of the Great Pyramid; Prince Kha-em-uas, the favorite son of Rameses the Great; King Amasis, who gave Naukratis to the Greeks; and even the great Alexander himself, figure among the *dramatis personæ.*

Of the popular poetry of those far-off times we will take but two specimens, the one a love-song, from a papyrus in the British Museum; the other a rustic ditty, supposed to be sung by the driver of a pair of oxen, while they tread out the corn on the threshing-floor.

The love-song is sung by a girl to her lover. Each strophe begins with an invocation to a flower, thus curiously resembling the *stornelli* of the Tuscan peasantry, of which every verse begins and ends with a similar invocation to some familiar blossom or tree:

"Oh, flower of henna!
  My heart stands still in thy presence.
  I have made mine eyes brilliant for thee with kohl.
  When I behold thee, I fly to thee, oh my Beloved!
  Oh, Lord of my heart, sweet is this hour. An hour passed with
      thee is worth an hour of eternity!

"Oh, flower of marjoram!
  Fain would I be to thee as the garden in which I have planted
      flowers and sweet-smelling shrubs! the garden watered by
      pleasant runlets, and refreshed by the north breeze!
  Here let us walk, oh my Beloved, hand in hand, our hearts filled
      with joy!
  Better than food, better than drink, is it to behold thee.
  To behold thee, and to behold thee again!"

This is literally "the old, old story;" and the story this time is yet older than the song.(")

15

Our threshing-song dates from about 1650 B.C. It is carved on the walls of the tomb of one Pahiri, at El Kab in Upper Egypt, and it belongs to the early years of the Eighteenth Dynasty. In the wall-painting which illustrates the text, we see the oxen at work, just as in the Egypt of to-day, treading in a measured circle, with the driver seated on his revolving stool in the middle.

It is a simple chant of but four lines many times repeated.([*]) We know not the air to which it was sung; but no one who has listened to the monotonous songs of the Egyptian laborers as they ply the *shadûf* or the water-wheel, can fail to be struck by their evident antiquity. Doubtless, the cadenced chant intoned of old by Pahiri's laborers survives to this day among those so often heard by the modern traveller, as his boat glides along the broad waters of the sacred river. These are the words:

> " Thresh the corn, oh ye oxen !
> Thresh for yourselves, oh oxen !
> The fodder for eating,
> The grain for your master !"

It has been thus paraphrased by Mr. Gliddon:

> " Hie along oxen,
> Tread the corn faster !
> The straw for yourselves ;
> The grain for your master !"

The Religion of ancient Egypt is still very imperfectly understood. Every year, almost every day, we find ourselves compelled to abandon some long-established theory which, up to that moment, we had believed to be as self-evident as the pyramids, and as well understood as the law of gravitation. The opening of a tomb, the discovery of a papyrus, may at any moment put us in possession of religious texts older than the oldest yet known, and subversive, perhaps, of our best-founded assumptions.

This is precisely what happened when the pyramids of
Unas, Teta, and other very early kings were excavated in
1881 and 1882. Because the Great Pyramids of Ghizeh are
destitute of inscriptions, it had been rashly concluded that
all pyramids must be blank. Great, therefore, was the stu-
pefaction of those who pinned their faith upon that theory,
when the sepulchral chambers and passages of this group
were found to be lined with graven prayers and invocations,
some of which are more ancient than any religious texts previously known. Again, it had been laid down as one of the
fundamental facts of the Egyptian religion that certain gods,
whose renown was great at a later period, were as yet un-
born, so to speak, in the time of the Pyramid Kings. Thebes
was not founded till the beginning of the Eleventh Dynasty,
and Amen was the Great God of Thebes. Consequently,
Amen had no existence when the pyramids of Unas, Teta,
and Pepi, of the Fifth and Sixth Dynasties, were built. But
when those pyramids were laid open, Amen was found there
as a member of the cycle of great deities.

We cannot, in fact, exercise too much caution in formulat-
ing general rules, or in making use of elastic definitions. We
speak, for instance, of " the Egyptian religion ;" but there can
hardly be a much more misleading phrase. Just as Professor
Revillout has said of the Egyptian language that " it is not
one language, but a whole family of languages," so I would
say of the Egyptian religion, that it is not one religion, but a
whole family of religions. This family springs, it is true,
from one very ancient stock ; but it branches out into innumerable varieties. It is not too much to say that there was
in Egypt a Religion of the Pyramid Period, a Religion of the
Theban Period, a Religion of Saïs, a Religion of the Ptolemaic age, a Popular Religion, a Sacerdotal Religion, a Relig-
ion of Polytheism, a Religion of Pantheism, a Religion of
Monotheism, and a Religion of Platonic Philosophy. And
these religions were not revolutionary. The new did not
drive out the old, as the bud pushes off the dead leaf in autumn. On the contrary, the Egyptians, who were nothing

if not conservative, clung with the strictest fidelity to the old, even while ardently embracing the new. It did not matter in the least, if the dogmas of one school were diametrically opposed to the dogmas of half a dozen other schools; they continued to believe them all.(⁶⁰)

The one great and crucial question—the question which we are most keenly concerned to resolve—is whether the ancient Egyptians believed in one God, or in many gods. In Ra, the supreme solar deity, are we to recognize the Egyptian synonym for "Almighty God, Maker of Heaven and Earth, and of all that in them is?" Are the other deities of the Egyptian Pantheon mere personifications of his divine attributes? Does Knum represent his creative power? Does Amen, the Hidden One, signify his unsearchable mystery? Does Thoth, the ibis-headed god of letters, typify his wisdom, and the bull Apis his strength, and the jackal Anubis his swiftness? Are these animal-headed and bird-headed and reptile-headed forms mere hieroglyphs, of which the secret meaning is the unity and omnipresence of God?

This theory was elaborated in the first instance by M. Pierret, in his *Essai sur la Mythologie Egyptienne;* and it has been still further developed by Dr. Brugsch in his recent work on *The Religion and Mythology of the Ancient Egyptians.* As it is the most attractive exposition of the Egyptian Pantheon, so it is undoubtedly the most popular, and I therefore doubly regret that I am unable to follow M. Pierret and Dr. Brugsch in their proposed solution of this deeply interesting problem. This solution is founded on the assumption that the religion of the Egyptians was, from first to last, absolutely homogeneous; and that in all its complex developments it merely presented varying aspects of one simple, fundamental, and God-given truth. In this sense, all the gods of Egypt are one and the same, the name merely changing with the seat of worship. Animal worship becomes mere symbolism; and Knum, Sebek, Horus, Thoth, Anubis, and the rest, are but reflections of an omnipresent Deity.

The Egyptians were, unquestionably, the most wonderful people of antiquity; but they would have been infinitely more wonderful had they started in life with notions so just, so philosophic, so exalted, as these. The earliest Egyptian monuments to which we can assign a date are the monuments of a people already highly civilized, and in the possession of an alphabetic system of writing, a grammar, a government, and a religion. It must have taken them long ages to arrive at this advanced stage of their national development; and of those ages a few vague traditions and the names of three dynasties of kings have alone survived. Yet there must have been a time when these people were mere unlettered barbarians, like the forefathers of other nations. They did not spring fully civilized from the mud of the inundation, like Athena from the head of Zeus. As a matter of fact, the barbarian origin of the Egyptians is more distinctly traceable than the barbarian origin of any other highly civilized nation of antiquity. It is traceable in their laws, in their customs, and even in their costumes. Above all, it is traceable in their religion.

We have but to turn our eyes to the far West of America in order to discover the living solution of some of our most puzzling Egyptian problems. Just as the northern half of that great continent was originally possessed by tribes of Indians, so the land of Egypt, in the ages before history, was divided into many small territories, each territory peopled by an independent clan. The red man had, and has, his "totems," or clan crests; these "totems" being sometimes animals, as the bear, the wolf, the beaver, the deer; and sometimes birds, as the snipe, the hawk, the heron. So, in like manner, the prehistoric tribes of ancient Eygpt will have had their "totems," taken from the familiar beasts, birds, and reptiles of the Nile Valley—the jackal, the crocodile, the ibis, and so forth.

Now, a distinctive appellation is one of the first necessities of life, whether savage or civilized; and in an age when proper names, and the occupations from which proper names

are largely derived, are yet unknown, the tribal name is of
extreme importance. For this tribal name, the savage naturally adopts that of some creature whose strength, subtlety,
swiftness, or fearlessness may symbolize such qualities in
himself. These facts are true of barbarian and semi-civilized
races in all parts of the world. The Bechuanas of South
Africa, the Kols of Khota Nagpar in Asia, the Yakats of
Siberia in Northern Europe, the aborigines of Australia, are
all divided into clans, each clan being affiliated to some beast,
bird, fish, or reptile. They all regard the "totem" animal
as sacred. They forbear to eat it; and if compelled in self-
defence to kill it, they ask its pardon for the act.

Here, then, we have the origin of animal worship—animal
worship being the direct outcome of totemism.

Now, what is true of these American, South African, Asiatic, European, and Australian tribes, must surely be true
also of the prehistoric Egyptians. They began with totemism — the Bull-clan at Memphis, the Crocodile-clan in the
Fayûm, the Ibis-clan at Hermopolis, and so forth.(") As time
went on and civilization progressed, they explained away the
grosser features of this creed by representing the totem animal as the symbol, or incarnation, of an unseen deity; and
there is no clearer proof of the extreme antiquity of their
civilization than the fact that they had already reached this
point in their spiritual career when Mena, the first king of
the First Dynasty, laid the foundation-stone of the Temple
of Ptah, at Memphis.

But, having started from totemism, animal worship, and
polytheism, did they not rise at last to higher things — to
monotheism, pure and simple?

Yes; they did rise to monotheism; but not, I think, to
monotheism pure and simple. Their monotheism was not
exactly our monotheism : it was a monotheism based upon,
and evolved from, the polytheism of earlier ages. Could we
question a high-priest of Thebes of the time of the Nineteenth
or Twentieth Dynasty on the subject of his faith, we should
be startled by the breadth and grandeur of his views touch-

ing the Godhead. He would tell us that Ra was the Great
All; that by his word alone he called all things into existence; that all things are therefore but reflections of himself
and his will; that he is the creator of day and night, of the
heavenly spheres, of infinite space; that he is the eternal es-
sence, invisible, omnipresent, omniscient; in a word, that he
is God Almighty.

If, after this, we could put the same questions to a high-
priest of Memphis, we should receive a very similar answer,
only we should now be told that this great divinity was Ptah.
And if we could make the tour of Egypt, visiting every great
city, and questioning the priests of every great temple in turn,
we should find that each claimed these attributes of unity
and universality for his own local god. All, nevertheless,
would admit the identity of these various deities. They
would admit that he whom they worshipped at Heliopolis
as Ra was the same as he whom they worshipped at Memphis as Ptah, and at Thebes as Amen. We have proof of
their catholicity in this respect. Ptah and Apis were, of
course, one and the same; but Apis was also recognized as
"The Soul of Osiris, and the Life of Tum." Again, Amen
and Knum and Sebek were made one with Ra, and became
Amen-Ra, Knum-Ra, and Sebek-Ra. This, however, was but
a compromise, and they never got beyond it. That individual theologians rose to the height of pure monotheism cannot be doubted. Those who conceived and formulated the
exalted pantheism of Ra-worship cannot have failed to go
that one step further; but that one step further would be
heresy, and heresy was not likely to leave records for future
historians in a land where the governing classes were all
members of the priesthood. In a word, it is certain—absolutely certain—that every great local deity was worshipped as
the "one God" of his own city or province; and it is also
certain that, to whatever extent these gods were identified
one with another, the Egyptians never agreed to abolish
their Pantheon in favor of one, and only one, supreme deity.([20])

There is, however, one central fact which must never be over-looked in any discussion of the religion of the old Egyptian people. They were the first in the history of the world who recognized, and held fast by, the doctrine of the immortality of the soul. Look back as far as we will into the darkness of their past, question as closely as we may the earliest of their monuments, and we yet find them looking forward to an eternal future.

Their notions of Man, the microcosm, were more complex than ours. They conceived him to consist of a Body, a Soul, a Spirit, a Name, a Shadow, and a Ka—that Ka which I have ventured to interpret as the Life ;* and they held that the perfect reunion of all these parts was a necessary condition of the life to come. Hence the care with which they em-balmed the Body; hence the food and drink offerings with which they nourished the Ka; hence the funerary texts with which they lined the tomb, and the funerary papyri which they buried with the mummy for the instruction of the Soul. But none of these precautions availed, unless the man had lived a pure and holy life in this world, and came before the judgment-seat of Osiris with clean hands, a clean heart, and a clean conscience.

"Glory to thee, O thou Great God, thou Lord of truth and justice!" says the dead man, when brought into the presence of the eternal Judge. "Lo! I have defrauded no man of his dues. I have not oppressed the widow. I have not borne false witness. I have not been slothful. I have broken faith with no man. I have starved no man. I have slain no man. I have not enriched myself by unlawful gains. I have not given short measure of corn. I have not tampered with the scales. I have not encroached upon my neighbor's field. I have not cut off the running water from its lawful channel. I have not turned away the food from the mouths of the fatherless. Lo! I am pure! I am pure!"

This is from the Negative Confession in the 125th chapter

---

* See chap. iii.

of the most famous religious book of the ancient Egyptians
—*The Book of the Dead.* It gives the measure of their standard of morality. The teachers who established that standard,
and the people who endeavored faithfully to live up to it,
may have had very childish and fantastic notions on many
points; they may in one place have put gold rings in the
ears of their sacred crocodiles ; they may have shaved their
eyebrows when their cats died; but as regards uprightness,
charity, justice, and mercy, they would not, I think, have
much to learn from us, if they were living to this day beside
the pleasant waters of the Nile.

VIGNETTE FROM THE BOOK OF THE DEAD.

VII.

THE HIEROGLYPHIC WRITING OF THE ANCIENT EGYPTIANS.

A CELEBRATED definition of the *genus homo* classifies man as "a cooking animal." It is not a bad definition. Cooking implies the knowledge and use of fire; and not even the most intelligent of monkeys has yet been known to evoke sparks from a stick and a block. I should prefer, however, to define man as "a writing animal;" for writing implies language as its starting-point, and literature as its goal. Given the first barbarian attempt at transmitting intelligence by means of signs scratched on rocks or graven on the bark of trees, it is but a step—a long step, I admit—from the drift-man to Shakespeare.

The infancy of writing has much in common with the infancy of language. Of the actual beginnings of language we have no positive knowledge beyond such evidence as is furnished by the syllabic particles known as "roots;" but it is quite certain that all speech was at first extremely simple —that words were monosyllabic, and that prehistoric man eked out his limited vocabulary with gestures. He was, in fact, a natural and involuntary pantomimist; and pantomime is picture-action.

Now, the immortal Dogberry, when he said that reading and writing came by nature, told quite half the truth. Writing is a spontaneous growth, like speech ; and, like speech, it is the offspring of necessity. Man needs to communicate with his fellow-man ; and when distance, or any other cause, makes *viva voce* intercourse impossible, he sets his brains to work to find a substitute for spoken words. No matter in what country, in what age, or under what circumstances, this problem is invariably solved in the same manner.

Just as prehistoric man supplements his lack of words with what I have ventured to call "picture-action," so, at a later stage of his career, he inevitably invents "picture-writing." This is true of every ancient script of which we have any knowledge. The writing of the Egyptians undoubtedly began as a picture-writing, pure and simple; and notwithstanding the many phases through which it passed in the course of thousands of years, a picture-writing, to some extent, it continued to the end of the chapter. The writing of the Hittites was a picture-writing; and even the arrow-head writing of the Babylonians and Assyrians, and the contorted characters of the Chinese, are abridged picture-writings in which the pictorial forms are yet in some instances discernible. But even the rudest stage of picture-writing must have been preceded by some yet more primitive effort, and the direction taken by that primitive effort may probably be traced in a curious story told by Herodotus. He relates how Darius, when he invaded Scythia, was led on continually by the retreating foe, till he and his army were outwearied by guerilla warfare without being able to bring the Scythians to a

pitched battle. At last, the Scythian princes despatched a
herald to the Persian camp with gifts for the great King of
Kings. These consisted of a bird, a mouse, a frog, and five
arrows. In vain the Persians interrogated the herald. He
but made answer that, if they were wise, they would find out
the meaning of these things for themselves. Then Darius,
the self-confident, proclaimed that the Scythian gifts signi-
fied that they gave up land and water, the bird for swift
flight, the mouse for land, the frog for water, the arrows as
a surrender of arms. But one Gobryas, wiser than Darius,
interpreted the message thus:

"Unless, O Persians, ye can turn yourselves into birds
and fly through the air, or become mice and burrow under
the ground, or be as frogs and take refuge in the fens, ye
shall never escape from this land, but die pierced by our
arrows."(⁶³) And this interpretation was the true one.

Now, in what way were these objects conveyed to Darius?

Were they strung in a leash, like game; or carried as a
horseman might be supposed to carry them, in a saddle-bag?

I do not think so. I believe that they were pinned down
upon a piece of board, so forming a high-relief group composed of natural objects.

Now, we may be very certain that this message of the
Scythian generals was no isolated instance. It was the customary style of polite letter-writing in Scythia at that period, the Scythians being in just that stage of barbarism
which the Persians, the Egyptians, and the other great nations of the East had left behind and forgotten. I imagine
that all those nations had once upon a time invented the
very same method. To pin objects on a board would always have been easier than to draw them; and our prehistoric man, of whatever race or climate, would assuredly have
recourse to symbolism by means of *things* before he dreamed
of symbolism by means of *signs*. Thus, "object-writing"
would naturally precede "picture-writing."

The earliest writing of which we have any historic example is the hieroglyphic writing of the ancient Egyptians;

and the earliest of early hieroglyphs are carved *in relief*. I cannot help thinking that this fact is profoundly significant —significant of the origin of those hieroglyphs, a long way back, as "object-writing." The oldest Egyptian inscriptions are older than the Great Pyramid. The earliest date from the Second Dynasty, and carry us back to full four thousand three hundred years before the Christian era. But they testify to a foregone time, the extent of which it is impossible to estimate. For, although they are the oldest extant, the language they embody has already passed through its first stages of evolution. Its grammar is formed; its rules are fixed; the foundations of style are laid. As for the writing, it is already systematized, and the methods are fully developed by which sense and sound are expressed.

Some day, perhaps, as the work of exploration goes on, our labors may be rewarded by the discovery of yet earlier records. We have reason to believe that the most ancient necropolis of all—the necropolis of the kings of the First and Second dynasties—lies buried under a hundred feet of sand round about the base of the Great Sphinx. This huge amphitheatre is in course of excavation; and it is quite possible—possible and probable—that inscriptions in the earliest stages of the hieroglyphic writing may there be discovered.

Till then, if we desire to realize what the first attempts at writing were like in the East, we must turn for light to the West. We must go to America for specimens of the earliest picture-writing of Mexico, and for the picture-writing of the red Indians. In these we behold groups of what are called in Egyptology "ideographs;" that is to say, pictures of objects arranged for the purpose of conveying sequences of ideas, but without any of those connecting links which language supplies. The tribute-lists of the Mexican kings consist of long catalogues, in which there are signs for numerals, but nothing resembling a word. Thus, one hundred strings of beads, two hundred pitchers of honey, sixteen hundred cacao-nuts, and eight hundred loads of feather mantles are represented by a string of beads, a pitcher, a basket of nuts, and a feather mantle neatly drawn and colored, with numeral signs to show how many of each were received. This is the merest picture-writing; yet, as a system of exact book-keeping. it leaves nothing to be desired.

Other Mexican documents of the same period contain accounts of battles, executions, sacrifices, and even family histories, in which every fact is a picture. We see a youth bidding good-bye to his father; starting upon a journey; sitting at the feet of the sage by whom he is to be educated; serving his apprenticeship as a woodman; sending an old woman to treat with the parents of the girl whom he desires to wed; and, finally, the marriage ceremony, where bride and bridegroom are bound together by a scarf. This is neither more nor less than a " nutshell novel," and it is written in pictures only.

But the picture - writing of the North American Indian, though less graphic, is often more ingenious than the picture-writing of the Mexicans. I will take, for example, a petition addressed by certain Indian chiefs to one of the Presidents of the United States, reclaiming possession of a chain of lakes in the neighborhood of Lake Superior.

In this curious document, the head man of each tribe is figured by the "totem," or symbolic animal, of his clan; as

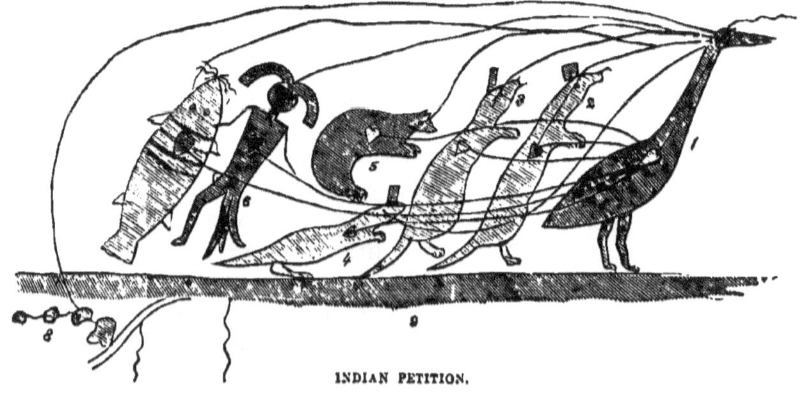

INDIAN PETITION.

the Crane, the Marten, the Sloth Bear, the Catfish, and so on. These creatures are represented as walking in procession, the Crane taking the lead, and the Catfish bringing up the rear. The eye and the heart of each is carefully indicated, the heart being just such a heart as we absurdly depict on our playing-cards and valentines. Beneath their feet is seen a sheet of water—probably intended for Lake Superior—and this sheet of water communicates by a tributary stream with the little lakes for which our Indians are making their petition. Now, from the eye of the Crane is drawn one line leading round to the coveted lake district, and another line going off into space, and supposed to lead to the eye of the President. Then, from the eyes of the Martens, the Sloth Bear, and the rest are drawn similar lines leading to the eye of the Crane, thus indicating that their views and his are the same. A line is also drawn from the heart of each creature to the heart of the Crane, showing that the heart's desire of all is identical. For combined simplicity and subtlety this is the best example of pure picture-writing with which I am acquainted.

And here let me say a word about the parallel so frequently drawn between the savage and prehistoric man, and about what is erroneously called the "picture-writing" of prehistoric times. A few fragments of bone scratched with spirited outlines of the cave-bear, the mammoth, and other extinct animals—a few specimens of delicate bone-carvings —a few rude attempts at depicting boats, men, and animals, cut here and there upon the face of a cliff in Scandinavia or Siberia, or the Maritime Alps, have come down to us from the ages before history. The immense antiquity of these is self-proven, since they can only have been executed by men who were contemporary with the animals they depicted. Those men were the cave-dwellers of the palæolithic period —that far-distant time when the hairy rhinoceros, the mammoth, the reindeer, and the hyena ranged the forests of France and Belgium; when there was as yet no English Channel; when the Thames was a tributary of the Rhine;

and when the bed of the German Ocean was one vast plain over which great herds of these formidable beasts migrated from north to south, or from south to north, as summer was succeeded by winter, and winter by summer. There are few things in this world more interesting than these pathetic relics of our remotest ancestors. They bring very near to us the life of the cave-man—that life which was a daily warfare with beasts of prey; and they are certainly the most ancient specimens of fine art in the world.

PREHISTORIC INCISED OUTLINE REPRESENTING THE MAMMOTH ON A FRAGMENT OF BONE.
From Sir J. Lubbock's *History of Civilization.*

But they are not picture-writings. They are sketches— sketches done with a flint point by an artist clad in skins, who fashioned his own stone hatchets, chipped his own arrow-heads, and lived in an age when there was neither society nor government.

This cave-man was not, strictly speaking, a savage; nor is the argument either just or scientific which likens him to the red man, or the bush-man, or any other race of untamable aborigines. He was simply a man whose foot was on the lowest step of the ladder, but who was steadily working his way upward to civilization.

The historic age in Egypt begins with Mena, the first king

of the First Dynasty; but, as there was a prehistoric age in Europe, so there was also a prehistoric age in Egypt — the age of the " Horshesu."(")

The land was divided at this time into petty principalities governed by hereditary chieftains. That was, in all probability, the era of mere picture-writing. How long it took the ancient Egyptians to emerge from this first stage of the art. it is impossible even to guess. Perhaps they had already emerged from it when Mena reduced the primitive chieftains to a state of vassalage, and converted their territories into the provinces of his new Empire. Be this as it may, we do know quite exactly, step by step, how the art and mystery of the scribe's craft was developed in the Valley of the Nile; and if we are unable to put a date to those successive stages, we can at all events trace them with unerring certainty.

The first stage is " ideography," or mere picture - writing, in which a man stands for a man, a ship for a ship, a camel for a camel, and so forth. But to construct a sentence by means of pure ideography is impossible. Tenses, parts of speech, and all those grammatical contrivances whereby we connect or separate ideas are wanting. The very pictures are liable to misinterpretation. Even now, the helpless tourist in a foreign land is sometimes reduced to picture-writing to express his modest requirements; but the result is seldom satisfactory. The Englishman who sketched a mushroom on the margin of the bill of fare at a Paris restaurant, was naturally disappointed when the waiter brought him an umbrella.

A long course of umbrellas, so to speak, and the confusion to which it must have led, paved the way for another kind of picture-writing, in which *sounds* were expressed instead of things — namely, pictorial phonetism; and pictorial phonetism registers the second stage in the art of writing. Now, in pictorial phonetism each figure stands for the sound of the word denoting the object represented, that word being generally, though not necessarily, used in a far-fetched sense.

16

The illustration gives us an example in our own language: an eye, a can, a sail, a round, and a globe.

If we but look at these figures, they have neither sense nor sequence. They are intelligible only when pronounced: "I can sail round the globe."

This is pictorial phonetism; and pictorial phonetism is, in fact, pictorial punning, of the sort commonly known as the rebus, or charade.

From picture-writing to pictorial phonetism was an enormous stride; but as we know nothing of the condition of the Egyptian vocabulary at that remote time, we cannot possibly estimate to what extent pictorial phonetism supplied a means of coherent communication between man and man. That the language contained a very large number of monosyllabic words is, however, certain; and as phonetism is necessarily syllabic, we may assume that the earliest Egyptian scribes had a rich mine of syllabic forms to draw upon. These syllabic forms represent the common objects of daily life, the names of which belonged to the earliest period of the language, when all words were monosyllabic; as: *mer*, a hoe; *ma*, a sickle; *neb*, a bowl, and so forth. These, and

such as these, were readily adapted for phonetic syllables, and had the advantage of being so well known that a summary representation in outline was at once recognizable. In the autumn of 1889, and again in the autumn of 1890, I had the pleasure of examining Mr. Pe-

tric's most interesting collection of domestic objects discovered in the ruins of Kahun—a site of which I have already
had occasion to say something in Chapter IV. of this volume
—and I well remember the thrill with which I saw and
handled some of these very objects. There was a hoe, for
instance, exactly like the hoe of the hieroglyphs—a simple
implement enough, of old brown wood, with the ancient
cord of palm-fibre yet in its place.

There, too, was the handle of an adze — a very familiar
hieroglyph, signifying *sotep*, ⌐— which often occurs in royal
names; and, above all, there was one perfect sickle, the han-

dle and blade of wood, with three little flint saws cemented
into the inner side of the curve—a most interesting implement, and the first of its kind yet discovered. All these
tools and implements were of the extremely ancient period
of the Twelfth Dynasty, about two thousand eight hundred
years before the Christian era. That is to say, they were close
upon five thousand years old. But that sickle carried with
it a yet older history. It carried on the traditions of a time
when the use of metals was unknown; and it pointed back,
as with Time's own finger, to that far-off prehistoric age
from which its shape and make had been handed down without alteration.

Just as pictorial phonetism was evolved from ideography, or picture-writing, so was alphabetism evolved from pictorial phonetism. Now, when writing has reached the alphabetic stage, it enters upon the last, and by far the most important, phase of its development. Every real obstacle to the free transmission of thought is overcome. The foundations of history and science are laid. The instrument of literature is found. And it was the ancient Egyptians who found and fashioned that instrument. To them we owe the invention of the first alphabet—the most precious and momentous invention of all time. And they invented it so inconceivably long ago that they were in the full possession of vowels and consonants. and of the art of spelling words by means of letters instead of syllables, when they carved the oldest inscriptions in existence.

Other ancient writings passed through the same three stages of development—picture-writing, pictorial phonetism, and alphabetic writing; but the oldest alphabets of other nations are modern when compared with that of the Egyptians. The cuneiform writing of Babylonia and Assyria, after crystallizing for ages as a syllabic script, ended by becoming an alphabetic writing in the hands of the Medes and Persians; but by that time the Egyptians had been using their alphabet for some three thousand five hundred years. Again, the cuneiform never overleaped the great mountain range which divides Asia Minor from Asia; whereas that other alphabet whose origin lies so far back in the darkness before dawn that we cannot discern its beginning—the alphabet of the ancient Egyptians—was the parent stock of the Phœnician, of the Greek, and of all the alphabets of Europe, including, of course, our own.

But how was the Egyptian alphabet constructed? Upon what principle was it founded?

These are questions upon which Egyptologists differ; for even Egyptologists (who are by far the most amiable people on the face of the globe) do sometimes, like doctors, disagree. According, however, to the theory most commonly accepted, the process was effected in this way. A monosyllabic word was selected, as, for instance, *bu*, the Egyptian for "leg," represented in simple picture-writing by a leg, thus: To convert *bu* into *b*, it was but necessary to drop the final vowel, and let the leg stand for *b* only. The same with *ro*, the mouth, represented thus in the picture-writing. The vowel sound being dropped, they obtained the letter *r*. A reed of the sort which grows abundantly in the Delta was called *aak*. It was conventionally represented thus. By preserving only the initial sound they obtained the vowel *a*. In this way, a certain number of vowels and consonants were detached from the old phonetic words, some being dropped from the beginning, and some from the end, of a familiar monosyllable. They were thus formed into a regular alphabet—the parent alphabet of all our European series.

But the parent was, in some respects, very unlike its children. It contained no letter *e*, no *g*, no *d*, no *z;* but it made up for these deficiencies by extreme liberality in other ways. It contained no less than three forms of *a*, three forms of *t*, and two forms each for *i*, *u*, *m*, *n*, *k*, and *s*. After this, it is some relief to know that they had but one *b*, one *p*, and one *f*.

Here is the hieroglyphic alphabet as it was commonly in use :

Vowels ...   *a*,   *a*,   *ā*,   or \\ *i*,   or © *u*.

Labials ...   *b*,   *p*,   *f*.

Liquids ..   or *m*,   or *n*,   or *r*.

Palatals ..   *k*,   *k*,   *q*.

Gutturals .   *h*,   *h*,   *χ*.

Sibilants ..   or *s*,   *s* (= English *sh*).

Dentals ...   *t*,   *t*,   *θ*,   *t'*.

All these letters must have stood originally for monosyllabic words belonging to the earliest stage of the language; but it is no longer possible to identify the source of every letter, owing, doubtless, to the fact that many of the oldest words had become obsolete by the time when the alphabet had reached that point of development at which our knowledge of it begins.

And now it will naturally be concluded that our Egyptians threw aside their old childish picture-writing, their clumsy phonetic picture-punning, and all the swaddling-clothes in which their infant literature had till then been smothered. Not in the least. The Egyptians were, of all nations, the most conservative. A custom, a belief, a method once adopted was never wholly relinquished. Being in possession of an alphabet, they proceeded, of course, to write words as we do, spelling them letter by letter; but they still clung to the old ideographs, tacking them on at the end, so as to make quite sure that there should be no mistake about the meaning—like those sign-board artists who take the wise precaution of adding, "This is a lion," or "This is a cow."

Thus, in writing the word *hetra*, which is the Egyptian for "horse," they began by spelling it letter by letter, omitting only the vowel *e*, which did not exist in their alphabet.

The word being now spelled, they next added the figure of the horse—a distinct survival of the old picture-writing. Finally, not being content with the word and the ideograph, they added the determinative sign representing a hide, a hide being the conventional symbol for all four-footed animals.

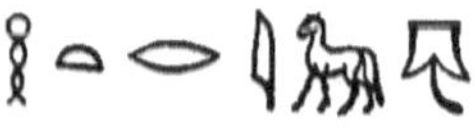

We will take another example. *Ab*, "thirst," is spelled *a-b*. Now *ab*, spelled in the same way, also signifies a kid. We would therefore expect to see the figure of the kid placed after the word when used in this sense, but we would not expect to see it if the word were used in the sense of "thirst." It was retained, however, all the same, merely to express its original syllabic value; that is to say, the figure of the kid is added to emphasize the pronunciation of the word *ab*.  Next, to show that the kid has nothing to do with the sense of the word, but that *ab* stands for "thirst," they added the hiero-glyphic sign for "water." Even this was  not enough. To clinch the sense of the whole, they finally added the figure of a man with his hand to his mouth, indicating his desire to drink. Thus, to a monosyl-labic noun of two letters only, we have three determinatives: a determinative of *sound*—namely, the kid, signifying *ab*; a determinative of *sense*—namely, water; and the generic determinative commonly in use to denote actions performed by the mouth, such as speaking, eating, and drinking. A more cumbrous system could not be con-ceived; yet in so far as we are concerned, its complexity is its greatest recommendation. Had the Egyptians been less conservative, had they rejected their early methods when they invented the alphabet, we could not have traced the stratification of the language or the writing. In such an example as the last we clearly read the history of both.

Perhaps the most remarkable feature of the hieroglyphic writing is the extraordinary number and variety of the signs. Of these characters there are about 3000, including 29 alpha-betic letters, 140 phonetic signs, and upward of 200 deter-minatives. This strikes us as an embarrassment of riches. It is certainly not the sort of writing which advertisers un-dertake to teach in twelve lessons. At the same time the study of hieroglyphs is much more fascinating, and much less difficult, than might be imagined.

The signs, we must remember, are not mere arbitrary and meaningless figures. They are more or less pictorial; and they represent an immense number of interesting objects of all kinds—tools, weapons, plants, and the like. The amount of information locked up in these little figures is quite incal-culable. They show us with what kind of plough the ancient

Egyptian husbandman tilled the soil; the sickle with which he reaped his harvest; the wine-press in which he crushed his grapes. There, too, we see the drill and auger and chisel of the carpenter; the spear and shield of the soldier; the crown and sceptre of the Pharaoh; the harp and lute of the minstrel; the ink-bottle and pen-case of the scribe. And there, also, are the lotus lily and papyrus plant; the crocodile, the hippopotamus, and the fishes of the Nile; the jackal and hare of the desert; the hawk, the pelican, the crane, the ibis, the vulture, and every other bird that haunts the banks of the great river. The sacred beetle, the hooded cobra, the eared cerastes, the scorpion, the lizard, and all creatures that burrow in the sands or lurk in rocks and caves, have likewise their place in this wonderful picture-gallery—for that is just what it is. A hieroglyphic dictionary, or a list of hieroglyphic characters, is in fact a pictorial encyclopædia of all the objects, natural or artificial, animate or inanimate, which were known to the Egyptians.

The human figure plays a conspicuous part in the hieroglyphic system, being employed as a determinative sign in many different ways.

It continually occurs, for instance, as a determinative of gender. After such words as "youth," "slave," "father," "scribe," there follows the figure of a man sitting.

After "wife," "queen," "daughter," "sister," "maiden," and the like, we find the figure of a seated woman. These are generic determinatives.

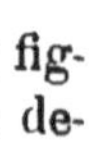

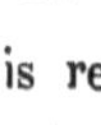

But there are also special determinatives. Say that an inscription refers to some high official, that official's name is followed by the figure of a man walking with a staff; the staff being the emblem of authority, as, indeed, it is in Egypt to this day. Or say that an old man is in question, then his name is followed by a stooping figure, leaning heavily upon a stick; this being the determinative for age or infirmity. An act of worship is recorded, and straightway the scribe adds a figure in the attitude of adoration. A man standing with his arms flung up above his head signifies joy or exultation. A man with his hands and arms in the position of repelling means dissuasion, turning back, repudiation. It is a question of eating, drinking, or speaking, and we have a squatting figure with the hand to the mouth. Or it is a question of singing or declaiming, and the determinative figure at once assumes a parliamentary attitude.

Now, there is a special and peculiar interest attaching to these determinatives, which are of extreme antiquity, and belong to the earliest known stage of the writing. They are evident reminiscences of the old "gesture language"—that "picture action" to which I have referred as coeval with the beginnings of human speech. In this fashion our "rude forefathers" supplemented their scanty vocabulary. The gestures first employed as a necessity were continued at a later period as a matter of habit; and thus, when primitive man had so far advanced upon the path of civilization as to attempt picture-writing, he naturally had recourse to the representation of picture action in order to indicate emotions and conditions of being for which, in the absence of an alphabet, he had no other means of expression.

In addition to hieroglyphs of the whole figure, there is a considerable series representing only parts of the figure.

A nose, for instance, was the determinative for smelling or breathing; an ear stood for hearing; a head for command, precedence, superiority. Any reference to walking or travelling was followed by a pair of legs; and if it were a question of returning. the legs were reversed. Thus, when it is said in *The Book of the Dead* that the virtuous Soul is privileged to go in and out of Hades, the sentence concludes with both determinatives.

And this reminds me of a similar device in the Mexican picture-writing, where the act of going to and fro is indicated by footprints—such footprints as are made by a bare foot upon the sands.

It may be objected that these are not in the least like footprints, for that is an observation frequently made ; but it only shows how seldom we see the print of a bare foot, and how little we cultivate our powers of observation. For the Mexican ideogram is, in truth, strictly correct. We do not touch the ground with the inner side of the sole of the foot; consequently that side leaves no mark. Neither does the little toe make any sensible impression. It is, therefore, only the four first toes, the flat "tread" beneath them, and the outer side of the sole which are printed off at each step.

But to return to our Egyptians. Here is a sign composed of two arms, with the hands open and the palms turned downward. This is the determinative sign for denial. Here we have a palpable survival of the "gesture language." It is precisely the action of the modern conjuror who assures his audience that he has nothing whatever in his hands; and it distinctly points to an age when force was the law of the strong, and theft was the resource of the weak, and every man's hand was against his neighbor. Such an example is a piece of fossilized history.

To those who know anything (though never so little) about this curious and interesting subject, it sometimes happens to be asked whether the study of hieroglyphs is not, in truth, of extraordinary difficulty. To this question it may be replied that the study of hieroglyphs is sufficiently easy up to a certain point, after which it becomes more, and increasingly more, difficult. It needs but a very little perseverance to enable the student to master so much knowledge as may suffice for the translation of the ordinary run of funerary or dedicatory inscriptions ; but it is when he comes to deal with the archaic forms of the earliest periods, or the corrupt and complicated forms of the latest periods, that his troubles may be said to begin. Apart, however, from archaisms and corruptions, there is, as it seems to me, another and a very real difficulty which we moderns have to encounter when we begin to study the language and writing of the ancient Egyptians. It is not that the grammar is abstruse; on the contrary, the grammar is singularly elementary. It is not that the hieroglyphs are puzzling, or hard to remember. Being pictorial, they tell their own story, and are as easy to remember as the objects they represent. It is not even the alarming fact that there are 3000 of them; for of those 3000, only a limited number were in common use. It is for none of these reasons. Our real stumbling-block is the amazing and utterly childlike simplicity of the whole thing. It is a simplicity which belongs to the time "when all the world was young;" and now that all the world is old, we do not know what to make of it. We are born with nineteenth century brains; and we cannot put our brains back, as if they were the hands of a clock. Yet it is only by putting our brains back that we can possibly contrive to get behind the simplicity of ancient Egyptian thought. That simplicity of thought, joined to admirable powers of observation, a speculative turn of mind, and a curiously literal method of reasoning, led this singular people to construct a theory of the universe and an elaborate system of religion which so strongly affected their arts, their literature, and even their hieroglyphs, that unless one knows what they thought and believed on a great many subjects, it is impossible to grasp the meaning of many an ordinary looking character.

Here, for instance, is the ideograph   for *pet*, the "sky." It represents a ceiling, or,   rather, a crossbeam supporting a ceiling. This looks like a metaphor; but it is nothing of the kind. The Egyptians conceived the sky to be a ceiling, or overhead platform of iron, along which flowed the waters of the heavenly ocean. Daily, from east to west, this heavenly ocean was traversed by Ra, the sun-god, in his golden bark. But at night the iron ceiling was lighted by lamps, each star in the firmament being a lamp watched over by an attendant god. We add a star suspended by a string (the loose end of the string hangs down at the other side of the beam), and this sign—the sign *pet* with the star added—is the determinative hieroglyph signifying "night," "darkness," "gloom," and all such notions. These suspended lamps were the fixed stars, and the gods of the fixed stars were stationary; but the planets were lamps carried on the heads of wandering gods who sailed the heavens as earthly mariners sail the seas, steering their barks by the divine chart, and following fixed courses according to the seasons.* In the mean while the iron ceiling, which formed the bed of the great upper ocean, was supported at the four corners by the four sons of Horus—the gods of the four cardinal points. They upheld it by means of four props shaped thus: —forked boughs, in fact, such as were used to support the roof of the primitive house. When it rained, the rain was taken to be an overflow from the superincumbent ocean: and if it rained heavily (which is very unusual in every part of Egypt except the Delta), then every one was terrified lest the props should be giving way, and the ceiling and the ocean should both be coming down together.

Here we have the hieroglyph for rain, consisting of the ceiling and the four props. The props should, of course, stand at the four corners of the heavenly platform; but the Egyptians were hopelessly ignorant of perspective, so they placed them in a row. These props, it will be observed, support nothing, because the ceiling is in the act of descending, in order to convey the notion of rain. To express a heavy storm (*shena*), the ceiling is shown as half-way down. We ourselves are wont to say, when it rains very heavily, that "the sky is coming down." The Egyptians believed that it was literally doing so.

Now, they had also a word for "clear," "light," "crystalline," "shining," and the like —the word *tahen*. They spelled this word

t a h [e] n

alphabetically, but they required, as usual, a determinative of the sense, and for that purpose they had
recourse to another hieroglyph, which represents
the iron ceiling safely supported *on* its four props.
This represents the clear sky of Egypt, when all is bright
overhead.

It remains to be told how there came to be an overhead
ocean. At the dawn of creation those waters covered the
face of the earth, so that there were no living things except
such as peopled the sea. Then came the god Shu, and he
separated the waters from the earth, and uplifted them by
main strength, "as a great god can;" and behold, the gods
of the cardinal points stepped in with their four props and
fixed it up forever. Thus we see how a whole chapter in
the history of human thought may be preserved, like a fly
in amber, in two or three little hieroglyphs. Here we have
the Egyptian cosmogony, the Egyptian theory of the fixed
stars and the planetary system, and their explanation of the
familiar phenomenon of rain.

We will now turn to *ta*, the hieroglyph for "land." This
sign is not of such far-reaching meaning as the last;
but it is a very interesting sign, and I believe that it
has not been analyzed till now. Here we see the level
plain—the surface of the earth. The lower signs indicate
what is below the surface. The object shaped as an acute
angle is a cutting instrument—a wedge; it indicates mining. The three small balls stand for metals. The vertical line means a sunk shaft—the boring, perhaps, for an
artesian-well. So here we have the earth and its riches,
metals and water, and the little implement which symbolizes the enterprise and industry of man.

This is the ideograph for a city, used also as a determinative sign after the name of any special city. This
object is described in hieroglyphic dictionaries as a "cake,"
and it certainly does resemble a kind of hot cross-bun frequently represented in pictures of offerings; but the sign
(pronounced *nu*) is really intended for a walled town, with

its two main streets crossing at right angles. At Benha, the site of the ancient city of Athribis, the lines of these two main streets are yet clearly distinguishable, as doubtless they are in other places.

Strange as the statement may seem, it is nevertheless true that we are all, quite unconsciously, using many and many an ancient Egyptian word to this day, like Molière's Monsieur Jourdain, who had been talking prose all his life without knowing it. For instance, the land of Egypt was known by many names to its ancient people — as *Ta-meri*, the "Beloved Land;" *Nehi*, the "Land of the Sycamore;" *Khem* or *Khemit*, the "Black Land," meaning the rich, dark soil annually deposited by the inundation; and so on. In the same way, Ireland, Erin, Hibernia, and the Emerald Isle, mean one and the same. Now, this word *khem, khem-t, khemit,* or *khemi,* has many applications. It is the name of a god, Khem,(*) the deity who presided over productiveness and "the kindly fruits of the earth." In this sense, he was also the god of curative herbs and simples, and so became associated in the popular mind with the arts of healing. 'Hence, from *khem,* our chemist and chemistry. But *khem* also meant "black," and in this connection it survives in "alchemy," the "black

art." Here we have the hieroglyphic group for *Khem-t*, Egypt. The first sign is a syllabic hieroglyph standing for *khem*—"black." The owl, *m*, confirms the final consonant; and the half sphere, *t*, is the feminine determinative — a country, a province, a city, being feminine in Egyptian, as in many other tongues, both ancient and modern. The first sign has never been satisfactorily explained, but I venture to think that its meaning is not far to seek. In the square marked off by two diagonals, I recognize an ideograph for territory; and in these parallel lines the levels at which the dark alluvial mud is freshly deposited every year. The uppermost line is the shortest, because the Nile begins to subside again as soon as it has touched its highest point; and the lowest line is the longest, because it represents the nor-mal level of the river. These words have come to us by a somewhat circuitous route, through the Arabic; the original word *khem* having first been picked up by the Arab conquerors of Egypt, and by them handed on to the Barbary Moors, who carried it to Spain, whence it has spread through Europe.

The word "camel" is Egyptian. It is spelled thus: *k-a-ma-a-a-l.* The  *a* was evidently very broad, for it is repeated four times, the whole ending with the generic determinative of a hide, as in the word *hetra*, or "horse."

Although the cocoa-palm is not native to the soil, the name of the cocoa-nut, strange to say, is of Egyptian descent. A well-known text mentions a palm sixty cubits high, the fruit of which contained nuts in which there was water; and these nuts are called *ku-ku.* The little circle is the ideograph of the nut, and the three vertical strokes signify plurality.

The Egyptian for "knife" is *kat;* whence our "cut." And here is the name of a precious wood which often figures as tribute brought by Ethiopian vassals, and which is invariably painted black. Here we have a phonetic syllable pronounced *IIa;* the leg, *b;* the zigzag line, *n;* the two slanting lines for the vowel *i*, pronounced "e;" and finally the conventional determinative of a tree. The whole spells *habni*, which is "ebony." So here again is a word in which every stage of the hieroglyphic writing is present—the old picture-writing, preserved in the determinative tree; the punning phonetic syllable, of which the actual meaning is "house;" and the alphabetic spelling in *b, n,* and *i.*

Another coveted Ethiopian product was *kumi,* a substance imported from the Somali coast and from the Soudan. This word passed into the Greek as *kommi;* thence into the Latin as *gummi*, and now it is "gum." This is the gum which we call "gum-arabic;" and it continues to be an article of commerce, exported from the Soudan through Egypt, to this day. At Assûan, on the frontier of Nubia, we may see the swarthy Soudanese traders camping out, surrounded by great bales of this gum sewn up in buffalo hides, waiting for the cargo-boats which shall carry their goods to Cairo, just as in ancient days they journeyed with the self-same article of tribute or commerce to Thebes and Memphis.

This brief sketch of the origin and development of the hieroglyphic writing has already run to so great a length that I must pass but lightly over much else on which I would fain have dwelt longer. Nothing has yet been said about the cursive writings of the Egyptians; but they had two cursive writings—namely, the "hieratic," and the "demotic." For, as time went on, and the requirements of social and political life became more complex, there inevitably arose the demand for a popular script. It would have been impossible for literature to flourish, as it did flourish in Egypt from the Eleventh Dynasty onward, had the scribes, the poets, the letter-writers, and the professional copyists been fettered by a system so complicated and so cumbrous as the hieroglyphic. They were bound to discover some way of abridging it—of rendering it more flexible, more rapid, more simple. At what time they made their first efforts in this direction we know not. But we do know that by the time of the Eleventh Dynasty they were already in possession of a bold cursive writing, and of a material upon which to employ it. That writing bears the same relation to the hieroglyphic writing as our running-hand bears to printed matter. It is known as the hieratic script; and the material invented for the use of the scribe was papyrus.

Just as our own systems of cursive writing have undergone many changes in the course of centuries, so the hieratic writing of the Egyptians varied from age to age, the tendency of these variations being persistently in the direction of economy. It was massive and square-cut under the Eleventh and Twelfth dynasties; that is to say, from about two thousand eight hundred to two thousand five hundred years before our era. Under the Eighteenth and Nineteenth dynasties it lost something in the way of force, and gained something in the way of elegance. Later still it became small and cramped, and, if I may be permitted the use of a word so unacademic, "niggling."

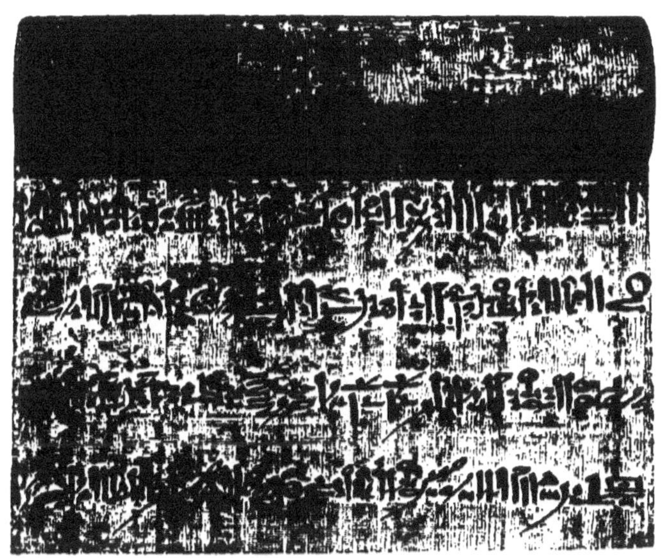

HIERATIC PAPYRUS OF PRINCESS NESIKHONSU.
Twenty-first Dynasty.

But even the hieratic—itself an abridgment—ceased by-and-by to satisfy the demand for increased simplicity and speed, and a third form of writing, which was an abridgment of the hieratic, came into use. This abridgment of an abridgment—which stands to hieratic as our short-hand stands to ordinary running-hand—is called the "demotic." It makes its first appearance as a fully developed system about the time of the Twenty-fifth Dynasty, some seven

17

hundred years before our era. By this time the Egyptians had become a highly commercial, and an extremely litigious, people. They bought and sold, borrowed, mortgaged, and lent with feverish activity, and were so perpetually quarrelling over their bargains, their leases, their securities, their marriage-settlements, and their inheritances, that a writing better adapted to legal and commercial purposes than the literary hieratic was urgently needed. As usual, the demand

DEMOTIC WRITING.

From a funerary inscription written with the reed pen upon a wooden tablet.

created the supply, and demotic became the ordinary script of the people. In the mean while neither the hieroglyphic nor the hieratic writings had wholly died out. The hieroglyphic continued in use for stone-cut inscriptions as long as the ancient language endured; that is to say, it is found on monuments of the later Roman period, the names of all the Cæsars, from Augustus to Decius, being transliterated into Egyptian, carved in hieroglyphic characters, and enclosed in the royal ovals of the Pharaohs, on temples and tablets dating from the twenty-seventh to the two hundred and fiftieth year of the Christian era.

The hieratic writing was more short-lived than the hieroglyphic. Beginning from the time of the Eleventh Dynasty, it continued to be employed for literary purposes down to the period of the Twenty-fourth or Twenty-fifth Dynasty, when it was finally superseded by the demotic. Our museums contain thousands of hieratic papyri, consisting chiefly of extracts from *The Book of the Dead*, besides works on medicine and mathematics, tales, poems, essays, hymns, magical formulas, correspondence, State-papers, and the like ;* and it is not too much to say that there are tens of thousands of demotic documents in the museums of Turin, Berlin, Vienna, Paris, Leyden, and London. These are chiefly law-deeds, accounts, letters, and the miscellaneous memoranda of a trading population. The hieratic documents are principally written on papyrus. The demotic documents are scrawled on all kinds of materials — on papyrus, parchment, flakes of limestone, potsherds, and the like.

Just as I have compared the three writings of the Egyptians with type, running-hand, and short-hand, so I may roughly classify them as the monumental, literary, and commercial scripts of that ancient people.

Of the language itself, and of the laws by which it was governed, a few words must be said. The actual source of the Egyptian language is wrapped in obscurity. Some great authorities make it of Aryan origin, while others class it with the Semitic tongues. In all probability, neither classification is strictly correct. The Egyptian belongs, however, to what is called the "Khamitic" family of tongues—a group which includes the Ethiopian, Libyan, Berber, and other African languages. In all these the feminine takes the letter *t* either as a prefix or a suffix; and they all conjugate the verb by agglutination. The one and only really certain fact is that the Khamitic and Semitic languages are derived from a common source. Their grammatical system is, in certain essential points, the same. Many of their roots are identical; their plural forms are closely related; and in all the feminine determinative is alike. But these two linguistic families—off-shoots from one parent stem—separated in the ages before history, that parent being itself but a prehistoric idiom of very limited range and unknown antiquity. Whether its home were in the Hindoo Kush, or the plains of Mesopotamia, or the highlands of Scandinavia, may perhaps forever remain an open question.

The Egyptian grammar is of most elementary barren-

* See chap. vi.

ness.   Its structure, as compared with the grammar of other languages, is like the structure of the polyp as compared with the complex organism of the higher animals. Some parts of speech are altogether lacking.   In the series of personal pronouns, for example, there is no first person plural.   It exists as a suffix to the verb, but not as a word. Among the conjunctions there is no equivalent for "and." If an Egyptian needed to say "and" he used "with;" so that instead of saying "you and I," he would say "you with me."   As a rule, however, he omitted the conjunction in this sense.   As for the Egyptian verb, it has been concisely described by Mr. Le Page Renouf as "expressing being or action without any reference to time, or to the conception of the speaker," and as having "neither tenses, moods, voices, nor conjugations."   The stock of prepositions and of compound prepositions was, however, very considerable, consisting of some sixteen or seventeen simple forms, and over thirty compound forms, many of which appear to us quite superfluous.

It must not be supposed for a moment that the rudimentary character of the Egyptian grammar helps to make it one jot easier.   On the contrary, it would be a great deal easier if it were a little more difficult.

THOTH.

The Egyptian god of writing.

VIII.

QUEEN HATASU,

AND HER EXPEDITION TO THE LAND OF PUNT.

QUEEN HATASU has been happily described as the Queen Elizabeth of Egyptian history; and she was undoubtedly one of the most extraordinary women in the annals of the ancient East. A daughter of Thothmes I., third Pharaoh of the Eighteenth Dynasty, and of his wife, Queen Ahmes Nefertari, she inherited sovereign rights in virtue of her maternal descent from the old Twelfth Dynasty line. (⁶⁶)

It has pleased historians to rank Thothmes II. as the immediate successor of Thothmes I., and to place the reign of Queen Hatasu between the reigns of her two brothers, Thothmes II. and Thothmes III. By some she is described as Queen Consort during the reign of Thothmes II., and as Queen-regent during the earlier years of the reign of Thothmes III. By others, and most emphatically by Dr. Brugsch, she is stigmatized as a usurper. As a matter of fact, however, Hatasu was actually Queen, and Queen-regnant, during the lifetime of her father. Her accession, therefore, dates from a time long preceding that of her brother, Thothmes II. An important historical inscription sculptured on one of the pylons of the Great Temple of Karnak records this event in eighteen columns of hieroglyphic text, which were copied and translated by the late Vicomte E. de Rougé in 1872.

The inscription is preceded by a bas-relief sculpture representing Thothmes I. in adoration before the Theban triad, Amen, Maut, and Khonsu. The bas-relief and the upper part of the inscription are still in fair preservation, but the lower part of the text is unfortunately much mutilated. When perfect this inscription would seem to have contained a detailed history of the King's life and reign up to the time at which it was executed. It records his birth, and relates that he put down various rebellions which had broken out in Lower Egypt and in the foreign provinces. Suddenly, in the eleventh column of the text, the narrative form is dropped, and Thothmes I. addresses the god Amen face to face.

"Behold," he says, "I make offerings unto thee; I prostrate myself before thee; I bestow the Black Land and the Red Land (⁴⁷) upon my daughter, the Queen of Lower and Upper Egypt, Makara, living eternally. As thou hast done for me."

Further on, in the seventeenth and eighteenth columns, Thothmes reverts to the throne-name of Hatasu, saying that it is given to her by the decree of Amen himself, to which he adds: "Thou hast transmitted the world into her power; thou hast chosen her as King."

In these passages there is more than meets the eye at first sight. A "throne-name," sometimes called a "solar-name," inasmuch as it affirms the direct descent of the reigning monarch from Ra, the greatest of the solar deities, was never assumed by a mere regent, but marked the actual accession of a sovereign. It was equivalent to the act of coronation, and probably was in general accompanied by some such ceremony. De Rougé, in translating this very significant text, remarks that Thothmes I., actuated, no doubt, by some reason of State policy, had "during his lifetime presented his daughter as Queen to the god Amen, and had given her a solar cartouche or throne-name;" that is to say, he had invested her with all the insignia of actual royalty, not making her a mere regent or coadjutor. Hence it would seem that De Rougé recognized in this act of Thothmes I. a solemn transfer of the regal power;(**) and this transfer was evidently made before the altar of the god in the Great Temple of Amen. It is not, perhaps, difficult to guess what those "reasons of State policy" may have been by which Thothmes I. was actuated in taking this strange and important step. It may well have been that Queen Ahmes Nefertari, his wife, was dead, and that his own position was therefore less stable, hers being the direct legitimate right in the female line. By placing his and her daughter upon the throne, he thus re-established the continuity of that line and strengthened his own hands, which probably none the less continued to hold the reins of government.

The title assumed by Hatasu on the occasion of her proclamation affords a good example of the principle upon which these throne or solar names were framed. It is composed of three hieroglyphic signs—MA, represented by the sitting figure of the Goddess of Truth, Law, and Justice; KA, represented by the hieroglyph of the uplifted arms, and signifying Life;* and the sun-disk, representing RA, the supreme solar god of the universe. This combination of hieroglyphs, though apparently so simple, is capable of several interpretations. By some it would be translated as "Ma, the Image of Ra;" by others as "Ma, the Soul of Ra;" by others, again, as "Ma, the Double of Ra;" but the interpretation which most commends itself to me is "Ra, the Life of Ma," with the meaning that Truth, Law, and Justice are the vital manifestations of Ra. The main point as regards the solar cartouches is, however, as I have already said, the direct affiliation of the sovereign to the visible source of Light and Life. And this, be it observed, was in no mere symbolic sense. The Pharaohs claimed to be literally and lineally descended from Ra; and, which is yet more strange, their subjects appear to have believed in this amazing dogma.

Whether the marriage of Hatasu took place before or after her proclamation in the Temple of Amen we do not

* See Lecture IV., on "The Origin of Portrait Sculpture."

know; but she was, at all events, wedded while yet quite young to her eldest brother, Prince Thothmes, afterwards Thothmes II. A recent discovery has for the first time revealed the exact relationship which subsisted between this prince and Hatasu. A funerary chapel dedicated to the memory of Prince Uatmes, a deceased son of Thothmes I., as well as to some other members of that king's family, was discovered in 1887 by M. Grébaut, a little to the northward of the Ramesseum at Thebes.(**) Many interesting historical stelæ and other monuments were found in the course of the excavation of this chapel, the most important being a life-sized sitting statue of a certain Queen Mautnefer, hitherto unknown to history. This Mautnefer proves, according to the inscription on her statue, to have been a wife of Thothmes I., and mother of Thothmes II., by whom her effigy was erected in the chapel of Uatmes. It would thus appear that Thothmes I. had two legitimate wives—namely, Ahmes Nefertari, the royally descended mother of Hatasu, and Mautnefer, a lady evidently of inferior lineage, the mother of the elder Prince Thothmes. As for the younger Thothmes, afterwards Thothmes III., he was of quite humble descent maternally, being a son of Thothmes I. by a Lady As-t, whose name was discovered ten years ago upon the inscribed winding-sheet of Thothmes III., now preserved in the Museum of Ghizeh.(**) This lady is therein entitled *Suten Maut* (Royal Mother), but not also *Suten Hem-t* (Royal Wife), as would have been the case with an actual queen; thus indicating that she was merely a lady of the royal hareem. The elucidation of this piece of family genealogy is very valuable, inasmuch as it shows Hatasu to have been but half-sister to her two brothers, while it at the same time emphasizes the inferior rank of the elder prince, and the vastly inferior rank of the younger. Hatasu, in short, was not only "Heiress-Princess" in right of her maternal descent, but she was also the only surviving offspring of Queen Ahmes Nefertari; and this, in any case, would have furnished an important reason for her marriage with Thothmes

SITTING STATUE OF HATASU.

In the Berlin Museum.

II., whose succession must otherwise have lacked the prestige of old historic descent.

Hatasu appears to have been the mother of only two children, both daughters—Hatasu-Meri and Neferu-Ra. The latter died in infancy, whereas Hatasu-Meri inherited the legitimate rights of her royal mother and became "Heiress-Princess," thus excluding the younger Thothmes from the order of succession. Hereupon, having regard to the interests of the empire and to the further consolidation of family ties, Hatasu wedded her little daughter to the younger of her two half-brothers. This marriage took place during the lifetime of Thothmes II., and it would even seem as though the juvenile couple were nominally associated with their elders upon the throne of Egypt, since it is not possible otherwise to account for the fact that the cartouches of Thothmes II. and Thothmes III. are found in conjunction upon certain monuments of this period. We thus see how carefully Hatasu protected the interests of that younger brother whose throne she is supposed to have usurped.

After a reign of about a dozen years, Thothmes II. died, and was buried with his fathers. Then, for fifteen years, Hatasu seems to have resumed her full hereditary rights, and to have reigned alone. From this time forth, she assumed the style and title of a Pharaoh; and it is literally as a Pharaoh that we find her represented on monuments of this period. In contemporary wall-paintings and bas-relief sculptures, we see Queen Hatasu in male attire, wearing the short kilt and sandals, and crowned with the *Kepersh*, or war-helmet, habitually worn by the Pharaohs on the field of battle. Sometimes we see her adorned with a false beard; but this is perhaps a touch of delicate flattery on the part of the artist.

Meanwhile, the Queen's younger brother, who had been brought up in the Great Temple of Amen and dedicated to the service of the Chief God of Thebes, took, apparently, no share in the government of the country. It is not, in fact, till the sixteenth year after the death of Thothmes II. that we find the name of Thothmes III. occurring in conjunction with that of Hatasu upon a rock-cut tablet in Sinai. Four years later still, in the twentieth year of his nominal reign, when it is probable that the great Queen either died or abdicated—we know not which—Thothmes III. began that extraordinary military career which carried the fame of his arms into the farthest corners of the known world of his time. How long Hatasu continued to hold the reins of government it is impossible to say, as we have no record of the exact length of her reign.

Throughout the years of Hatasu's sole reign the land of Egypt appears to have enjoyed an interval of profound peace, during which she taxed the resources of her empire by repairing those shrines and temples which had gone to ruin during the period of Hyksôs rule; by embellishing and enriching Karnak; and by erecting a sumptuous temple in Western Thebes. In those works she proved herself to be one of the most magnificent builder-sovereigns of Egypt. Of the victories of Thothmes III., there remain only the long lists of conquered nations and captive cities which he caused to be sculptured on the pylons of Karnak; but the Temple of Dayr-el-Bahari and the two great obelisks of Karnak, much as they have suffered at the hands of Time the Destroyer, are to this day permanent records of the tranquil reign of Hatasu.

Numerous and stately as were the obelisks erected in Egypt from the period of the Twelfth Dynasty down to the time of Roman rule, those set up by Hatasu in advance of the fourth pylon of the Great Temple of Karnak are the loftiest, the most admirably engraved, and the best proportioned. One has fallen; the other stands alone, one hundred and nine feet high in the shaft, cut from a single flawless block of red granite. An inscription engraved on the plinth of the one yet erect states that:

"Amen Khnum Hatasu, the Golden Horus, Lord of the two Lands, hath dedicated to her father Amen of Thebes, two obelisks of Mahet stone [red granite], hewn from the quarries of the South. Their summits [pyramidions] were sheathed with pure gold, taken from the chiefs of all nations.

"His Majesty gave these two gilded obelisks to her father Amen, that her name should live forever in this temple.

"Each is one single shaft of red Mahet stone, without joint or rivet. They are seen from both banks of the Nile, and when Ra arises betwixt them as he journeys upward from the heavenly horizon, they flood the two Egypts with the glory of their brightness.

"His Majesty began this work in the fifteenth year of her reign, the first day of the month of Mechir, and finished it on the last day of the month of Mesore, in her sixteenth year."([71])

The shaft of this obelisk bears on its western and southern sides long dedicatory inscriptions in the name of Hatasu only; whereas on the eastern side we find, to the right and left of the central column of hieroglyphs, two outer columns in which Hatasu and Thothmes III. are represented together in adoration before various manifestations of Amen - Ra. The fact that the name of Thothmes III. here appears with that of his sister in the sixteenth year of her reign acquires an especial interest when it is remembered that this is the same date at which we meet with it on the before-mentioned tablet of Sinai. It seems, therefore, to mark the precise time at which he was finally recognized.

With regard to the dates recorded in the inscription on the plinth, they show that these magnificent monoliths were extracted from the quarries of Syene, thence conveyed to Thebes (a journey of one hundred and thirty-three miles), engraved, and placed in position within the amazingly short period of seven months—*Mechir* being the sixth month of the Egyptian year, and *Mesore* the twelfth; which is just as though we were to say that some great public work was begun on the first of June, and finished on the thirty-first of December. It is, however, only when we consider the enormous size and weight of these obelisks that the magnitude of that task can be fully appreciated, each of them measuring one hundred and nine feet in the shaft, without counting the plinth. The one yet standing is, in fact, the highest in the world; the great obelisk brought from Egypt to Rome in the reign of the Emperor Constantine, and now standing in front of the Church of Saint John Lateran, measuring only one hundred and six feet.

One startling peculiarity in the inscriptions of Hatasu, not only upon her obelisks at Karnak, but upon the walls of her temple at Dayr-el-Bahari, consists in the employment of masculine titles with feminine pronouns. As hereditary sovereign of Egypt, she was Pharaoh and King, head alike of the sacerdotal and military castes. Hence, in one and the same sentence, she appears as *Hon-f* (His Majesty), while the suffixes used in the grammatical construction are feminine.

The broken obelisk differs from its fellow in no longer bearing the name of Hatasu; Thothmes III. having, during his own sole reign, erased her cartouches and substituted his own. Yet, despite his usurpation, these sculptured fragments are still the property of Hatasu. In the bas-relief groups wherein she is represented as performing acts of worship before Amen, her spirited and characteristic profile is preserved. The name may be the name of Thothmes, but the face is the face of Hatasu. If we turn back to the full-face portrait of this queen, given in Lecture IV., and compare it, feature by feature, with this profile, their identity is at once recognizable. Even the little dimple in the chin, which is so strongly marked in the front face, is carefully indicated by a depression in the chin of the outline profile.

The most magnificent historic monument of the reign of this great queen was, however, the temple which she constructed on the western bank of the Nile, nearly opposite the Great Temple of Karnak. This superb structure is architecturally unlike any other temple in Egypt. It stands at the far end of a deep bay, or natural amphitheatre, formed by the steep limestone cliffs which divide the Valley of the Tombs of the Kings from the Valley of the Nile. Approached by a pair of obelisks, a pylon gate-way, and a long avenue of two hundred sphinxes, the temple consisted of a succession of terraces and flights of steps, rising one above the other, and ending in a maze of colonnades and court-yards uplifted high against the mountain - side. The Sanctuary, or Holy of Holies, to which all the rest was but as an avenue, is excavated in the face of the cliff, some five hundred feet above the level of the Nile. The novelty of the plan is so great that one cannot help wondering whether it was suggested to the architect by the nature of the ground, or whether it was in any degree a reminiscence of strange edifices seen in far distant lands. It bears, at all events, a certain resemblance to the terraced temples of Chaldæa.

PROFILE PORTRAIT AND ROYAL OVALS
OF QUEEN HATASU.

From the pyramidion of her fallen obelisk at Karnak. She wears the *Kepersh*, or war - helmet worn by the Pharaohs in battle, with the golden "uræus," or so-called "basilisk," on the brow.

As the statue of Bak-en-Khonsu in the Glyptotheca of Munich preserves for us the name of the architect of the Ramesseum, so the obelisks of Hatasu at Karnak immortalize the name of Sen-Maut, the architect of her temple at Dayr-el-Bahari. His tomb has not been discovered, and his personal history is unknown; but enough remains of his work in this unique temple to show that he was not only possessed of consummate taste and ability, but that he also originated a new departure in his art, which, had it been followed, might have revolutionized the architecture of ancient Egypt.

Few of the great buildings erected by the Pharaohs of the later Theban line have suffered more deplorably at the hand of the destroyer than this temple, which is now only known by its Arabic name of "Dayr-el-Bahari." Dayr-el-

Bahari signifies the Convent of the North, and the ruins of the old Coptic monastery which give it this name still encumber part of the site. (") Of its two hundred sphinxes, though nearly the whole of them were prostrate on the ground when the French Commission visited Egypt in 1798, not one is now left. (") The long and stately flights of steps are represented by a steep hill strewn with rubble and fragments of limestone. Of the pillared colonnades, only a few columns are yet standing in the shelter of the cliff-side; and the ruin of the whole is so complete that the casual visitor can with difficulty recognize the plan on which it was built. By means, however, of close and patient study on the spot, M. Brune, a distinguished French architect, has

TEMPLE OF HATASU AT DAYR-EL-BAHARI.
(Restoration from a design by M. Brune.)

succeeded in making a restored elevation of this beautiful temple, as it appeared in the days of its splendor. (")

The dromos of approach, the long avenue of sphinxes, the obelisks, and the pylons, are necessarily omitted from M.

Brune's design. But we here see two great flights of steps leading from terrace to terrace, each step guarded by two couchant sphinxes; the two colossal statues of Hatasu seated on either side of the steps which rise from the second

HATHOR-HEAD CAPITAL.

From one of the fallen columns at Dayr-el-Bahari. (From a photograph by Mr. W. M. Flinders Petrie.)

terrace; and the pillared portico in the centre of the third terrace, marking the entrance to the rock-cut sanctuary beyond. The columns which supported that third terrace were surmounted by Hathor-headed capitals, and of these columns only a few shattered shafts and two or three fallen capitals now strew the ground. The color on those capitals is still brilliant.(*) The long wall facing the spectator at the upper end of the temple where it adjoins the mountain-side, and another wall bounding the second terrace on the left of the picture, are covered with bas-relief sculptures, which in the

18

illustration are of necessity but slightly indicated. These bas-relief tableaux, or rather what remains of them, are most delicately sculptured and vividly colored; but full two-thirds of the upper part of the walls are gone.

The traveller who now visits the wreck of this temple can with difficulty identify its wide-spread ruins with M. Brune's elegant restoration. That part, however, which is best preserved does not appear at all in our illustration—namely, the rock-cut chamber, commonly called "The Chamber of the Cow," which is entered from the third terrace. Hewn out of the solid cliff-side and lined with blocks of the finest limestone, this little speos contains two bas-relief subjects representing Queen Hatasu, in the costume of a royal prince, kneeling beside the Goddess Hathor, who is represented as a large red cow. The Queen, with a naïveté peculiar to Egyptian art, is shown as in the act of sucking the milk of the Divine Cow, thus signifying that she was the very foster-child of the goddess. One leg and hoof and part of the body of the cow are seen in our next illustration. The figure of the Queen is excellently proportioned, and her face, although it differs from her other portraits in being more conventionally rendered, is historically valuable. On her brow she wears the Uræus of royalty, and on her head the wig of close-laid rows of curls usually worn by youthful princes. Her cartouche is sculptured in the space between her right arm and left knee, but the hieroglyphic characters have been erased, and it is no longer legible.

By some authorities, the Temple of Dayr-el-Bahari is supposed to have been begun during the lifetime of Thothmes II., and by others it is believed to be the work of Hatasu, during her sole reign. The cartouches of Thothmes II. appear, it is true, in some of the inscriptions. Whether Thothmes II. had, or had not, any share in the founding of the temple, it is at all events certain that the bulk of the building, and its decoration, was due to Hatasu. The cartouches of Thothmes III. also appear in many of the inscriptions, and notably on that of the red granite gate-way leading to the rock-cut chambers on the uppermost terrace. But these are usurpations, and date from some period subsequent to the reign of Hatasu; her successor, Thothmes III., having caused the names of his sister to be obliterated and his own to be engraved in their place. The building is dedicated in part to Amen, the Great God of Thebes, and in part

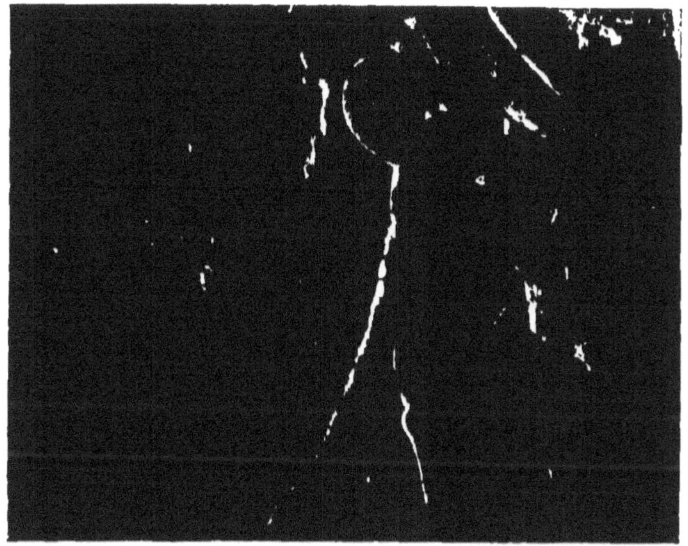

HATASU AND THE DIVINE COW.

Bas-relief sculpture representing Hatasu in the costume of a youthful Prince, sucking milk from the Divine Cow (emblematic of Hathor), from the south wall of the rock-cut sanctuary of her temple at Dayr-el-Bahari. (From a photograph by Mr. W. M. Flinders Petrie.)

to Hathor, the Lady of the West, the nurse of Horus, and the presiding deity of the far-distant Land of Punt. It was under this last aspect that Hathor was especially reverenced in the Temple of Dayr-el-Bahari.

It is in the sculptured and painted tableaux upon the walls of the two uppermost terraces of Hatasu's temple that we find depicted every incident of the most remarkable event of her reign. That event was the building of a fleet of sea-going ships, and the despatch of an exploring squadron to the Land of Punt; a region identified by Maspero and Mariette with that part of the Somali country which is situate on the eastern coast of Africa, bordering the Gulf of Aden. This region, rich in incense-bearing trees, in costly gums and resins, in myrrh and amber, gold, lapis-lazuli, ivory, and precious woods, is the *Cinnamomifera regio*, sometimes called the *aromatifera regio* of the ancients.(")

At this time, the province of Yemen, on the south-west coast of Arabia, was the great general meeting-place of Indian and Asiatic commerce. Thence the Phœnicians, the Arabs, and the Arameans carried the merchandise of the great trading nations of the East by sea and land to Mesopotamia, to Syria, to Egypt, and to the coasts of Asia Minor. Here, too, the mysterious products of the Land of Punt found their market; and, being transported from the east coast of Africa to the west coast of Arabia, were brought back to Africa by a circuitous route to the great Egyptian port of *Touaou* (the modern Kosseir), whence the merchants of Coptos conveyed them to Thebes.

Inspired, as one of the temple inscriptions states, by the direct command of Amen himself, Hatasu resolved no longer to be dependent upon the uncertain trade of Arabia for the valuable products from which the incense used in the service of the temples was made. She therefore resolved herself to despatch an expedition to the Somali coast; and for this purpose she built and fitted out five ships, the largest and the best equipped yet built on the banks of the Nile.

These ships were built with a narrow keel, the stern and prow rising high above the water. Their length was about seventy feet, and they were evidently without any sort of cabin accommodation. A raised platform with a balustrade, erected at both prow and poop, served for a lookout fore and aft; and under these platforms there was probably some kind of shelter for the officers. These vessels had no decks, the hull being fitted up with seats for the rowers. The ends of

the planks which formed the seats were fixed through the
ribs of the ship, as may be seen in our illustration. There
was probably some kind of hold for the storage of provisions,
ballast, etc., under the feet of the rowers; but this, of course,
would be below the water-line. There is but one mast, hewn
from a massive palm-trunk, and measuring about twenty-
seven feet in height. This is fixed in the middle of the ship,
and lashed strongly to the deck. Each vessel mounts but a
single sail, and has two spars, the top one straight and the

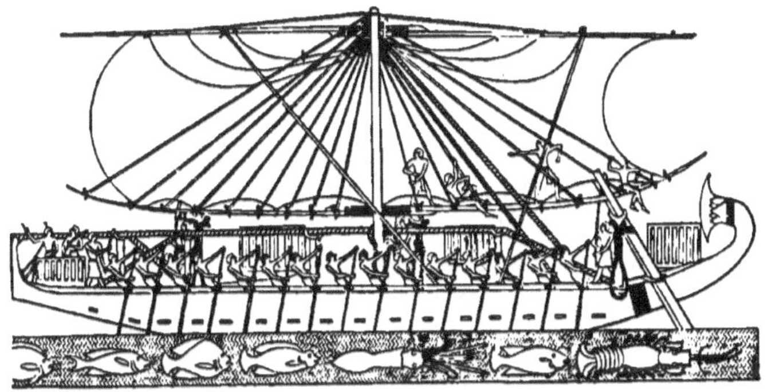

FIRST SHIP OF OUTGOING SQUADRON BOUND FOR PUNT.
(From Mariette's *Deir-el-Bahari*, plate 12.)

lower one curved. The helm is made of two very large oars,
firmly bound to a kind of bracket in front of the rear platform, and worked by a long curved stick. The crew consists of thirty rowers, fifteen on each side, four reefers, two
steersmen, a pilot, an overseer of the rowers, and a captain.
A small detachment of military, numbering about eight or
ten soldiers and an officer, accompanied the expedition.
These served as a guard of honor to the envoy sent by
Queen Hatasu to the Prince of Punt. Soldiers and sailors
all counted, the expedition consisted of about two hundred
and ten men to the five ships.
Our illustration shows the departure of the leader of the

squadron. Each rower is in his place. Their overseer, standing with his back to the platform at the prow, directs the rise and fall of their oars, probably, as at the present day, by leading a chant in which all join. The steersman is stationed at the stern, and holds in his hand the long curved handle by which the helm is worked. The captain, baton in hand, stands on the platform at the prow, looking forward in the direction that the ship is going. A brief hieroglyphic inscription above the carved lotus which decorates the stern states that they "make head for the large "—in other words, for the "open." The great sail is spread, and is evidently filled by a favorable wind, and all promises well for the success of the voyage.

Every part of the vessel shown in our illustration is elaborately rendered, down to the minutest detail. We see how the spars are spliced, and where the reef-bands are tied; and we also see the great cable passing over the heads of the rowers, to which, doubtless, the anchor was attached. Some allowance must, perforce, be made for the conventionalities of Egyptian art. The sail, which here appears as though parallel with the length of the vessel, should, of course, be set at an angle to it; but the naval draughtsman of Hatasu's time was as anxious to display every part of his subject as was his compatriot the figure-painter, who represented a front-wise body in conjunction with profile legs and head. The water through which our gallant vessel is ploughing its way is, as usual, represented by zigzag lines. Those in the original are painted of a light blue, and represent the Nile; blue being the color symbolical of fresh-water. The fishes, too, are the fishes of the Nile. The admirable accuracy with which these fish are drawn compensates for the incongruity of their proportions as compared with those of the crew of the vessel. There is not one of them who could not swallow a couple of sailors whole without the smallest inconvenience.

The original wall-sculpture from which our illustration is taken shows the whole squadron in full sail, and is accompanied by a few columns of explanatory text, which read as follows:

"Departure of the soldiers of the Lord of the Two Worlds traversing the Great Sea on the Good Way to the Land of the Gods, in obedience to the will of the King of the Gods, Amen of Thebes. He commanded that there should be brought to him the marvellous products of the Land of Punt, for that he loves the Queen Hatasu above all other kings that have ruled this land."

Before we go farther on our way towards the Land of Punt, it will be well to consider by what route the squadron reached its destination. This is a very interesting question. Many of the upper courses of these sculptured and painted walls are so hopelessly mutilated as to break the continuity of the narrative. Thus, although it is distinctly stated that the ships returned to Thebes and there disembarked their cargo at the close of the expedition, the inscription which should inform us as to the point of their departure is lost. Seeing, however, that they returned to Thebes, it may be taken for granted that they sailed from the same port, and this supposition is confirmed by the blue color of the water and the presence therein of the fishes of the Nile. But what course did they take when they had turned their backs upon "hundred-gated Thebes?"

That the squadron should have descended the Nile, sailed westward through the Strait of Gibraltar, skirted the west coast of Africa, doubled the Cape of Good Hope, and reached the Somali shores by way of the Mozambique Channel and the coast of Zanzibar is absolutely incredible.

Such an achievement at so early a stage of naval history,

would be far more wonderful than the building of all the pyramids or temples of Egypt. It would, in fact, imply that Queen Hatasu's squadron twice made the almost complete circuit of the African continent. We are compelled to reject this hypothesis. Rejecting it, we must fall back upon the only alternative possibility, which is that they went out by some ancient water-way connecting the Nile with the Red Sea.

Now, the surveys recently made by Lieutenant-colonel Ardagh, Major Spaight, and Lieutenant Burton, of the Royal Engineers, have rendered it certain that the Wady Tûmilât was at some very distant time traversed by a branch of the Nile which discharged its waters into the Red Sea—the majority of geographers being now of opinion that the head of the Gulf of Suez formerly extended as far northward as the modern town of Ismaïlia. Whether that branch of the Nile was ever navigable, we know not; but we do know that it was already canalized in the reign of Seti I., second Pharaoh of the Nineteenth Dynasty, and father of Rameses II.

This ancient canal started, like the present Sweetwater Canal, from the neighborhood of Bubastis, the modern Zagazig; threaded the Wady Tûmilât; and emptied itself into that basin which is now known as Lake Timsah. When M. de Lesseps laid down the line of the Sweetwater Canal, he, in fact, followed the course of the old canal of the Pharaohs, the bed of which is yet traceable. When I last saw it, several blocks of the masonry of the old embankment were yet *in situ,* among the reeds and weeds by which that ancient water-way is now choked.

This canal is represented in one of the most celebrated wall-sculptures of the Great Temple of Karnak, (") and it is there called *Ta-Tena,* or "the cutting;" and because King Seti is shown to be returning to Egypt from one of his Syrian campaigns by way of a bridge over this same canal, it has been universally taken for granted that he was the author of that important engineering work. There is, however, no kind of evidence to justify the assumption. As reasonably

might it be supposed that Napoleon the First was the builder of the Pyramids, because in Gérome's great picture he is
represented as seated on horseback, and contemplating them
from a distance. The canal may have existed, and in all
probability did exist, long before the time of Seti I. It would
seem, indeed, as if the great woman-Pharaoh who first conceived the daring project of launching her ships upon an unknown sea, was by far the most likely person to canalize that
channel by which alone, so far as we can see, it would have
been possible for them to go forth. For my own part, I have
not the slightest doubt that Queen Hatasu was the scientific
ancestress of M. de Lesseps; and that it was to the genius
and energy of this extraordinary woman that Egypt owed
that great work of canalization which first united the Nile
with the Red Sea.

In the sculptured tableau from which our illustration of
the ship is taken, four other vessels are shown: the first, as
we have seen, leads the way with a swelling sail; the last
is not yet fully laden, but lies at anchor, waiting for a small
boat into which some sailors are conveying large jars.

In the next tableau, the expedition has reached its destination. The voyage being omitted, the ships are once
more seen at anchor, and the ancient draughtsman, in one
of the very few known examples of Egyptian landscape
art, has carefully depicted for us the characteristic scenery
of the unknown country to which the squadron has made its
way. The ground is flat and thickly wooded, the conical
huts of the inhabitants being built on piles and approached
by ladders. A cow reposes peacefully in the shade of a tree
to the right, and a bird, known by its characteristic tail-feathers as the *Cinnyris metallica*, wings its flight towards the
left. Of the five trees here represented, two are conventional
renderings of the date-palm. The trunks and branches of
the other three are most carefully drawn. An enclosing line
carried round each indicates the outline of the foliage, the
details of which are left to the imagination. It has been
supposed that this landscape represented some spot on the

shores of the Red Sea ; but M. Maspero has pointed out various reasons to show that we are here on the banks of a river. The three last-named trees, for instance, precisely reproduce the structure of the odoriferous sycamore, which

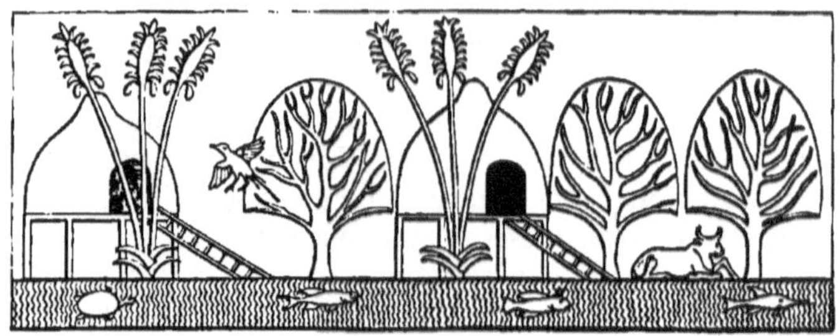

VIEW OF A VILLAGE IN PUNT.

(From Mariette's *Deir-el-Bahari*, plate 5.) The huts of the natives are built on piles and approached by ladders, and, according to Dümichen, closely resemble the *Toquls* of the modern Soudanese. The trees are two date-palms in fruit, and three myrrh-trees (odoriferous sycamore), the foliage of the latter being indicated by a line bounding the tops of the branches. The bird flying to left is identified with the *Cinnyris metallica*, a native of the Somali country, having two long tail-feathers, of which only one has been given by the ancient Egyptian artist.

does not grow by the sea-side, but on the borders of rivers ; and he concludes that the Egyptian squadron, after sailing down the Red Sea and rounding the headland called Ras-el-Fil, had made its way up the mouth of the Elephant River. The water in the original is painted green, which may be taken to indicate a tidal river; green being the Egyptian color for sea-water, and blue for fresh-water. The fishes, it is to be observed, are not the fishes of Egypt, while among them is seen a fine turtle, a cetacean unknown to the waters of the Nile. ([78])

The royal envoy having landed, accompanied by his military escort, arranges on a table, or stand, the gifts which he has brought for presentation to the Prince of Punt. These gifts consist of bead necklaces, bracelets, collars, a hatchet, and a dagger of state. We may suppose the beads to be of that beautiful variegated glass, in the manufacture of which the

Egyptians of the Eighteenth and Nineteenth Dynasties particularly excelled. The collars and bracelets are painted yellow, to represent gold, the former being torque-shaped and closely resembling the "toqs" worn by the Egyptian women of the present day. The envoy is in civil dress, and leans upon his staff of command. The soldiers are armed with spear and hatchet, and carry a large shield rounded at the top — the ordinary equipment of infantry of the line. Their captain carries no shield, but is armed with a bow, in addition to the spear and hatchet of his followers. The inscription states that these are "all the good things of His Majesty, to whom be Life, Health, and Strength, destined for Hathor, Lady of Punt." This is a circuitous manner of stating that the said good things are intended, not for the goddess, but as a means of exchange for the coveted products of Punt.

THE ROYAL ENVOY, ATTENDED BY HIS BODY-GUARD, DISPLAYS THE GIFTS SENT BY HATASU TO THE PRINCE OF PUNT.

(From Mariette's *Deir-el-Bahari*, plate 5.)

We next see the approach of the native chief, accompanied by his family and followers. They advance with uplifted hands, this being the accepted attitude of deprecation and homage. The chief wears a collar of large beads, a small dagger in his belt, and a *shenti*, or loin-cloth, of the same fashion as that worn by the Egyptians. Unlike them, however, he wears a beard; and this beard is curved slightly upward, like those with which the Egyptians represented their gods and deceased Pharaohs. The inscription engraved in front of his body states that he is "The Great of Punt, Parihu;" a name apparently derived from an Arabic root. He is followed by his wife, his two sons, and his daughter, to each of whom is attached a short inscription. The two youths are simply described as " his sons," and the young girl as " his daughter." His spouse, a very singular and unbeautiful person, is described as " his wife, Ati." She wears a yellow

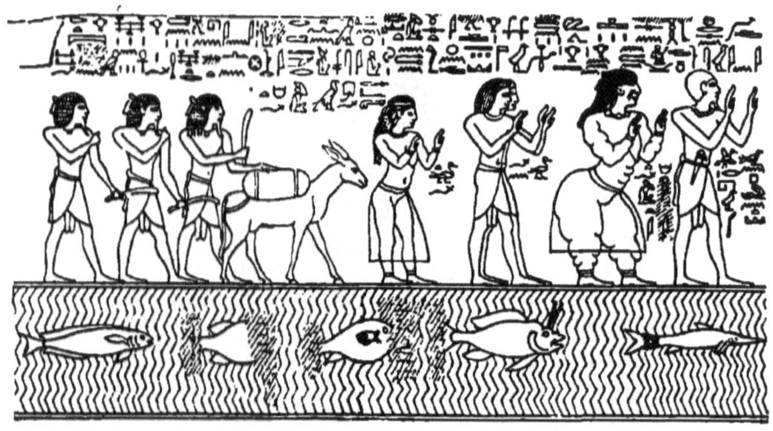

PROCESSION OF THE PRINCE OF PUNT,
accompanied by his wife, family, and followers. (From Mariette's *Deir-el-Bahari*, plate 5.)

dress, bracelets on her wrists, anklets on her ankles, and a necklace of alternate bead and chain work round her throat. Her hair, like that of her daughter, is bound with a fillet on the brow. Her features are repulsive, and her cheek is disfigured by two lines of tattooing on either side of the mouth. She is hideously obese, her limbs and body being weighed down by rolls of fat. Her daughter, though evidently quite young, already shows a tendency towards the same kind of deformity.

This strange portrait of the Princess Ati has been the subject of much discussion, it being a doubtful point whether she is to be considered as a diseased monstrosity, or as a paragon of beauty. It is the opinion of some authorities that she must have been the living realization of the highest type of female loveliness, according to the taste of the natives of certain parts of Central Africa. Chabas compares her with Speke's description of the favorite wife of the brother of the King of Karagoué, whose fat hung in large puddings about her arms, and whose weight was too great to allow of her standing upright. Beauty of this class was formerly supposed to belong exclusively to the fair ladies of the Hottentot race; but Schweinfurth, in his "Heart of Africa," describes the Bongo women in words that would almost seem to have been suggested by the subject of our illustration. Maspero suggests that the Princess Ati may be suffering from *elephantiasis;* but Mariette is of opinion that the Egyptian artist has here represented not merely the wife of the chief, but the most admired type of the women of the Somali race. The complexions of the whole family are painted of a brick red, and their hair black, thus showing that they are not of negro race. The superimposed hieroglyphic inscription, which extends to some length beyond that of our illustration, states that "Hither come the Great [ones] of Punt, their backs bent, their heads bowed, to receive the soldiers of His Majesty." Then follow the words which are supposed to come out of their mouths: "How have you arrived at this land unknown to the men of Egypt?(") Have you come down from the roads of the Heavens? Or have you navigated the sea of Ta-nuter?* You must have followed the path of the sun. As for the King of Egypt, there is no road which is inaccessible to His Majesty; we live by the breath he grants to us."

An ass, saddled with a thick cushion, and three attendants carrying short staves, bring up the rear of the procession. Over the ears of this beast of heavy burden is engraved in hieroglyphic characters, "The great ass that carries his wife;"

* The Land of the Gods.

the great ass, if the ancient artist is to be relied upon in his
scale of proportion, bearing about the same relation to
Princess Ati as Falstaff's half-pennyworth of bread to his
"intolerable deal of sack." The men who guide and follow
the ass wear the upcurved beard everywhere characteristic
of the natives of Punt in Egyptian art. On the sculptured
pylon of Horemheb, at Karnak, we find a Prince of Punt of
one hundred and six-
ty years later, with
features closely re-
sembling those of
Parihu. He wears
the same curved
beard, and even the
close-fitting cap,
which was apparent-
ly the distinguishing
badge of the chief-
dom.([60])

CHIEF OF PUNT.

From the Pylon of Horemheb, at Karnak. This fine
head of a chief of Punt is photographed from a
cast taken by Mr. W. M. F. Petrie from the group
of foreign tributaries sculptured on the Pylon of
Horemheb, at Karnak.

The gifts sent by
Hatasu having been
presented by the en-
voy and accepted by
the Prince of Punt,
the latter proceeds to
offer in return five ship-loads of the special products of his
country. The inscription states that the Chief of Punt piles
his tribute by the water-side.

From this point, the sculptured tableaux form a continuous scene, those in the lower register being almost perfect,
whereas those in the upper register are unfortunately so
much broken away that in many places there remain only
the feet of the figures and the water lines of the river. In
several of the best preserved, we see the Egyptian sailors
carrying half-grown saplings which have been taken up
with a ball of earth about the roots, and are being transported in baskets slung upon poles, each pole carried by

four men. These, as they wend their way towards the ships, are accompanied by natives of Punt, some carrying large logs of ebony, others leading apes, and one a giraffe. In one place where there is a great gap in the wall, the remains of the inscription show that an elephant and a horse were among the animals embarked from Punt for the gratification of Hatasu. This Queen doubtless shared in that lively interest which, as

MEN CARRYING SAPLINGS OF THE "ANA-SYCAMORE" IN BASKETS, FROM THE SHORE TO THE SHIPS.

(From Mariette's *Deir-el-Bahari*, plate 5.)

it is well known, her brother Thothmes III. entertained for all kinds of foreign birds, beasts, and plants.(") A running commentary of short inscriptions is interspersed here and there between the figures. "Stand steady on your legs, Bohu!" says one of the bearers. "You throw too much weight upon my shoulders," retorts Bohu.

Over the saplings which are being carried in baskets, is inscribed *Nehet Ana;* that is to say, the Sycamore of Ana. Elsewhere we see the full-grown trees. The trunk is massive; the leaf is a sharp-pointed oval; and at the junction of the trunk and the larger branches are seen little copper-colored lumps of irregular form, representing the resinous gum which has exuded through the bark. A passage in Pliny, to which Mariette especially refers in his memoir on Deir-el-Bahari, shows that this tree, the odoriferous sycamore, can be none other than the myrrh-tree, whose gum was brought by the ancients from the so-called "land of the Troglodytes." According to the old naturalist, the myrrh-tree is found

"... in many quarters of Arabia; also there is very good myrrhe brought out of the Islands; and the Sabeans passe the seas and travell as far as to the Troglodites countrey for it. ... The plant groweth ordinarily five cubits high, but not all that length is it smooth and without prickes: the bodie and trunke is hard and wrythen; it is greatest toward the root, and so ariseth smaller and smaller, taper-wise. Some say that the barke is smooth and even, like unto that of the Arbute Tree: others againe affirme that it is prickly, and full of thornes. It hath a leafe like to the Olive, but more crisped and curled, and withall it is in the end sharpe-pointed like a needle. ... The myrrhe trees are twice cut and launced in one year; the slit reacheth from the very root up to the boughes, if they may beare and abide it."

Further on, he says that, of all the wild kinds of myrrh-trees, "the first is that which groweth in the Troglodites countrey;" and this, "the Trogloditike myrrhe, they chuse by the fattinesse thereof, and for that it seemeth to the eie greener. ... The best myrrhe is known by little peeces which are not round; and when they grow together, they yeeld a certain whitish liquour which issueth and resolveth from them, and if a man breake them into morsels, it hath white veines resembling men's nails, and in tast is somewhat bitter."([82])

That the *Ana* was undoubtedly the resinous gum of the myrrh-tree is still further confirmed by the above passage from Pliny, which describes it as of a green color; the "green Ana" being constantly named in Egyptian inscriptions as the most precious and desirable kind.

One very interesting tableau, which is yet happily in good preservation, represents a group of three large trees of this species, *i. e.*, the *Nehet Ana*, or odoriferous sycamore. On the ground, in the shade of their boughs, are piles of panther-skins and elephant-tusks, logs of ebony in stacks, and rings and ingots of precious metal. Above the tops of the trees is shown a row of sycamore saplings in tubs, with an inscription stating that "thirty and one growing trees of the *Ana* were taken as marvels of Punt to the holiness of this God [Amen]. Never was there seen the like since the world began."

And now, while the Egyptian sailors, assisted by the natives of Punt, are busily engaged in loading the ships, Hatasu's envoy offers an official reception to Prince Parihu, his wife and family. This parting interview is conducted with great ceremony on both sides. A huge heap of myrrh, two trays of massive gold rings, and a pile of elephant-tusks are brought by Parihu, probably as a farewell *bakhshish* to the envoy himself. The Lady Ati is apparelled as before, but the right leg of Parihu is covered from the ankle to above the knee with a close succession of metal rings resembling

GIFTS PRESENTED TO THE ROYAL ENVOY BY THE PRINCE OF PUNT.
(From Mariette's *Deir-el-Bahari*, plate 5.)

the *dangabor* of the Bongo people, as shown in an illustration to Schweinfurth's *Heart of Africa*.(") The sons of Parihu, one of them carrying a bowl of gold-dust; an attendant bearing a large jar on his shoulder; and the ass, which has again enjoyed the unenviable privilege of carrying the Lady Ati, bring up the rear. The pile of *Ana* is here represented in a very summary fashion by a mere outline, but in some of the other subjects the little irregularly shaped lumps of the precious gum are all elaborately defined. The envoy stands in front of his pavilion—omitted in our illustration—and is apparently in the act of inviting his guests to partake of the banquet which, by order of Hatasu, he has prepared for them. This consisted, according to the accompanying inscription, of "bread, beer, wines, meat, vegetables, and all good things of Egypt, by command of His Majesty, to whom be Life, Health, Strength."

In the very interesting subject now before us, we see the Egyptian sailors, some carrying the saplings in baskets slung

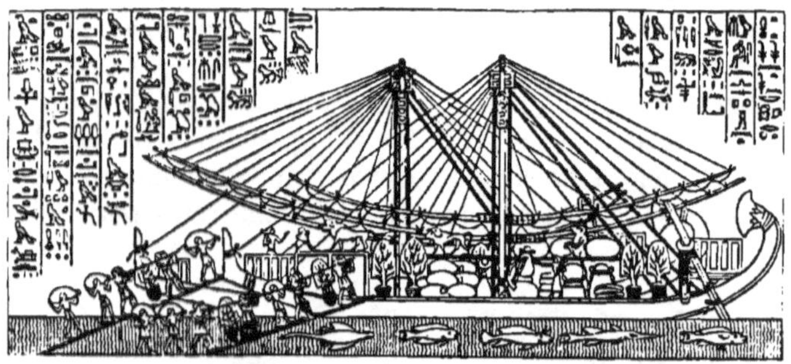

SHIPS OF THE EGYPTIAN SQUADRON BEING LADEN WITH THE PRODUCTS OF PUNT.
(From Mariette's *Deir-el-Bahari*, plate 6.)

from poles, as before; others laden with big jars; and all hurrying on board along inclined planks reaching presumably from the shore, which, however, is not shown in the picture. The decks are already piled high with their precious cargo, among which may be observed three large apes, who make themselves perfectly at home. Slung to the main-mast of the nearest vessel, a harp is depicted, of a shape which may even now be seen in the hands of native musicians in Cairo and other large towns. The captain stands on the platform at the prow, issuing his commands; and, small as is the scale, the very natural action of the man in front of him, who shouts the order with his hand to his mouth, must not be overlooked. The long inscription engraved in vertical columns at either corner of the picture reads as follows:

"Very great lading of the ships with the marvels of the Land of Punt, and with all the good woods of Ta-nuter; with heaps of *kami* of *Ana*, with trees producing green *ana;* with ebony and pure ivory; with gold, and green agates found in the Land of the Amu; with blocks of the wood *tascheps;* with *ahem* perfumes; with *tasem* dogs; and with hides of the panthers of the South; and with natives of the country, their women and children. Never since the beginning of the world have the like wonders been brought by any king." (")

While these last two vessels are receiving their cargoes, the other three have already weighed anchor, and are seen with their sails set and filled by a favorable wind. A short inscription states that this is "the peaceful and prosperous voyage of the soldiers of his Majesty returning to Thebes, bringing with them the men of Punt. They bring such marvels of the Land of Punt as have never been brought by any King of Egypt, on account of the greatness of the King of the Gods, Amen, Lord of Thebes."

The return voyage, like the outward voyage, is passed over; and the next incidents of this curious panorama in stone take place in Thebes. We are shown nothing of the arrival of the squadron, nor of the unlading of the ships; the rest of the tableaux consisting mainly of processions of priests, soldiers, and sailors. The order in which these processions meet and succeed each other is somewhat confusing. The hieroglyphic inscriptions in this part of the building are also greatly mutilated, so that the subjects in many instances have to be taken as their own interpreters. It seems possible that they do not all represent the return of the expedition from Punt, but that some may have reference to the ceremonies which accompanied the opening of the temple. The unity of the composition as an historic whole is moreover impaired by the introduction of other foreign. tributaries besides those brought from Punt; whence it may be concluded that the artist. in order to produce a more brilliant effect, introduced the representatives of various nations who

on other occasions, had laid their tribute at the feet of
Hatasu.

In one tableau we see the Sacred Bark of Amen, carried by
twenty - five priests and preceded by libation-bearers, divine
standard-bearers, and priests carrying bunches of lotus-lilies.
In another, the sailors of the expedition march in single file,
armed with hatchets, and carrying green boughs in their
hands—probably of the *Ana* sycamore. A drummer goes before, and the inscription says that "the sailors of the royal
squadron shout for joy. They cry aloud ; the heavens rejoice.
May Amen grant long life to his daughter, the Builder of his
Temple."

Following the sailors, comes the deputation from Punt, the
native Somalis distin-
guished by their curved
beards. Some of these
bring trays of the *Ana*
gum; others carry
large jars, probably
filled with gold-dust;
others, again, lead apes
of the two species in-
digenous to Punt, *i.e.*,
the *Cynocephalus Ha-
madryas*, and the *Cy-
nocephalus Babuinus*,
called in the inscrip-
tion the *Ani* ape, and
the *Kafoo* monkey. To

TRIBUTARIES OF PUNT WALKING IN THE PROCES-
SION TO THE TEMPLE OF AMEN.

(From Mariette's *Deir-el-Bahari*.)

this part of the procession belong the figures of men leading the horse, the giraffe, and the elephant, which, as before-
mentioned, are unfortunately almost destroyed. Last of all
come more sailors, carrying the sycamore saplings in baskets as before.

Marching in the contrary direction, as if coming to meet
and welcome the sailors on landing, we are shown a body of
young soldiers, representing no less than three different regi-

ments. They are armed with axe, bow, and shield; while some, belonging apparently to a Nubian corps, brandish the boomerang. All carry green boughs in token of festivity. Besides this procession, which may be called the Procession of Welcome, there is another and a very interesting cortege which may be distinguished as the Procession of the Queen.

First come the troops of the royal household, designated in the inscription as the soldiers of the *Per-aa*, or palace.([13])

PROCESSION OF THE QUEEN.

Her Majesty's fan-bearers, quiver-bearer, sandal-bearer, and grooms with hunting leopards. (From Mariette's *Deir-el-Bahari*.)

Her Majesty's throne-chair carried by twelve bearers. (From Mariette's *Deir-el-Bahari*.)

Next follow the Queen's fan-bearers, carrying long-handled flabellæ of conventionally rendered ostrich-feathers. After these come the Queen's quiver-bearer and sandal-bearer, and two grooms leading her Majesty's hunting leopards. Her throne-chair, carried by twelve bearers, brings up the rear.

The chair, with its footstool, stands on a portable platform, and is evidently used as a *chaise-à-porteurs*, and not as a mere emblem of royalty. The inscription beneath the chair describes the Queen as "this good God," and enumerates her titles as "Lord of the Two Lands," etc.

Hatasu has presumably been carried to the Temple of Amen, where she is seen in the next tableau standing, staff in hand, in the full costume of a Pharaoh, face to face with Amen enthroned. The inscription which fills the space between these two figures is cast into the form of a dialogue between the god and the Queen. Hatasu, reverting to the origin of the expedition, proclaims her intention of exploring the ways of Punt, that there may be *Ana* in abundance for the service of the temple. The god,

THE QUEEN RECEIVING HER TROOPS.

CEREMONY SUPPOSED TO TAKE PLACE IN THE TEMPLE OF AMEN AT KARNAK.
(From Mariette's *Deir-el-Bahari*, plate 11.)

in reply, congratulates her on the success of her expedition, and states that he himself, together with Hathor, the Lady of Punt, and Urtheku, Vice-Regent of the Gods, guided the Egyptian explorers to the land of the myrrh-trees.(⁷⁶)

An ox is then sacrificed to Amen, the sacrificial act being depicted in a bas-relief, from which, unfortunately, the next block is missing, thus carrying away one corner of the subject. Here we see the altar of the god loaded with offerings, among which may be noted a haunch, a goose, and various kinds of cakes. Four priests uplift their hands in adoration; another carries a small stand; while two more cut the slaughtered ox limb from limb.

After this the tribute of Punt is formally transferred to

MEASURING THE PRECIOUS GUM.
(From Mariette's *Deir-el-Bahari*.)

the treasury of the temple; the *Ana* gum (specified in the inscription as "green *Ana*") is measured and registered by the temple servants; while the bags of gold-dust, the bricks of electrum, the ingots of pure gold, and the ivory tusks, are, by a conventional fiction, being weighed in the presence of Horus by no less a sacred scribe than Thoth himself.

The ceremony at the Temple of Amen being concluded, the expedition is rowed across the Nile in a flotilla of State galleys, and proceeds to render homage to Hathor in that part of the temple at Dayr-el-Bahari over which she especially presides. They are accompanied by a detachment of troops composed of the flower of the Egyptian army.

And thus, to the sound of trumpets and drums, with waving of green boughs and shouts of triumph, the great procession lands on the opposite bank of the Nile, and, followed by an ever-gathering crowd, takes its way between avenues of sphinxes, past obelisks and pylons, and up one magnificent flight of steps after another, till the topmost terrace of the Great Temple is reached, where the Queen herself welcomes them to the presence of Hathor the Beautiful, the Lady of the Western Mountain, the Goddess-Regent of the Land of Punt.

Such is the story told in the sculptured decorations of this most interesting and beautiful ruin. Until it was partially excavated by Mariette, only a few of the less interesting sculptures were visible above the sand and débris in which it was entombed. Even now, a systematically conducted excavation would probably bring to light more inscriptions, and possibly more sculptures, than could be discovered by Mariette with the limited means at his command. In the slight but interesting work in which he has commemorated the results of his labor at Dayr-el-Bahari, he expresses his regret that he never had the opportunity there to conduct any properly organized work, such as his excavations of the temples of Karnak, Denderah, and Edfû.

Beyond the fact that Hatasu rebuilt and restored many ruined shrines and temples in various parts of her kingdom, and that the celebrated Speos Artemidos ([6]) was her work, and not, as is generally supposed, the work of Thothmes III., we know little or nothing more of the events of her reign. Seventeen years after the death of Thothmes II., her name, as already said, disappears from the monumental records, and we may assume that she had either ceased to live or ceased to reign.

However this may be, her successor, Thothmes III., endeavored systematically to efface her memory from the minds of the Egyptians and her cartouches from the public monuments on which they had been emblazoned. It is her name which underlies the names and titles of Thothmes III. not only in the Speos Artemidos, but in hundreds of cases at Dayr-el-Bahari. Only in one single instance has the royal oval containing her family name escaped the chisel of the mason; and her solar name, though traceable under the chipped surface, is almost invariably erased. The mere grammatical construction of the texts bears witness, however, to the wholesale forgery committed by Thothmes III.; for, combined with the Pharaonic style in which the inscriptions are couched, the feminine suffixes which are so curiously appended to masculine nouns everywhere remain to show in whose honor these innumerable columns of hieroglyphs were engraved.

The tomb of Queen Hatasu was discovered by Mr. Rhind, in 1841, excavated in the cliff-side, in the near vicinity of her temple; but its identity appears since then to have been forgotten.(") Although the mummies of her father, Thothmes I., of her husband and half-brother, Thothmes II., and of her half-brother and successor, Thothmes III., were discovered in 1881, in the famous tomb of the Priest-Kings, within a stone's-throw of her temple at Dayr-el-Bahari, the mortal remains of Hatasu were missing from the ranks of the illustrious dead with which that sepulchre was crowded. A small wooden cabinet, inlaid with ivory and carved with both her cartouches, was found among the minor objects there concealed. It contains, strange to say, a dessicated human liver—probably hers. This would look as if at one time the mummy of Hatasu had there been deposited, in company with the mummies of her kindred.

A few scarabæi dispersed through various public and private collections; a draughtsman of red jasper, in the form of a lion's head engraved with her two cartouches, which was found at Karnak, and is now in the Museum of Ghizeh; her signet-ring, engraved on turquoise and mounted in gold, in the possession of an English gentleman; and a funerary statuette, or Ushabti, inscribed with her name and titles, in the Museum of the Hague, are, with one exception, the only authentic mementos of Hatasu which have come down to our time.

The exception is a splendid one, and of great historic and archæological value, being an object of no less importance than the throne-chair of this great Queen. It was discovered by some Arabs in 1885 or 1886; brought to England in 1887, and exhibited at the Jubilee Exhibition in Manchester that year. At the close of the exhibition it was presented by Mr. Jesse Haworth to the British Museum, where it now occupies a conspicuous place in the upper Egyptian gallery.

THRONE-CHAIR OF QUEEN HATASU.
(From a photograph from the original in the British Museum.)

Specimens of ancient Egyptian stools and chairs, some beautifully inlaid with marqueterie of ivory and various woods, may be seen in several European museums; but in none do we find a Pharaonic throne such as this, plated with

gold and silver, and adorned with the emblems of Egyptian
sovereignty. It is not absolutely intact. The seat and back
(which may have been made of plaited palm-fibre or bands
of leather) have perished ; but all that remains of the original
piece of furniture is magnificent. The wood is very hard and
heavy, and of a rich dark color resembling rosewood. The
four legs are carved in the shape of the legs of some hoofed
animal, probably a bull, the front of each leg being decorated
with two royal basilisks in gold. These basilisks are erect,
face to face, their tails forming a continuous coil down to the
rise of the hoof. Round each fetlock runs a silver band, and
under each hoof there was originally a plate of silver, of
which only a few fragments remain. The cross-rail in front
of the seat is also plated with silver. The arms (or what
would be the arms if placed in position) are very curious,
consisting of two flat pieces of wood joined at right angles,
so as to form an upright affixed to the framework of the
back and a horizontal support for the arm of the sitter.
These are of the same dark wood as the legs and rails, having a border-line at each side ; while down the middle, with
head erect at the top of the upright limb, and tail undulating
downward to the finish of the arm-rest, is a basilisk carved
in some lighter colored wood, and incrusted with hundreds
of minute silver annulets, to represent the markings of the
reptile. The nails connecting the various parts are round-
headed and plated with gold, thus closely resembling the or-
namental brass-headed nails in use at the present day. The
gold and silver are both of the purest quality.

Of the royal ovals which formerly adorned this beautiful
chair of state, only one longitudinal fragment remains. This
fragment, which measures some nine or ten inches in length,
is carved on both sides, and contains about one-fourth part of
what may be called the field of the cartouche. Enough, however, remains to identify on one side the throne-name, and
on the other side the family name, of Queen Hatasu. The
carving is admirable, every detail—even to the form of the
nails and the creases of the finger-joints in part of a hiero-

glyph representing a hand—being rendered with the most perfect truth and delicacy. The throne-name, " Ra-ma-ka," is surrounded by a palm-frond bordering, and the family name, " Amen-Knum Hatasu," by a border of concentric spirals. The wood of this cartouche is the same as that of the basilisks upon the arms, being very hard and close-grained, and of a tawny, yellow hue, like boxwood. Some gorgeously colored throne-chairs depicted on the walls of a side-chamber in the tomb of Rameses III. at Thebes show exactly into what parts of the framework these royal insignia were inserted, and might serve as models for the complete restoration of this most valuable and interesting relic.

It is a significant fact that the dark wood of the chair and the lighter wood of the basilisks are of growths unknown to Egyptian soil; and it may well be that both originally formed part of that very cargo which the exploring squadron of Queen Hatasu brought home to Thebes, some three thousand five hundred years ago, from the far distant shores of the Land of Punt.

LITTLE CABINET OF HATASU.

NOTES.

Note 1, page 5.—Dr. Birch's calculation was based upon the supposition, then universally accepted, that embalmment was not practised in ancient Egypt till after 2000 B.C., no earlier specimens of embalmed and bandaged mummies having been discovered at the time when he wrote. See Birch's *Guide to the First and Second Egyptian Rooms of the British Museum*, 1878. When, however, the Pyramid of King Pepi (Sixth Dynasty, *circa* 3500 B.C.) was opened in 1880, the mummied remains of that very ancient king were not only found to be impressed by bandages, but portions of these actual bandages were found strewn on the floor of the sepulchral chamber. "On a mis au jour les sépultures du dernier roi de la Vme Dynastie, Ounas, et de plusieurs rois de la VIme, Teti, Pepi Ier, Merenra, Pepi II. La momie de Merenra a été trouvée dépouillée de ses bandelettes, qui avaient été arrachées à une époque ancienne; mais la trace de ces bandelettes, imprimée en relief sur la peau, est restée parfaitement visible et prouve que les procédés d'embaumement déjà constatés pour les époques postérieures, étaient en usage dès la VIme Dynastie." See M. Maspero's paper on Egyptian Exploration, addressed to the Académie des Inscriptions et Belles-lettres, in the *Revue de l'Histoire des Religions*, vol. iv., No. 4, 1881. See also "Lying in State in Cairo," by Amelia B. Edwards, *Harper's Monthly Magazine*, July, 1882.

Note 2, page 5.—For some particulars respecting the shipping of mummies for manure during the reign of the Khedive Ismail, see MacCoan's *Egypt as It Is*, chap. viii., p. 168.

Note 3, page 18.—The colossal seated statue of Rameses II. in black granite, and the remarkable headless sphinx here referred to, are now in the Museum of Fine Arts at Boston, U. S. A.

Note 4, page 23.—Many of these interesting fragments are preserved in the Museum of the Louvre.

Note 5, page 24.—Ancient Egyptian flint weapons and implements have been found in large numbers in various parts of Egypt, but they do not indicate what is understood as a Stone Age, since they all belong to historic times. Flint saws, flint fruit-scoops, etc., have recently been found in large numbers by Mr. Petrie, in the Twelfth Dynasty town of Kahun. Flint chisels are also found in large quantities in the turquoise mines of Wady Maghara, dating apparently from the earliest to the latest time at which these mines were worked, thus showing that flint was not superseded by bronze where flint was equally effectual. See Chabas's *L'Antiquité Historique*, chap. v.; also Lord's *Peninsula of Sinai*, p. 433, *et seq.*

Note 6, page 30.—By such as desire to become better acquainted with the styles and devices of these fascinating amulets, Mr. Petrie's illustrated *Hand-book of Historical Scarabs* will be thoroughly appreciated.

Note 7, page 31.—For illustrations of the various stages of the lotus pattern on the potsherds of Naukratis, see the plates to *Naukratis*, Part I., by Mr. Petrie, and the plates to *Naukratis*, Part II., by Mr. Ernest A. Gardner. See also Prof. W. H. Goodyear's paper on "The Origin of the Ionic Capital and the Anthemion in Greek Art," published in the *American Journal of Archæology*, vol. iii. (1888); also Mr. Goodyear's important forthcoming work, entitled *The Grammar of the Lotus*.

Note 8, page 31.—"Amasis was partial to the Greeks, and, among other favors which he granted them, gave to such as liked to settle in Egypt the city of Naukratis for their residence. To those who only wished to trade upon the coast, and did not want to fix their abode in the country, he granted certain lands where they might set up altars and erect temples to the Gods. Of these temples the grandest and most famous, which is also the most frequented, is called 'The Hellenium.' It was built conjointly by the Ionians, Dorians, and Æolians, the following cities taking part in the work: the Ionian States of Chios, Teos, Phocæa, and Klazomenæ; Rhodes, Cnidus, Halicarnassus, Phaselis of the Dorians, and Mytilêne of the Æolians. These are the States to whom the temple belongs, and they have a right of appointing the governors of the factory; the other cities which claim a share in the building claim what in no sense belongs to them. Three nations, however, consecrated for themselves separate temples—the Eginetans one to Zeus, the Samians to Hera, and the Milesians to Apollo."—*Herodotus*, Book II., chap. clxxviii.

Note 9, page 36.—See *Naukratis*, Part II., by Ernest A. Gardner.

Note 10, page 38.—The Great Sphinx is attributed by Mariette to the mythic ages before the advent of Mena, the first king of the First Dynasty; and Maspero considers it to be, if not actually prehistoric, at all events the oldest monument in Egypt. The Sphinx has been several times cleared from the ever-drifting sands of the desert. The first occasion of which we have any record was in the time of Thothmes IV., that king having celebrated the fact by a votive tablet placed against the breast of the Sphinx, and which yet remains *in situ*. He therein relates that, having been upon one of his hunting expeditions, he lay down to rest in the shadow of the huge image. He there fell asleep and dreamed a dream wherein the Sphinx conjured him to clear away the sand in which it was nearly buried. After this it was cleared again in the time of Pisebkhanu, a king of the Twenty-first Dynasty, who has also left a tablet on the spot; and it must have been cleared again in Roman times, when the paws and breast were repaired with slabs of lime-stone. From that time till the opening of the Suez Canal, the sand continued to accumulate without being disturbed; but it was once again cleared down to the paws in honor of the visit of the Emperor and Empress of the French in 1869.

Note 11, page 44.—Tum, or Atum, the God of the Setting Sun, was also wor-shipped at Heliopolis. He is represented as a man walking, with a head-dress composed of the lotus, with drooping calyx leaves, surmounted by two straight feathers.

Note 12, page 44. The hieroglyphic spelling of "Thukut," or "Sukut," has given rise to much discussion among Egyptologists, the initial hieroglyph of this name being capable of a twofold reading. M. Naville has, however, shown by anal-ogy that this sign must have been used to express the sibilant S as well as the diphthong *Th;* as, notably, in the Greek transcription of the Egyptian name of the city of Thebnuter, which must have had the sibilant pronunciation, as it was tran-scribed *Sehennytus* by the Greeks. See *The Store-City of Pithom and the Route of the Exodus*, 3d edition (1888), by E. Naville.

Note 13, page 47.—The Septuagint was the official and authoritative Bible of Hellenistic Jews, accepted by the Jewish high-priest at Alexandria, and author-ized by the high-priest at Jerusalem and the seventy elders. These latter were, in fact, responsible for the work, and are accredited with the performance of the task of selection and translation. According to a well-founded tradition, the Sep-tuagint was undertaken by order of Ptolemy Philadelphus (286–247 B.C.), and be-gun, if not completed, at Alexandria, the law being the part first translated. We quote the following from the author of the article "Septuagint," in the *Encyclo-pædia Britannica*, 1886: "From Ecclesiasticus it appears that about 130 B.C. not only the law but the 'prophets and other books' were extant in Greek. With this it agrees that the most ancient relics of Jewish-Greek literature all show acquaint-ance with the Septuagint. The later translations of prophets and other books were private enterprises, as appears from the prologue to Ecclesiasticus and the Colophon to Esther. It appears also that it was long before the whole Septuagint was finished and treated as a complete work. The work of translation was gradual, and not uniform. Philo, Josephus, and the New Testament writers use the Septuagint."

Note 14, page 50.—See Josephus's *Antiquities of the Jews*, xiii., 3.

Note 15, page 54.—See *Tanis*, Part I., chap. ii., by W. M. Flinders Petrie. See also "Tanis," by Amelia B. Edwards, *Harper's Monthly Magazine*, October, 1886.

Note 16, page 58.—See *Goshen and the Shrine of Saft el Henneh* (1887), by E. Naville.

Note 17, page 73.—For an admirable account of the methods of ancient Egyptian painting, see Maspero's *Egyptian Archaeology*, chap. iv., pp. 164–201.

Note 18, page 75.—See Pliny's *Historia Naturalis*, Book XXXV., chap. iii. See also Woltmann's *History of Painting*, chap. i.

Note 19, page 75.—See *Plinie's Naturall Historie*, translated by Philemon Holland, Book XXXV., chap. iii., London, 1601.

Note 20, page 78.—See *Les Origines de l'Historie d'après la Bible*, chap. xiii. François Lenormant. See also Note 27.

Note 21, page 79.—See "Les Attaques dirigées contre l'Égypte," *Revue Archéologique, nouvelle sér*, Vol. XVI., by E. de Rougé.

Note 22, page 80.—For a full account of these discoveries, and fac-similes of the archaic alphabetic signs scratched on the potsherds of Kahun and Gurob, see Mr. Petrie's new volume, entitled *Kahun, Gurob, and Hawara*; Trübner & Co., 1890.

Note 23, page 81.—Mr. Lepage Renouf has recently cast grave doubts upon the usually accepted significance of the papyrus and lotus groups, which he maintains in nowise stand for Upper and Lower Egypt. It has also been suggested by M. Grébaut that another well-known group of hieroglyphs, signifying "the two lands," may refer not to Upper and Lower Egypt, but to the right and left banks of the Nile.

Note 24, page 83.—From the earliest date at which we have any knowledge of the manners and customs of the ancient people of Syria, we find them delighting in rich and picturesque raiment, after the fashion of the garments worn by the typical Syrian in our illustration. Joseph's coat of many colors was, we may be sure, a fringed and embroidered garment such as these; and that this kind of embroidery was carried to a point of great perfection at a later period is shown by the enumeration of the booty taken from Sisera in the "Song of Deborah," where we read of "a prey of divers colours of needle-work on both sides meet for the necks of them that take the spoil."—Judges, chap. v., verse 30. See also Psalm xlv., verses 13 and 14: "The King's daughter is all glorious within: her clothing is of wrought gold. She shall be brought unto the King in raiment of needle-work." See also the descriptions of the hangings of the tabernacle and the garments of the priests in the books of Exodus and Leviticus.

Note 25, page 84.—The Libyan tribe, called the Maatsaiu (thus spelled phonetically in the hieroglyphs), are represented by the Mâazehs of the present day. They were employed by the Pharaohs as gendarmes, or armed police. See "La Carrière administrative de deux hauts fonctionnaires Egyptiens," *Journal Asiatique*, Avril–Juin, 1890, by Professor Maspero.

Note 26, page 91.—Mr. Ernest Gardner, referring to this beautiful Sphinx plate in *Naukratis*, Part II., writes as follows: "This is a plaque-painting rather than a vase design. It is executed with the utmost delicacy and ease in four colours—yellow, brown, purple or red, and white; these are the typical four colours of early painting, and we can hardly doubt that they were the four that characterized the technique of Polygnotus and other early masters. Here, then, we have an example closely approaching to a panel picture, showing us exactly how these colours were used. Perhaps the most remarkable thing of all is the use of touches of white to bring out the high lights. Unfortunately it is hardly possible to see this now; but when the plate was first taken out of the ground such touches were distinctly visible in some places, especially on the front of the fore-legs and paws. The use of the other colours may be pretty clearly seen on the plate. The outlines are drawn in brown with a brush, but incised lines are also used, especially to indicate the plumage on the breast. Above the head of the sphinx two small holes were bored through the rim of the plate, clearly indicating that it was intended to be hung up, in all probability as a picture to decorate the wall of the temple. If so, we may with yet more certainty regard this plaque as affording us invaluable information as to the style prevalent in the free paintings of the period—if, indeed, any existed in the sixth century which were not purely decorative in their subject and treatment." See *Naukratis*, Part II., chap. v., p. 45, by Ernest A. Gardner.

NOTE 27, page 92.—According to *Herodotus*, Book I., chap. xciv., there was a great famine in Lydia in the time of Atys, son of Menes, wherefore the King divided the nation in two halves, and it was decided by casting lots which half should remain in Lydia, and which should go into exile. The lots being drawn, he gave his son Tyrsenos to the emigrants for their leader, and they built ships, and put out to sea in search of some fertile place in which to settle. Having touched at the ports of many nations, they at last colonized Umbria, and there founded cities which they still continued to inhabit in the historian's own time. He further goes on to say that they ceased to call themselves Lydians, and, taking the name of their early leader, called themselves Tyrsenes. This is the same people whom we meet with in the Egyptian hieroglyphic chronicles as the Tursha. And here, again, we find them evidently in search of a new home in which to establish themselves as a settled colony. During the reign of Meneptah Egypt was invaded by the Libyans, in alliance with the Achæans, the Tursha, and other tribes from the coast-lands of Asia Minor. In this coalition the Tursha appear as emigrants under arms, rather than as mere invaders in search of plunder; for it is expressly said in the great inscription which records the defeat of the invaders that "the Tursha took the lead in this war, all the warriors from that country having brought their wives and their children." If, however, the Tursha, or Tyrsenes, were in search of a new country in the time of Meneptah, they seem to have found a home by the time of Rameses III., some sixty years later; for, in the great invasion of Egypt by the Græco-Asiatic and European tribes, which took place during the reign of that Pharaoh, the Tursha occupy but a secondary place, and send only a small contingent to the war. This, as Lenormant observes, points to the fact that the bulk of the nation had by this time found their long-sought place of settlement in Central Italy. According to this authority, it was towards the fifteenth or fourteenth century, B.C., that the Tursha, or Tyrsenes, who up to that time had inhabited the western coast of Asia and the islands of the Ægean, emigrated *en masse* in a westward direction, and settled in Central Italy. See *Les Origines de l'Histoire d'après la Bible*, chap. xiii., by François Lenormant.

NOTE 28, page 94.—It was Apollodorus who first combined landscape and figures, and who first abandoned the old system of monochrome background. He was also the first of the Greek painters who mastered the difficulties of light and shadow. "Apollodorus was the first to give his pictures a natural and definite background in true perspective; he was the first, it is emphatically stated, who rightly managed chiaroscuro and the fusion of colors. Hence he earned the title of *Skiagraphos*, or shadow painter. He will also have been the first to soften off the outlines of his figures, and thus no longer to draw and tint merely, but, in the true sense of the word, to paint with his brush. For this reason we may, with Brunn, in a certain sense call Apollodorus the first true painter."—Woltmann's *History of Painting*, chap. ii., p. 46.

NOTE 29, page 96.—For a more detailed account of these portraits and their discovery, see *Biahmu, Hawara, and Arsinoë*, by W. M. Flinders Petrie, chaps. iii., vi.

NOTE 30, page 104.—In the Græco-Roman cemetery at Hawara, in which these portraits were discovered, Mr. Petrie found a large number of mummies inwrapped in garments both woven and embroidered in rich colors and elegant designs, many in extraordinary preservation. Woollen socks, various kinds of shoes and sandals in leather and palm-leaf, as well as a number of head-scarfs and hair-nets in delicate netted thread-work and woollen-work were also found. Specimens of these hair-nets and netted head-dresses are to be seen at the South Kensington Museum, London. These very curious relics of wearing apparel, etc., date from 200 A.D. to

300 A.D.; they are therefore of later origin than the portraits, and belong to subsequent interments. The manufacture of netting for trimming purposes, etc., may, however, have been common long before.

Note 31, page 116.—For full particulars of these early tombs and their contents, see *Les Mastabas de l'ancien Empire*, by A. Mariette Bey.

Note 32, page 118.—See Mr. Lepage Renouf's volume of *Hibbert Lectures*, 1879. Lecture IV., p. 147 *et seq.*

Note 33, page 119.—The tablet of Pepi-Na is in the Museum of Ghizeh.

Note 34, page 120.—The tablet of Napu is in the possession of Jesse Haworth, Esq.

Note 35, page 140.—The presence of these statues of servants in tombs of the ancient empire may very possibly point to a far distant prehistoric time, when the servants were themselves sacrificed and buried in the tombs of their masters.

Note 36, page 143.—See Sir Charles Newton's description of the treatment of the human figure by Greek sculptors, *Essays on Archæology*, chap. viii., p. 360 (1880).

Note 37, page 149.—The first Sallier Papyrus (British Museum), after having been long regarded as an historical document, has been shown by Professor Maspero to be a popular story, based probably upon fact, but indebted for some of its incidents to the common stock of Oriental folk-lore. Of this king, Apepi, we only know that he repaired and embellished the Great Temple of Tanis, that he built a temple to Sutekh, a Semitic deity, and that it was in his time that the Theban princes, headed by Sekenen-Ra-Ta-a, commenced that war of independence which resulted in the expulsion of the Hyksôs. The first Sallier Papyrus, which is unfortunately much mutilated, begins by describing how "the whole land did homage to King Apepi, and how the King took unto himself Sutekh for lord, refusing to serve any other God in the whole land." It then goes on to say how he called his counsellors and magicians together, to assist him in framing a fantastic message to Sekenen-Ra-Ta-a, in which he desired that prince to hunt down the hippopotamuses of Upper Egypt, because they prevented his sleep by day and by night. Sekenen-Ra-Ta-a received this message with dismay, and summoned his captains and generals to advise him as to its meaning, whereupon they were all struck with silence and terror. Here the manuscript breaks off abruptly, and we are left with the enigma unsolved. It is evident, however, that Apepi imposed an impossible task upon the Theban prince, in order to compel his acceptance of some unwelcome alternative, such as the abjuration of his national faith, and his conversion to the worship of Sutekh. What the historic kernel of this story may have been it is impossible to say, but it seems probable that Apepi endeavored to abolish the worship of the Gods of Egypt, in order to impose upon his subjects the exclusive worship of Sutekh. Such a proposal, if addressed to the tributary princes of Thebes, who were the direct descendants of the great Twelfth Dynasty Pharaohs, would have been sufficient to precipitate that great rising which was already inevitable. The first Sallier Papyrus has been translated into English by E. L. Lushington, in *Records of the Past*, vol. viii.; into German by Brugsch, in his *Geshichte Ægyptens unter den Pharaonen;* and into French by Professor Maspero, in his *Contes Populaires de l'Egypte Ancienne*. There are also translations by Ebers, Chabas, and others.

Note 38, page 149.—See M. Naville's *Bubastis*, being the Eighth Annual Memoir published by the Egypt Exploration Fund.

Note 39, page 157.—See "Lying in State in Cairo," in *Harper's Monthly Magazine* for July, 1882.

Note 40, page 157.—The highest honor which an Oriental can bestow upon a stranger or a friend is to abnegate in his favor the tomb prepared for his own mortal remains. It was thus that Joseph of Arimathea gave up his own sepulchre, as related in Matthew xxvii., 57-60; Mark xv., 43-46; and Luke xxiii., 50-53. An interesting modern instance of how the modern Arab still prepares his tomb during his own lifetime, and how, when influenced by friendship, he offers to dedicate it not only to the remains of a stranger, but to a stranger who is a woman and an infidel, is recorded in the experiences of Lady Duff Gordon.

20

Note 41, page 160.—"'Yavan' is the Hebrew rendering of 'Ionia,' and is employed in the Bible in a generic sense, designating the Greek nationalities collectively." See Lenormant, *Les Origines de l'Histoire d'après la Bible*, chap. xiii.

Note 42, page 164.—See "Mémoire sur les Attaques dirigées contre l'Egypte," *Revue Archéologique*, 1867, by De Rougé.

Note 43, page 168.—The wall-paintings and inscriptions of these extremely interesting tombs have just been exhaustively copied by means of photographs and colored tracings by Messrs. Newberry, Fraser, and Blackden, agents of the Egypt Exploration Fund, this being the first series of monuments undertaken for the great Archæological Survey of Egypt.

Note 44, page 169.—See Mr. W. M. Flinders Petrie's Lecture on Naukratis, delivered at the Annual General Meeting of the Egypt Exploration Fund, October 28, 1885. Printed in the Third Annual Report of the Society, pp. 14–32.

Note 45, page 170.—For the Orchomenos ceiling, see Schliemann's *Orchomenos;* Leipzig, 1881, Pl. I.

Note 46, page 171.—See Dr. Schliemann's *Orchomenos.*

Note 47, page 174.—"The age of the Doric temple at Corinth is not, it is true, satisfactorily determined; but the balance of evidence would lead us to believe that it belongs to the age of Cypselus, or about 650 B.C. The pillars are less than four diameters in height, and the architrave—the only part of the superstructure that now remains—is proportionately heavy. It is, indeed, one of the most massive specimens of architecture existing, more so than even its rock-cut prototype at Beni-Hassan, from which it is most indubitably copied. As a work of art, it fails from excess of strength, a fault common to most of the efforts of a rude people, ignorant of their own resources, and striving, by the expression of physical strength alone, to obtain all the objects of their art."—*History of Architecture,* vol. i., Book III., chap. ii., p. 220, by Fergusson.

Note 48, page 181.—See *American Journal of Archæology*, vol. iii., Nos. 3 and 4.

Note 49, page 195.—An excellent translation of this papyrus, published, with commentary, in the *Bibliotheca Sacra*, 1888, has been made by Professor Howard Osgood, of Rochester, N. Y.

Note 50, page 196.—Mr. Petrie has more recently found at Gurob fragments of the Phædo of Plato and the Antigone of Euripides—certain portions of the latter part of the play being hitherto unknown.

Note 51, page 213.—It was the opinion of De Rougé that this papyrus is a later copy, and that the date and signature are mere transcriptions from an earlier document. Erman, basing his opinion upon the fact that a well-known scribe named Pentaur lived some 70 years later during the reign of Meneptah, doubts not only that the copy was made in the 7th year of Rameses II. but that Pentaur was the author. It is, however, quite possible that the Pentaur of Meneptah's time was a son of the original Pentaur, inheriting his profession and his office. In any case, the name of Pentaur was not uncommon; and the fact that there was a Pentaur in the time of Meneptah is really no reason for dismissing as mythical the Pentaur of the preceding reign. In the mean while the colophon can only be accepted as it stands.

Note 52, page 217.—Besides the better known transcriptions of this poem on the pylon-walls of Luxor and the Ramesseum, and in the great hall at Abû-Simbel, there are some remains of other transcriptions in the Temples of Rameses II. at Abydos in Upper Egypt, and Derr in Nubia.

Note 53, page 218.—See Chabas, in *Zeitschrift für Ægypt: Sprache*, 1864. Also Lieblein, in a paper entitled "Les Anciens Egyptiens Connaissaient-ils le Mouvement de la Terre?" Transactions of the Congrès Provincial des Orientalistes Français, 1 Bulletins, vol. ii.

Note 54, page 220.—The Prisse Papyrus has of late been admirably translated into French from the original Egyptian by M. Philippe Virey (1887).

Note 55, page 221.—Translated by M. Pierret, *Recueil des Travaux*, 1870.

Note 56, page 222.—These sixteen tales, some of which are fragments only, are all to be found in the latest edition of M. Maspero's delightful little volume of *Contes Egyptiennes*, 1889.

Note 57, page 223.—See *Études Egyptiennes*, G. Maspero, Tome I, Fascicule 3, 1883.

Note 58, page 225.—The flowers mentioned in this love-song are identified by Professor Maspero with "Sweet Marjorum," Purslane, and Mugwort, all sweet-smelling herbs. In adapting my translation to the English language, I have ventured to substitute Henna, one of the Lythracea, for the less poetical original.

Note 59, page 226.—We may even know how the words of this song actually sounded in the mouths of the men who sang them 3540 years ago. The old tongue is strange enough to our modern ears, but thanks to its close relation to the Coptic, and to the researches of modern Egyptologists, we are enabled to call back its far-off echoes.

<table>
<tr><td>

1.

Hi ten enten,
Hi-ten enten,
 Aha-u! Aha-u!

</td><td>

2.

Hi-ten enten! Hi-ten enten!
Tehen en amu!
Shesu en Nebuten, Shesu en Nebuten,
 Aha-u! Aha-u!

</td></tr>
</table>

Note 60, page 228.—See, for many important papers on the religion and mythology of the ancient Egyptians, Professor Maspero's contributions to the *Revue de l'Histoire des Religions* during the past ten years.

Note 61, page 230.—See Tyler's *Primitive Culture*, the chapter on Totemism.

Note 62, page 231.—Bulletin de la Religion d'Egypte in *Revue de l'Histoire des Religions*, 1st year, vol. i., No. 1.

Note 63, page 236.—See *Herodotus*, Book IV., chap. cxxxi-cxxxii.

Note 64, page 241.—For an account of the Horshesu, see chap. ii., "The Buried Cities of Ancient Egypt."

Note 65, page 254.—The God Khem, also by some Egyptologists called Min and Am. He was identified by the Greeks with Pan, and by the Romans with Priapus.

Note 66, page 261.—That Hatasu was not their only daughter is shown by a funerary bas-relief sculpture representing Thothmes I. and Ahmes-Nefertari with their daughter, the princess Neferu Kheb, who died in infancy. Whether Hatasu was the elder or the second daughter we do not know; but in either case, as the survivor, she was heiress to the throne.

Note 67, page 262.—"The Black Land and the Red Land" signifies Lower and Upper Egypt; the Black Land being the dark mud of Lower Egypt, and the Red Land the sandy deserts of Upper Egypt.

Note 68, page 263.—See "Études des Monuments du Massif de Karnak," by E. de Rougé, in the *Mélanges d'Archéologie*, vol i., page 50.

Note 69, page 264.—See *Le Musée Egyptien*, by E. Grébaut, Part I.; see also an article by G. Maspero, in the *Revue Critique*, No. 49, December, 1890.

Note 70, page 264.—For a description of the winding-sheet of Thothmes III., see *Les Momies Royales de Deïr-el-Baharî*, Part I., p. 548.

Note 71, page 269.—Compare various translations of this inscription in *Records of the Past*, in *Cleopatra's Needle*, by Sir Erasmus Wilson, and in *The Egypt of the Past*, by the same author.

Note 72, page 272.—The lofty tower which is yet standing of this ruined convent has been the temporary abode of Lepsius, Champollion, Rosselini, and Sir Gardner Wilkinson, while they were prosecuting their researches.

Note 73, page 272.—One whole sphinx, and part of another are in Berlin.

Note 74, page 272.—See *Deïr-el-Baharî*, by Auguste Mariette, folio, 1877.

Note 75, page 273.—In 1874 two of these prostrate Hathor-head capitals were in admirable preservation, the hair being colored yellow, the eye-balls white, with a black disk for the iris; and the necklace, if I remember rightly, black, green, and red. By this time, probably, they are scored over with travellers' names, or chipped to pieces by relic-hunters.

Note 76, page 276.—See *Deïr-el-Baharî*. Mariette, p. 31.

Note 77, page 280.—This celebrated subject forms one of the great historic series relating to the reign of Seti I. sculptured in bas-relief on the north outer wall of the Hypostyle Hall at Karnak. The canal is represented by two vertical lines enclosing a narrow space of water, conventionally rendered by zigzags, the banks being each planted with a row of trees. The only bridge known to be represented in ancient Egyptian art is here shown as crossing the canal in front of the fortified gates of a strong frontier fortress, named El Khetam, or "The Key." For an exact reproduction of this important sculpture, see Rosselini, *Monumenti Storici.* A part of the subject is also given in Eber's *Egypt*, vol. ii.

Note 78, page 282.—Dr. Doenitz, in his remarks on the fishes, contributed to Dr. Dümichen's work, *Die Flotte einer Ægyptischen Königin*, writes of these turtles as tortoises, and classifies the crawfish as the *Palinurus penicillatus* of the Red Sea. He remarks, however, that the Egyptian artist has here and there mixed up the fishes of the Nile and the Red Sea in a curiously arbitrary manner, having more than once introduced the sacred *oxyrhinchus* of the Nile among the fishes of Punt.

Note 79, page 285.—The speech which the Egyptian lapidary scribe has here put into the mouth of Parihu gives to Hatasu the glory of being the first ruler of Egypt whose representatives visited the Land of Punt; the tablet of Sankhara (Eleventh Dynasty) in the Wady Maghara refers, however, to an expedition, despatched by this Pharaoh to the Land of Punt in quest of the "green anu." The tablet states that the King's explorers started from Coptos and crossed the Arabian desert by the old trade route to a port on the Red Sea, the site, no doubt, of the more modern city of Berenice. Here they built and launched the vessels which conveyed them to the coast of the Somali country. See the Wady Maghara Tablet in Lepsius' *Denkmäler.*

Note 80, page 286.—The Egyptians entertained an extreme reverence in the abstract for the Land of Punt, which apparently formed part of a larger district known generally as Ta-nuter, or the Land of the Gods. Hathor and Bes, two of the principal deities worshipped by the Egyptians had their divine origin in Punt, and Hathor was adored under a special form as "The Lady of Punt." Bes, in his grotesque features and general characteristics, is clearly a barbaric divinity, and is occasionally represented as nursing or devouring the large cynocephalus apes depicted in the wall-sculptures of Dayr-el-Bahari as indigenous to the Land of Punt. The Egyptians appear to have cherished a vague tradition of their own origin as natives of Ta-nuter at some extremely remote period; and it is interesting to note that the curved beard characteristic of these natives of the Land of the Gods is a special attribute of divinities as well as of deified personages in Egyptian art.

Note 81, page 287.—An inscription at Karnak, which gives a long list of the booty brought to Egypt after a victorious campaign of Thothmes III., especially mentions a certain curious bird "which delighted the heart of his Majesty more than all other things." The architraves of this Pharaoh's Hall of Pillars, also at Karnak, are covered with elaborate representations of foreign flowers, trees, and plants brought by that king from Syria for planting out in the great botanic garden attached to the Temple of Amen at Thebes. A wood-cut in Maspero's *Egyptian Archæology* admirably reproduces some of these very curious designs. (See English translation, 2d edition, p. 89, fig. 100.)

Note 82, page 288.—See *Plinie's Natural Historie*, translated by Philemon Holland, 1691, Book XII., chaps. xv. and xvi.

Note 83, page 289.—See Schweinfurth's *Heart of Africa*, vol. i., p. 271.

Note 84, page 291.—See Chabas, *Antiquités Historiques*, chap. iii.

Note 85, page 293.—The Egyptian word *Pera*, signifying literally "Great House," is the invariable name for a royal palace. It is also used as a synonym for the King himself, and gives us the origin of that title which is transliterated in the Hebrew Bible by "Pharaoh." This employment of the name of the palace as a synonym for the name of the King is exactly paralleled at the present day by our own use of the term "Sublime Porte," or "Great Gate-way" for the title of the Sultan of Turkey.

Note 86, page 295.—Urtheku, or "Great Charmer," is a Goddess of Magic but rarely met with in the inscriptions.

Note 87, page 296.—A somewhat similar inscription on the face of the cliff above the entrance to the celebrated Speos Artemidos in the province of Minieh, which is in part effaced, has recently been copied and deciphered by M. Golenischeff. This sanctuary had hitherto been attributed to Thothmes III.; but M. Golenischeff has discovered that the royal ovals of this king are resculptured over those of some earlier sovereign, who, to judge by the mention of Hathor of Punt, and the products of the Land of Punt, can have been none other than Hatasu. In the course of the same inscription it is said that she had restored the temples of the Gods in various parts of Egypt where they had been ravaged and overthrown by the enemy, whom we may presume to have been the Hyksôs.

NOTE 88, page 297.—See Rhind's *Thebes, its Tombs and their Tenants.*

INDEX.

Aahlu, Fields of, idea borrowed by Greeks, 186.
Ab, 117.
Abode of Tum, 48.
Abraham, 38, 196.
Abû-Simbel, 53, 79; battle-piece, with Rameses II., 213–217; portraits at, 86, 87.
Abydos, 17.
— Great Temple of, 211.
— Lord of, 120.
Achæans, 76, 160, 167, 191.
— first appearance of the, 163.
— or Akaiusha, 79.
— pictures of, 163.
Achilles, 163.
Ægean, Islands of the, 199.
Æsop, indebtedness of, to Egypt for "Lion and Mouse," etc.; Brugsch and Maspero on, 223.
"Agib, Prince, and Lodestone Mountain," 224.
Ahmes Nefertari, Queen, 263, 264; mother of Hatasu, 261; portrait described, 156.
Aimia (the Ionians), 79.
Akaiusha (the Achæans), 79.
Akerit (the Carians), 162.
Alcæus, 23, 196.
Aleppo, 204, 206, 208; portrait described, 216, 217.
Alexander, 75, 114, 222; Thothmes III. the Alexander of ancient Egyptian history, 160.
Alexandria, 6, 7, 26, 37, 40, 101, 179; art at, 35.
Algeria, 84, 199.
Alphabet, hieroglyphic, given, 245.
Am, City of, 18, 34.
Amasis, 30, 61, 179, 180, 223.
— as a hero of fable, 225.
— II., 28, 33, 76, 88.
— last of the Saïte kings, 165.

Amasis, Naukratis and the Greeks, 180, 225.
Amen, 102, 156, 206–208, 262, 270.
— address of the Great God, 160; brigade of, 204, 216; coming to aid in battle; idea borrowed by Greeks, 205.
— Great God of Thebes, date of existence, 227.
— Great Temple of, 262, 267, 294, 296.
— High-Priest of, 157.
— Lord of Thebes, 291.
— of Thebes, 279.
— one with Ra, 231.
— oxen sacrificed to, 295.
— Sacred Book of, 292.
— speculations about, 228.
Amenemhat I., 52.
— II., 18.
Amenemhats, dynasty of, 168.
Amenhotep III., 125, 126, 128, 150.
Amen-Knum Hatasu, 300.
Amen-Ra, 126, 199, 269.
American Journal of Archæology, 170.
Amorites, 205.
— frontier of the, 204.
Amr, 41.
Amu, Land of the, 291.
Amulets, 4.
Anacreon, 194, 196.
Ana sycamore. See Nehet Ana.
Ani, ape, 292.
— scribe, maxims quoted, 221.
Ankh, 127, 128, 156.
— as Father of Ma, 125.
— associated with Ka, 126.
— as symbol of life, 126, 187.
— identified with Ka, 127, 128, 129.
— — with King, 128.
Au-Tursha, 77–79.
Anubis, 187, 228.
— speculations about, 228.
Apelles, 71, 75, 112.
Apepi, face identified, 148.

Aphrodite, Temple of, at Naukratis, 20, 29, 35.
Apis (Ptah) as Greek Serapis; identified with Zeus, 102.
— as Soul of Osiris and Life of Tum, 231.
— speculations about, 228.
Apollo, 35.
— at Naukratis, 191.
— at Tenea, 190.
— at Thera, 190.
— Strangford, the, 190.
— temple to, 29.
Apollodorus, 94, 97.
Arabia, 146, 199, 288, 298.
Arabs, 5, 6, 8, 11, 13, 14, 39, 41, 64, 68, 69, 84, 255, 276.
— at tombs, 98, 142.
Aradus, 203, 206.
Arameans, 276.
Archæology defined, 24.
— Egyptian, period of, 24.
— requirements for study of, 24–26.
— school of, at Athens, 29.
Archipelago, 78.
Ardagh, Lieutenant-colonel, survey of, 280.
Argolis, 160, 161.
Ari-n-Amen (Ammonarin), 102.
Aristides, 75.
Arsinoë, City of, 105.
Art, Alexandrian, 35.
— Assyrian. See Assyrian.
— decorative designs. See Decorative designs.
— early examples, 132.
— Egyptian. See Egyptians.
— Greek. See Greeks.
Artemidorus, 96.
Aryan Hellenes, 168.
Ashmolean Museum, Oxford, 195.
Asi, 120.
Asia Minor, 73, 202.
— — light on history of, 80.
— — tribes of, 80.
Asiatic Greeks, 73.
Asiatics, 200.
— influence of the, on Egyptian art, 133.
— types of, on tombs, 82.
Assûan, 53, 54, 176, 256.
Assyrians, 68, 69, 159.
— art of the, 74, 132.
— — influenced by Egypt, 81.
— early works in sculpture of the, 132.
— empire of the, 38.
— sculpture of the, 114.
— writing of the, 244.
As-t (Lady), mother of Thothmes III., 264.

Astronomy, 217, 218.
Ateta, King, author of anatomy, inventor of hair-wash, 218.
Athena, 90, 229.
Athenæus, 29.
Athens, 30, 37, 74, 75.
Athribis, City of, 254.
Ati (wife of Prince of Punt), 284, 289.
— Chabas on, 285.
— Maspero and Mariette on, as type, 285.
Atmu (Tum, Tumu), 81.
Augustus, 258.
Australia, aborigines of, 230.
Auvergne, 6.

Ba (Egyptian, soul), 117.
— Greek misinterpretation into harpy, 187, 188; into siren, 189.
— representation and office of, 187, 188.
Baal, 206, 208.
Babylon, 61, 63.
Babylonians, 62, 159.
— designs borrowed, 171.
— inscriptions of the, 68.
— writing of the, 244.
Bakakhiu, 57.
Bak-en-Khonsu, 271.
Balât (brickwork), 68.
Bechuanas of South Africa, 230.
Bedouin, Mound of the (Tell Bedawi), 17.
Benha (site of Athribis), 254.
Beni-Hasan, 168, 169, 172, 174, 191.
— columns of, 180.
— decorative designs at, 170, 172.
Berlin, Museum of, 190, 259.
Bible, the, 42, 50, 58, 63.
— its account of Pharaoh's house verified, 68.
— its history of the Hebrews verified, 40.
Bibliothèque Nationale, Paris, 195, 220.
Birch, Dr., 4.
Bitter Lakes, 46.
Bodleian Library, 23.
Book of the Dead, The, 14, 187, 196, 198, 233, 249, 258.
— its "Negative Confession" quoted, 232.
British Museum, 33, 92, 111, 155, 162, 180, 189, 190, 212, 225, 298.
Browne, Sir Thomas, 5.
Brugsch, Dr., 46, 118, 197.
— finding fable, "Lion and Mouse," etc., 223.
— on Hatasu, 261.
— theory about Egyptian religion, 228.
Brune, M., at Karnak, 274; restorations at Dayr-el-Bahari, 272, 273.
Bubastis (modern Zagazig), 6, 26, 45, 50, 133, 146, 280.

Bubastis, Temple of, 8, 148.
Bûlak, 27.
— "Wooden Man of," Ra-em-ka, 139, 140.
Bull-clan of Memphis, 230.
Burton, Lieutenant, survey of, 280.
— Sir Frederick, 158.
— — on panel portraits, 106.

Cadmean Greek inscriptions, 77.
Cæsars, 14, 37, 114.
Cairo, 6, 7, 16, 26, 39, 40, 116, 141, 168, 176, 179, 256.
Canaanite, A, 82.
Canal, branch of Nile existing in Nineteenth Dynasty; Author believes it was built by Hatasu, 281.
— course of, described, 280.
— represented as Ta-Tena, walls of Karnak temple, 280, 281.
Caria, 206.
Carians, 58, 76, 167.
— as the Akerit, 162.
— troops of the, 66, 88, 164.
Castellani, Signor, 108.
"Castle of the Jew's Daughter," 64, 68.
Central Africa, 285.
Ceremonial deposits, 31, 32.
— — time of Philip Arrhideus, 34.
Cervetri, 92.
Chabas, on Princess Ati, 285.
Chaldea, 271.
— art of, 132.
Chaldean governor, 61.
"Chant of Victory," 198, 199.
— Mariette on the, 202.
— ranked with Pentaur by Brugsch, 202.
— recording conquests of Thothmes III., 198.
—· text given, 199–202.
— where found, 198.
Charles II., 153.
Chaucer, 114.
Cheops, 71.
Children of Israel, 80, 105, 191.
Christianity, introduction of, 9.
Cinderella, Egyptian origin of story, 223.
Cinnamomifera regio, sometimes aromalifera regio, 276.
Cinnyris metallica, the, 281.
Clans, Bull, Crocodile, 230.
Cleopatra, 38, 39.
Collignon's Archéologie Grecque, 87.
Colossi of the Plains, 53.
Colossus of Rameses II.; described, 53, 54.
Combs, 4.
Coptic monasteries, 272.
— memoranda, 10.

Coptic monks, 9.
Coptos, 276.
Copts, the, 5, 112.
Corinthian capitals, 186.
— — compared to Egyptian, 174.
Crocodile-clan, Fayûm, 230.
Cross-legged scribe, 140, 143.
Cuirasses, Egyptian Tarena, 163, 164.
Curium, 26.
Cyclopean temples, 167.
Cynocephalus Babuinus, 292.
— Hamadryas, 292.
Cypriote alphabet, 77, 78; ancestry, 110; art, 35; pottery, 77; relics, 26; schools in decorative designs, 183; sculpture, early examples of, 132; settlers, 167.
Cyprus, 80, 186, 201.

Damietta, 7, 176.
Danai, or Danæans (descendants of Danaos), 76, 77, 201.
— first appearance as Greeks under Thothmes III., 76, 160.
— history of name, 160, 161.
Daphnæ, 50, 61, 62, 76, 90, 92, 180, 184, 187.
— colonization of, by Greeks, 191.
— founded by Psammetichus I. for Carian troops, 88.
— Greek, Daphnæ of Pelusium; Arab, Tell Defenneh, 58.
— history of, 58–63, 165, 166.
— identified as the Biblical Tahpanhes, 58, 63, 165, 166.
— Jeremiah quoted, 65–67.
— lotus design by potters of, 183.
— Petrie's discoveries at, 63–69.
Dardanelles, 163.
Dardani (Dardanians), 163.
— as Asiatic Greeks by Thothmes III. and Homer, 78.
Dardania, 208.
Dardanians, 76, 163.
— history and laws of, 3, 191.
Darius and Scythians, Herodotus on, 235, 236.
Dayr-el-Bahari—Arabic, signifying Convent of the North, Coptic monastery, 271, 272; illustrations from, 277, 293; Mariette at, 296; restorations by Brune, 272–274; Temple of Karnak at, 271, 274, 275, 297.
Decius, 258.
Decorative designs, 169–171.
— — comparison of Greek and Egyptian, 170–172.
— — Egyptian, Egg-and-dart pattern, 184.

Decorative designs, Egyptian. Goodyear on (*The Grammar of the Lotus*), 172.
— — Greek, as affected by lotus (examples), 181, 182.
— — honeysuckle-pattern, 169; first appearance of, 183.
— — identity of Greek with Egyptian, 173.
— — key pattern, 160, 170, 183.
— — lotus (see flower also), 172, 181, 183; discussed and described, 176, 179.
— — Orchomenos, 172.
— — palmette, 171, 172, 185; the royal, 181.
— — Petrie on, 169.
— — Petrie's discoveries at Tell Defenneh, 182.
— — Rhodian type, 182, 183.
— — rosette, 169, 171, 172.
— — Schliemann quoted, "on long bud," 172.
— — spiral, 169, 172.
Defenneh vase, 184.
Deir-el-Bahari, Mariette on, 287.
De Lesseps, M., 280.
— following in canal-course of Hatasu, 281.
Delos, 167, 174.
Delta, 4, 6–8, 15, 16, 26, 31, 40, 41, 58, 176, 185, 245, 252.
— Eastern, 57, 88.
— history and resources of the, 41, 42.
— marsh canals, 18.
— Western, 166, 179.
Demetrius, 96.
Denderah, 11, 296.
Dessûk, 26.
Diocletian, 57.
Diogenes (artist), 104.
— Flute of Arsinoë, 105.
Dodecarchy, the, 164.
Doric columns, development of shaft in Egypt, 191.
— Ferguson quoted on, 173, 174.
Dürer, Albert, 114.
Dynasty I., 38, 218, 230, 237, 241.
— II., 135, 195, 237; tablets of, at Oxford, 135.
— III., 135, 195.
— IV., 116, 135, 136, 139, 177; Tombs of, 195.
— V., 116, 140, 177.
— VI., 52, 116, 177, 195.
— XI., 52, 76, 150, 195, 227, 256, 258.
— XII., 11, 18, 52, 77, 145, 148, 168, 220, 222, 242, 257, 261; date of founding, 168; School of sculpture, 145.
— XIII., 52, 146.

Dynasty XVII., 146.
— XVIII., 76, 77, 84, 92, 125, 129, 150, 151, 256, 257, 261; poetry of, 226.
— XIX., 8, 10, 52, 80, 151, 152, 155, 179, 188, 230, 257, 283; Pharaohs of, 194; sepulchres of, 82.
— XX., 17, 53, 75, 77, 80, 82, 86, 151, 182, 194, 230; sepulchres of, 82.
— XXI., 157.
— XXII., 43.
— XXIV., 258.
— XXV., 257, 258.
— XXVI., 18, 29, 58, 130.
— XXX., 44.

Ebers, Dr., 26, 98, 178.
Edfû, 39, 296; Temple of, 9.
Egypt, 3–5, 10, 11, 15, 16, 20, 22, 23, 33, 37, 42, 43, 62, 63, 67.
— ancient names of Tamari, Nehi, etc.; as Ta-meri, Neri, Khem or Khemit, 254.
— comparative history of, 37, 38.
— divisions of, 40.
— historic age of Horshesu, 241.
— history as a nation, 38, 39, 63.
— topography of, 39–41.
— under Hatasu, 268.
Egyptian artists, 70–72, 100; methods, 73; with new types, 86.
— Exploration Fund, 15, 50, 57, 67, 218.
— — history and place of, 40.
— Hall (Piccadilly), 106.
— manuscripts, 57.
— panel portraits with process, 98–101.
— pigments, etc., 99.
Egyptians, 14, 67, 96.
— art of the, compared to Greek, Assyrian, etc., 74.
— — early examples of the, 71, 132.
— — effected by Hadrian, 97.
— — emancipated from old traditions, 94.
— — exponent of religious beliefs, 134.
— — influence on Greeks, etc., 81, 87–91.
— — influenced by Asiatics, 133.
— — light thrown by Greek inscriptions on the, 79.
— — manner and methods, 71–73.
— — painting, 75, 97.
— — Petrie's discoveries of the, 79.
— — potters, 78.
— — relation to Ka, 134.
— — religious origin of the, discussed, 115, 134.
— — schools classified—Memphite, Saïte, etc., 133, 134, 139–141. ·
— — sculpture compared with the Greeks, 134, 135.

Egyptians, art of the, summary, 94.
— — superiority of early schools, 184.
— — Theban period, 81.
— belief of (parts of man, destiny after death), 186.
— character of the, discussed, 222.
— early, 6, 194, 229.
— love of meditation, 195; of songs and stories, 222.
— on tombs, 82.
— types of, 100.
Eisenlohr, Dr. August, 218.
El Defenneh, 64–66.
Elephant River, 282.
Elizabeth (Queen), 261.
— Hatasu as the Elizabeth of Egyptian history, 261.
El Kab, 112, 226.
El Kasr el Bint el Yahûdî (the "Castle of the Jew's Daughters"), 64.
Erastosthenes, 166.
Erectheum, 186.
Ero Castra, 46.
Etham, 46.
Ethiopia, 73, 80.
Ethiopians, 84, 154.
— on tombs, 82.
— portraits described, 85.
Ethnological Department, South Kensington, 23.
Etruscans, 78; Egyptian Tursha, 79, 92; Greek Tyrrhenes or Turseni, 92.
— alphabet of, 78, 79.
— art of, 74, 80.
— — affected by Greeks, 91; by Egyptians, 81.
— — compared to Egyptian, 92.
— — history of, 91, 92, 163, 193.
— — necklaces, 108.
— — painting on tombs, 92, 93, 95.
— — sculpture, 79.
— — standards, 93, 94; summary, 94.
Eudoxus, 166.
Euphrates, 199.
Eusebius, 198.
Exodus, the, 8, 41, 42, 45, 79.
— later, the, 62.
— route identified, 46.
Explorers, requirements for and trials of, 20–26.

Falstaff, 286.
Fayûm, 23, 77, 79, 94, 98, 99, 104, 147.
— described, 96.
— mummies at, 96.
— panel-portraits at, 102–104, 112.
— Petrie at, 77.
— site of Labyrinth at, 95, 96.

Fellows, Sir Charles, 188.
Fields of Aahlu, 186, 187.
First empire, 115.
Food, 4.
Fresh-water Canal, 42.
Funerary tablets, etc., 4, 119, 120.

Galen, 218.
Galerius Maximian, 44.
Gardner, Ernest A., 19, 23, 29, 35, 36.
Genesis, 46.
Germanicus, 112.
Gérome, 281.
Geschichte Aegyptens unter den Pharaonen, 197.
Gezireh, 8.
Ghizeh, 116.
— Great Pyramid of, 71, 131, 136, 227, 237.
— museum at, 136, 155, 264, 298.
— necropolis of, 137.
— sphinx of, 11, 38.
— tombs of, 156, 195.
Gibraltar, Strait of, 279.
Gliddon, M., paraphrasing poem, 226.
Glyptotheca of Munich, 190, 271.
Gnostic gems, 10.
Gobryas, 236.
Goodyear, W. H., 170, 181.
— Egyptian origin of Ionic column, 170.
— Lotus, origin of, 172.
Goshen (modern Saft el-Henneh), 58; identified with Kes, 58; land of, 58.
Graeco-Asiatic alphabet, 77.
Graeco-Egyptian panel-painting, 97.
Graff, Herr, 98.
Grammar of the Lotus, The. See Lotus.
Great Oppression, the, 58.
Great Pyramid, 71, 131, 136, 227, 237.
Grébaut, M., 264.
Greece, 97.
Greeks, the, 5, 9, 14, 96.
— alliance with Hittites, 162; disappearance under Rameses and second alliance (first chapter European history), 162, 163.
— alphabet of the, 79, 80.
— architecture of the, 173; columns compared to Egyptian, 173–175; Ferguson on, 174; indebtedness to Egypt, 186 (see also designs); Ionic discussed, 176, 179, 180; Perrot on, 175.
— at Daphnae, 165, 166.
— at Naukratis, 165, 166, 181.
— early colonies, 30, 76, 77.
— first appearance in Egypt, 159.
— gems of, 10.

Greeks, gentleman and lady (costume), 102, 103.
— in Egypt as Danai or Danæa, 160, 161; as the Hanebu, the Hebrew îyé haggóim, 159, 160.
— invasion under Psammetichus and founding of Daphnæ of Pelusium (Biblical Tahpanhes), 164, 165.
— language of, 199.
— manuscripts of, 57.
— meeting point of, 63.
— of Asia Minor, 78.
— of the Ægean, 78, 193.
— of the Archipelago, 76.
— papyrus of (Ptolemaic times), 196.
— Petrie on evidence, 78.
— Petrie's discoveries as evidence in art, 79.
— prehistoric, 191.
— relics of (coins, etc.), 22, 28, 30, 35, 65, 66, 77.
— towns of, 58, 61.
— transcriptions of, 45.
— art of the, 36, 80.
— — adaptation and alteration of Sphinx, 90.
— — ceramic history of, 30, 31, 36.
— — compared to Egyptian, 75.
— — decorative designs: affected by lotus, 181; history of, 31; identity with Egyptian established, 173; indebtedness to Egypt, 169–172, 181; summary of evidence, 185.
— — early specimens, 87, 89.
— — evidence quoted, 190.
— — indebtedness to Egypt, 81, 88, 89, 167, 189.
— — painters of portraits, 41, 74, 75, 100, 101.
— — sculpture, 79, 132.
— — summary, 94.
— — work of Apollodorus, 94.
Griffiths, F. Llewellyn, 57.
— Mr., 16, 22, 34; explorations described, 19, 20.

Hadrian, 97, 103, 112.
Hair-pins, 4.
Halicarnassus, 26.
Hall of Columns, 199.
Hanebu (Egyptians as Greek Hellenes), 76, 161, 189.
— (Hebrew îyé haggóim) as Greeks in Egypt, 159–161.
Harpakhrat, 18.
Harpy, Greek misinterpretation of Ba, 187–189.
— tomb of, at British Museum, 187, 188.

Hatasu, Queen, 125, 261.
— as builder, Temple of Karnak, 270.
— as Pharaoh, 267.
— conjectures of Mariette on, 150.
— daughters of, Hatasu-Meri, Neferu-Ra, and marriage of one daughter with Thothmes III., 267.
— Egypt under, 268.
— expedition to Land of Punt, explanatory text quoted, and speculations about route, 276, 279, 280; pictures of, explained, 281, 296.
— fame destroyed by Thothmes III., 297.
— history, genealogy, and marriage with Thothmes II., 263–268.
— identity established, 262, 263.
— obelisks of, with inscriptions quoted, 151, 268–270, 271.
— only relics of, 279, 298.
— portrait described, 150, 151.
— "Procession of the Queen," 293.
— Rougé, Dr., on 262.
— royal oval of, 297, 299.
— scientific ancestor, De Lesseps as builder of the great canal, 281.
— ships of, 276–278.
— Speos, Artemidos, 296.
— statue of, 273; with cow, 274.
— throne-chair, 298.
— tomb of, 297.
Hathor, the beautiful goddess, 125, 126, 224, 274, 296.
— as Lady of Punt, 283, 294.
— Karnak dedicated to, as Lady of the West, deity of Punt, etc., 275.
Hawara, graves at, 23, 105.
— Petrie and panel-portraits of, 102–112.
Haworth, Jesse, 208.
— relics, 22.
Hebrew settlers, 42.
— transcriptions, 45.
Hebrews, 40, 42, 48, 58, 131.
— history of the, 63; light on, 40.
Heidelberg, 218.
Heliodorus, 28, 57.
Heliopolis, Great Temple and Sacred College of, 198.
Hellas, 30, 38, 75, 76, 168.
Hellenic tribes, 28.
Hera, 29.
Her-Hor, High-Priest of Amen, 157.
Hermonthis, 208.
Herodotus, 8, 14, 29, 84, 166, 176.
— credulity of, 222.
— on Daphnæ, 165.
— on Naukratis, 179.
— on Tel Defenneh, 64.
— quoted on Labyrinth, 95.

Herodotus, story of Darius and the Scythians, 235.
— story of Rhodopis and the sandal, 223.
Heroöpolis, 47.
Herusha, 202.
Hindoo Kush, 259.
History, none of Egyptian, Manetho in Greek, 197, 198.
Hittites, 188, 203, 216, 217.
— against Rameses, 205.
— allied with Lycians, Mysians, Carians, Ionians, and Dardanians, 162, 163.
— battle-piece of Abû-Simbel, 214.
— leagued with Greeks in Egyptian wars, 162.
— war-chariots, 205.
Homer, 23, 77, 191.
— Papyrus found under a woman's head, now in British Museum, 197.
Homeric vases, 87.
Hophra, refuge of daughters of Zedekiah in Egypt, 165.
— service of gold, 67.
Horace, 37, 194.
Horemheb (Pharaoh), 150, 152, 161, 189.
— inscription on Pylon, 286.
Hor-pa-khroti (Hor-the-child), borrowed by Greeks as Harpocrates, 186.
Horshesu, 38.
Horus, 90, 127, 128, 202, 252, 295.
— child of, 80.
— followers of, 38.
— Greeks borrowed as God of Silence, 182.
— the Victor "hut" as an emblem, 127.
Hotep-hers, Lady, 137.
Hottentot, 285.
Houses, decoration of, described, 7.
Hui, 84, 112.
Huts of mud described, 8, 9.
Hyksôs (Shepherd Kings), 147–149
— invasion of the, 194.
— kings, history of the, 146–150.
— race of, 148.
— rule of the, 268.
— school of sculpture, 146; finest specimens of, 148.

Ibis-clan, Hermopolis, 230.
Ibrem, 101.
Iliad, 160, 191, 202.
— buried with lady, 23.
— Second Book of the, 23; found by Petrie, 196.
Ilion, 208.
Images, Greek and Egyptian, 10.
Immortality believed by Egyptians, 131.
Indians, Red, picture-writing of, 237, 238.

Inscriptions describing Prince of Punt, 291.
— early examples of, 77.
— of Maskhûtah, 42–44.
Ionians, the (Aiunu), 76, 79, 163.
— columns of, discussed, 179; earliest examples of, 180.
— decorative designs identified with lotus. See Decorative Designs.
— of Daphnæ, 166.
— troops of, 58, 66, 88, 164.
— volute, 185.
Ireland, Erin, etc., 254.
Isarous, Lady, 101, 102.
Isi-ari-s or Ast-ari-s, 102.
Isidora (Isadore), 102.
Isis (Ision), 102.
Ismaïlia, 41, 46, 280.
Ismel, 62.
— children of, 48, 80, 105, 191.
— — in Egypt, 58.
Israelites, 42, 48.
Italy, Alps of, 77; an early nation, 193; tribes of, 79.

Jacob, 41, 47.
Jeremiah, 62, 67, 68, 165.
— prophecy of, quoted, 62, 63.
Jerusalem, 61.
Jewellers, 30.
— workshop of the, 30.
Jewels, 4.
Jewish guests, 67.
— types, 105.
Jews, antiquities of the, 198.
Johanan, 61, 62.
Joppa, taking of, like Ali Baba, 223.
Joseph, 46, 47.
— oath of, 131.
Josephus, 50, 198.
Journal of Hellenic Studies, 92.
Judah, 62, 63.
— royal line of, 68, 69.
Julius Cæsar, 112.
Jupiter, 102.

Ka, 186, 187.
— and the "Ankh," 126–130.
— as life, 131, 232, 263; summary of argument about the, 130–132.
— as Oath of Pharaoh—Joseph, 131.
— association with the "Ankh," 126–130.
— as Suten-ka (Ankh Neb Taui), Life of, Lord of Two Lands, Royal Ka, 128.
— Brugsch, definition of the, 118.
— chambers, 142.
— different interpretations of, 122.
— discussion of the, 117–119.

Ka, dogma of the, 128–134.
— fidelity of likeness in Ka statues, 132, 133.
— Greeks and the Kha and Khai, 131.
— hieroglyphic for the, 118.
— Maspero defines the, 118.
— relation to portrait statues explained, 122, 132.
— Renouf, Le Page, defines, 118, 129.
— statues, 141.
— supplication tablets, etc., 119, 121.
— theory of author on the, 123–130; of Maspero, 122.
— relating to the, 124–130.
— Wiedemann defines the, 118.
Kadesh, 162, 202–206.
Kadeshites, the, 208.
Kafoo (monkey), 292.
Kahun relics described by Petrie, 243.
Kalynb, 7.
Kami, Greek kommi, 255.
— Latin gummi, 256.
Kareah, 61.
Karkhemish, 202, 208.
Karnak, 153, 163, 185, 199, 268, 270, 296, 298.
— built by Hatasu, 270, 271.
— column and Temple of Thothmes III., 175, 179.
— dedicated to Amen, Great God of Thebes, and to Hathor, Lady of Punt, 275.
— Great Temple of, 28, 151, 154, 160, 198, 212, 261, 268.
— pictures and sculptures of canal and great expedition on walls, 280–296.
— present aspect of, 272–274.
— pylon of Pharaoh (Horemheb), 189.
— restored by Brune, 272.
— speculations as to building, 274.
Kati, 203.
Ken-un, 135.
Kes, 58. See Goshen.
Kha-em-uas, Prince, hero of fable, son of Rameses II., 225.
Khafra, 11, 136.
Khaïbit, 117.
Kha, Khai, 131.
Khamatic family of languages, including Syrians, Ethiopians, etc., 259.
Khem, or Khem-t, Khemet, Khemi, ancient hieroglyphic name of Egypt, 254.
— god of productiveness, 254.
— survival in chemistry, and carried by Arabians to Moors and Europe, 254, 255.
Khepersh, war-helmets, 154, 267.
Kheta, or Hittites, 203, 204, 208.

Kheta, prince and people of; princess of, wife of Rameses II., 205, 211.
— soldiers of, 213.
Khonsu, 262.
Khou, 117.
Khufu, 11, 135, 136.
— "Ankh," 83, 136. See Ka.
— king of, as builder of Great Pyramid and hero of fable, 71, 225.
— priest of, 131.
King of Karagoné, 281.
Kings, Pyramid, 11.
— Shepherd. See Shepherd Kings.
Kitchen of Pharaoh at Tell Defenneh, 65, 66.
Knum, speculations about, 228.
— with Ra, 231.
Kols of Khota Nagpar, in Asia, 230.

LABYRINTH, The, at Fayûm, 95, 96.
— destroyed by Romans, 95.
— Petrie at, and portraits from, 69.
— plateau of, 98.
Land of Canaan, 7, 40, 41, 42, 47, 203.
— of Punt. See Punt.
Language, Grammar of the, 259.
— Semitic and Khamatic one source, 259.
— theories as to origin of the, 259.
Latium, 78, 92, 100.
Leather, 4.
Leku (Lycians), 79, 188.
Lenormant, François, 78, 79.
Lepsius, 41, 42, 46.
Leyden, 259.
Libyan Range, 4.
Libyans, 73, 77, 159.
Life, Egyptian and Greek theory of, 131.
Linen, 4.
"Lion and the Mouse." See Æsop.
— Brugsch on, 223.
Literature, Egyptians first in field of, 195.
— "Chant of Victory," 190.
— "Cinderella" borrowed from, 223.
— comments on growth of, 191–193.
— compared to Greek, 196.
— difference between writing and, 195.
— Ebers's discoveries, 219.
— fables borrowed from, 228. See Æsop.
— indebtedness of Æsop to, 223.
— inscriptions of 4200 B.C. on stone, 195.
— London, in, 259.
— love songs and romances, 222; "The Doomed Prince," 224; "Tale of Two Brothers;" "Taking of Joppa;" "Shipwrecked Mariner," all borrowed by Greeks, 222–224.

Literature, mathematical papyri found at Tanis and Thebes, 218.
— medical books, 218.
— moral philosophy, 219; maxims quoted, 220.
— necessity for convenient writing material, 194.
— no history (Manetho's in Greek), 198.
— Papyrus of Homer, where found, 197.
— Pentaur, poem of, 205.
— Petrie's discoveries, 196.
— poetry — examples quoted: Prisse Papyrus (oldest book in the world), 195.
— scientific, remarks on, 217; astronomical, 217, 218.
— subjects always historical and religious, 197.
Lord of Abydos, 120.
Lotus: as a flower, 176, 177.
— as designs affecting Greek decorative art, with examples, 181–183, 186.
— Defenneh vases, 184.
— first appearance in architecture, 184.
— Grammar of the Lotus, The, 172.
— Marquand, Prof. Alan, on, 186.
— Petrie's discoveries, 179.
Louis XIV, 153.
Louvre, Museum of the, 57, 190; Egyptian Department of the, 218.
Lower Egypt, 4, 14.
Lucius Verus, 112.
Luxor, Great Temple of, 211.
Lybia, 163, 199, 201.
Lybians, 163, 188.
— on tombs, 82.
— types described, 83, 84.
Lycia, 76, 77, 188, 206, 208.
Lycians (the Leku), 79, 92, 162, 163, 167; first alliance, 163; amnesty, 211.
Lydia, 203.

Ma, 125.
— Goddess of Justice, 263.
Macedonian rule, 101.
Makara, 262.
Man, definition of, 234.
Manetho, High-Priest of Ra, wrote history of Egypt in Greek, 11, 197, 198.
Marcus Aurelius, 112.
Mariette, 4, 26, 116.
— at Meydûm, 142.
— at tomb of Nefert, 142.
— conjectures about Hatasu, 150.
— excavations at Dayr-el-Bahari, 296.
— on "Chant of Victory," 202.
— on Land of Punt, 276.
— on sycamore, 287.

Mark Antony, 39.
Marquand, Prof. Alan, 186.
Martial, 194.
Mashuasha, 84.
Maskhûtah, Tell-el-, 42.
— described, 48.
Masonic deposits, 18; at Tell Nebesheh, 33; where found, 32. See Petrie.
Maspero, Professor, 4, 69, 116, 118; finding fable of "Stomach and Members," 223; identifying Land of Punt, 276; on the Ka, 122; speculations about canal, 282.
Maten, located, 201.
Maut, 120, 127, 162.
Mautemhatmest, 120.
Mautemua (Queen-mother), 125.
Mautnefer, Queen, wife of Thothmes I., mother of Thothmes II., 264.
Maxims on demotic papyrus (Lowe), 221; of Ptah-hotep in Prisse Papyrus, 220; of Scribe Ani, quoted, 220, 221.
Maxyans, 84.
Medes, writing of the, 244.
Medinet-Habû, 86, 87, 133.
— temple of, 156.
Medit, 16.
Mediterranean, 8, 77.
Memphis, 4, 17, 37, 58, 61, 133, 164, 165, 219, 223, 256.
— medical library, 218.
— mounds of, 6, 11.
— school of, typical series, 138.
Memphite school, 145.
— compared to Florentine, 145.
— compared to Greek, 143.
— school of sculpture, 133, 134, 141; its character drawn, 141.
— school summarized, 143–145.
— statues as bodies for Ka, 134.
Memphites, the, 148.
Mena, Prince of Thebes, 24, 38, 230, 241.
— history begins with, 240.
Meneptah (Pharaoh of Exodus), 162, 167, 173, 188.
Menthu, 208.
Menzaleh, Lake, 58, 63.
Mertetefs, Queen, 125, 135–137.
Mesopotamia, 140, 199, 200, 259.
Mexico, picture-writing, 249.
— described, 237, 238.
Meydûm, 116, 142.
Michael Angelo, 114.
Middle Egypt, 4, 40.
Migdol, 48.
Milesians, 29.
— at Naukratis, 166.
— colonists, 28, 36.

Models, ceremonial and industrial, buried at Naukratis, 32, 33.
Mohammedan invader, 39.
Monasteries, Coptic, 272.
Mongolian types, 11, 148.
Mosaic books, 160.
Moses, 38.
Mounds, 11, 12.
— contents of, described, 4, 6, 17, 18.
— estimates of, 5.
— excavating of, described, 10–14.
— growth of, and geological strata, 7–9.
— of Bedouins, 17.
— of Bubastis, 6.
— of Lower Egypt, 40.
— of Maskhutah, 48–50.
— of Memphis, 6.
— of Nebireh (city of Naukratis), 26.
— of Tanis, 6.
— of Tell Defenneh, 63.
— of Twenty-sixth Dynasty, 18.
— of Wady Tûmilât, 41.
— situations of, 15, 16.
— with temples, 11.
Mozambique Channel, 279.
Mummies, 4.
— at Fayûm Labyrinth, 96, 98.
— bandages of, 11.
— of Roman and Pharaonic period, 108.
— statistics about, 5.
Museum : Athens, 190.
— Berlin, 190, 259.
— Bibliothèque Nationale, Paris, 195, 220.
— Ghizeh, 136, 155, 264, 298.
— Glyptotheca of Munich, 190, 271.
— Hague, the, 298.
— Leyden, 125.
— Louvre, the, 102, 141, 212.
— Naples, 121.
— Oxford, 195.
— Paris, 259.
— South Kensington, 197.
— Vienna, 259.
Mycenæ, 168, 169, 171.
Mycians, the, 76.
Mysia, 206, 208.
— tribes of, 203.
Mysians, the "Masu," 162.

Napoleon the First, 281.
Napu, 119, 121.
— funerary tablets of, 120.
National Egyptian Museum (Ghizeh), 69, 115, 116.
Naukratis, 20, 23, 30–35, 36, 50, 57, 58, 61, 76, 92, 165, 181, 184, 185, 223.
— colonized by Greeks, 191.
— description of, 26–31.

Naukratis, fragments at, 36.
— Herodotus on, 179.
— history of, 28, 180.
— locality of, 26.
— mounds of, 26, 28.
— plate described, 90, 91.
— pottery of, 31.
— sculpture found at, 34.
— Sheikh of, 16.
Naville M., 4, 22, 34, 41, 42, 46, 48, 57.
— discoveries in Saft-el-Hennch, 57.
— discovery of Hyksôs portraits, 148.
— — Jewish cemetery, 50.
Nebireh, 26, 28. See city of Naukratis.
Nebuchadnezzar, 61–63, 68, 69.
Necropolis, 2, 3, 7.
Nectanebo I., 44.
— II. (monolithic shrine of), 57.
Nefert, statue of, described, 142.
— Princess, portraits of, described, 137–139.
Nehet Ana (sycamore of Ana), 287, 288, 292–295.
— as gifts, 288–291.
— Mariette on, 287.
— Pliny quoted on, 287, 288.
Nehi (ancient Egypt), 254.
Neko, 65.
Nelumbium speciosa (rose lotus), 176.
Nemhotep, 132, 133.
Nenuphar, 176. See white and blue lotus.
New Testament, 10.
Newton, Sir Charles, paraphrase quoted, 143.
Nikias, 74.
Nile, 5, 7, 16, 37, 39, 70, 164, 176, 269, 280, 296.
— branch of canalized in Nineteenth Dynasty, 280.
Nile Valley, 3, 4, 9, 11, 31, 71, 101, 197, 218, 229, 241.
— relics of the, 80.
— stone age of the, 24.
Nilus, 126.
Nineveh, 26.
"Nomes" (provinces), 38.
Notem-Maut, Queen, 157.
Nubia, 11, 40, 112, 200, 256.
— types of, 100.
Nubian corps, 293.
— fashions in hair, 84.

Obelisk, 8.
— at Rome, 270.
— in Central Park, 53.
— of Tanis, 54.
— on Thames Embankment, 53.
Odysseus and the Sirens, 189.

Œdipus of the Daphnæ, 92.
— and the Sphinx, 89.
Olympiad, the, 79, 159.
Olympus, 205.
Onias, 50.
Orchomenos treasury and ceiling, 168, 170-172, 185, 191; decorative designs, 172.
Orontes, 162.
Oscano, the, 193.
Osiris, 119, 120, 186, 219, 232.
Osorkon II., 43, 52, 53.
Ovals, royal, of Hatasu, 297, 299.

Pa-Bast, defined, 45.
Pahiri, at El-Kab, songs in stone, 226.
Palestine, 112.
Palmetto, Oriental, 181.
Pames Isis, 44.
Pandarus, 188.
Panel-portraits, 97-111.
— — comments on, 112.
— — Egyptian lady, 104.
— — speculations about, 108, 111, 112.
Pan-Hellenian, 29, 31.
Papyrus: first knowledge of use of, 195.
— found by Petrie, Twelfth Dynasty, 196.
— Great Harris, creation of Ptah, 218.
— Greek and Roman, 10.
— necessity for, 194.
— oldest papyrus (Prisse), 195.
Parihu, the Great, of Punt, 283, 289.
Pa-Tum, 44.
— meaning of, defined, 45.
— of Sukut, 46.
Pausanias, 74.
Payni month, 212.
Pedasos, 203.
Pelasgi, the, 171; speculations as to origin of, 84, 168.
Pelasgic Greeks, 76.
Peloponnesus, 163.
Pelusiac, bank of the Nile, 58.
Pelusium, 63, 77.
Pentaur: edition in papyrus, 212.
— Epic of (The Great Iliad), with contents described, 173, 202.
— Greek and Hittite invasion, 162.
— identity of man, 212.
— poem quoted, 205, 210.
— where found, 212.
Pepi Merira, 52.
— Pepi-Na, funerary tablet of, 119-121.
— Pyramid, 11, 227.
Pericles, 37, 174.
Perrot on Corinthian architecture, 175.
Persepolis, sculptures of, 114.
Persians, the, 14, 236.

Persians, the, as invaders, 39.
— tablets of, 10.
— writing of, 244.
Petrie, M., 16, 17, 22, 29, 30, 32, 53, 64, 66-68.
— at Daphnæ, 166, 184.
— at Fayûm, with value of discoveries, 77, 79, 80.
— at Lake Menzaleh, 58.
— at Naukratis, 26, 166, 179-181.
— at Tanis (Zoan), 51, 57.
— at Tell Defenneh, 63, 64.
— at Tell Nebireh, 80, 179.
— contradicting Herodotus, 165.
— dates of Temple of Apollo, 184.
— discoveries of, 50; of Greek alphabet signs, 79.
— explorations and excavations described, 19, 166.
— finding Lady of Iliad, 23.
— Masonic deposits, 32, 33.
— on designs, lotus, etc., 169, 182, 183.
— on standards, in relation to false doors and Ka, 123, 124.
— panel portraits and pictures on tombs, 82, 84, 88, 90, 96, 98, 111, 112.
— papyrus, mathematical, 218; Twelfth Dynasty at Fayûm, 196.
— Rameses II. colossus, 53.
— relics of Kahûn, 243.
Pharaoh III., 18.
— Hophra, 68.
— Usertesen II., 73, 78.
Pharaohs, the, 4, 38, 48, 76, 80, 114, 131, 157, 167, 258.
— costumes of, 294.
— crown and sceptre of, 90, 248.
— days of, 4, 153.
— house of, in Tahpanhes, 19, 63, 67, 68.
— kitchen at Tell Defenneh, 66.
— land of, 84.
— last of, 57.
— of Twelfth Dynasty, 145, 168; dates given, 169.
— of Twentieth Dynasty, 152, 194.
— prisoners of, 80.
— three names of each, 123.
— verifying Bible accounts of, 68.
Pharaonic canal, 48, 50.
Phidias, 143.
Philadelphus, 41.
Philip Arrhidens, ceremonial deposits of the time of, 34
— of Macedon, 174.
Phœnicia, 201.
Phœnicians, the, 159, 171, 276.
— alphabet of, 78.
— sculpture of, 77, 132.

Piccadilly, 106.
Pierret, theory about religion, 228.
Pigments in panel-portraits, 99.
Pihahiroth, 46, 48.
Pikeheret, 48.
Pindar, 196.
Pithom (treasure-city), 41, 42, 45, 48.
— bricks of, 49.
— identified with Bible account, 50.
— of Succoth, 46.
Plato, 14, 37, 71, 166.
Pliny, 74, 77, 79.
— historical views justified, 76, 77.
— on art of Greeks, 97; of Egyptians, 75.
— on Sycamore Ana, 287, 288.
— reasons for prejudice, 77.
Polygnotus, 74, 91.
Portrait sculpture, at Fayûm, 98, 99.
— — oldest examples of, 135.
Potters, 31.
— factory at Naukratis, 30.
Praxiteles, 143.
Prince of Punt. See Punt, Prince of.
Prisse Papyrus (oldest book in the world), 220.
Prometheus, 131.
Protogenes, 74.
Proto-Homeric vases, 75
Psammetichus I., 61, 64–66, 76, 88.
— dynasty of, 119, 130.
— founder of Daphnæ of Pelusium (Biblical Tahpanhes), 164, 165, 180.
— founder of the Twenty-sixth Dynasty, 164.
— palace-fort of, 182.
Ptah, 218.
— brigade of, 204, 205.
— the Memphis, the Ra of Heliopolis, 231.
Ptah-hotep, 221.
— maxims of, 220.
Ptolemaic Greeks, 96.
Ptolemies, the, 9, 10, 14, 46, 223.
— time of, 161.
Ptolemy Lagus, 74.
— Philadelphus, 32, 33, 47, 50, 198.
Punt, as Parihu, 823.
— Land of, 276, 279, 300.
— later prince of, 286.
— located, 201; by Maspero and Mariette as Somali, 276.
— presents to Hatasu, 291.
— Prince of, 277, 287.
— tableau of expedition described, 281–296.
— wife of, 284.
Pyramid Kings, the, 11, 116, 132, 227.
— Period, 118, 166, 218.

Pyramids, the, 38, 76, 218.
Pythagoras, 166.

Ra, 123, 126, 131, 212, 219, 251, 262, 269.
— as Amen-Ra, Knum-Ra, Sebek-Ra, the Great All, 231.
— brigade of, 204, 205.
— speculations about, 228.
— worship of, 231.
Raamses (treasure-city), 41, 45.
Ra-em-ka, "Wooden Man of Bulak;" portrait described, 83, 139, 140.
Ra-hotep, General, 137, 142.
— portraits described, 83, 139, 142.
Ra-ma-ka (throne-name), 300.
Ra-men-Kheper, 200.
Rameses I., 18, 151.
— history of, 11, 51, 52.
— II., The Great, 10, 13, 18, 38, 43, 44, 52, 79, 80, 86, 87, 152, 155, 163, 188, 204, 205, 225.
— as hero of Pentaur, 202–205; Pentaur quoted, 205–210.
— as Pharaoh of the Great Oppression, 162.
— at Tanis, 52.
— exploits given in battle - piece, Abû-Simbel, 213–217.
— portraits and statues, 53, 153, 154.
— Temple of, 57.
— where buried, 155.
— wooden mask of, 157.
— III., 75, 77, 80, 86, 173, 300.
— and the Greeks, 162.
— history of, and Twentieth Dynasty, 155.
— tomb of, 82.
— Mer-Amen, 212.
— of Tanis (colossus), 53, 54.
Ramesseum at Thebes, 53, 211, 217, 264, 271.
Ramses, 42.
Ras-el-Fil, 282.
Red Sea, the, 48, 280, 282.
Religion (Egyptian), first to recognize immortality, 231.
— idea of the Ka, 232.
— identity of Rah, Ptah, Amen, 231.
— in relation to sculpture, 117.
— of man divided the body into Khat, Ba, Khon, Khaïbit, Ren, Ka, Ab, Sahu, 117.
— microcosm of man, 232.
— morality, standard of, 233.
— polytheism and monotheism, with speculations about Ra, etc., 228, 281.
— Ra as Great All, 231.

Religion (Egyptian), theories of Brugsch and Pierret, 228.
—— the author on, 227, 229–231.
— Totemism, 228, 230, 231.
— unsettled present knowledge of, 227.
Ren, 117.
Renouf, Le Page, 118.
— on Egyptian verbs, 260.
— on the Ka, 129.
Revillout, Prof. Eugene, 57, 218, 227.
Rhind, tomb of Hatasu, 297.
Rhodes, 186.
Rhodian school, Greek only in Greek art, 183.
Rhodopis, 223.
Romans, the, 5, 14, 44, 96, 107.
— coins of, 10.
— growth of period, 9.
— language of, 199.
— rule of, 46.
Rome, 8, 37.
Rosetta, 176.
Rotennu, 201.
Rouge, Vicomte de, 261.
Rubaiyat, 98.

Sabeans, 288.
Safekh, 126.
Saft el-Henneh, 57, 58.
Sahu, 117.
Sailors, Egyptian, 290.
Saïs, 26, 58, 164.
Saïte Kings, 165; Period, 10, 119.
Sakkarah, 78, 116.
Salatis, 147.
Salhadscher, 26.
Sallier Papyrus, 149.
Sandals, 4.
Sàn, description of, 50.
Sàn-el-Hagar, 51.
Sankhara, King, 76, 159.
Santorin, ancient cemetery of, 79.
Sappho, 23, 194, 196.
Sarapis (wrong for Serapis), 102.
Sardinia, under foreign rule, 86.
Sardinians, 77.
— chieftains of the, 86.
— first alliance of the, 163.
Sayce, Professor, 171.
Scandinavia, 239.
Scarabs, 11, 166.
— described, 30.
— makers of, 30.
Schersehell, 199.
Schliemann, Dr., on decorative designs, 170, 171.
Schweinfurth, *Heart of Africa*, 289.
— on Bongo women, 285.

Sculpture, Egyptian, compared with Greek, 134, 135.
— Hyksôs school of, 146.
— Middle Empire school of, 145.
— of Prince of Punt expedition, 281–296.
— relation to the Ka of sculpture portraits, 134.
— religious origin of portraits, 115.
— Theban school of, 151.
— wooden portrait-masks, 156.
Scythias, 147.
Sebek, with Ra, 231.
Semites, the, 87.
— types of, 100, 152.
Sennefer, 83, 137.
Seneca, 112.
Seneferu, last king of Third Dynasty, 135.
Sen-Maut, architect, Dayr-el-Bahari, 271.
Septuagint, 46, 47.
Sepulchres, Twentieth Dynasty, 82.
Set, 202.
Seti I. (father of Rameses II.), 77–79, 126, 152, 157, 280, 281.
Seti II., 18; portrait described, 154, 155.
Set-nekht (Rameses I.), 18.
Severus, 44.
Shabtûn, 203, 205.
Shakespeare, 114, 234.
Shalûf, 46.
Shepherd Kings (Hyksôs), 11.
— history of the, 146.
Sheshonk I., 43; Sheshonk, 52.
"Shipwrecked Mariner" likened to "Sindbad the Sailor," 225.
Shishak, 43.
Sicilians, the, 77.
— first alliance of, 163.
Sinai, 199, 268.
"Sindbad the Sailor," 225.
Siptah, 155.
Siren (Greek misunderstanding of Ba), 189.
Siût, 11.
Smith, Cecil, 107.
Solon, 166.
Somali, 255.
Soudan, the, 85, 255, 256.
Spaight, Major (survey of), 280.
Speke, description of, wife of Karagoué, 285.
Speos Artemidos, 296, 297.
Sphinx, the, at Ghizeh, 11, 38, 89, 239.
— headless, 18.
— type described, and Greek alteration of, 90.
St. Albans, 44.
Standards, military, Egyptian, Roman, etc., 93, 94.

Statues, 8.
"Stomach and Members" (Æsop), Maspero on, 223.
St. Peter's, 8.
Strabo, 71.
Stratford-on-Avon, 114.
Stuffs, 4.
Suez, Gulf of, 16, 280.
Sukut, 44, 46.
Susa, sculptures of, 114.
Sutekh, 204, 208.
— brigades of, 205.
Sweetwater Canal, 48, 280.
Syene, 101.
Syria, 50, 62, 80, 199, 200, 202.
— provinces of, 162.
Syrians, the, 73, 96, 204, 217.
— chiefs, 204.
— costumes of, 83.
— medical lore of, 219.

TA-AN (Tsan). See Tanis.
Ta-art (gift of Isis), Isidora, 102.
Taha (Gaza), location of, 200.
Tahpanhes identified, 58, 63. See Daphnæ and Defenneh.
Taluti (general to Thothmes III.), 223.
Taking of Joppa. See Joppa.
"Tale of Two Brothers," the foundation of "Cinderella," 155, 223.
Ta-meri (ancient name of Egypt), 254.
Tanis (Ta-an or Tsan, Hebrew Zoan, modern Sàu), Great Temple of, 146.
— history, site, remains, etc., 20, 50–57, 133, 153.
— mathematical papyrus at, 218.
— mounds of, 6.
— sphinx at, 149.
Tanûter, Land of the Gods, 285, 291.
— location of, 201.
Tarena, Egyptian for cuirasses, 153, 164.
Ta-Tena, 280. See Canal also.
Teans, 29.
Tell Abû Suleiman, 42.
Tell Bedawi, 17.
Tell Defenneh (ancient Daphnæ), 18, 58, 68, 182.
— as a meeting-point in history, 63.
— Petrie at, 58, 63, 64.
Tell el Amarna, 22.
Tell el Barûd, 26.
Tell el-Maskhûtah (site, relics, etc.), 42, 43.
Tell el-Yahudieh, 80.
Tell Farûn, 17.
Tell Gemayemi, 34.
Tell Gurob, 77, 78, 167.
Tell Kahun, 77.
Tell Nebireh (Arab, Naukratis), 179

Tell Quarmus, 34.
Temple of Abû-Simbel (Nubia), 211.
— Cyclopean, 167.
— of Abydos, 8, 211.
— of Amen, 263, 267, 294, 296.
— of Aphrodite, 22.
— of Apollo, 179, 180, 184, 199.
— of Bubastis, 8,
— of Dayr-el-Bahari, 268.
— of Derr (Nubia), 212.
— of Edfû, 9.
— of Karnak, 126. See Karnak also.
— of Luxor, 125, 128.
Temples as places of worship, 5.
— in mounds, 11.
— sites, 78.
Teucrians, the, 76.
Thales, 166.
Theban triad, Amen, Maut, Khonsu, 262.
Thebes, 4, 11, 17, 73, 76, 97, 112, 119, 126, 133, 155, 166, 167, 198, 219, 230, 256, 260, 291, 300.
— founded in the Eleventh Dynasty, 227.
— kings of, 159.
— nobles and tombs, 84.
— paintings on tombs, 81 ; on walls, 178.
— period in Egyptian art, 81.
— princes of, 149.
— sculptured illustrations at, 216.
Theodosius I., 24, 118.
— abolishing of religion by, 134.
Thera, 79.
— inscriptions at, 79.
Thespis, 196.
Thinis, Prince of Mena, 38.
Thoth (scribe), 228, 295.
Thothmes I., 129, 261, 263.
— marriages of, 297 ; wives of, 264.
Thothmes II., 261, 264, 296.
— marriage with Hatasu, 264.
— mummy of, 297.
— reigning with Hatasu, 269.
— Temple of, at Karnak, 274.
— III. (Alexander of Egyptian history), 13, 76, 78, 150, 160, 167, 173, 179, 191, 202, 223, 224, 270.
— as brother of Hatasu, 266.
— as husband of Hatasu's daughter, 267.
— character and conquests of, 198, 199, 268.
— effacing records of Hatasu. 296, 297.
— Great Temple at Karnak, 175, 274, 275.
— mummy of, 297.
— son of Thothmes I. and Lady As-t, 264.
Thrace, 163.
Ti (gentleman of the Fifth Dynasty), 140.
Tii (Queen), wife of Amenhotep III. ; Mariette, wife of Horemheb, Maspero, 150.

Timotheus, 196.
Timsah, Lake, 280.
Titus, 96.
Tombs, 4, 12, 84.
— of Priest-Kings, 297.
— painting of Theban times, 81.
Totemism, Bull-clan, Crocodile-clan, etc., 230. *See* Religion.
Touaou (modern Kosseir) 276.
Treasuries of Athens, Mycenæ, Argolis, Minyas, etc.,167–170. *See*, also, Raamses and Pithom.
Troad, 203.
Troglodytes, 288.
Troy, 26, 171, 205.
Tsàn (Ta-an), Greek Tanis, Hebrew Zoan, Petrie at, 50.
Tum, 44.
— as Tumu, Atmu, description of, 81.
Turanians, 168.
— types of, 147.
Turin, 259.
Turks, 5.
Tursha (Egyptian Etruscans), 77, 79, 92.
— identity of the, 77.
Tuscan poetry, 225.
Tyrrhene Sea, 78.
Tyrrhenes, Turseni (Greek Etrurians), 92.

Uabra, 61.
Uatmes, chapel of, 264.
— Prince, son of Thothmes I., 264.
Unas II., 227.
Upper Egypt, 4, 14, 40, 46.
Urtheku, 295.
Usertesen II., 77, 78, 168.
Ushabti, funerary statuettes at, 298.

Valleys of the Hamamat, 76.
— the Nile. *See* Nile.
— the Tombs of the Kings, 153, 155, 270.
Vases, 4.
Verulam, 44.
Victory, Chant of. *See* "Chant of Victory."

Wady Tûmilât, 42, 46, 48.
— located, 280.
— mound of, 41.
Weapons, 4.
Wellington, 114.
Wiedemann, Dr., 117.
— on Egyptian ideas, 130.
Wigs, 4.
Wilkinson, 178.
Wilson, Sir Erasmus, 40.
Woltmann's *History of Painting*, 87.
"Wooden Man of Bulak," 139, 143.
Writing, Demotic, 256, 258.
— compared with Mexican, 249.
— earliest examples in relief, 237.
— examples given, 243, 247, 251–253, 255.
— explained as gesture language, 249.
— first alphabet invented by Egyptians, 244.
— general development among Egyptians, Hittites, etc.; Herodotus quoted, 234, 235.
— generic determinatives illustrated, 248, 249.
— Hieroglyphic, alphabet given, 245.
— history of, 256–258.
— ideography, 241.
— indebtedness of Greeks, 244.
— its simplicity its stumbling-block, 250, 251.
— of Mexico, 237, 238.
— of Paleolithic period, Europe, 239, 240.
— of the Phœnicians, 244.
— papyrus for, 256.
— subjects and materials, 258, 259.
— theories about origin of, 236, 245–247.

Xanthean tombs, 189.
Xanthus, 188.
Zeuxis, 74, 106, 112.

Yakuts of Siberia, 230.
Yavan, 160.
Yemen as a centre of commerce, 276.
— on coast of Arabia, 276.

Zagazig, 19, 41.
— ancient Bubastis, 280.
Zanzibar, 279.
Zedekiah, 61.
— daughters of, history given, 61–69, 165.
Zeller, Professor, 171.
Zeus, 29, 75, 90, 102, 229.
Zoan, 6, 50.

BIN TRAVELER FORM

Cut By: _Rosa Castillo   #12_ **Qty** _20_ **Date** _07/23/26_

Scanned By: ___________________ **Qty** _______ **Date** ___________

Scanned Batch ID's

____

Notes / Exceptions

____